A **TOM MARLOWE** THRILLER

STEALTH STRIKE

NEW YORK TIMES #1 BESTSELLER **TONY LEE** WRITING AS

JACK GATLAND

Hooded Man MEDIA

INSPIRATION ● PRODUCTION ● PUBLICATION

Published by Hooded Man Media.

Cover design by L1graphics

First Edition: February 2024

PRAISE FOR JACK GATLAND

'This is one of those books that will keep you up past your bedtime, as each chapter lures you into reading just one more.'

'This book was excellent! A great plot which kept you guessing until the end.'

'Couldn't put it down, fast paced with twists and turns.'

'The story was captivating, good plot, twists you never saw and really likeable characters. Can't wait for the next one!'

'I got sucked into this book from the very first page, thoroughly enjoyed it, can't wait for the next one.'

'Totally addictive. Thoroughly recommend.'

'Moves at a fast pace and carries you along with it.'

'Just couldn't put this book down, from the first page to the last one it kept you wondering what would happen next.'

There's a new Detective Inspector in town...

Before Tom Marlowe had his own series, he was a recurring character in the DI Declan Walsh books!

An EXCLUSIVE PREQUEL, completely free to anyone who joins the Jack Gatland Reader's Club!

Join at bit.ly/jackgatlandVIP

Also by Jack Gatland

For Mum, who inspired me to write.

For Tracy, who inspires me to write.

CONTENTS

PROLOGUE

OVER THE LAST COUPLE OF WEEKS, TOM MARLOWE HAD HAD quite a few things sent through his letterbox. Death threats, warnings, even bullets with his name written on them.

The last thing he expected was a letter with written text beautifully created with top-class calligraphy on it.

It had been an interesting few weeks following the events that had happened in America. Marlowe and his allies, Trix Preston, Marshall Kirk and his daughter Tessa, and Brad Haynes – a rogue CIA agent, and "sort-of" friend who now seemed to be working on behalf of a mysterious and mainly unnamed agent "named" Sasha Bordeaux – had all assisted in the process. But during the mission – well, he would call it *adventure*, but it felt more like an off-the-books mission than anything exciting – his dying and incredibly estranged father, Taylor Coleman, had given him a gift. The gift was unwanted but simple; Coleman's own position on the High Council of a super-secret agency known as *Orchid*, an agency that Marlowe had been tasked with destroying.

Marlowe had realised at the end of the mission, however,

that MI5 and MI6 had "fifth columns" inside that were just as corrupt as Orchid was, riddled with agents and compromised from within. He'd taken a leave of absence from the service, pretty much moments before they kicked him out anyway, stepping back and letting the others carry on. If he was being honest, it was a bit of a relief to do this, as even when he was trying to save the world, MI5 and MI6 were still treating him like some kind of pawn in a game of chess, where nobody knew what colour the squares were ... and he was pretty sick of it now.

There had been a suggestion, one given to him by Tessa Kirk before she left, that Marlowe should use this to his advantage. Orchid was fractured now, the billionaire who was funding some of the more right-wing aspects of it – Lucien Delacroix – now dead, his loyal followers scattered to the winds, and the High Council themselves friendless, their virtual world meeting place now revealed as a game server on a long-forgotten network, one which, curiously, Marlowe now controlled.

If he had wanted to, Marlowe could have possibly even taken his toys elsewhere, created a new Orchid from scratch, taken over and been a modern-day Blofeld against James Bond, causing problems for MI6 and MI5 as he did so.

But that wasn't Marlowe's thing. Because, no matter what people said about him, Tom Marlowe was a *patriot*.

That said, there was still an opportunity to use this gift, this cursed poison chalice that he'd been given, for good.

The problem was, he hadn't yet worked out how to *do* that.

Therefore, Tom had stayed off the grid, waiting to see what happened next. His church apartment was now finished, a bedroom mezzanine above what was once the altar, a hallway and dining area to the right as you entered, a kitchen to the left, and a sitting area complete with TV and sofa in the middle. Even some pews, the ones that hadn't been sold to antique dealers, were used along the walls as seating for guests. It was the "public" face of Marlowe, a simple location with the most minimal of secrets. If you were to break in and have a good nose around, you'd perhaps find a single gun hidden under a kitchen counter, and a large array of "middle class" furnishings to give you a character assessment that couldn't have been more wrong if you tried.

He'd spent most of his time in his *other* apartment, the one based in a crypt underneath the church, a crypt that nobody knew about unless Marlowe himself had given the information on how to find it. This was Marlowe's *Batcave*, his *sanctum solitaire,* his *fortress of solitude.* Well, it would have been if Trix Preston hadn't kept using it as some kind of gaming room, claiming that his network speed was far better than her own, and therefore it was only fair he allowed her to use it. In fact, she'd even created a corner of the room where she'd sit in her gaming chair – which had appeared out of nowhere one day – with her headphones on, playing for hours at a time.

Marlowe knew she wasn't actually *playing.* She was currently running through *Crime City*, a popular first-person shooter game used by Orchid as a virtual world, checking every inch of the map, looking for anything else that had been left by Orchid in the game server before it had been wrenched from their grasp. She'd been told it was clean, but even Ciaran Winston, the creator, couldn't be sure that Orchid hadn't added items, and so she'd spent the last three weeks checking every available spot of the map for secret locations, tunnels, and buildings.

She had found five so far, all of which held files within the server, and were currently being encrypted by both Trix and Ciaran.

Marlowe had to smile. Trix was an expert hacker and had broken into some of the biggest and most dangerous places in the world, yet her greatest hacking achievement seemed to be in playing a game where teenagers ran around online in cat masks and stole cars during high speed, car-destroying chases. The irony hadn't been wasted on her either. When she wasn't with him, she was visiting Ciaran. The two of them seemed to be quite close now, and Marlowe hoped that maybe this was somebody she could start a relationship with. She'd been alone as long as he'd known her, and it was about time she found somebody she could converse with, in her own weird, tech-savvy language.

When the invite came, Marlowe was alone.

He'd been sitting downstairs watching the monitor screens, trying to work out what next to do when a black car had arrived at the front of the church. The CCTV he'd set around it was secure and state-of-the-art for obvious reasons. He'd been trying to figure out what to do next with Orchid at the time, and he was quite surprised to see that when the person holding the envelope in their brown leather gloves climbed out of the car, the face was pixelated.

This was some kind of technology that even Marlowe hadn't seen before. It impressed him. He was also impressed when they walked up to the door to his church/apartment and opened it as if it had been unlocked, walking into the apartment upstairs, placing the envelope on the table with their leather gloves on, likely to avoid fingerprints, and walking back out as if it was the simplest thing possible.

As soon as they'd left, Marlowe clambered up the steps

into his main apartment, walking to the front church door and checking it was locked. More than that, it was still the original door, made from heavy oak. Even opening it was an effort, let alone picking the large Victorian lock without breaking a stride.

Impressive trick, he thought to himself. *You can teach me that when I find out whoever you are.*

Looking now at the table, he'd seen the black envelope. It was slightly smaller than an A5 sheet, and in gold letters on the front, it said,

THOMAS MARLOWE
HIGH COUNCIL

Next to it was a freshly plucked orchid.

Marlowe had pulled on a pair of latex gloves and started visually scanning the letter before he picked it up. The person who had placed it was wearing gloves on the screen, and Marlowe didn't want to pick up anything that could have something on it, maybe a toxin that could slowly kill him – the gloves might not have just been to hide the identity, after all. He'd spent too much time pissing people off to lose his life in such a pedestrian way, so, after he examined it closely, he moved an ultraviolet lamp onto it, scanning all sides, picking it up with tweezers as he slowly slid down the line with a sharp blade to open the envelope.

With another pair of tweezers, he pulled out the card within and his eyes widened in surprise as he read it.

It was an *invitation*.

The invite was a black card with gold writing, unadorned with any logos. The text was simple, made from some kind of monotype font and all it said was,

THOMAS MARLOWE

YOU HAVE BEEN INVITED TO THE WAKE AND MEMORIAL SERVICE OF
TAYLOR COLEMAN
GOLD STRIKE HOTEL & CASINO, LAS VEGAS, NEVADA.

There was no date or time, but as Marlowe turned it over, he saw a QR code, again in gold. He knew this would probably provide the time, location, date, and everything else needed. But at the same time, he didn't really want to try anything, in case scanning the QR code sent him to some dodgy spyware site, or even turned on a bomb that had already been placed in the apartment somewhere.

He knew he was being overly paranoid, but this was Orchid, and Orchid were overly paranoid in the first place. Plus he had to admit, from a father who wanted nothing to do with Marlowe, and whose dying wish was to give him nothing more than pain and misery, becoming his father's replacement on the High Council of Orchid, it seemed strange that he would now be invited to a knees-up of any type.

Placing it back down carefully, he stared at it before finding an offline QR code reader. It was a device that wasn't connected to the internet, but it could take the information from the QR code itself, and this might give him the date he needed without risking the code affecting anything. Aiming it at the QR code, he was able on a small screen to pull up the information that the QR code linked to. It was base code, but it was easier than opening up a website.

Unsurprisingly, all it gave him was a time, a date, and a

comment that *black tie was appreciated, but not enforced.* The date itself was a week away, and Marlowe sat back on a chair, staring at the piece of card on the table, as if it was going to burst into flames like a message in *Mission Impossible.*

He had conflicting thoughts about Taylor Coleman.

No, that wasn't exactly correct. They weren't conflicting at all. Coleman was a prick, always had been a prick, and his last act had been to *be* a prick. But Marlowe, having seen the organisation Taylor Coleman had been involved in, was realising his estranged father possibly didn't have the choices Marlowe thought he'd had.

Taylor Coleman had been an arms dealer for most of his life, and had met Marlowe's mum, Olivia, while she was undercover on a mission in Kosovo. They'd had a short but passionate affair, but Taylor disappeared when he found out she was pregnant.

Olivia had found him two years later, and the first thing he asked was if she'd had an abortion. She'd punched out two of his teeth.

Understandably, Taylor was gone by the time Marlowe was born. In fact, Taylor had been away from his life for most of it, turning up on Marlowe's doorstep on his eighteenth birthday. He had a four-pack of Tennent's Special Brew with him, took Marlowe to a local park and chugged two down on a park bench. He'd explained it was his task in life to "make Marlowe into a man," and Marlowe had punched him hard in the face, taken a butterfly blade to his throat, and told him he'd succeeded. Tom Marlowe was now a man; a man who told Taylor to never come close to him or his mother again.

It was only a few months earlier that Taylor Coleman, terminally ill and looking to finish his loose ends, had arranged to meet with Marlowe in a New York diner. And by "arranged to meet," Marlowe presumed he meant "send a rubbish hitman to try to kill him, purely to lead Marlowe towards him."

During this meeting, however, Marlowe had learned that Taylor had not only kept a close eye on Marlowe all of his life, a fatherly eye that didn't involve contact because of Marlowe's late mother's request, but that he also had a family; half-brothers and sisters he didn't know of. He'd informed Marlowe he was dying soon, had said he would give Marlowe a gift he didn't want when he died, and Taylor's last request before dying had been simple – to not contact his siblings in any way. They weren't part of his life, his world. They were *innocent*.

Marlowe had agreed, but it was only recently he'd wondered how much of a lie that had also been, as the last time he'd seen Taylor Coleman, at a secret party in Versailles, he'd announced to Orchid that Marlowe was his heir apparent, and the new member of the Orchid High Council.

But the man he'd been standing beside, a tall, gangly man that Marlowe had claimed the nickname "Ichabod Crane" for, had been revealed to be a half-brother.

So much for keeping the family out of the business, Marlowe thought to himself.

But Taylor Coleman was now dead.

Marlowe had been informed of this by a mysterious man named St John (pronounced "Sinjen") Steele, Orchid's ex-Arbitrator, sitting in the same room as he sat now, unaware of a secret crypt, but still able to walk through doors as if they were nothing.

For a second Marlowe wondered whether this invite had been sent by Steele. With the reputation the man had, it could explain how someone could walk through Marlowe's defences with such ease; and that single thought spurred Marlowe into action, walking over to his phone and picking it up as he sent a text to Trix, asking her when she had a chance to come and see him. There was every chance that this would need her experience.

Who was he kidding – this was totally her wheelhouse.

Marlowe then walked over to the bar, poured himself a whisky and sipped at it while still staring at the invite. There was a part of him that wanted to throw it away, to set fire to it, tear it into small pieces and make sure that nobody ever knew that they had invited him to the event. But again, there was another part of him who wanted to know more about his family, a part who wanted to know more about Taylor Coleman himself. Also, he had to admit, he wanted to know who currently was thinking of him.

If he'd been invited, he assumed he wasn't there to be the sacrifice. Or was he?

Walking back to the coffee table, he stared down at the note one last time before deciding that booking some flights might be an idea. He wouldn't do them as himself, though. Oh no. There was every chance that half a dozen security agencies would be watching for Tom Marlowe right now. Not because he had done something, but because they wanted to know what he was *going* to do. Tom Marlowe had become the barometer of shite things about to happen, it seemed.

Before he could do that, however, there was a knock at the front door to his apartment-church. Silently, Marlowe walked over to it, drawing his Sig Sauer from a concealed holster at the four o'clock position on his belt, a location it seemed to spend the majority of its time in. Cracking the door, he paused as he stared at the person standing in front of him.

'Monty?' he asked in confusion, releasing his hand and opening the door to let the man facing him in.

Monty Barnes was easily in his nineties. He'd been a mentor to Marlowe's mentors, he was ex-SAS and there was even talk he'd been attached to John F Kennedy's retinue on the day of the Dallas assassination, sixty years earlier – but you wouldn't have guessed, as the man looked like he was seventy still, sprightly, wiry, and muscled. His hair was dyed brown and straight in what people called "curtains," a middle parting showing the slight touch of white where it needed to be re-dyed, and he had what people call a "soul patch" of hair under his lip. He looked like a slightly aged hippie, but the only thing that gave his true age away were the lines around his neck and the fact that his ears had now drooped, as was typical for an elderly man, the cartilage in them softening, and gravity taking hold.

Monty slid past, and it was only as he did so that Marlowe noticed he was holding his side, which was bleeding.

'Sorry Marlowe, you're the closest person I knew around here, and I can't go to a hospital,' he said. 'Can I come in before I bleed out?'

1

MONTY

'CHRIST MONTY, WHAT THE HELL HAVE YOU BEEN DOING?'
Marlowe pulled Monty in, looking outside quickly before
closing the church door behind them. 'What's happened?'

'I offered to help family and, well, let's just say I got
stabbed for my generosity.'

Marlowe sat Monty down, grabbing a first aid kit and a
whisky from the kitchen.

'Let's have a look,' he said, pulling up Monty's jumper and
checking the wound.

'I'm fine, I just need some Savlon and a needle,' Monty
muttered.

'It's a side wound, hasn't pierced anything vital from the
looks of things. It's just bleeding,' Marlowe ignored the
protestations, working on it. 'What were you doing? You're
like a hundred and ten; you shouldn't be doing anything like
this.'

Monty chuckled as he winced, drinking down the glass of
whisky and waving for another one.

'I had agreed to have a word with one of Frank Maguire's

enforcers,' he said. 'I know, I know, he's bad news and I shouldn't have touched him. But my grandson's got in with his gang and I was trying to get him out.'

Marlowe leant back. He knew Frank Maguire very well. In fact, it was under another alias of his, that of Kieran Lachlan, ex-Real IRA and full-time money launderer, that Maguire, the head of one of the Southend crime families in Essex, knew Marlowe.

'Who stabbed you?' Marlowe shook the memory aside and re-examined the wound.

'There's a guy called Razor,' Monty grimaced once more as Marlowe administered to the wound. 'He's an up-and-comer in the gang, from what I can work out. Maguire doesn't even realise he's a threat right now. He's got Sammy – that's my great-grandson – under his thumb and he's pretty much told Sammy that if he tries to leave, he'll come after those he loves and wipe them out one by one.'

'Way to increase loyalty,' Marlowe said.

'Razor doesn't understand about loyalty,' Monty replied. 'All he cares about is power. Anyway, Sammy had come to me and said he didn't know how to get out, so I went and faced him.'

'You faced a gangland wannabe? At your age? Are you stupid?'

Monty laughed; it was more a cough than a laugh to start with, and for a second Marlowe thought he was having an attack.

'I took three of them down before they stabbed me,' he said. 'I collapsed to my knees, and they walked off laughing. I knew if I went to a hospital it'd just cause questions.'

'Why?' Marlowe looked up at him. 'An old man being stabbed isn't something that would usually cause issues.'

'I've got a couple of warrants out for my arrest at the moment,' Monty smiled. 'Nothing major.'

By the term "nothing major," Marlowe already knew that the things that Monty was probably being chased for were *quite* major and probably enough to have Marlowe assumed to be an accessory, now he'd patched up Monty's wound.

'Why did you come to me?' he asked.

Monty shrugged.

'First, you were closest,' he explained. 'Second, because you owe me from that time in Chechnya and I thought I ain't got many years left, I might as well call it in before it's too late.'

Marlowe chuckled at this. Monty had saved his life a good ten years earlier; he did owe him that at least. But the apartment was new, and he hadn't seen Monty for years.

How did he know where Marlowe was now, without checking?

'And third, well, I heard you've got powerful friends now,' Monty said, and at this, his eyes narrowed. 'Thought you might be able to use them.'

Marlowe stepped back. The wound wasn't that deep; it wasn't fatal, and it was almost as if it was made to bleed. Monty could have fixed this up himself with a needle and thread and some antiseptic wipes. Marlowe had known Monty for several decades now, ever since he was a child, but now he wondered whether Monty had done this deliberately to find a route to meet with Orchid. It would explain his knowledge of Marlowe's address. But was Marlowe over-thinking this? Monty also knew Marshall Kirk, and there was every chance he'd passed the details.

'Your information's wrong,' he said coldly. 'I don't deal with anybody like that.'

Monty nodded, as if accepting the answer, but Marlowe wondered whether this was still the case.

'Either way, you still owe me,' he said. 'You must be able to do something. Maguire needs to know that Razor's a loose cannon and Maguire isn't going to listen to me, but ...'

Marlowe knew where this was going.

'I patch you up, you go home, I'll come back to you when I've done it,' he said. 'Show me a picture of your great-grandson, and I'll get this done now.'

'Appreciate it, Thomas,' Monty smiled. 'You always were one of the good ones. I'll message you the photo.'

And with that, his wound now patched up for the moment, and groaning with pain, Monty clambered slowly to his feet and slowly winced his way back out of the apartment.

'Do you need a cab?' Marlowe shouted.

'I'm good,' Monty smiled back. 'I appreciate the help.'

The door shut, and Marlowe gave out a kept-in groan. On a normal day, he would have felt that Monty had turned up to him because he needed his help – but now everyone was a potential assassin.

A threat.

No longer a friend.

He poured himself another whisky and downed it before heading back to his staircase behind the fuse box. The identity he needed was downstairs, and with luck, wouldn't be needed after tomorrow.

IT WOULD HAVE BEEN STRAIGHTFORWARD TO GO STRAIGHT TO Frank Maguire as Kieran Lachlan, and demand that Razor sort himself out. But Marlowe had met Frank many times over the years as Kieran, and one thing he knew was that Frank Maguire didn't accept demands. Even if Frank owed Marlowe, he would have still played up about this.

No, this would take some *research*.

Luckily for Monty, and in a way his great-grandson, Marlowe's MI5 training gave him all the patience he needed, and the skillset to not only find Razor but also work out what his average day was. The following morning, Marlowe woke up early and started contacting his assets and contacts in the London crime world. He wasn't wearing the legend of Kieran Lachlan yet; he didn't want to bring that identity out until it was time. The last thing he wanted was for Frank McGuire to hear that an Irish gunrunner was trying to find out information about his own people, after all.

By lunchtime, Marlowe had found out that Razor was actually Raymond Gibson, a onetime enforcer for Frank Maguire who had risen the ranks, primarily after the fight that Marlowe himself had instigated when rescuing Deacon Brodie's brother Barry, months earlier. Marlowe hadn't meant to change any power structure that day – all he did was solve a problem in order to gain information from an asset. But, during that gunfight where Marlowe had turned Conor Clarke and the Chelmsford Crewz, one of Maguire's allied gangs, into an enemy to the Southend gangster with rumours and lies about Conor allying with enemies, it had resulted in a five-in-the-morning gunfight in the London suburbs.

Apparently, Raymond, or "Razor," had come out of this well, and was now positioned at the forefront of Maguire's organisation.

Marlowe winced at this. There wasn't a lot he could do when it came to cause and effect. But now that he knew

Raymond Gibson was Razor, he could now use his own information sources to find and follow him for the day.

For most of the day, he stayed in his recently repaired 2015 Burgundy Jaguar XJ, monitoring the gangland leader as he fulfilled tasks for Frank Maguire. There was even a young man reluctantly with him who bore an uncanny resemblance to Monty; Marlowe knew from the photo he'd received that this was the "Sammy" that Monty had mentioned, and could already see from how Razor treated him that there was no love lost on either side. If anything, Sammy seemed more like a hostage than a member of his crew.

Marlowe had spent most of the day keeping at a distance, but there was one moment, shortly after lunch, when he decided to risk it and enter a bar that Razor had gone into on his own.

Watching from across the road, the *Shoreditch Light Bar,* a onetime power station-turned-bar and restaurant, had been an easy target to observe from a car across the High Street. Watching Razor stop his own men from entering with him, however, made Marlowe sit up.

Usually, when going into an open scenario like a bar, restaurant, or other places where the public would be – possibly including someone with their own agenda against you – it was wise to take a couple of goons at least, if only to use them as meat shields as the bullets started flying. But here, Marlowe watched as Razor stopped his men from coming with him. This was interesting and, more importantly, something that Marlowe believed he could use to his advantage.

Exiting the car and walking into the Light Bar itself, Marlowe paused as he glanced around. Shoreditch Light Bar had been revitalised over the last few years, merging its historical roots with a contemporary touch. The interior was built as a kind of tribute to the power station's past, with elements like the original mechanical pulley system, exposed steelwork, and glazed brick adding to its "rustic yet modern charm," according to the sign on the glass door.

Another sign indicated the levels of the bar itself; there was the "Engine Hall" on the main ground floor, where the space was open and lively, buzzing with the chatter of patrons enjoying their meals and drinks. Above, the "Copper Bar" looked to offer a more intimate setting, built as a space where cocktails and memories of early millennium East London parties mingled, while the top floor apparently housed the "Timber Loft," a more secluded area with skylights that bathed the space in natural light.

Marlowe noted that although the top floor seemed the most secluded, it served as a cozy dining and events area, and a sign at the base of the stairs mentioned it was usually reserved for private gatherings. This, to Marlowe's espionage-trained ears sounded like the perfect backdrop for discreet conversations away from the curious eyes and ears of the public – however, to his gangland-trained ears as Kieran, booking a space for a private meeting just made you stand out, if you were trying to keep your head down.

Not seeing his target in the Engine Hall, Marlowe walked up the steps to the Copper Bar, where he saw Razor sitting at a table to the left of the long bar. He moved to the side, within sight but still close enough to hear if anything happened, and took his own position. He was near the stairs, and could see anyone coming in or going out, while getting a better idea of what was happening.

Razor sat alone for five minutes, ordering himself a beer

and drinking it ... and then something very *interesting* happened.

Arun Nadal was a minor league player from West London. Arun and his gang had been building up a reputation as fixers, expanding an income from drugs, illegal immigrants, and female trafficking. He was a scumbag of the highest order, and all of this at twenty-four. He was young, ambitious, and dangerous to know.

He was also a known enemy of Frank Maguire, Marlowe remembered.

He watched as Arun entered the bar, looked around, and immediately walked up the stairs, heading over to Razor. Unlike Razor, however, Arun had three of his men with him, and Marlowe knew because of that, this was a meeting Arun was happy to have, but one Razor didn't want his boss to know he was having. If the men with Razor – men who also had a loyalty to Frank Maguire – had seen who the meeting was with, the chances were Frank would already know, as someone would have texted him within seconds.

Razor was playing his cards very close here.

Marlowe considered what this meant. Razor could have been making a play, or alternatively, he could have been trying to broker a peace. Brokering some kind of ceasefire agreement for Frank Maguire was a job that would have elevated him, but if he *was* doing that, he would have brought his own muscle in. It would have been known to them, and likely commanded by Maguire himself.

No, this was definitely something that Razor wanted under the radar, and Marlowe knew without a doubt he'd be able to use it as leverage.

He took a couple of crafty shots with his phone, enough to prove that such a meeting had happened, immediately sending one to a cloud backup site. He'd noticed one goon on Arun's side see this, and in a way, he hoped it would play out the way he expected.

Razor finished his conversation, rose, and left, walking past Marlowe without a sideways glance, and after a couple of seconds, Marlowe got up to follow.

As he left the Light Bar, however, one of the muscle that had been standing with Arun Nadal grabbed him by the arm.

'I think you should tell me what you're doing, mate,' the muscle said in his most fearsome, gravelly voice.

Marlowe relaxed, smiled, and looked back at the muscle. He decided now was the time to bring out the legend.

'I think you want to let go of my arm there, buddy,' he said, his voice now becoming tinged with a harsh Northern Irish accent. 'Before I go tell your boss there that you laid hands on me.'

Goons were used to paparazzi, investigative reporters, even small-time gangsters trying to gain a bit of leverage. They would usually stop them, have a go at them, scare the piss out of them, and then walk away. To have the intended target turn around and effectively do the same back wasn't a common occurrence, and Marlowe could see the muscled goon already playing through the conversation.

'Who are you?' he asked.

'If you don't know, then you're not on my pay scale,' he replied. 'I'd hazard a guess Nadal in there knows, though. So, why don't you go back and guard him, rather than bother me—'

The muscle had finally had enough, it seemed, and reached for the phone, deciding to remove the photos himself; it was a bad move. Waiting for this, Marlowe spun around, twisting the muscle's arm, flipping him to the floor, kneeling down, resting on his chest.

'You tell Master Nadal that Kieran Lachlan said he needs better trained muscle, okay?' Marlowe hissed, rising. 'And if he wants these images, he can come call for them. Okay?'

The muscle nodded, terrified, as Marlowe smiled and walked off.

'Good talk,' he said.

2

ROBIN HOOD

Frank Maguire was in his usual office – a disused restaurant on the northern end of Southend seafront. On entering, Marlowe was reminded of childhood trips to the seaside with ice creams, and those ring doughnuts that could only be found at places like this, or at carnivals; recently battered, and fresh out of the fryer.

Maguire looked up from his seat. He was currently eating lunch, which today seemed to be battered sausage and chips with either gravy or some kind of curry sauce on the side.

Marlowe sat down, smiling at Maguire, waiting for him to speak. Maguire had known he was here; he wouldn't have been allowed into the restaurant without the muscle informing their boss, but currently, Maguire had no idea exactly why Marlowe, in his guise as Kieran Lachlan, was visiting.

'When I heard you were here, I was surprised,' Maguire said conversationally, not looking up from his food. 'I thought to myself, "surely Kieran Lachlan, the man who had cost me time and effort at five am, taking out a rival who didn't even seem to be aware he *was* a rival in the first place, wouldn't come back and darken my door without a serious goddamn apology happening," and then I hear you're here.'

'Good to see you too, Frank,' Marlowe smiled, keeping his "Kieran" accent strong. 'It was a fine state of affairs when I saw you last, and I hasten to add, completely out of my hands.'

Maguire looked up from his meal.

'Completely out of your hands,' he repeated tonelessly. 'You had nothing to do with the fact you had me and my men turn up at five in the morning to take out a fictitious bad guy, while you stole whoever he had hidden.'

He pointed a fork at Marlowe, curious.

'Who was it, by the way, that they had hidden away in a basement?'

Marlowe didn't need to keep this secret. In fact, letting Maguire know could even help him. So he shrugged.

'Deacon Brodie's younger brother.'

'Deacon Brodie, that two-bit arms dealer? I thought you'd be happy to see his brother go,' Frank was surprised. 'Enemy of my enemy and all that.'

'Deacon owed me a favour,' Marlowe shrugged again. 'And I buy where I can get the best deal. Deacon Brodie had the best deal, especially after I got his brother back.'

'You didn't have to use me,' Maguire snapped. 'You didn't have to lie to me.'

'Oh, Frankie, I didn't lie to you,' Marlowe smiled. 'The Chelmsford crew were moving on you. What happened after you spoke to them isn't my problem. The moment you arrived, they started firing on you.'

'Yes, and why was that, do you think?' Maguire glowered at Marlowe. 'Some random gunshot, which the Chelmsford crew reckon wasn't them. But if it wasn't them, who would it be?'

'I wasn't there. I was keeping to the shadows, waiting for my moment,' Marlowe grinned. 'I wasn't gonna start a fight.'

'Certainly benefited you though, didn't it?' Maguire pushed his plate away, no longer hungry. 'What do you want, Kieran? I'm busy.'

'I wanted to give you an apology,' Marlowe replied, pulling out his phone gently with two fingers, showing the goons that he wasn't reaching for a weapon. 'I felt bad over what happened and I wanted to find a way to make it up to you. I think I found it.'

'And how would that be?'

'One of your men is siding with the enemy.'

'Is this another enemy like the Chelmsford muppets?' Maguire trailed off as Marlowe turned the phone to show the picture of Razor meeting with Arun Nadal.

'As I said,' Marlowe replied calmly. 'I'm here to apologise.'

'And what exactly do you want with this apology?'

'Young lad, works for Razor, I'd like him removed from the family,' Marlowe explained. 'And I don't mean in a bad way, I mean given some money and told to go home and start afresh. Find a new vocation. This isn't his life.'

'So you're once again trying to take somebody out of a sticky situation,' Maguire chuckled to himself. 'How do I know that's a real photo?'

'You could always check the security footage of the Light Bar in Shoreditch,' Marlowe suggested. 'Although you may find that at the time stamp that they met, the security footage will have mysteriously disappeared.'

'That would be a problem,' Maguire replied, looking once more at the picture. 'Who's the lad you want out?'

'Goes by the name of Sammy.'

'The great-grandkid of the old guy they attacked?' Frank nodded. 'I heard about that. Tore Razor a new one over what he did. You don't attack your elders, especially old-school lads like him.'

'Well, I'd appreciate it if you allowed Sammy to leave your employ once Razor was removed,' Marlowe leant back in the chair, wondering if he could risk snagging one of the remaining chips, or whether that was a step too far.

'I can do that,' Maguire smiled. 'You have my word in front of witnesses. The moment Razor no longer works for me, and is removed from my employ, young Sammy will be allowed out of whatever deal he's been forced into.'

Marlowe frowned. *This was too easy.*

'You knew already,' he said, a statement more than a question. 'You already knew about his chats with Nadal.'

Maguire said nothing in reply, simply smiling.

Marlowe went to rise from the chair, but only then did Frank Maguire do anything, as he held a hand up.

'I haven't finished yet,' he said. 'You've turned up to apologise and you've given me another favour you require. Sure, you've shown me a traitor in my ranks, but ...'

He sniffed, looking away.

'You haven't shown me the way to fix this.'

Marlowe groaned. He knew what this meant. Maguire *had* known about Razor's meeting. Maybe even *meetings*, plural. But he needed someone who wasn't part of his organisation to do it.

He'd played Marlowe.

'For something like this, you need a removal specialist,' he said.

Maguire thought about this for a moment, picked up a chip and munched on it as he pondered the statement.

'True,' he said. 'But I know about you Irish types, and I know how good you are at removing people. I want him gone, without a trace. Once Razor is gone, then your boy can leave.'

'I'm not a hitman,' Marlowe growled.

'You're whatever you need to be to get your debt cleared,' Maguire snapped back. 'I didn't come to you with this, you came to me. Dealer's choice.'

Marlowe nodded. He understood what Frank was saying, and the request was valid.

'You want him gone ... or murdered?'

'I'm happy for him to run for his life,' Frank said. 'As long as he never comes back here again. You find a way to put the fear of God into that obnoxious little scroat, I will happily leave it as is.'

Marlowe sighed.

'Fine,' he finished. 'The lad will never bother you again, one way or the other.'

Maguire smiled, grabbing another chip and ramming it into his mouth.

'Grand,' he said, munching away as he did so. 'Anything else?'

'Aye, I'm having one of these,' Marlowe finally grabbed a lone chip to the side and ate it, watching Maguire as he did so, his eyes widening as he chewed. 'No vinegar on your chips? You monster.'

'So I've been told,' Maguire laughed as Marlowe walked out. 'So I've been told.'

Marlowe had no qualms about killing Razor. It wasn't his first, and it certainly wouldn't be his last; he was aware of that. However, it was a favour for Monty, not a mission on behalf of the King or government. Also, Marlowe didn't really want the police hunting him. Razor hadn't attacked him; this wasn't self-defence. This was a request from a gangster.

Therefore, the second option, that of making sure Razor never came back, was the only viable one.

However, the only way he'd be able to do this would be with shock and awe.

Returning to his church apartment, Marlowe quickly snuck in through the back door, avoiding any front entrance observers. He didn't know if there would be anyone, but the last thing he needed was rogue Orchid agents or MI5 jobsworths seeing him as an Irish gunrunner. He opened his small and dwindling armoury and pulled out a few items he needed, mainly lumps of C4 with Bluetooth detonators. He checked into the details he had of Razor, or, rather, Raymond Gibson, confirming and memorising some small pieces of information he might need later while bluffing his way either in or out of the meeting. As well as this, he checked DVLA records and memorised any car number plates he needed to monitor. There were only two: a Land Rover and a BMW 5 Series.

This done, he returned to his Jaguar, piled the small bricks of C4 into the side passenger seat, and travelled back into Essex to find Razor.

After an hour of checking around, he found him in a pub, the *Robin Hood*, just outside Loughton on a roundabout off the Epping Road, and beside the expanse of ancient woodlands known as Epping Forest. It looked like a standard country pub, the walls painted a mixture of green and grey, giving it an almost blueish look, but the many mentions of "Thai Food" changed your impressions of what to expect. Marlowe had actually been here before, and knew most of the inside was indeed a Thai restaurant, complete with gold wallpaper and ornate Thai woodcarvings next to the flagstone floors, low beamed ceilings and comfortable seating giving a relaxed ambience for enjoying a chat and a drink next door in the bar itself.

In front of the restaurant entrance were car parking spaces but, as he continued around the roundabout, Marlowe saw two cars parked to the right of the building, in a wide expanse of lay-by just past the roundabout, and that bordered onto the beer garden. One was a Land Rover, the other a BMW X5 Series; it looked like Razor was having a drink today.

Marlowe continued back around the roundabout, parking in the area outside the main restaurant, but then, after examining the doors to the entrance, he walked casually over to the two cars on the side of the road. It was a weekday and early in the afternoon, and there was still traffic heading past on the roundabout, although by the time they were hitting their turnoffs, they weren't looking at the man standing beside the beer garden entrance, crouching quickly beside both cars before entering the pub through the back entrance. He headed straight up to Razor, ignoring the goons who, surprised by this sudden arrival, turned to face him.

Sitting down, Marlowe smiled widely. It was a humourless smile, one to give concern and suspicion, and it succeeded in what it needed to do.

'Who the hell do you think you are?' Razor said.

'Kieran Lachlan,' Marlowe replied calmly, letting the Northern Irish accent flow out slightly. 'I've been having a chat with Frank Maguire. He said I should come and have a talk with you.'

'I know your rep, Lachlan. You're a Paddy hardman, right? Well, if you've got a request for something, you don't turn up like you own the place,' Razor snarled. 'You don't own the place. I do.'

'That's the problem with ownership,' Marlowe replied, pulling out his phone slowly, so as not to scare the goons into doing anything rash. Out of the corner of his eye, he saw the pub's bar staff watching; he got the impression they disagreed with Razor's opinion about "owning the place", but were too scared to do anything, in fear of reprisals. 'It's always a transitional situation.'

He opened the phone and showed Razor the photos he'd taken.

Razor scowled at them.

'I knew I'd seen you before,' he said. 'You were that bitch in the pub. I reckoned I'd see you again.'

Now Marlowe looked back at Razor.

'Wow, you're like Sherlock Holmes,' he said mockingly. 'How did you work it all out? We need to know.'

Razor ignored him.

'What do you want?' he asked. 'I'm guessing you've shown this to Frank already?'

'I have,' Marlowe replied as he looked around the room, spying Sammy to the side. 'It's real simple. He's asked me to kill you.'

At this, Razor laughed, as his goons, unsure whether or not to do anything, stood ready.

'You?' he chuckled, looking around. 'Mr. Beardy here is going to come and take me out, along with all my men?'

'Again, with the *transitional*,' Marlowe quipped. 'Are these *your* men, Raymond, or are these Frank Maguire's men?'

He turned to stare at the now suspicious goons.

'Come on, speak up. Are you Frank Maguire's men, or are you Raymond Gibson's men?'

There was a concerned look among the goons at this. Many of them had probably been brought up through the ranks of Frank Maguire's empire. And although they currently worked for Razor, their loyalty was still to the man himself.

'Because Frank Maguire wants this man dead,' Marlowe continued, turning his attention back to Razor now, lowering his voice, forcing Razor to lean closer. 'He wants you removed. He wants you gone.'

'Bullshit,' Razor said. 'He doesn't know what was going on. The photo's out of, what's it called, context, yeah. The photo's out of context. I could have been doing anything.'

'He knows exactly what you were doing,' Marlowe smiled. 'Because I had a chat with Arun Nadal right after you did. Nice long chat, found out everything.'

Marlowe was lying, but he didn't need to continue. Razor stood up, furious, pulling out a blade as he did so.

'You little bitch—'

'No, no, no, for God's sake, you're a bloody child,' Marlowe leant back, shaking his head sadly, his phone still in his hand. 'Haven't you ever seen the film *The Untouchables?*'

Razor glowered once more at him.

'You *what?*'

'The film with Kevin Costner, Sean Connery, Robert DeNiro? Eliot Ness and Al Capone? No? Shame. Anyway, there's a line in it about bringing a knife to a gunfight, and how it shows how inexperienced you are as a gangster.'

He nodded at the blade in Razor's hand.

'Like that knife, for example.'

'This knife is going to cut you—'

Razor didn't go any further, because Marlowe pressed a button on his phone, a button on an app Trix had created, that instantly connected to one of the Bluetooth detonators he'd brought and caused a massive explosion outside.

'That's your Land Rover going up in flames,' Marlowe said, glancing at the bar and giving them a reassuring wink as they stared out of the window. 'You said you know who I am. That I'm a "Paddy hardman," right? So, you know what I trade in, yeah? You know what I'm capable of doing?'

He pressed the button on the app again, and a second explosion happened.

'That's your BMW X5 going up,' he smiled.

Razor was furious, fighting the urge to just stab Marlowe, or run outside to see the full extent of the damage. Marlowe knew it wouldn't be much though, as the amount of C4 he'd used hadn't been that great, just needing the loud bang.

The last thing he wanted was to take out the pub, or anyone walking past it, after all – although being on a round-about, the chances of that happening were minimal.

'I'm gonna slice you up—'

'I've placed four devices,' Marlowe interrupted, holding a hand up, phone visible in it, the screen showing the button, his thumb hovering over it. 'Where do you think the third one's going to be?'

'I've only got two cars here,' Razor said with a dark smile. 'So, you screwed up, didn't you?'

'True, your cars here are toast,' Marlowe nodded. 'But your sister Michelle has a car, right? And your mum, Debbie? She has a car, too.'

He counted off his fingers.

'Three, four ... tick tick boom.'

'Don't you dare bring my family into this,' Razor was still all bluster, but Marlowe could see genuine fear in his face at the mention of his mother and sister.

'You're the one who brought family into it,' Marlowe stood up, facing Razor and nodding at Sammy. 'You took your goons and beat up his great-grandfather, a man nearly a hundred years old, a war veteran, leaving him bloodied and on his knees, while you laughed at him, purely because he asked you politely to let his great-grandson out of your control.'

As Razor looked over at Sammy, both of them finally realising what was going on, Marlowe continued.

'Well, here's the thing, Mister Gibson. He's now out of your control.'

He turned back to Sammy.

'Frank Maguire says you're released from whatever this prick's got on you, and you can go home now. No problems, no comeback. And Razor here will give you your severance package. Whatever's in his wallet.'

Razor went to reply, but Marlowe just held up his phone.

'The problem with this app,' he said, 'is it does it in order: one, two, three, four. And I can't remember which of your family members was number three. I mean, is Mum in the car right now? Or is Michelle having a drive? She's got a kid, hasn't she? Single mum? Shame if something bad happened. But it's a coin toss, really. You need to ask yourself if you can risk this.'

Razor stopped, placed the knife carefully on the table, and pulled out his wallet.

From the back of it, he yanked out a handful of what looked to be fifty-pound notes.

'I'm going to kill you,' he said, his voice strangely calm. 'I'm going to find you, you Mick bastard. And I'm going to—'

'I've heard it before,' Marlowe smiled, not allowing the young man to continue. 'Many times, in fact. And it's always *so scary* when I hear it.'

He took the money from Razor.

'I'll do you a deal. I don't have to kill you, if you leave right now – and never darken the door of Frank Maguire again.'

'I ain't going nowhere.'

'That's your choice,' Marlowe said. 'But it also means your air supply is gone. Someone in this bar is likely to get a call about replacing you, and from that point on, you're powerless. And a *threat*.'

He passed the wad of money over to Sammy, who took it, stepping back quickly in case Razor tried to take it back.

Now, it's up to you to decide whether you start from scratch here, or somewhere else. You could even take your friends with you, the ones who don't want to work for Maguire anymore – but trust me, you're done. There is no save point, no second go.'

He looked back at the men and noticed that nearly all of them had moved away from Razor at this point. Only two men, roughly around the same age and probably childhood friends, stood beside the man.

'All you've lost today is a couple of cars and a few quid,' Marlowe said. 'You leave now, you keep whatever else you have. But you don't "own this" anymore. This is *my* place now.'

Sighing, Razor nodded.

'Fine, whatever,' he said, chuckling to himself. 'You think you're some kind of bad man? You'll get yours.'

'Oh, I know.' Marlowe laughed. 'But it won't be from you.'

With that, he turned and started walking away, heading back towards the front entrance. He knew what was going to happen next. Razor wouldn't be able to help himself; he'd attack.

Marlowe had been waiting for this, though.

As he walked through the pub's entrance, out into the main car park, away from the two smoking cars already gathering a crowd – and likely a quick visit from the fire brigade – Razor charged at him, blade in hand.

Before Razor even got to the door, however, Marlowe pressed the third button, and two minor charges placed on either side of the doorway exploded out, catching Razor in the blast, and with a yelp he went down.

The C4 charges were tiny, nowhere near big enough to kill Razor or do any damage, but they were enough to knock him to the floor and hurt him.

As he crouched next to the prone, bleeding ex-gangster, Marlowe patted him on the shoulder.

'Next time,' he said, 'it's bigger, and it's you, your sister, your baby niece, your mother, or anyone I deem a friend of yours. Walk away, take what you have, start afresh. I won't repeat myself again.'

He hadn't realised, but his Irish accent had dropped. And although burnt and in pain, Razor stared at him.

'Who are you?' he said. 'You're not Irish.'

'I'm whoever I want to be,' Marlowe continued, leaning into this. 'I'm a shadow. I'm a ghost. And you'll never know I'm there.'

He looked up to Razor's friends, now standing inside the

pub watching out as, in the distance, the sound of sirens could be heard.

'Get him to a hospital, get him patched up, and get him the hell out of Essex,' Marlowe commanded. 'I suggest somewhere nice, like Weston-Super-Mare, Lowestoft, or maybe York. Otherwise, I'll come back.'

The threat finished, he turned and carried on over to his car. Driving away, heading north, towards Epping, he saw Sammy running down the pavement as fire engines and police cars drove the opposite way. Slowing down, he beeped his horn and waved to Sammy to get in.

Sammy clambered in, staring at him in shock.

'I don't know who you are, but thank you.'

'I'm a friend of your great-granddad's,' Marlowe said. 'You tell him the job's done. And from now on, don't make stupid decisions about who you hang out with again.'

'Yeah,' Sammy nodded. 'Can you drop me at—'

He stopped as Marlowe laughed.

'I'm not a cab company,' he said. 'You've got at least a thousand pounds in your pocket now. Get a bus.'

Sammy went to argue, but then shrugged and got out of the Jaguar as it stopped at the kerb, then headed north. Marlowe nodded to him before driving off towards the M25 – and home.

He'd helped Monty out, and this had been a nice warm up for him – but now he needed to prepare for the real thing.

Now he needed to prepare for Las Vegas.

3

VIVA LAS VEGAS

It took another day for Marlowe to make his arrangements for Las Vegas.

He could have hopped on the first flight there, but he wanted to ensure that he was prepared for whatever was coming. This might have been a sombre event, but he knew there would be many other things happening simultaneously. Most of the High Council of Orchid would likely be there, people he hadn't seen for several weeks – not since he had taken down a rogue Orchid agent's plan to destroy the US Presidency.

He was also aware the High Council had been both mixed and unhappy with the plan, and many of them had sided with Marlowe on this, but he still didn't know exactly where his position stood in the grand scheme of things.

That Orchid hadn't contacted him since then was a clue they were probably happy for him not to turn up to company days out.

So, a day later, Marlowe flew business class to Las Vegas from Heathrow.

Business class was a habit he'd gotten a bit too used to. When working for MI5, he'd often fly as a civil servant, and civil servants were given the lowest economy bookings, with their air miles going into a pot so other civil servants could use them. This usually meant MPs could upgrade their flights and have jollies while the civil servants stayed in "cattle class". But they often gave Security Service agents business class seats when on operations, knowing that once they landed, they wouldn't have time to acclimatise; they'd be straight on to the job, "boots on the ground".

If they were undercover, they would be in whatever class their cover required, usually economy, staying out of the spotlight; but the last few times Marlowe had flown to America, he'd flown on a slightly higher class of flight.

Brad Haynes had flown him business class to New York, and Sasha Bordeaux had given him a private jet the last time they'd crossed paths. He knew that wasn't something to get used to; after all, she'd also dumped him in the hold of a courier plane once too, but he liked the fact he could go into the lounge before getting on the plane.

The flight itself was uneventful; he kept to himself, read a book, and tried to take his mind off what was about to happen. Once in Las Vegas, he quickly moved through security, using an identity he'd picked up in France a few weeks earlier from Helen Bonneville, one of a handful of identities he knew were golden.

Once out of the airport he caught a cab to the Las Vegas Strip. The invitation had mentioned the *Gold Strike Hotel and Casino*, but there was no way Marlowe was going to stay there; it was too open and too obvious – and more importantly too *new*, having not even had the official launch yet. Instead, he picked the *Horseshoe Las Vegas*, a lower-level casino opposite the *Bellagio* on the Strip, and about a half mile from the wake location. Once known as *Bally's*, it was still undergoing renovation, and was a cost effective and convenient place to stay. He used a different fake name to check in, booked a suite, and used the online check-in section at reception once arriving to avoid bumping into anyone.

However, as he started checking in, he realised there was some kind of problem ...

There had been an alteration made to his booking.

Walking over to the reception desk, he smiled at the receptionist.

'Can I help you?' she asked.

'Yes,' Marlowe replied, giving her his most helpful smile. 'I was just checking into my suite in the tower, and it says there's been an alteration. It's booked under Colin Baker.'

The receptionist searched her screen, tapped on the keyboard, then nodded.

'Yes,' she said. 'We had your email last night. The one about your daughter.'

'My daughter?'

'Yes, your daughter, who's now staying with you. We've upgraded your suite to the two-bedroom Penthouse Suite.'

'Ah,' Marlowe nodded. 'That makes sense. Thank you, I hadn't realised that had happened. Has she checked in yet?'

The receptionist checked the screen.

'About an hour ago,' she said.

'Brilliant,' Marlowe kept the fixed smile on his face, as the receptionist passed him his own set of room cards, pointing him in the direction he needed to go to the penthouse suite and thanking him "for his service". He'd seen when booking the original room that a night in the suite was about fifteen hundred dollars; after working out who'd done this, he'd be passing the bill to them. He wouldn't be paying for this one alone.

Before he reached the elevators, however, Marlowe stopped in the hotel boutique. It was a standard tourist shop with fake casino chips, T-shirts, and baseball caps with the "Welcome to Las Vegas" sign on them, but he avoided these, looking instead for a few helpful items to use.

One of them was a metal camera tripod pole, sold mainly for anyone who'd forgotten their own. It was a portable one, only a foot in length, but Marlowe picked it up, anyway. It was made from an aluminium base, and it felt heavy when held.

He hadn't yet reached a point in his trip where someone could provide him with a weapon, and he hadn't risked bringing his more recent favourite hand to hand weapon, a security bracelet that uncoiled into a metre long steel whip. If somebody had been playing around with his room, he wanted to make sure he wasn't walking in unguarded. The last time he'd had someone in his room before he entered had been in San Francisco.

And he definitely didn't want another repeat of *that* attack.

So, with a weapon in his hand, Marlowe walked up to the elevators, preparing himself as he headed towards his suite. There weren't many people in Las Vegas who knew he was going to be in town, so he wasn't sure if this was actually going to be a problem or not, but Orchid had a long reach, and if someone had already worked out he was going to be staying here rather than the Gold Strike, there was every possibility that this was going to be a welcome gift he didn't want.

Arriving at his door, he paused and crouched by the lock

area. He saw no elements of tampering, but then if they'd given his "daughter" a card key, the chances were there wouldn't need to be. He looked around the corridor and noted that someone had placed a small portable webcam into the corner of the ceiling and wall opposite his room. It was small and basic, only an inch and a half in diameter, and if you weren't looking for it, you wouldn't have noticed it. But Marlowe knew the moment he saw it that this would be connected by the hotel's Wi-Fi to a laptop inside his room and lowering his guard, he grinned, opening the door with the key and entering his suite.

As Marlowe stepped into the penthouse suite, the first thing that struck him was the sheer size of the place. Spanning an impressive amount of square feet, the suite was definitely some kind of testament to luxury and space. Two living areas, each distinct in their layout and design, offered a clear view of the bustling strip below, once he'd walked through the marble-floored hallway, past a bathroom and into the main living area. The furniture in these areas was modern and comfortable looking, with plush sofas and elegant coffee tables littered around an empty bar, as if someone had got bored with laying things out and simply dumped them anywhere. Marlowe assumed this was a planned and orchestrated randomness.

To the right were the two bedrooms, each with a king-size bed, the frames crafted from rich, dark wood that contrasted with the white linens. Beside the bed in the closest room stood a writing desk, its surface clean and uncluttered.

Throughout the suite, the little things caught Marlowe's attention – a sleek fifty-five inch HD TV, a coffee maker behind the small, marble-topped bar, and a refrigerator discreetly tucked away while the air conditioning hummed quietly in the background, a subtle reminder of the desert heat outside.

Marlowe took a moment to absorb his surroundings. The suite was more than just a place to stay; it was a statement of power and elegance in a world where appearances were as important as reality.

Trix Preston looked up from the dining room table as he did so. She smiled, and Marlowe could see on the screen that her camera, the one she had placed in the corridor, had already tipped her of his arrival.

'Thought you'd be here earlier,' she said.

Marlowe sat his suitcase down and placed his hands on his hips, glaring at her.

'My daughter,' he said.

Trix shrugged. She was young, in her early twenties, and her long blonde hair had been pulled up into a bun, but her face was young for her age, something she had used to her advantage frequently. And Marlowe could see that with his bearded, greying, mid-thirties appearance, his face now slightly weathered with the life he'd lived, the irritatingly fresh-faced Trix could easily pass as a late teen daughter.

'What can I say,' Trix said. 'If I'd said I was your girlfriend or your wife or anything else ... well, first, they would have wondered how you managed to get such a catch, and second, we would only have had one bed.'

Marlowe walked to the coffee machine.

'There's no coffee machine yet,' Trix smiled, nodding over to the sink in the bathroom, where Marlowe could see a small kettle. 'It's broken. I've asked them to fix it, but I don't think it's a priority. Lucky for you, I've brought a travel kettle and some instant sachets.'

'Why isn't coffee a priority?'

'Las Vegas don't like you having coffee machines in your room,' Trix shrugged, staring at the screen as she typed. 'They want you out of your room and on the casino floor where the coffee stores are next to the slot machines. Why would you want to stay in your room when you have a chance to gamble?'

Marlowe grimaced.

'Fine,' he said as he turned, placing his hands on the table, facing Trix across it. 'So why don't you tell me why you're here? Last I recall, you were still playing games in the corner of my room and waiting for your opportunity to return to MI5.'

'Yeah,' Trix smiled. 'I don't think that's going to be happening anytime soon. Apparently, I'm a loose cannon.'

'You surprise me.'

'MI5 wanted to discuss with me about moving into Regent's Park, and bedding in with the analysts. You know, connecting with GCHQ and all that,' she shrugged. 'What can I say, working with you out in the field, it corrupted me. I'm used to the good things now; business class flights, hotel suites.'

She waved a hand around as she did so.

'Yeah, I'm not paying for this,' Marlowe growled.

'You don't need to,' Trix grinned. 'It was a free upgrade. I may have hacked into their systems and convinced them you were a long-term patron, war hero and big money player.'

Marlowe shook his head.

'That'll explain the "thank you for your service" line I received,' he muttered. 'You'll get us killed. Not by enemy spies, but the bloody Mafia.'

'I got your message.' Trix changed the subject. 'About the

man who left you the invite. I also checked the invite as well, and it's legit.'

'And how would you know that?'

'Ciaran still has some connections in Orchid, and I had him reach out to see if anybody was heading to Vegas this week. Quite a lot, apparently. It seems it's quite a convention going on.'

Trix leant back in her chair, watching Marlowe.

'I checked the feed, too. Saw the man with the pixelated head. He's big money.'

'How did you work that out?'

'The gloves,' Trix showed an image on the screen, a closeup from Marlowe's security footage. 'They're Hermes *Hapi* gloves, super expensive. You can tell from the stitching and the square silver buckle at the wrist. You want a pair? They'll cost you almost as much as this room costs for a night. And anyone who has a grand to throw on a pair of gloves ...'

She trailed off, watching Marlowe, making sure he understood the implications here. Once she saw he did, she continued.

'I knew you weren't going to invite me. You'd go off on this damn fool, "get this done on my own" kind of suicide mission. So I decided if you weren't going to ask me to be your backup, I'd come along, anyway.'

'I don't need backup,' Marlowe snapped, walking over to the bar again, this time picking a can of sparkling water from the fridge and opening it.

'You always need my help,' Trix shook her head. 'For once, accept the fact I've decided to help you, rather than you claim, erroneously, you don't need me.'

'And are you the only person backing me up I have so far?'

'Yes,' Trix nodded. 'I got in last night while you were playing silly bastards with Frank Maguire, and scoped the place, got some information, put a couple of webcams around. You know, usual spy shit.'

'Any friendlies?' Marlowe asked.

'Nobody yet that I recognise,' she replied. 'But I reckon we'll probably have Sasha Whatsherface turn up. Oh, there is one thing, though.'

She smiled now, tapping on her keyboard.

'There's a conference on this weekend, same time as the funeral. Not at the Gold Strike, but across the road at the Las Vegas Convention Centre.'

'Should I care about this other conference?' Marlowe raised an eyebrow. That Trix had mentioned it meant there was something going on here; he just didn't know what it was.

Trix's smile widened as she turned the laptop to show him the screen. On it was a familiar face.

'One of the guest speakers is someone we know,' she said, as the smiling face of an olive-skinned woman, with shortcut brown hair and blue eyes, stared out of the screen at him.

Roxanne Vasquez.

'Thought you might like to catch up,' Trix cooed. 'There's a lot of places you can go for dinner in Las Vegas.'

'If I realised you were here to sort out my love life, I would have called you a lot earlier,' Marlowe laughed. 'Let's see what happens with everything else before we start working on our evening dinners, yeah? We've got more important things to look into.'

'Like what?'

'Finding me a weapon,' Marlowe shrugged, nodding at his makeshift club on the table. 'I don't know anybody in Vegas.'

'Luckily for you, I do,' Trix said. 'I checked into it before I left. Marshall did some close security work off the books about ten years ago. He said one of the guys he worked with was solid; an ex-military-turned-actor guy named Ryan Gates. Comes from the UK, now lives in Las Vegas. Still does a bit of security work here and there, so I gave him a call. Mentioned Marshall's name, and he's providing you with something.'

'Great,' Marlowe said. 'Time and place?'

Trix grinned as she looked at her watch.

'In about half an hour,' she said. 'As I said when you arrived, I thought you'd be here earlier.'

MARLOWE WALKED INTO THE CAR PARK OF THE ATOMIC Museum in Las Vegas, its modern architecture a stark contrast against the desert backdrop. The building stood ominously under the bright Nevada sun; housing exhibits on the atomic testing era, it served as a reminder of the city's pivotal role in the Cold War's nuclear history.

It was only a half-mile walk from the hotel for Marlowe, which meant he had an opportunity to take in the sun as it set. It was late in the day already; Marlowe had planned to arrive, settle in, and start the following day. But if he could start things a little earlier, he wasn't going to say no.

As he arrived, he saw a red Corvette parked to the side, a man sitting inside it. Marlowe couldn't make him out that well through the tinted window, but he assumed that this had to be the man that Trix had arranged. And so, with a nod, Marlowe walked over, opening the passenger door and climbing into the car.

'Are you Gates?' he asked.

'I am,' Ryan Gates replied. 'You must be Marshall Kirk's protégé.'

'Oh, I wouldn't say protégé as such,' Marlowe smiled. 'I like to think of myself more as a slightly younger equal.'

'That's not what Marshall said when I called him,' Gates smiled. 'You know, I had to check you out and stuff. He was quite pissed that you'd gone on a jolly without him. Reckoned he's getting on the next plane.'

'This wasn't really the kind of thing Marshall could be used on,' Marlowe replied. 'It's a wake. A social event.'

'Yet one you need a gun for?'

'I don't need the gun for the event,' Marlowe shrugged. 'I need the gun for the people who might be at the event.'

Gates chuckled at this.

'Yeah, I get that,' he said.

A car pulled into the car park, and Gates turned to monitor it. As he did so, Marlowe took a moment to examine the man. He was in his sixties, stocky and with short, almost-shaved hair over a whitening beard. He was tanned, looked like he could keep his own in a fight, and wore chinos and a pale-blue polo shirt.

He looked back to Marlowe as the car drove off, simply using the car park as a turning circle, wincing as he did so.

'You okay?' Marlowe asked.

'Yeah, sorry,' Gates replied. 'Old wound. Had a speargun to the gut. Still aches when I turn sometimes.'

'A speargun?' Marlowe frowned. 'Some kind of war wound? Were you SBS? Boat squad?'

'Oh no, I was with my wife at a Robin Hood convention,' Gates chuckled. 'Long story, don't worry. We're still together.'

Marlowe decided that this was a conversation he probably didn't want to have. Sensing this, Gates turned, reaching behind him and pulling out a small black box. Marlowe recognised the style. It was a small gun case with most likely an automatic pistol within. With a smile, Ryan Gates placed the box on Marlowe's lap.

'Marshall said that you have an affinity for the Sig Sauer,' he said. 'Unfortunately, I don't have any right now, and the Glock's a second-rate gun if you ask me. But I've got this, it's off the books, always been a personal favourite.'

Marlowe opened the box, looking down at the gun inside.

It was a CZ 75BD. Pretty much the same size and weight as the Sig P226, it was a de-cocker, just like the Sig, and had the double action first round, with a single action follow up.

Gates was speaking as Marlowe pulled it out, examining it.

'Magazine capacity is sixteen to nineteen rounds, as you prefer, and any full size CZ magazine will work in this gun,' he explained. 'There's a reason the CZ's the most copied pistol in the world – it's tough, battle tested, and the ergonomics are second to none, no pistol sits better in the hand.'

'I've used this before,' Marlowe said. 'Kosovo, a few years ago. They're excellent guns, you don't see many of them about these days.'

'Not like this,' Gates said proudly. 'The trigger job was done by a custom shop out of Mesa, Arizona – took a decent trigger and made it smooth as butter, with a seven-pound double-action pull and three-point-five pound single, reduced reach and shorter reset.'

'Sounds like it's personal.'

'All my guns are personal so you'd better take good care of it now it's yours,' Gates grinned, passing over a box. 'Here, a chunk of ammo for you, although I'm guessing you can probably find your own places for that.'

Marlowe nodded, placing that into his pocket.

'If anyone ended up being shot, would it come back to you?'

Gates shook his head.

'If it comes back to anyone, it'll be someone long missing and buried in the Arizona desert,' he said. 'Actually, it's probably a good thing *you're* taking it on, just in case.'

Marlowe knew better than to ask if Ryan Gates was involved in the buried body.

'What do I owe you?' he asked.

'Marshall's already paid the bill,' Mark said. 'And we have a mutual friend who I owe, so it goes to that debt, too.'

'Do we?' Marlowe frowned.

'Yeah, you see, when my wife shot me with a spear gun, it was a DI called Walsh and a DCI called Monroe that got me off,' he said. 'I understand you're Monroe's nephew.'

'Small world,' Marlowe chuckled. 'Although it's complicated.'

'It always is. Anyway, all I ask is when you get back and see him, give him a nod from me.'

Gates watched as a minibus appeared, and a small group of tourists left it, heading into the museum.

'Who are you worried about?' he asked. 'To need this?'

'Let's just say I have a family event I don't trust,' Marlowe smiled. 'At the Gold Strike.'

'The Gold Strike?' Gates narrowed his eyes and looked as

if an unpleasant taste had entered his mouth. 'You want to be careful there. That's Gabriel Rizzo's new hotel.'

'As in the Rizzo family?'

Gates nodded.

'I keep away from it, but an old buddy works there, part of his security. You can't miss him, scar down his cheek. Anyway, he's an ex-Marine, worked with me a couple of times when I was in ... well, let's say a line of work similar to yours, and he says it's a horror show, so stay alert and watch your six at all times, because he grew up in Hell's Kitchen when it matched the name, and if he's worried ...'

He let the sentence trail off, the message given.

'I will do,' Marlowe closed up the box, went to leave and then paused. 'This might sound strange, but have we ever met before? You look familiar.'

'That depends,' Ryan Gates grinned, 'on if you ever watch TV. I'm on it here and there.'

'That must be it,' Marlowe nodded. 'I might call on you again while I'm here, is that okay?'

Gates nodded and started the car, an unspoken suggestion for Marlowe to leave. Pushing the gun box into his backpack, Marlowe stepped away from the Corvette, closing the door as it drove off, and started heading his way back to the hotel.

He'd been walking for three minutes when he realised he was being followed.

4

LINGERIE DEPARTMENT

HE DIDN'T HAVE TIME YET TO TAKE THE GUN AND PREPARE himself, and so, noticing a bar on the other side of the road, he quickly hurried across, walking in before anyone could catch up.

It was a low-class joint, what Marlowe would usually call a *truck stop bar*, far enough away from the strip to not gain the average tourist, but clean enough to avoid some of the more dubious locals.

He placed a five-dollar bill on the counter.

'Beer,' he said. 'And your restrooms?'

The barman, a beefy-looking black man with a growing beard and bald head, cleaning a glass with a dirty rag, used the rag to point to a room at the back. Marlowe nodded appreciatively and followed the direction, entering a rather murky and battered-looking bathroom that had definitely seen better days and more than its fair share of fights inside if the chipped sink was anything to go by.

Quickly, he moved into the cubicle, closed the door behind him, pulled out the CZ 75 and hit the mag release.

Confirming it was full, he reinserted the magazine and press checked the slide, confirming a round in the chamber. Usually, he'd want to check over the weapon, but he hoped Gates had done this for him. This done, he placed the box back in his bag, and slid the CZ into his waistband at the four o'clock position. He didn't know if he was going to need it, but if someone was following him already, he damn sure wanted to make sure he was ready.

He didn't want to return to the Horseshoe Casino before he knew what was going on. After taking the bought drink and pacing himself, allowing the men following to get tired outside for around another ten minutes, he then left the bar with a slightly faster pace now. He carried on walking to the Strip, heading past the Horseshoe Casino on the left, moving towards the fake Eiffel Tower that stared out over Las Vegas, with the Bellagio's Fountain on the other side of the road. Here it was busier, the tourists were in force. And here was an opportunity for him to take a moment and observe the men who were following him.

It was a two-man crew, both young, likely inexperienced. He didn't recognise either of them, but one of them, he noticed, kept checking a picture on his phone. He couldn't see what the picture was, but the phone had flashed in his direction once while he was glancing, pretending to look into a window, and he could see the blurred motion of a face on it.

The chances were they were trying to confirm if the man in the image was Marlowe. This was promising, as it meant they'd been sent out to look for people with his description, rather than they'd been following him since he'd left the hotel. There was no way to prove this though, unless he confronted them – and currently, confronting was the last thing he wanted to do.

Instead, he slid through the crowds, entering the inside shopping mall and restaurant area beside the Paris Eiffel Tower, heading quickly through the bustling tourists. As he did so, he walked into a boutique before they could see him, pulling off his thin denim jacket, stuffing it into his backpack. He quickly grabbed a brown leather coat in the style of a bomber jacket, and a red supreme backpack. It was slightly larger than the one he had, and he used this to place the smaller backpack into, while pulling the brown jacket, and a hastily grabbed Las Vegas branded baseball cap on, paying for all items while the cashier took the security tags off. Now with a new jacket, bag, and cap, he slipped out of the second entrance, moving back into the crowd.

It wasn't the look he wanted; he knew that his hair and beard still stood out, but it was enough to move him away from their observation.

He was about to continue, considering stopping at one of the inside diners, expensive but secluded slightly in the corners, when he saw another face, one he recognised for the second time that day.

Roxanne Vasquez saw Marlowe and her eyes widened in fear.

Marlowe had to be honest with himself, this wasn't the expression he'd expected her to give when seeing the man who had saved her life once in New York, and he started towards her, but she turned and hurried in the other direction.

Marlowe frowned, glancing behind him and seeing the two men were still on his tail. He still couldn't go back to the hotel, so this time he decided to follow Roxanne and find out what was truly going on. It took him another three or four minutes of hurrying through the Paris shopping mall before he finally stopped her, standing at the back of a woman's clothing shop waiting for him to pass by.

'You know, for someone who I haven't seen for a while,' he said, 'you're really making it feel like I'm not wanted.'

Roxanne looked at him.

'You ghosted me,' she said. 'I tried to call you and you ignored me.'

'I've been busy,' Marlowe replied as he looked back at the door. The two men were now standing there, looking around. 'Can you stay there for a moment? I need to fix something.'

With Roxanne looking confused, Marlowe walked back to the front of the shop, heading towards the two men who, once they looked up, didn't seem that surprised to see him walk towards them, still staring at the image on the phone.

His disguise wasn't that good, though, and this confused him. *Surely they'd have clicked he was the same man.*

Reaching into his pocket, he pulled out an old faithful.

'Guys,' he said, holding up his fake US Marshal badge. 'Dexter Garner, US Marshals. Can I ask what you're doing?'

'We're tourists,' the first of the two men said. He didn't continue as Marlowe grabbed the phone from him, looking down at the photo.

Nodding, he looked back up at them.

'So here's the deal,' he said, opening his jacket and flashing the CZ riding on his hip. 'I'll give you your phone back, and the two of you are going to turn around and walk for three minutes, no more, no less, in any direction. Then feel free to turn around and come back.'

'I—' the first of the two men started again, but Marlowe held a hand up.

'No,' he replied. 'No negotiations – or do I need to take you both in and find out what's really going on here?'

The men shook their heads.

'Why were you at the Atomic Museum?' Marlowe asked.

'We weren't,' the first of the men said. 'We were walking from the Gold Strike Casino.'

Marlowe nodded casually, as inside he tried to work out the angles here. *Were they Orchid? Had they been sent by someone to escort him, or murder him?*

'So, seeing me was purely by chance?'

'Dude, we don't even know who you are,' the second of the two men said, nodding at the pocket where Marlowe had placed his Marshal's card. 'Until we saw that, anyway.'

This surprised Marlowe, but he did a good job of hiding it.

'Well, it's your unlucky day then, isn't it?' he replied. 'Go back to the Gold Strike Casino and tell whoever sent you that today's jaunt around Las Vegas has been cancelled because of inclement weather.'

The two men looked confused at the last section, and Marlowe leant in closer.

'I mean lads, if you don't piss off right now, an absolute storm is going to land on you and whoever sent you.'

Placing the phone away, the two men turned and left.

Marlowe then gave it a moment, turned and walked back to where he had left Roxanne. Unsurprisingly, she wasn't there anymore. There was a door to the back though, that led into the service areas and Marlowe hurried into them.

He'd guessed she would move the moment he turned his back, but the confrontation with the men had taken just that little too long for him. It only took him a minute though, before he saw her once more, now stopped at a door that barred her way, frantically pushing at the bar as if hoping that, by jiggling it even harder, the door would magically open.

She looked at him, sighed and lowered her shoulders.

'Are you with them?' she asked.

'The men? No,' Marlowe said. 'In fact, fun story, I thought they were following me until the moment I saw they had your photo on their phone.'

'Ah. So why are you in Las Vegas, then?'

Marlowe walked closer.

'Family business. Unconnected to you,' he said. 'But now it seems that you need my help. So why don't you tell me why two muscles from the Gold Strike Casino, which I believe is owned by Gabriel Rizzo of the Rizzo family, have your photo on a phone and seem to want to have a serious word with you?'

'A serious word?' Roxanne chuckled, but it was a dark, bitter one. 'Is that what you call it?'

'Well, why don't you tell me what they want?'

Roxanne sighed. 'They were after me because Gabriel wants me dead,' she said. 'And currently, it's looking like he'll get what he wants.'

'Then it's your lucky day,' Marlowe smiled. 'Why don't we come back to my hotel suite and have a chat about this?'

Roxanne raised an eyebrow.

'We see each other for five minutes and already you're bringing me back to your room.'

'Oh, don't worry,' Marlowe said. 'We won't be alone. It'll be just like old times.'

'I DIDN'T THINK YOU MEANT YOU'D BE BRINGING YOUR girlfriend as well,' Roxanne joked as she entered the suite, nodding over to Trix, who was now seemingly building some kind of computer network out of her laptop.

Marlowe paused at the door, staring at the screens.

'When I left, you had a laptop,' he said. 'Now you seem to have two different screens on either side. How did you ...'

'It's called multitasking,' Trix replied with a smile. 'These fold up, and I can attach them. I've added a quick-release camera bracket to the back of one of them, and I can use a portable tripod to stand it up if I need to. Either way, it gives me three screens of real estate. If I need more, I've got some augmented glasses in my bag that I can throw out.'

She sighed theatrically.

'You didn't think I was going to destroy the world with just a laptop, did you?'

'No. And at the same time, please don't destroy the world,' Marlowe said as he escorted Roxanne in.

Trix chuckled.

'I will say, however, that when I said that Roxanne was in town, I didn't expect you to go find her immediately.'

Marlowe flipped Trix the finger as he walked to the wet bar, pulling out his CZ 75 and placing it on the counter.

As he did so, he heard an intake of breath from Roxanne.

'Are you sure you're not here for anything dodgy?' she asked.

'I didn't say I wasn't here for anything illegal,' Marlowe replied. 'I just said I wasn't connected to the gangster who's trying to kill you.'

At this, Trix looked up, interested.

'Now I'd like to know some more,' she said. 'Who's trying

to kill you, why are they're trying to kill you, and when they *do* try to kill you, how do we destroy them?'

'You see,' Roxanne said as she looked back at Marlowe, 'that's how you get someone on your side.'

Marlowe shrugged, reaching into the minibar and pulling out a can of beer. He noted that there were more drinks in there than there had been the last time he'd looked. Glancing back at Trix, she shrugged.

'I asked room service to send up a few extra things. I knew that without the coffee, you'd get irritable without some sweet, sparkly drinks to drink. Oh, and they fixed the coffee machine, too, so maybe you didn't need them after all.'

'So I guess asking you why you're here, and why you have a gun, isn't going to give me an answer I like?' Roxanne asked.

'Believe it or not, I'm here for my father's wake,' Marlowe replied.

'Your father?' Roxanne looked quickly at Trix, unable to hide her shock. 'The guy you met in New York who basically told you to piss off and he never wanted to speak to you again?'

'Yes, that one,' Marlowe nodded, opening the can and drinking a mouthful of beer.

'And he's dead?'

'Well, that's usually what a wake entails,' Marlowe replied. 'I saw him a few weeks back before he died. I was involved in an undercover case, I can't really talk about it. And he was my way into a meeting.'

'It turned out he was on the High Council of a secret, secret society,' Trix grinned. 'But when Marlowe turned up and said, "hello Daddy, I love you, I haven't seen you for years," his father gave him a gift, the hereditary seat on the High Council.'

Marlowe grimaced at the thought.

'Either way, I've been invited to his wake or memorial service, and it's at the Gold Strike Hotel and Casino tomorrow.'

At the name, Roxanne paled – most likely thinking of Gabriel Rizzo and his apparent hatred of her, and Marlowe took the moment of silence to lean back against the bar, watching Roxanne.

'I've shown you mine, why don't you show me yours?'

Roxanne waved for a can of beer to be passed to her as well, and Marlowe did so, pulling a fresh one out of the fridge and resisting the urge to toss it, allowing it to spray everywhere when she opened it.

Opening it and taking a long draught, she sighed.

'I'm here for an environmental law conference,' she explained. 'I wasn't going to be involved in anything else, but then, another lawyer who was attending, one who works here, she didn't show up.'

'Was she supposed to?'

'She's the keynote speaker,' Roxanne replied, a little too condescendingly. Marlowe let it slide. 'Suffice to say, she should have been here, and she wasn't. But she's local, so I went and checked her out, and I found her house was gutted. Burned to the ground.'

'She was in it?'

'Yeah, and she was in hospital. I visited her yesterday.'

'I'm guessing she's not great,' Marlowe said. 'I'm guessing burns?'

Roxanne nodded, taking another mouthful of beer.

'Third degree, some first. They used accelerant, Marlowe. Poured it all over the outside of her house while she was asleep. Lit it up like a candle. She only just got out, but she's lost a chunk of her face, her shoulders, her upper arms, and she's in a medical coma. It'll take a couple hundred grand worth of skin grafts and plastic surgery to fix, and even then she'll never look the same.'

'So someone was trying to kill her, or send a warning?' Trix now asked, the anger audible in her voice.

'You mean, did they know she was in there?' Roxanne shrugged. 'I don't know. And currently Lexi Warner – that's the woman – she's not speaking.'

'Because she can't, or because she won't?'

'You remember the bit literally seconds ago when I mentioned the word "coma," right?' Roxanne said snarkily. 'Anyway, I asked around to find out what was going on, and I learned she'd been involved in a couple of cases for a casino on the outskirts. Not one of the big ones, but family-controlled.'

'By family, you mean the Rizzos,' Marlowe nodded, noting that Trix was already typing on her computer. 'That's where the goons came from. They told me when I—'

'Wait, what goons?' Trix looked around now, confused. 'What exactly did I miss when you went for your stroll?'

'Well, I gained myself a nice new gun, found some people were following me, realised they weren't following me, learned they worked for the Rizzo family and were actually following Roxanne, and there you go.'

Trix let out a whistle.

'First Nathan Donziger, now the West Coast Rizzo family,' she replied to Roxanne. 'When you pick people to piss off, you really go platinum level, don't you?'

'Yeah, it was the Gold Strike,' Roxanne nodded. 'Gabriel Rizzo had employed her services a few times. However, it seemed this was a few times too many. She'd ...'

She paused, as if trying to find the right words.

'Let's just say from what I can work out, the official story is she found herself tempted when she was in control of the budget on one of the cases,' she continued tactfully. 'She brought in a few million from an unpaid source, but some of it, well, it fell away.'

'How much fell away?'

'A few grand, maybe fifty.'

'They did all this for fifty grand?' Trix was surprised.

'It's more the optics,' Marlowe added, understanding. 'Doesn't matter what the amount was. She stole from them, and they couldn't let it stay out there like that.'

'But that's the problem,' Roxanne replied. 'I've known of Lexi for years. She's a straight arrow, makes seven figures a year. She wouldn't risk everything for fifty grand.'

'You think she's being set up?'

'I know she is.' Still holding the beer, Roxanne rested her free hand on her hip. 'Which means something else is going on, and she found something she wasn't supposed to.'

'Still doesn't explain why they want you now?' Trix was typing again.

'I may have been a little blunt,' Roxanne admitted sheepishly, taking a long draught from the can before continuing. 'Confronted Gabriel in public. Told him I was going to get the truth, find some vengeance for her.'

'Let me guess, mob types are less likely to negotiate than New York corporations?'

'I learned she's not the first he's taken out this way,' Roxanne glowered at Marlowe now. 'I know she didn't take the money, and this was set up to discredit her. Asking around, I heard she'd found something out. Something bad.'

'Like what?' Trix asked. 'And, more importantly, from who?'

'A source,' Roxanne said evasively. 'Someone I think Marlowe should speak to.'

'So, your friend Lexi found out something about Gabriel Rizzo, maybe spoke to him about it, or he learned she'd found his secret out, and then he tries to kill her, blaming a theft?'

'We can't prove he tried to kill her,' Roxanne shook her head. 'He's claiming she was working with a rival firm and they probably tried to kill her when she didn't come through for them.'

'Clever,' Trix pursed her lips. 'He places blame on a rival, maybe takes them off the board, too. Or at least keeps them busy while he does something else at the casino.'

She glanced at Marlowe knowingly.

'Maybe even through your wake. The website says his official launch is in a couple of days.'

'If it helps, my source mentioned another gang,' Roxanne added now. 'She didn't hear it clearly, but she thinks they're called the *War Kids*. Rizzo apparently owes them big time.'

Marlowe had to force his face to stay emotionless this time.

War Kid.

Orchid.

Before he could reply, however, Trix frowned as a new thought went through her mind, looking back at Marlowe.

'Hold on. Are you telling me that in a city like Las Vegas, with millions of people, you walked into the exact two people who were chasing Roxanne?'

Now, Trix spun slowly in her chair, focusing on the American lawyer, standing, nervously sipping her beer.

'That isn't how Las Vegas works. So why don't you tell me what actually happened?'

Roxanne went to argue, and then paused, sighing.

'I saw him,' she nodded at Marlowe. 'At the airport. I was waiting for a colleague, someone who could help me with the problems with Lexi, but he decided not to turn up.'

'Let me guess, scared off by the Rizzo family name?'

Roxanne nodded.

'He was a private eye I'd dealt with a few times in New York, and I thought he'd be strong enough to take on these guys. Seems he wasn't. Anyway, I was about to leave, and I saw Marlowe walking out, calling a cab. I followed, saw he was at the Horseshoe, but when I went in, I lost him. I didn't want to turn up on his doorstep and ask for help, so I thought I'd see if I could find something out myself.'

Roxanne flushed as she continued.

'I'd been camping out around the area, playing a few slots, hoping he'd come out, do whatever he needed to do, and I'd be able to speak to him.'

'Well, I'm here,' Marlowe placed his can on the counter. 'And it looks like our stars are aligned again.'

'Yay,' Trix said, but there was no enthusiasm in her tone whatsoever. 'So, what now?'

Marlowe went to reply, but stopped.

Actually, he had no idea what to do next.

———

5
_____

BROTHERLY LOVE

As the evening was drawing on, Roxanne had decided she needed to head back to her room at the Gold Strike Hotel and Casino, if only to gather some things. Marlowe hadn't been happy about this, especially with the knowledge now out that Rizzo wanted her either to be tortured for information, or dead. Even so, she was adamant that she had to return. After all, she was at a conference that started the following day, and if she was staying here, with Marlowe once more on the couch, she needed to grab her items – which were in the hotel room.

Marlowe had even considered going alone to her room, picking up the items and bringing them across, like the friend or the brother of a girl who was leaving their partner, picking up their items from the apartment so that she didn't have to meet her ex again. But in the end, nobody could make the final decision on what should be done. Marlowe wanted one plan, Roxanne another, and Trix, wisely, kept her head glued to her monitor screens.

Marlowe was about to decide for everyone and be

damned with the consequences when his phone beeped. It was a message from an unknown number.

Bellagio Fountain, now.

He wasn't sure who it was, as the Caller ID had been withheld, but the chances were it was somebody he knew, and who knew he was in Vegas. That left a small list of people. Maybe it was Gates, having learned something already? He wouldn't know who it was from until he saw them face to face, and with everything else that was going on this week, he knew it was probably a meeting he needed to take. So, grabbing the CZ and tucking it in his waistband, he told Roxanne to wait, wandered out into the Horseshoe Casino's ground floor, and followed the Paris shopping centre out to where the Bellagio Fountains were on the main strip.

Arriving there, he looked around. It wasn't one of the set times for the Bellagio fountain performances, where the fountain performed various programmed movements to music with lights flashing around it. Instead, it was quieter, with only a few tourists around, some waiting optimistically, some just taking photos before moving on.

However, there was one man standing there that Marlowe recognised.

It was his half-brother. Marlowe had never found out his real name, just remembered him as "Ichabod" because of his strange resemblance to the animated Ichabod Crane from *The Legend of Sleepy Hollow*, the Disney cartoon rather than the live-action movie. Marlowe hadn't seen or heard from his half-brother since his father's death; he'd assumed the family wanted it kept that way, and it wasn't until the card had appeared, inviting him to this Vegas wake, that he'd even considered the ramifications of Taylor Coleman's passing.

Ichabod stood strangely formal amidst the other tourists, wearing a black suit, white shirt, and black tie. Seeing Marlowe approach, he turned, nodded slightly, and walked over, meeting him beside the railings of the Bellagio fountain.

'Thank you for coming,' he said. 'I didn't think you would.'

'I'll be honest,' Marlowe replied. 'I did consider refusing, but it was a coin toss. I didn't know if I'd even been *accidentally* invited, if it wasn't for the guy who broke into my apartment to leave the note.'

'I meant coming here now,' Ichabod frowned. 'I wanted to know why you were in Las Vegas.'

Marlowe went to reply, but paused, confused.

'If you weren't expecting me, how did you know I was in town?' he asked. 'I used an ID you didn't know.'

'And then you told people you were a Marshall named Dexter Garner,' Ichabod shrugged. 'Go figure, super spy. Still doesn't explain why you're here.'

'You invited me,' Marlowe pulled the invite out of his pocket, passing it over, but noting the fact that Ichabod had ears on the ground in Vegas; in particular, the people who worked for Gabriel Rizzo.

Ichabod squinted at it, peering closely.

'It definitely looks like ours, or a very good fake,' he said. 'But you weren't on the list.'

Marlowe hadn't been sure, but he thought he saw Ichabod smile at this. At the same time, he wondered why someone had gone to such lengths to get him here.

'Still, I suppose you should be here, with your position

and everything. Consider this a verbal invite. I'll make sure security knows.'

'Thanks, I suppose,' Marlowe replied tersely as Ichabod passed the invite back, now examining Marlowe, as if expecting him to be hiding something.

'I noticed you're not staying at the Gold Strike,' he said.

Marlowe shook his head.

'I never stay where an event's being held,' he replied. 'The last couple of times I've done that, things have gone wrong.'

'I get that,' Ichabod nodded. 'But I'll arrange a room for you to be booked there if you do require it.'

'Good to know,' Marlowe looked out across the lake.

Ichabod watched him for a second.

'Is there a problem?'

'Actually, yes,' Marlowe looked around, making sure they were alone for the moment. He couldn't see any black-suited goons around and didn't know if Ichabod was as guarded as his father was. 'Gabriel Rizzo. What's his connection to your father?'

'Rizzo ...' Ichabod considered the name. 'He and my father worked together quite a lot. It was Rizzo who suggested his casino be used for the wake. Why do you ask?'

'It's not the first time his name's turned up today,' Marlowe replied. 'A lawyer I know had her house burned down, believed to be by Rizzo and his men.'

It was an exaggeration. Lexi was a lawyer he knew *of* rather than knew, but he wanted to see what happened if he pushed buttons.

If Ichabod knew about this, he was a very good poker player, however, and shrugged.

'I have no knowledge of what Mister Rizzo or his family

do when we're not around,' he said. 'But Mister Rizzo has been a very loyal friend to both my father and to Orchid.'

'Of course he has,' Marlowe sighed. 'Bloody Orchid yet again.'

'On that subject,' Ichabod reached into his inside jacket pocket, rummaging around. 'The reason I called you here once I heard you were in town.'

After a moment of rummaging, he pulled out a coin. It was about the size of a one ounce bullion coin, around an inch and a half in diameter, but it was a metallic black, almost like someone had charred it – and Marlowe could see from the moment Ichabod revealed it, that the coin was specially forged.

On one side was a selection of numbers and barcodes, and on the other was a single image engraved into the surface – that of an orchid.

'This was my father's,' Ichabod carried on. 'It's his High Council coin. It's what you need if you're attending a High Council meeting.'

'I didn't need one in the virtual world.'

'That's because it was virtual, Thomas,' Ichabod almost smiled as he mocked. 'And the Palace of Versailles was a larger scale event, where the coins weren't needed. But know this, my father – *our* father had it on his person at all times. Even when he passed the reins to you.'

Marlowe didn't take the coin, watching Ichabod carefully.

'You should be on the High Council,' he said. 'Not me. This should be yours.'

Ichabod actually laughed at this.

'And what makes you think I want it?' he asked. 'Besides, even if I did, a simple surreptitious giving wouldn't work.

You've seen how Orchid operates now. They would expect something vocal and public.'

'I can do that.'

Ichabod shrugged.

'Our father pointed out this was a gift that you wouldn't want, and it was given to you to clear his own family from the curse he'd created. By you, his bastard, taking this coin, his legitimate heirs can be free of Orchid, of the past, and left to build our own industries, our own legacies, while you take on the poison chalice and issues our father left in his wake.'

Marlowe clenched his teeth at this; he knew the family he never had thought little of him, believing him the result of a brief affair, but it stung to hear it stated so matter-of-factly.

'Wow, you almost make it sound exciting,' he said, picking the coin from Ichabod's outstretched hand, and looking at it. 'Do you really think so little of me?'

'Honestly, Thomas, your half-brothers and sisters, including myself? We don't think of you at all,' Ichabod replied calmly. 'The wake starts at midday tomorrow. It's up to you whether or not you attend. The coin will gain you admittance to anywhere you need to go. Be aware that any, as you say in England, *shenanigans* will be replied upon in kind.'

Marlowe nodded, placing the coin in his pocket.

'I am sorry about Taylor's passing,' he said. 'He was a shit father to me, and I hated his guts for most of my life, but I'm sorry for your loss.'

He saw Ichabod draw in a breath through his teeth.

'Oh, don't look so surprised,' Marlowe continued. 'I think you're aware of that as well. But, that said, the way he went, it shouldn't have been—'

'He chose his path,' Ichabod had already turned and was

walking away as he interrupted. 'I hope to see you at the wake, Thomas. It would be nice to say goodbye.'

'You make it sound like we'll never see each other again,' Marlowe laughed, shouting loudly after him.

But Ichabod had already left.

Marlowe sighed and decided to return to the hotel. That Ichabod had asked to meet at the Bellagio fountain, a short walk from the Horseshoe, made him suspicious it was already known where he was staying. But then again, it could simply be a case of knowing that the Bellagio fountain was smack bang in the centre of the Las Vegas strip, and no matter where he was staying, he could reach it.

He stared at the coin. He knew Ichabod had made a thing about not wanting this, but there was the slightest of hesitations when giving it. Marlowe might have imagined it, but it felt as if Ichabod, for a moment, had wanted to take whatever was behind door number two.

Interesting. Almost as interesting as who'd worked hard to get a fake invite to him.

Walking back into the suite, Marlowe noticed a hamper at the side of the door.

Checking it, he saw inside was a bottle of champagne and some deli meats and bread, some chocolates – expensive ones – and a card. Pulling it out, he opened it up and read the message on the inside.

We're grateful for your service. The Horseshoe Casino.

Marlowe frowned as he opened the door, taking the hamper with him and placing it onto the table.

'When you upgraded me,' he said to Trix, looking up from her screens, 'what did you tell them?'

'I might have embellished a few things,' Trix laughed. 'Mister Baker might have turned from a bearded, scraggly man to a purple-heart-wielding veteran who was—'

'I don't want to hear anymore,' Marlowe waved a hand at the item, now on the dining table. 'The Horseshoe's sent us a basket with meats and treats in, and they rarely do that for simple veterans.'

Trix smiled, rising, walking over to the basket, reaching in to grab something.

'You might want to check it first,' Marlowe held a hand up. 'Just because it says it's from the hotel doesn't mean it is.'

Trix paled, the piece of cheese she was about to eat dropping from her hand. Marlowe smiled slightly. It was likely from the hotel, but it was the minor battles that made the winning worthwhile, as Trix now sniffed the hamper like some kind of poison sniffer dog.

'Who was the meeting with? Your brother?' she asked, deciding to throw caution to the wind and eating the piece of cheese.

'Yes,' Marlowe replied, initially ignoring Roxanne's interested expression from the sofa across the suite, but then turning to face her. 'I have a half-brother. It's very strange. I call him Ichabod. I don't think he likes it. Apparently the invite to the wake I received was fake, given by a man wearing obscenely expensive gloves. Again, don't ask. Have we decided yet?'

Roxanne nodded, rising.

'I want to go back to the hotel,' she said.

'Okay, we can do that,' Marlowe replied, looking back at Trix. 'You good to hold the fort?'

'I am,' Trix said, reaching into a black canvas zip bag and pulling out what looked to be some kind of earbud. 'Fifteen-mile range, goes on several frequencies. Even if you're in the middle of a casino with steel and concrete all around you, we'll get through to you here.'

'Thank you,' Marlowe said, placing it into his ear, tapping it twice to test it. Trix nodded, seeing it blip twice on her screen.

This done, Marlowe looked back at Roxanne.

'So, the plan is, we get you to your hotel room, we grab your items, we bring you back here,' he said.

'Hey,' Trix said. 'Your half-brother, did he explain why the wake's being held at the same hotel as Roxanne's fatal attraction?'

'Apparently, Gabriel Rizzo worked with Taylor Coleman as some kind of financier,' Marlowe said. 'It looks like both cases are merging into one right now.'

'Well, that always seems to be the case, doesn't it?' Roxanne laughed. But it was a nervous one, like Roxanne already knew this. Marlowe noted this in the back of his mind; he'd consider that more fully later, but first they had a job to do.

'We get your items, and then we speak to your source,' he said, grabbing a piece of cold meat and chewing on it. 'Tomorrow is going to be an interesting day.'

6

GOLDEN STRIKES

THE GOLD STRIKE CASINO WAS EXPANSIVE AND NEW, BUILT ON the land where the Stardust Casino had once been. The Stardust Casino itself had been a location of gangsters and crime, and all the press for the Gold Strike had been about how this was a change, a new guard, and how crime was a thing of the past in Sin City.

That it was owned by the Los Angeles Rizzo family, a long-time player in Las Vegas crime culture had been handily swept under the table, at least for those who didn't care anyway, it seemed, as Marlowe walked up to the casino with Roxanne nervously walking beside him.

It was bright and flashy, with lights illuminating the entrance. Marlowe was surprised to see that in the doorway there were bodyguards stopping people as they walked in.

Marlowe frowned. *Most casinos actively welcomed people in, rather than turning them away.*

He looked back at Roxanne, who seemed as confused as he was.

'The hotel is on soft launch for a couple of weeks before

the opening,' she whispered. 'But it wasn't like this when I left.'

'I don't think they've done all this for you,' Marlowe thought to himself as he replied.

Maybe this was because of the guest list for Taylor Coleman's wake.

He was sure there would be quite a few dignitaries and billionaires turning up to pay their respects. Was this an extra level of security brought on? Marlowe wasn't sure, but he knew also that the metal detectors he could now see at the entrance would easily notice the gun in his back waistband. Still, this was Vegas, Nevada, and guns weren't illegal. He even had a fake gun permit he could use if needed, and a marshal badge he could use if things got hairy.

Taking a breath, Marlowe walked up, joining the queue to enter on the right-hand side, while Roxanne started along the left-hand side. She had little on her, no bag or anything else, so Marlowe assumed she would go through quickly, as long as she wasn't picked up by someone in relation to her connection to Lexi Warner, or the scene Marlowe assumed she'd made when confronting Rizzo.

Two people in the queue ahead of Marlowe, a man was having an argument with the guard. He'd placed his gun, what looked to be a 9mm semiautomatic in a leather holster in a plastic box about to be fed through the machine, but was now being told by the guard the other side of the table that he couldn't take the gun into the casino. He was raising an argument, pointing out that "this was Nevada and he could do what he damn well pleased," while the guards were quite patiently explaining that "yes, he could do whatever he wanted, just not here and just not this week."

Marlowe knew he was about to lose his gun, but there

was nothing he could do about this. Watching, he saw them take the man's gun, allow the man, still angry but reluctantly complying in, and give him a chit to claim his gun back when he left.

It had all the hallmarks of a common situation and Marlowe assumed that quite a few people wielding guns of various kinds had found themselves in a similar situation – a casino that was tightening down, if only for the week, apparently. Marlowe didn't want to be in the casino weaponless, but there was nothing more he could do.

When it came to his turn, he smiled at the man behind the counter, set up to look almost like a TSA security arrival at an airport. There was a small plastic tray to place his pocket items in, and a second larger one to place any bags that he might own. Laptops and iPads were being brought out by other people in the queues, and these were being examined more intently by the guards before being passed through. This was understandable, as many casinos were worried about tech-heavy grifters coming in to rip them off.

But Marlowe didn't need to worry about that. He needed to worry about the possibly serial numberless and illegal weapon in his pocket.

With a sigh and a smile, Marlowe pulled out his items from his pockets, placed them into the grey container, and went to pull his gun out from the back of his jeans.

'I have a gun,' he said. 'It's concealed, but I have a permit.'

He stopped as the guard held a hand up.

'Could you come with me, sir?' The guard spoke softly, taking the plastic box with Marlowe's items and moving to the side. Marlowe glanced back at Roxanne, who hadn't quite reached her point of entry yet, and saw her expression was one of horror as she watched Marlowe being escorted with two men on either side to a table across from the entranceway.

Marlowe walked with them, preparing himself, checking the men on either side. One was burly and looked like he was built out of brick, but the other was slim, wiry. He would be the trouble one. The brick guy would just absorb punishment but would be slow to react. The wiry one would be quick to attack. Marlowe needed to take him out first, even if the larger one was going to hit him.

But instead, the man with the plastic box stopped at a table, placed it down, and looked up at Marlowe.

'Our apologies, sir,' he said. 'Please take your items and enter the casino.'

Marlowe frowned.

'Why did you take me away?'

'You mentioned you had a weapon, sir. We can't let anybody see us allow someone with a gun to enter the casino,' the guard apologetically explained. 'We've been told that in cases like yours, we bring you over here, out of sight.'

Marlowe narrowed his eyes as he stared at the man.

'What do you mean?' he asked. 'When you say, "cases like yours?"'

The guard said nothing else, but tapped with his finger on the black coin of Orchid, the one Ichabod had given Marlowe less than an hour earlier, as if by doing this, all Marlowe's questions would be answered.

'You know what this is?' Marlowe asked.

'No, sir,' the security guard replied. 'And I don't want to know. All I know is we've been told by our superiors that if anybody turns up with one of these, we're to let them in without question.'

For the first time, possibly ever, Marlowe was actually grateful to have spoken to Ichabod.

One guard, however, paused Marlowe as he went to leave.

'Sir, you shouldn't have the gun tucked away like that,' he suggested, looking around and pulling a belt holster off one of the confiscated guns to the right. 'Here, use this one.'

Marlowe gave a brief nod of thanks to the guard as he took the holster, clipped it to the inside of his belt, and slid the CZ 75 into it.

'Where's reception?' he asked.

The guard nodded over past the brightly lit bandit machines and arcades to a wall at the far end.

Marlowe nodded thanks again and started out, but stopped as he noticed that on the other security section, Roxanne had passed through, but was now being surrounded by three suited men, one of whom he recognised as the goon who had been following her earlier that day.

Walking over, he must have given serious "get-lost" vibes, with an expression as dark to match, because the moment he started towards them, the goons standing on either side of her, and the third facing her, stopped and glared at him.

'This isn't your problem,' one goon said. 'You should back off.'

'This woman's under my care,' Marlowe said.

'You might be the law outside,' the goon who had met him earlier on in the day said, 'but you've got nothing here. This is a private estate and security covers this.'

One of the other goons looked confused, and the one who had met Marlowe earlier turned and said, 'he's a US Marshal.'

'The woman you're surrounding is under my care,'

Marlowe continued. 'I'd appreciate it if you took your hands away from her.'

Roxanne wisely kept quiet.

Nobody moved.

'Dude, you're in the wrong place at the wrong time,' the goon to the left, obviously unimpressed by the "US Marshal" line, snarled menacingly.

Marlowe simply stared at him, glanced around, and saw a security camera on the ceiling above them.

He looked up, directly facing it.

'I want to speak to Gabriel Rizzo,' he said.

At this, the goon who had met him earlier laughed.

'Everybody wants to see Mister Rizzo,' he said. 'Mister Rizzo doesn't want to see them.'

'Mister Rizzo will want to see me,' Marlowe continued. 'Tell him Thomas Marlowe is here.'

'That ain't the name you gave me earlier,' the goon frowned.

Marlowe gave an astonished look at him.

'Really?' he said innocently. 'I wonder why that was. Could it be that I didn't know who the hell you were at the time, and didn't want anybody to know I was in town until you forced my hand?'

At this, the goon frowned. He didn't understand what was going on; this was a US Marshal who now seemed to be something more, and something more meant *out of his pay grade.* Which was always a problem.

'It's very simple,' Marlowe said, waving a hand idly at Roxanne. 'I want to speak to Gabriel Rizzo right now about this issue.'

'There isn't an issue,' the goon snapped back. 'Miss Vasquez here is not welcome in the casino, and we—'

'*You* are doing nothing,' Marlowe finished for him. 'Miss Vasquez is still a guest of your hotel and casino, and unless you've emptied her room already, you will *not* be taking her out of the building or anywhere else. As I said, she is under my care.'

He looked back at the camera, this time pulling out the blackened coin, holding it up.

'I want to speak to Gabriel Rizzo,' he repeated, mouthing the words so that anybody watching through the camera would recognise them. The goon went to snap back another reply and then stopped as his radio earpiece buzzed.

He listened for a moment, looked at Marlowe, frowned, and then nodded to the two other goons.

'Back office wants to meet him,' he said. This was obviously unheard of, as the two other men seemed incredibly surprised at such a response. Marlowe, putting away the coin, looked back at them.

'As I said,' he repeated, calmly, 'this woman is under my protection. Let her go.'

The men on either side complied, but the third, the one who had met him as Dexter Garner, US Marshal, was still frowning.

'This is bullshit,' he said. 'I don't know what game you're playing here, but back office, they're going to tear you apart.'

'Maybe, maybe not,' Marlowe said. 'Let's go find out, yeah?'

With a nod, the goon sighed, motioning for Marlowe and Roxanne to follow him. Walking in step beside him now, Roxanne looked at Marlowe, confused and mildly horrified.

'You're taking me to the guy who wants to *kill* me,' she said. 'Are you crazy?'

'I've done crazier things before,' Marlowe said. 'And, I'll

be honest, I have a feeling at the moment, I'm untouchable. Let's see how far that goes.'

Once through the back door, Marlowe watched as the goons used a variety of different key codes and door cards to move into the back area. He was surprised that neither of the men tapping in numbers made any effort to change or to hide the numbers being tapped in. On noticing Marlowe watching, one of them laughed.

'Biometrical approved,' he said. 'You can know my number, but unless you're actually using my hand to open the door, the number won't work.'

'Nice,' Marlowe replied. 'Just better hope that someone doesn't cut your hand off.'

If this single line concerned the goon, he said nothing, instead opening the door and allowing Marlowe and Roxanne through. Now into a more lavish area, the corridors were carpeted, and it felt more like a convention centre than the back hallways of a building. There was an elevator at the end, and they escorted Marlowe and Roxanne into it, one goon pulling a small key out and clicking it into the metal lock.

Marlowe was impressed by this. Everything else seemed to be based on RFID, NFC or digital connections, but this was analogue. This was something that couldn't be hacked. Turning the key anti-clockwise, the goon pressed a button, and the elevator started moving. After a moment of absolute silence in the carriage, the doors opened once more, and the three men surrounding Marlowe and Roxanne suggested, quietly, with hand motions, that Marlowe and Roxanne follow them.

They were in a hallway leading to an ornate wooden door. Rapping on it twice, the goon Marlowe had known the longest stepped back as a new, more vicious-looking man opened the door. This man was in his late fifties, his hair peppered with white, cut short in a military cut, a scar running down from his temple across the side of his eyebrow. Marlowe guessed it was some kind of knife wound, but he wouldn't have sworn on the Bible about this, and wondered if this was the ex-Marine that Ryan Gates had mentioned earlier.

'Mister Rizzo will see you,' he said, and Marlowe noted that his accent was from New York. With the Rizzo family being West Coast based, Marlowe wondered whether this was by chance, or whether there was some kind of East-West exchange scheme going on, but the possible Hell's Kitchen origins of the accent gave even more credence to the fact this was Gates' friend.

Entering the room itself, Marlowe had expected to see some kind of casino nerve centre, with giant screens on the walls showing videos from the casino floor, but instead it was quite sparse. To the right of the entrance and against the white-painted walls was a black bookcase with a few ornaments and books on it. There were a couple of poster frames behind the desk, each showing Las Vegas related movies: the first was the Scorsese *Casino* film poster, while next to it was a poster for *Ocean's Eleven* – the Clooney version rather than the original "Rat Pack" one.

The desk was a basic, wooden-topped sit/stand desk, with a laptop, a lamp and a mug of probably coffee. There was nothing else, although beside it on the floor was a metal briefcase, currently closed.

Sitting at the desk was a man, watching Marlowe curiously as he entered, his hair short and cropped at the sides while slicked back on the top, a side parting giving volume.

He wore a pastel-blue shirt under a pale-cream suit, and Marlowe could see that under the desk, he was wearing Converse trainers.

This was not the look Marlowe expected a West Coast gangster to have unless he was reliving the hits of *Miami Vice* or *Scarface*.

'Thomas,' he said, smiling as he rose, holding a hand out for Marlowe to shake. 'I've heard so little about you, when I saw you were here, I just had to meet you.'

'Of course you did,' Marlowe smiled as he shook the outstretched hand. 'The fact I was telling your men to back away from Roxanne Vasquez there meant nothing, did it?'

Gabriel Rizzo stared at Marlowe for a long moment and then roared with laughter.

'You got me!' he exclaimed, almost excitedly, as he looked at the others in the room. 'You see that? The Brit has my number already! Better be wary of this guy!'

Marlowe wasn't sure whether he was being mocked, or whether this was genuine excitement by Gabriel, so he kept quiet, waiting to see what would happen next.

As it was, Gabriel Rizzo turned out to be a man of surprises.

'Right then,' he clapped his hands, returning to his desk. 'Someone shoot these pricks, and let's get on with things.'

7

EXECUTIONER

Marlowe's CZ was out of his holster and aimed at Gabriel Rizzo before anybody could make a move – but he paused.

No one had made a move.

Nothing had happened, and now he stood there lowering his gun, confused, as Gabriel turned to face him, smiling.

'You're as good as they say,' he said. 'Apologies for the cloak and dagger, but I had to see how fast the mysterious Thomas Marlowe was.'

'That was risky,' Marlowe replied, holstering the gun. 'I could have killed you.'

'And my men would have killed you, and one of my family would have taken my place,' Gabriel sighed, holding his hands out as if praying. 'My story would have ended. But such a tale to tell, Mister Marlowe, killed by a member of the High Council, during the wake of his own father.'

He looked across at Roxanne.

'You're lucky this man's with you,' he said. 'If he wasn't, we'd be having a different conversation.'

Roxanne simply nodded, her eyes wide like saucers. Gabriel looked back at Marlowe now as he walked to his desk and sat back in the chair, staring at the people in front of him.

'I assume you're here to negotiate on her behalf,' he said.

'I'm here to find out what the hell's going on,' Marlowe replied calmly. 'From what I can work out, she actually hasn't done anything except for have a go at you in the middle of a busy casino.'

'Her friend ripped me off,' Gabriel replied coldly.

'Her friend is currently laying in an intensive care ward covered in third-degree burns and unlikely to live the same life she ever lived,' Marlowe replied coldly. 'For fifty grand, that's a hell of a punishment, but we both know there's more, don't we? This isn't my first rodeo and it sure as hell isn't yours.'

Gabriel said nothing, but Marlowe could see he was angering at the tone being given to him.

'I understand you used to work with my father,' Marlowe continued, changing the subject quickly.

'Yes,' Gabriel replied. 'For several years now. He was a good man. I have yet to see whether this apple falls far from the tree.'

'This apple's fallen very far from the tree,' Marlowe said. 'Taylor Coleman would have negotiated with you, and then waited until you weren't watching, before sending in a team to stab you in the back. I, however, straight up tell you what I'm going to do.'

He leant his hands on the edge of the desk, moving closer, feeling the atmosphere change behind him as the goons, realising that their boss was about to be threatened, were shifting uncomfortably.

'Let's start afresh,' Marlowe said. 'My name is Thomas

Marlowe and I'm the son of Taylor Coleman, but I'm more than just some Orchid lackey or the latest Nepo Baby to gain themselves a pretty coin, which apparently gets me whatever I want in here. And if you've checked into me, as I'm assuming you have, you'll know damn well what I'm capable of, and what I've done in the past.'

Gabriel said nothing.

Marlowe glanced at Roxanne.

'Roxanne Vasquez here took down Nathan Donziger and his entire corporation in New York, after he tried to discredit and then murder her. When she did it, I was by her side. She wasn't there when Lucien Delacroix tried, after faking his death, to kill Anton McKay, the President of America, but I was. And you know what? He failed too.'

Gabriel smiled now.

'Is this a job interview, Mister Marlowe?' he asked. 'Because I'm impressed. I'll hire you. What are your rates? I have a briefcase of bearer bonds just waiting to be spent. Tax free and everything. Name your price. It'll be double, triple the pittance MI5 give.'

'You worked with my father,' Marlowe shook his head, ignoring the offer, 'and I'm not part of that business. I'm also guessing his family is trying to move out of it as well.'

'And why would you think that?' Gabriel asked.

'Because they gave me the seat on the High Council. And if they wanted to really make the money in the same area as my father did, I think they would have been fighting over the bloody thing instead.'

'Maybe they know something you don't,' Gabriel said, waggling his finger, and the way he spoke made Marlowe wonder if there was something that he knew Marlowe didn't.

Added to his concerns about Ichabod, Marlowe was now really wondering what the true game was here.

Gabriel rose to standing and Marlowe shifted his stance, hands now off the table as he faced him across it.

'Let me explain my situation here, Mister Marlowe,' Gabriel said. 'It's far easier if we just speak like men, rather than pussyfooting around, yes? Her friend discovered certain things that she shouldn't have found, and yes, fifty thousand dollars of my money was found in her account. It's believed that a lot more was taken. Millions, in fact.'

'Let me counter,' Marlowe replied. 'You're worried your family will learn you've been skimming the books. Maybe you've got a few vices you keep off the accounts and these millions that are missing, were actually you paying for things without people knowing. Maybe favours later on down the line. I seem to recall from a briefing a while back the Rizzo family is currently up for grabs, with your father now retiring. Maybe you're looking to build your own army. Either way, someone found out and now they want to know where the money is. You need a scapegoat. Conveniently, Lexi Warner is no longer talking.'

He smiled.

'But I wonder how long that'll be for? Don't think about trying to take her out at the hospital. I have experience in that area, and I already have one of the best agents I know there to keep her alive.'

It was a lie, but it was enough. Gabriel was not happy with this, and he glanced across at Roxanne.

'Lexi owes me money she stole from me,' he explained, ignoring everything Marlowe had said. 'And after her terrible accident, this woman came at me like a rabid dog, claiming publicly that I was corrupt, that I was part of the mob, that I'd stolen the money myself. It affected my PR, especially with the event happening this week that you are well aware of. I now have people looking to distance themselves from me and I'm unhappy about this.'

He snapped his fingers, and two of the guards at the back drew pistols. They didn't point them at Marlowe, but held them at a low ready position, expecting trouble at any minute.

'If you want to negotiate,' Gabriel said, his voice now calming and softening as he relaxed a little, 'here's my offer. You take your rabid dog and you get her the hell away from me. Teach her manners, give her a spanking if you have to. But if I hear her say one more slanderous thing about me, I will kill her and anyone she classes as a friend, including you, shiny coin or not. And when Lexi Warner wakes up from her magical coma, my lawyers will be demanding millions in stolen assets from her. I will destroy her. Her medical bills will be the least of her problems.'

Marlowe considered this.

'Strong words,' he said. 'But I get that. You think you hold the cards.'

He turned slowly in a circle, observing the men behind him.

'Here's how it's going to go,' he said. 'You heard me a minute ago point out that I state things in advance and, well, I don't want you to feel that I've caught you unawares.'

He looked at the first goon, the one he had seen when he was pretending to be a marshal.

'I'm going to take that gun, break your fingers and ram it down your throat,' he said, glancing now at the second goon. 'I'm then going to take your gun and I'm gonna ram it up your arse.'

He now turned to the East-coast accented muscle, the one that he was most concerned about here, and the one he reckoned was a friend of a friend – and someone he didn't want to take down because of that.

'You,' he said, 'I'm gonna leave alone. I'll disarm you, don't get me wrong, but I won't have the time to take you down the way I'd want to. Because I'll be too busy hunting this guy down.'

Marlowe nodded back at Gabriel, turning his attention back to him now.

'Because the moment I take apart your men, you'll run. They always do. And I'm not going to waste time killing more of your employees when you're my target. And Mister Rizzo, if you make me an enemy, you *will* be my target.'

And then, as if turning on a light, Marlowe smiled warmly, waving his hands in the air.

'But this is all hypothetical,' he said. 'Because I'm sure, Mister Rizzo, you do *not* want to cause a problem with the High Council of Orchid on the day of Taylor Coleman's wake.'

'There are people here who would be happy for me to kill you,' Gabriel said in response, his face completely emotionless.

'True, but I'll wager there are people who won't be,' Marlowe replied. 'Let me take Roxanne to her room, gather her items, and then we leave. If she says anything against you that is false or accusatory, then you can go for her in the courts. But if I smell one of your men anywhere near her, or if you try anything to strong-arm Lexi, then all bets are off.'

At this, the buzz-cut military man raised his gun.

He managed to get it halfway to Marlowe's face before

Marlowe spun, grabbing it, wrenching it, spinning it, and now aiming it back at the soldier.

'You might think that your military training is shit-hot,' he said, gun aimed at the man's face. 'But where I come from, we *trained* you, yeah?'

He flipped the gun back over, passing it to the man.

'I've got no problems with you. No trouble with any of you,' he completed, turning back to Rizzo. 'As long as you and I stay cordial.'

Gabriel Rizzo stared long and hard at Marlowe, as if trying to work out by looking at him what his options were, and then, with a chuckle, he sat back in his chair and waved his hands dismissively. It was a go-away wave, a flap of the hand to say that he was bored now and the fun was over.

'I thought you'd be more exciting,' he said, almost in dismay.

'This is me warming up,' Marlowe smiled. 'Keep going the way you will, and it'll get exciting.'

He turned back to the goons, who, watching their boss, moved to the side. Marlowe hadn't looked back to see what Rizzo had done, but he guessed there'd been some kind of movement to say, "let them out". With Roxanne beside him, Marlowe left the offices of Gabriel Rizzo.

'He's going to goddamn kill you,' she hissed as they walked out. 'You saw his face, right? There's no way he's letting you get away with what you did just then.'

'I know,' Marlowe nodded. 'Believe me, I'm very aware of what I've just done.'

'Why?' Roxanne couldn't understand. 'Why did you do it, anyway?'

Marlowe shrugged.

'First rule, kicking a fight off,' he said. 'If your friend is in the crosshairs, you make your crosshairs bigger. He's so pissed at me at the moment, he's going to forget about you for a while.'

'And that's a good thing?'

'Keeping you alive is a good thing,' Marlowe chuckled. 'Trust me, I've got enough people trying to kill me this week. Simply put, one more won't change a thing.'

MARLOWE HAD BEEN TRUE TO HIS WORD AND, AFTER HELPING Roxanne pack her bags, the two of them had left the Gold Strike Casino, catching a taxi back to the Horseshoe.

By now, Marlowe knew that people would have guessed where he was staying, and he was seriously considering moving locations once more. However, this was placed on hold when he arrived back at the suite, only to see a tense and nervous Trix waiting for him.

'I don't know what you did,' she said, 'but the chats have kicked off.'

'How do you mean?' Marlowe asked, as Roxanne took her bags into the bedroom.

'I mean, there's someone somewhere who wants you dead,' Trix continued. 'Your name's popping up in a dozen different places, on a few rather gnarly kill-lists. People have been checking your files, trying to work out what you'd do if *this* happened, or *that* happened. They're looking into ways to take you down.'

She shook her head.

'You've stirred a hornet's nest, Marlowe, and I don't know if I can keep you safe.'

'At the moment, we're keeping Roxanne safe,' Marlowe

nodded towards the bedroom as Roxanne returned into the main living area.

'I don't need to be kept safe,' she said. 'I was doing fine before you turned up.'

'You actively followed me to get my help,' Marlowe replied.

'Yes, to get your help,' Roxanne snapped. 'Not to have you tell me to sit in my room and shut up. Not to tell me that my story is over and I can just do the convention now and leave it all to you. The guy I'd hired was going to work with me, not tell me I was surplus to his needs.'

'Do you think that's what you are?' Marlowe asked, raising an eyebrow. 'Surplus to my needs?'

'Tell me I'm not.'

Marlowe shrugged.

'I'll admit you are a complication,' he said. 'But you're a complication I know can look after herself. Rizzo won't do anything for the moment. He'll be looking into his options, as I said. Even I don't know what kind of response I'm going to get from Orchid until I see them. He won't touch me until he knows if I am persona non grata or if I'm the prodigal son.'

'Can someone please explain to me what Orchid is?' Roxanne asked, and Marlowe realised he hadn't explained this, with everything that had happened.

'It's what your friend was saying. 'War Kid was Orchid,' he said. 'Talking of which, we need to have a chat with her.'

'She won't be around until tomorrow,' Roxanne shook her head. 'She works at the Charleston Swap Meet.'

'Your source works in a flea market?' Trix was surprised, but Marlowe nodded.

'People like that, ears to the ground, they hear everything,' he said. 'Fine, we go first thing tomorrow.'

'After breakfast, though, right?' Trix asked.

'You're not going,' Marlowe replied. 'I need you to do a few more things for me instead.'

'Of course,' Trix replied. 'How did I think I would leave this suite?'

'You're the one who picked it,' Marlowe chuckled. 'I'm sure you've already worked out what room service breakfast you can have tomorrow morning.'

Trix shrugged, and Marlowe knew he'd guessed right.

'So, you're sleeping on the couch then, yeah?'

'It's a pull-out,' Marlowe nodded. 'I'll be fine.'

'Good,' Roxanne folded her arms. 'So, now that's all sorted, how about you tell me what the hell Orchid is?'

Before Marlowe could reply, Trix spun in her chair.

'Oh, you had a gift arrive,' she said, nodding towards his room. 'Came from the front desk. Apparently, it'd got delayed when we upgraded rooms.'

Marlowe chuckled at the "we" line, and walked back to the room, using this as a distraction from speaking to Roxanne about Orchid.

On his bed was a brown box. Marlowe didn't need to check it for any traps, as not only did he know what this was, he'd bought it himself and had it sent it here a couple of days earlier, as he'd been aware that his own one wouldn't get through airport security.

It was a steel defence chain bracelet, a metre long, and secured by a dragon-head clasp. He'd stolen his one at a party in New York, and it had saved his life frequently. Released, it became a metre-long steel whip and garrotte, while when secured around his wrist like a bracelet, it could block a knife blade – and possibly worse. It had been a valuable tool, and when Marlowe first arranged to come to Vegas, it'd been his first purchase; after all, he didn't know how long he'd be without a gun for when he arrived.

As it was, he now had the gun, but it was never a bad thing to be too over-prepared, and so he placed it around his wrist, securing it tightly before returning to the suite's living room.

After all, he had a story about Orchid to tell.

———

LATER THAT NIGHT, LYING ALONE ON THE SOFA, PULLED OUT into a rather uncomfortable king-sized bed, Marlowe stared up at the ceiling, considering his next move.

Roxanne Vasquez was a complication, but she was somebody he liked. Not sexually, although there was a definite attraction, and she was stunning as hell, but he genuinely felt that she understood who he was. They'd gained a bond in New York, and then he'd ignored her, ghosted her every time she tried to contact him.

It was a common thing he did. The mission was over, and now it was time to move on. Especially when the person he was ghosting was someone he had started to fall for.

But now, he was wondering if this was something he *shouldn't* be doing, especially now he no longer seemed to have the advantages of being part of MI5.

He lay on the bed, shirtless, holding the coin and turning it in his hand.

He didn't understand what the importance was, but he knew there was *something*. People with this coin shaped the future of the world. They changed the direction of entire countries, corporations, lives. Marlowe wanted to hurl it as far away from him as he possibly could, but he knew that if he did that, then someone else would just pick it up and it would start all over again.

Placing it on the side table, he glanced at his watch. One-thirty in the morning, and still sleep wasn't coming.

He wondered if this was because of the flight and jet lag, though usually he was out like a light no matter where he was; a trait trained into him while in the Royal Marine Commandos.

He'd been tasked by Wintergreen to take down Orchid after Kate Maybury had turned out to be an agent for them. She had brought him in to remove a threat, and now he was *part* of that threat, whether or not he liked it. He understood why MI5 wasn't happy to have him around. It was almost amusing that MI5 also had several of their own agents compromised and working for the same network.

He almost considered calling Vic Saeed to see if he was in Vegas as well, but this didn't feel the same as the Paris event in Versailles that Lucien Delacroix had held.

This felt more personal.

Everything felt more personal.

Eventually, trying to clear his head, he shut his eyes, but all he could see was an image of his father firing three shots into Lucien in the middle of the Garden of Versailles. He knew with hindsight this had been a faked action made to convince the world that Lucien had been murdered, but it was also the last time he'd seen his father.

Was he calling him 'father' now?

Marlowe frowned. For so many years, he'd been "Taylor" or "that bastard". He hadn't really contemplated the fact that he was now an orphan.

Both his parents were dead.

Marlowe looked back at the coin on the side table.

'You were never my father,' he muttered to himself. 'Never.'

Feeling somewhat better for stating this aloud, Marlowe picked up his phone, searching for a number and then sending a message.

> I have a plan. Well. The starting of a plan.
> And if it goes wrong, I'll need you involved.

This sent, and the phone returned to charge, Marlowe shut his eyes and tried to sleep, albeit unsuccessfully.

He'd send details of his plan out early tomorrow, once he worked it all out, and convinced the others he wasn't on a suicide mission.

Well, *yet*, anyway.

8

SWAP MEET

THE CHARLESTON SWAP MEET WAS HELD IN A WAREHOUSE IN the north-east part of Las Vegas, ten miles from the hotel. It had taken him twenty minutes by cab to get there, and Marlowe was more worried about being hassled by panhandlers and drunks than he was assassins. Compared to the affluent Strip, this was a more downtrodden area of Las Vegas, which explained why it was the place where the information would be found.

He glanced across at Roxanne, who was wearing a pair of jeans, trainers, and a hoodie. Although a city lawyer, Roxanne was not foolish enough to turn up in this area looking well off. Marlowe himself had kept to his new leather bomber jacket, jeans, and trainers, with a t-shirt underneath and his CZ in his belt holster. He had also brought his US Marshal's badge in case things got troublesome.

He'd woken early, which, considering he'd gone to sleep late, hadn't been ideal. That said, he'd also woken up with a fully formed plan in his head, something he'd already set in motion with a couple of texts before leaving. He wasn't sure if he was moving in the right direction here, but if things changed, he could call things off as quickly as he'd started them, so that was okay.

Roxanne seemed to know where she was going, leading the way with an accuracy that belied multiple visits to the flea market.

'How did you find this place?' Marlowe asked as they walked. 'Don't take this the wrong way, but it doesn't really seem like you.'

'When I was checking into Lexi,' Roxanne replied, glancing around for a particular table. 'I found some parking receipts for this area. Lexi didn't live around here but would visit regularly, once a week, around this time in the morning, and around set up.'

'That still doesn't explain how you knew about your source,' Marlowe said. 'This is a big place; there's got to be a hundred stalls here. Did you walk up to each one and ask if they knew her?'

Roxanne laughed.

'Believe it or not, yes,' she began. 'I walked around looking for the source; the note Lexi had left about the Charleston Swap Meet mentioned a name, *Clarissa*. I just asked if anybody knew who Clarissa was. Eventually, I got pointed just down there.'

She indicated the third of the aisles, where, down the end, Marlowe could see a table filled with bric-à-brac and curios. Behind it was a woman, easily in her seventies, maybe even in her eighties. Her skin was leathered from the Las Vegas sun over many years, and her hair was wiry and grey, giving the impression of a slightly insane Brillo pad. She wore what seemed to be a sleeveless blue dress, prob-ably once darker, but now bleached to an almost pastel-blue, and she sat in a wheelchair, her legs hidden by the table.

'That's Clarissa,' Roxanne said as they started towards the table. 'I didn't even need to ask her name. She knew who I was the moment I arrived.'

'Psychic?' Marlowe asked.

'No, but she has a network. They knew Lexi had been taken out, and that I'd been asking around. By the time I arrived, she knew me better than I knew her.'

'This should be fun then,' Marlowe smiled.

Clarissa was setting up her stall as they approached. She smiled at Roxanne, but her smile faded as she noticed the bearded man beside her.

'You okay?' she asked Roxanne, foregoing any greetings.

Roxanne nodded.

'This is Tom. He's a friend of mine,' she said. 'He helped me in New York and is going to help me now.'

'And how are you going to help her, Tom?' Clarissa asked with a hint of disdain. 'Are you going to find who attacked Lexi, maybe take down that prick once and for all?'

'By that prick, I'm guessing you mean Gabriel Rizzo,' Marlowe said. 'We've already spoken.'

'Yeah, I know,' Clarissa laughed. 'Made him shit his pants, from what I hear. He wasn't expecting someone to take him down so quickly.'

Marlowe raised an eyebrow at this.

'Don't be so squirrely,' Clarissa chuckled. 'Coming in here bearded with your Hugh Grant plummy Brit accent, asking about Rizzo? It could only be you.'

Roxanne chuckled.

'Told you, Marlowe. This woman knows a lot.'

'Several of Rizzo's men owe me favours,' Clarissa said.

'Don't ask. It's better if you remain ignorant. Let's just say I know what happened last night. And I also know why you're here.'

'You do, do you?' Marlowe folded his arms, waiting to see what came from this.

'You're looking quite bright for a funeral, Mister Marlowe. Usually grieving children wear black.'

Marlowe didn't like that Clarissa knew more about him than he knew about her, something he was not comfortable with. But, as Clarissa moved to grab something else, he noticed something that gave him the answers to everything.

'Thank you for your service,' he said.

Clarissa paused, realising she'd exposed her forearm and the small tattoo on it: a faded tattoo of a dagger, point up and a heraldic sun composed of four straight and four wavy alternating rays, hidden behind a five-petal heraldic rose.

It was a tattoo Marlowe recognised from many people he'd worked with in US Military Intelligence.

'"*Always out front,*"' he said, now more respectful than he had been, as he gave the Intelligence Corps motto. 'I'm guessing you served in the seventies or eighties?'

Clarissa nodded, pulling back from the table, and Marlowe saw the reason for the wheelchair; she had a prosthetic leg from the knee down.

'Until I took an IED to the foot,' she nodded, taking a spanner from the table and tapping at her prosthetic shin with a *clang clang*. 'After that, I was pretty much my own boss.'

'A lot of bad stuff happening around then,' Marlowe continued. 'Enough to make someone go off the grid, decide to stay away. But you couldn't quite stop, could you?'

'Why would you say that?'

'Because if you were a sniper, all you'd do is grease your

gun, make sure it's in perfect working order every day. If you were a grunt, you'd work out, keep fit, make sure you were ready for action at a moment's notice, no offence intended. What *you* did was establish a small intelligence network.'

Clarissa laughed loudly and happily.

'Less of the small, Brit,' she said. 'I have one of the best intelligence networks on the West Coast.'

'Good to know,' Marlowe replied. 'Now how about you use that intelligence and tell me what the hell is going on here?'

At this, Clarissa lowered her voice so no one else could hear.

'Your man Rizzo,' she said, 'he owes money, big time money. The casino's shiny and new, but it hasn't made back the money it cost to build yet. And with Vegas filled to the brim with casinos, it's a dog-eat-dog world.'

She looked up at Marlowe.

'I know why you're here,' she continued. 'Your father's wake is only part of it. You've got a coin in your pocket, am I correct? A coin you didn't expect to have.'

Marlowe felt a sliver of ice slide down his back. Knowing something like that took Clarissa from "a crazy woman with some informants" to "dangerous at any level".

Clarissa grinned as she saw his expression.

'Don't you worry, honey,' she said, reaching into her pocket and pulling out a similar coin to the one Marlowe had been given. 'I have one too.'

Marlowe did a double-take at the coin. It looked exactly the same as his, and Clarissa rose from the chair now, the prosthetic leg supporting her as she passed it over, letting him look at it. It was an exact duplicate. There was no way this was a forgery.

Clarissa chuckled as Marlowe's inquisitive gaze returned to her.

'Don't worry, hon,' she said. 'I'm not part of your conspiracy group. I've got enough conspiracy theories of my own to last a lifetime. One of my contacts pinched this from a mark last night. Seems a few of you have come in for the party.'

'Do you know whose coin this is?' Marlowe asked.

'I do,' Clarissa replied casually. 'And I'm sure that you giving it back to them would make them mighty happy, possibly even make an ally. Or, you can use this for your own purposes, and screw them over. The question is, what's it worth to me?'

'What do you want?' Marlowe asked.

'I know you've got a fancy MI5 tech officer hidden away in a hotel room in Las Vegas,' Clarissa said. 'I'd like half an hour with her, with a laptop.'

'I think that can be arranged,' Marlowe replied.

Clarissa nodded.

'I'll go to her,' she said. 'The Horseshoe – yes, I know where you're staying, as does pretty much everyone – has a good accessibility track, but even if not, this boot works just as good.'

Marlowe looked back at the prosthetic foot.

'Why the chair?' he asked.

'Because I'm old and I've earned it,' Clarissa replied, sitting back in the wheelchair. 'When you go to the Gold Strike, look for Robert Chester Crown the Third. He'll be the confused and rather scared-looking dumpy man who's missing a coin.'

Marlowe nodded appreciatively, pocketing the coin. He made sure to keep it in a separate pocket, though. He didn't want to get the two confused; there might be a difference in the coins, and the last thing he wanted was to have someone else's details.

'Now,' he said, 'as you seem to know about my secrets, can we get back to what happened with Lexi?'

'Sure,' Clarissa replied. 'I've known her for a while. She visited the swap meet here and there, has a thing for uranium glass.'

Marlowe frowned, and Clarissa pointed at a couple of small glass vases and cups to the side that had a mottled dark-green hue to them.

'They're uranium glass, sometimes known as "Vaseline glass,' she explained. 'Big right now in retro-era collectibles. It's glass which has had uranium, usually in an oxide form, added to a glass mix before melting for colouration. Shine a UV torch on them and they glow up nicely. Big thing around here, you know, with the nuclear testing and everything.'

'How much uranium is in them?' Marlowe resisted the urge to back off.

Seeing this, Clarissa shook her head.

'The amounts are ridiculously small; our bodies are subjected to more radiation every day from the gamma rays that make it through our atmosphere. If you're really worried about the trace amounts of radiation on this table, sweet cheeks, you'd better cut out all those healthy spinach salads, 'cos they're packed with more radioactive potassium than these.'

Marlowe relaxed a little, and Clarissa continued.

'You can buy them pretty much anywhere, but you know how it goes – when in Las Vegas, you pay a premium,' she continued. 'Anyway, young Lexi, she was a good customer, but the last couple of times I saw her, she seemed stressed. I asked what was going on, pointed out I might be able to help her. When she thought she had an ally, she told me everything.'

'Everything being ...?'

'*Everything.* Lexi wasn't happy working for Gabriel Rizzo and he was in some kind of power struggle with his family,' Clarissa replied. 'His dad's retiring, he's got a sister, Angelina, and she wants him gone. She's looking for anything she can use to remove him from the family estate – preferably feet first, if you get what I'm saying.'

'No love lost there then.'

Clarissa shook her head.

'Honey, in a family like that, everybody wants to get to the top. There's no sibling love, more sibling rivalry, and it's a rivalry with a knife in the spine. A bit like yours, I hear.'

She grinned, and Marlowe knew she'd thrown the comments in just to keep him off guard. He smiled in response, trying to give the impression it didn't bother him.

'So, am I to understand that Rizzo owes Orchid?' he asked.

Clarissa paused as she considered the question.

'He had a couple of investors who helped with the building of the casino,' she said. 'He promised them quick turnarounds, good profits, high percentage, but he's not made good on this. As I said, it's not been a good year for casinos, and he's spent a lot on this building, as well as dipping into the funds for his personal expenses. He's shy maybe fifty million dollars, which he had until he spent it on goddamn everything *but* the debt payments.'

Clarissa laughed now, a throaty chuckle that caught the attention of a few of the surrounding stallholders. She waved them off with a glowering look and then turned her attention back to Marlowe and Roxanne.

'Gabriel's got expensive tastes,' she explained. 'Hookers, clothing, drugs, you name it, he lives that life. One reason he wanted to build the casino was so that he could be a casino boss. The problem was he expected to make loads of money from the casino, so, as far as he was concerned, it didn't matter that he was spending the money. He'd just take it out of the profits, you know?'

'Which don't exist, as the casino's only been open a couple of weeks,' Marlowe added.

'Bingo,' Clarissa nodded. 'He promised immediate results, so now his family is sniffing around, asking what's going on. Members of Orchid, the investors, are checking in to see what's going on. Suddenly, there's a man who's got to find maybe fifty, sixty million in the space of a week or two.'

She looked at Roxanne.

'And then Lexi Warner comes along sniffing about as well during the building process, trying to work out what's the story,' she said. 'She'd realised money was missing from the building funds, she went to Gabriel and confronted him about it. Not angry in the way you did, Missy, but more confused, trying to work out what was happening, so she could get ahead of it. Rizzo claimed nothing had happened, and she was mistaken. As she dug down, looked more, she started to find where the money was going.'

'So, he framed her.'

'That's for you to find out,' Clarissa mouth-shrugged. 'All I know is that two days after she found out what he was doing, she's hinting she has some kind of smoking gun, and he's suddenly telling everybody she stole money from him. Money turns up in her account, he claims that she's going to be taken to court, hints she stole millions upon millions during her time working for him, an Interpol agent appears looking into her, and then before she can say anything to anyone, her house burns down with her inside it.'

She sniffed, putting a couple of price tags on some items.

'I don't think he expected her to live, which is a definite fly in his ointment,' she continued. 'Someone's shitting in his pudding and he doesn't know what to do. So he hopes she'll go away. She's in a coma, there's no proof that she's going to live – and then Missy here appears and knows a lot more than he expected.'

Marlowe looked at Roxanne.

'Do you know what the smoking gun is?'

'No, but if an Interpol agent is connected, it isn't domestic,' Roxanne shook her head.

Marlowe nodded, looking back at Clarissa.

'So what happens next?'

'Next?' Clarissa shrugged. 'Your pop's wake happens next. Perfectly timed, too, like someone realised Rizzo needed a boost and held the party there as he launches this weekend. A big and impressive launch night, mainly to get a ton of money into the casino in one fell swoop. Happens in three days.'

'When Orchid is here.'

Clarissa nodded as she moved a couple of pieces around on the stall.

'Loads of high-ranking members of Orchid in his casino, where he gets to slide up next to them, maybe gain some loans that can cover the debts that he owes. He can pay off his family, keep Orchid at bay for the moment, and keep fighting for another day.'

'And if he doesn't?'

Clarissa shrugged.

'There's no *doesn't*. He'll make the money. The launch will be a big money event. He'll pull in fifty, maybe sixty million from that, including the uptick in gambling he'll get. Enough to cover the debt short term, and he can still claim that Lexi Warner stole his money. If the insurance pays out, he might even come out of it ahead.'

'So, we stop him,' Marlowe replied.

'And how are you going to do that, sweetheart?' Clarissa frowned. 'You gonna take your pretty little gun and shoot him in the head?'

Marlowe shrugged.

'We take away his cash source,' he said. 'You understand what happens when you burn a spy, right?'

'You cut their air supply,' Clarissa nodded. 'Leave them with nothing, freeze their accounts, stop their passports, make sure they can't go to anyone they used to know for help.'

'So, we do that to him,' Marlowe replied. 'If he doesn't make the money, then he can't pay his debts.'

He looked at Roxanne.

'Then you'll be the least of his problems. Orchid will want his head.'

'I like this idea,' Roxanne grinned. 'But how are we going to do that?'

'For the next couple of days, I'm going to be hanging out in his casino,' Marlowe replied. 'Gives me time to check it out and case the joint.'

'Case the joint?' Clarissa stared at him in surprise. 'You're not thinking ...'

She didn't finish as Marlowe smiled, picking up one of the uranium glasses on the table.

'You're damn right I'm thinking,' he said. 'How much is this?'

Clarissa, actually lost for words, waved the glass off as a gift.

'And what exactly are you thinking?' Roxanne, slow on the uptake, asked.

'I intend to find whatever this smoking gun is, and while I'm waiting, I'm going to remove fifty million dollars from Gabriel Rizzo,' Marlowe held up the glass, looking through it at the lights of the swap meet. 'Because if he doesn't have it, he can't pay it. And if he can't pay it, he's screwed.'

'Steal fifty million,' Roxanne looked back at Clarissa. 'He makes it sound so easy.'

'It's suicidal, that's what it is,' Clarissa replied, the slightest hint of a smile turning the edge of her mouth as she spoke. 'I knew I liked this guy from the moment I saw him.'

9

THE GRAVEDIGGER

GABRIEL RIZZO HAD EXPECTED NO OTHER VISITORS THAT morning, so when he was informed of the Gravedigger's arrival, he was quite surprised.

The Gravedigger was a man whose reputation preceded his appearance. He'd been a ghost, almost a legend, over the last twenty years. Nobody really knew who he was, or why he did what he did; just that he was one of the best out there, and when he arrived, you took the meeting, no matter what.

The information had been lacking in detail when his guards came to see him. Apparently, the Gravedigger had arrived early that morning, standing unarmed in the middle of the casino, stock still and motionless until a security guard, confused what was going on, asked him his business. The Gravedigger had spoken in gravelly tones, and announced he was here to create a business arrangement with Gabriel Rizzo – and that the guard could do everyone a service and inform Mister Rizzo that the Gravedigger had arrived.

The security guard, not really knowing what this meant, had passed the message on to his superior, who, having a better knowledge of crime in the area, immediately took the message to his boss.

Gabriel had been in the hotel gym when he'd received the message. Today was cardio day, especially as in the evening he intended to put on a show, and he'd considered making the unexpected visitor wait.

But you never made the Gravedigger wait.

Besides, there was that part of him that wondered if this was somebody stupid enough to pretend to be someone they weren't. It wasn't uncommon for chancers and fakers to turn up pretending they were part of something, seeing how far they could take the scam before they were found out.

They were *always* found out. And it never went well for them after that.

After grabbing a quick shower, when Gabriel arrived at his office, the man facing him looked to be the real deal.

He was in his late fifties, stocky and tanned. His eyes were piercing, and he had short black hair cut in a side parting. Rizzo wasn't sure, but it looked like the hair was actually a toupee. He wasn't going to comment on this, though; many people in the business wore wigs and hair weaves – it was a young man's world, after all, and looking old simply pushed you out of the job arena, no matter what your reputation and skill set was. If the Gravedigger wanted to look younger, who was he to judge?

The Gravedigger wore a charcoal-grey pinstripe suit, comfortable-looking black brogues, a crisp white Oxford shirt, and a tie. He looked like one of those jobsworth Nevada Gaming Commission pricks, here on a business trip rather than a jolly. And again, Gabriel assumed this was deliberate. In fact, the only thing that made him stand out from anybody else was his glasses, having what looked to be transition, or photochromic lenses, meaning they were slightly shaded under the bright lights of the casino. He held himself with a swagger that only soldiers held, but he didn't feel as intimidating as Gabriel had expected him to.

This could have been a meeting with an accountant, for all he felt from this gathering.

Again, that was probably the plan.

'I understand you're the Gravedigger,' he said as he entered his office.

The man turned and stared at him.

'Are you Mister Rizzo?' he asked, his voice only a gravelly growl.

Gabriel nodded, walking over to his desk, pouring himself water from a carafe at the side, and downing it.

'Call me Gabriel, please,' he smiled. 'Mister Rizzo is my father.'

The Gravedigger nodded, a barely imperceptible tip of the head.

'Why do I have such a legend in my casino?' Gabriel continued, warming up now.

'I have a contract,' the Gravedigger said. 'And I understand it might affect your business.'

Gabriel went to reply, but then paused, frowning.

'What contract?'

'Thomas Marlowe,' the Gravedigger replied, now walking over and sitting in the chair facing the desk, motioning for Gabriel Rizzo to do the same on his side. It was an unconscious gesture, but Gabriel found himself following the command, walking over and sitting in his seat like a good boy.

He looked over to his guards, to see if they were doing the same, but was surprised to see Atkins, his scarred, white-haired New York goon staring at the newly arrived and suited visitor with what could only be described as fear. He didn't think he'd ever seen Atkins scared before. But then he'd never seen him bettered before until the previous night.

'I find myself in a position,' the Gravedigger said, cutting into Gabriel's thoughts. 'A position which is unknown to me.'

'And that is?'

'Asking for help,' the Gravedigger replied, shifting in his chair as he looked at the men standing around. Rising, he walked to Atkins, and Gabriel wondered if he'd seen the expression on Atkins' face, and wrongly marked it down as disdain, rather than fear.

'You served, didn't you?' he said, his voice still gravelly and croaking.

Atkins nodded.

'I served,' the Gravedigger replied. 'It made me the man that I am. Did your service make you the man that you are?'

Atkins, now outed as an ex-soldier, nodded, and the Gravedigger smiled, looking back at Gabriel.

'You know my name, you know my reputation,' he said. 'I'm not here to show off and I'm not here to gain work. I'm here to do a job, but it might be on your property. I find it's best to make sure I don't cause any problems.'

'The Gravedigger I've heard of never usually announces their presence,' Gabriel replied. 'Why should I believe this is you?'

The Gravedigger considered this, nodded, and then sat back in the chair.

'I don't care if you believe me or not,' he said. 'It means nothing to me and doesn't affect my charter in any way what-soever. But I've been hired to remove Thomas Marlowe. Who currently is at an event in your casino and, from what I can work out, wasn't invited, even though he now has an invitation. And a coin.'

Gabriel hid his emotions well at this news – there was no way the Gravedigger could know this unless his sources involved Orchid High Council themselves. He'd only been told that Marlowe would be a guest at the wake and the surrounding events over the next few days, a couple of hours before the man himself appeared on his doorstep. For the Gravedigger to know this, and not be fazed, was more confirmation of his authenticity.

'I'd rather you didn't kill him in my casino,' Gabriel replied.

The Gravedigger nodded.

'I understand that,' he said. 'This is why I have come to you. I do not know your casino or your land that well. If I require space to perform my charter, I would appreciate a heads up on the best places to use.'

'Are you telling me you've never killed someone in Vegas before?' Gabriel raised an eyebrow.

The Gravedigger shook his head.

'I've never needed to,' he replied. 'Usually I've gained access and fulfilled my charter before I've even reached this place. At best, I'm thirty miles into the desert, with a spade and a torch.'

Gabriel nodded. Weirdly, this made him trust the Gravedigger even more. He'd heard of the name, of course, everybody had. He also knew the Gravedigger had never worked in Vegas. That this man knew this and hadn't tried to up the ante, claiming things he hadn't done, in a way proved that he was who he said he was.

In addition, the man wasn't asking for anything from Gabriel. He was just fulfilling a professional's commitment, alerting the bigger fish in the pool that he was about to swim.

'You know my father,' he said, as a statement rather than as a question.

The Gravedigger didn't reply.

'I said—'

'I know what you said,' the Gravedigger snapped back. 'But I will not answer that. You should know better, *Gabriel*, to ask me about my clients and my contacts.'

Gabriel smiled. It was a dark, menacing one.

'I could have my men pull out your fingernails one by one,' he said. 'I could—'

'Do you genuinely think that would scare me?' The Gravedigger laughed. 'I've acid-burned my fingerprints off three times. I've had my nails removed from my toes and my fingers multiple times over the years. Do you know what I call it?'

He leant closer.

'A *spa* treatment.'

There was an uneasy atmosphere in the room, and Gabriel couldn't help himself. He started to laugh.

'What do you need from me?' he eventually asked. 'I can't believe you're just here to say hi and mention the murder you want to do.'

'I need nothing,' the Gravedigger replied, rising and placing a card with a single phone number on the desk. 'Just your friendship, a heads up if the target outstays his welcome and, if needed, a location that can fulfil my charter.'

'I think we can arrange that,' Gabriel smiled. 'What if I need to hire you?'

'You couldn't afford me.'

'And if I wanted to hire you for someone like Orchid?'

At this, the Gravedigger paused.

'Taylor Coleman used me once,' he said. 'He couldn't afford me either.'

'Then who hired you to kill Marlowe?'

With a smile, the Gravedigger walked out of his office without answering. Gabriel watched the man go and turned to Atkins.

'And what the hell got into you there?' he snapped. 'You looked like you were about to piss yourself!'

Atkins nodded.

'I saw that man before,' he explained simply. 'Five years ago, in New York. There was this guy, right. Squealer. Real rat of a man. Everyone knew he was trying to screw the family. But he was untouchable, and he knew it. Name of Johnny Bucco.'

'I've heard of him,' Gabriel frowned. 'He went missing.'

'So the story goes,' Atkins nodded. 'I was in a club on the east side the night it happened. Saw him with about four goons around him. Nobody could get near. And then I saw the Gravedigger.'

'You sure it was the same man?'

'Different hair, but it was the same clothes, same creepy-ass glasses,' Atkins nodded quickly. 'Looked like a broker. Walked in, watched Johnny for about an hour, then around two in the morning I saw he and Johnny were both gone.'

'The goons?'

'All dead. Killed with a blade and dumped in the toilets,' Atkins shivered. 'He's the real deal and bad news, boss. We should burn that number and count our blessings we're not the ones he has the charter for.'

Gabriel considered the words.

'Christ, I hired some real cowards, didn't I?'

Atkins bristled at the insult.

'I ain't no coward,' he hissed.

'Good. In that case, gather your ball sack back out from inside your body and follow him,' he said. 'Find out where he is, where he's staying, and then get someone to look into who's hired him. I want the answer before I pass Tom Marlowe over to him.'

'You're thinking of doing that?' Atkins asked, frowning.

Rizzo stared at the goon. He knew that as an ex-military man, and as one that was actually bettered by Marlowe, he probably had some kind of misguided loyalty or affection for the Brit prick.

'What I decide to do with Tom Marlowe is none of your business,' he said. 'You work for me. Do the job and move on.'

Atkins reluctantly nodded and left the office, Gabriel staring after him.

The Gravedigger was in his hotel, and the Gravedigger was after Tom Marlowe.

'Get me Byron,' he said to another of his men. 'I need to check if he's been outsourcing recently.'

10

FAMILY COMMITMENTS

WITH THE MEETING WITH CLARISSA NOW OVER, MARLOWE AND Roxanne had returned to the Horseshoe Casino, where they had both changed for their respective events; Roxanne for the conference she was actually attending, and Marlowe for a wake for his estranged father.

He had originally considered turning up in the same clothes as he had worn to the swap meet, but no matter how he felt about his father—

was he still calling him 'Father' now?

—How he still felt about *Taylor*, he knew that he should at least be respectful. When he looked in the mirror of his bathroom, he also noticed that with his straggly hair and unkempt beard, he needed a trim; luckily, product tamed the hair, and a quick once over with his clippers turned him into a more hipster and less street hobo appearance.

Now groomed, it was with a black suit and shirt that Marlowe arrived at the Gold Strike Casino and Hotel later that morning. If he was being honest, he had wondered if they would even let him in following the events of the previous evening but, as he walked up to the main doors, seeing once more the security guards and metal detectors, Marlowe was quite surprised to find one doorman immediately waving him to the side, where a second guard, the one he had seen the previous day, nodded at him as he walked over and once more revealed the coin he'd been given.

That seemed to get him through doors better than any of the gold cards he had ever owned, and he wondered how Robert Chester Crown the Third had fared getting in without it, as the guard checked his watch, mentioning the "event" was starting at twelve. Which, as Marlowe looked at his own watch, was in about ten minutes. He'd just squeaked in, thanks to his swap meet diversion.

Once in the casino, Marlowe looked around, and realised the guards hadn't been super clever in knowing Orchid members as they arrived – they had simply taken anybody wearing black and moved them to the side. Most people at the casino, it seemed, were not into muted dark colours for their day of gambling.

Another guard pointed out that the event for Taylor Coleman was being held in the Venice Ballroom, and pointed off down the side. Marlowe thanked him and started towards it, wondering what the fixation was with Vegas and European locations.

He had a moment of disorientation as he walked through the casino, however; the brightly coloured fruit machines that were the mainstay of most casinos were not in the same place as they were the previous day. It was almost as if the entire place had been moved and changed around.

Marlowe realised, however, that this was actually most likely a policy by the casino; the last thing they wanted was for people to get comfortable, so every day it looked like a variety of fruit machines and gambling areas had been changed specifically to make sure that new devices and machines were picked up by gamblers, who wanted to try their luck on something new.

Good to know, Marlowe thought to himself as he walked through the gaudy, loudly carpeted area. *Maybe I can use this somehow down the line.*

Marlowe carried on through the casino area with no distractions; he wasn't there to gamble, although there was an element of chance and risk involved in what he intended to do. As he approached the Venice Ballroom, he recognised some faces, though. A woman to the side was the lady in her fifties who had spoken to him at Versailles: Senator Alison Pearson, the dark horse Democrat. Over by the bar, almost standing front and centre, was St John Steele.

Seeing Marlowe, Steele's face brightened, and he gave a visible smile.

'I wondered if you'd turn up,' he said, moving into step with Marlowe as he walked towards the ballroom.

'I thought you weren't involved with Orchid anymore,' Marlowe said. 'The last I heard, the term "arbitrator" was past tense with you.'

'I'm not here with Orchid, and this isn't an Orchid event,' Steele replied with the slightest hint of a smile. 'I am simply here to pay my respects to an old work colleague and friend.'

Marlowe smiled at this.

'Of course you are,' he replied. 'Everybody I see is purely here to pay their respects, and the fact most happen to be Orchid is completely coincidental.'

Across the room, he saw another familiar face; standing with an expensive-looking suit on, hideously blue, and as electric as you could possibly have, a pastel-pink shirt under this was Gabriel Rizzo.

Steele saw Marlowe's expression of disdain the moment he saw Rizzo and nodded.

'I see you've met the money man,' he said.

'Mister Rizzo,' Marlowe nodded. 'I had the delight of speaking to the man yesterday.'

'He's got a lot riding on this,' Steele looked around. 'Orchid has put millions into the place, hoping to find some extra money coming out of it.'

'Why would an organisation backed by billionaires look at a few million as a big investment?'

'Because you keep killing their billionaires, perhaps?' Steele suggested.

'I never killed Lucien Delacroix,' Marlowe growled. 'He took his own life when he realised he was screwed.'

'Either way, his billions are no longer able to be tapped into,' Steele continued. 'This isn't the only investment, either, I know Orchid has diversified into a hundred ventures just like this, and if they all bring in twenty, thirty percent profit, that's a hefty payout, hundreds of millions. And that convinces more people to buy in.'

He looked back at Gabriel.

'He was supposed to be paying them back this week. It's one reason Taylor's wake is being held here, to help him get the cash flowing.'

'I guessed there was another reason it was here,' Marlowe carried on into the ballroom with Steele beside him. 'Should you be seen with me?'

'You'd be surprised how many people are actually on your side,' Steele shrugged. 'You're the scrappy underdog, the person who wasn't expecting to get where they are. You're

Charlie Bucket and you've just been given Willy Wonka's chocolate factory. A lot of the members of Orchid in the room today actually identify with you.'

'They do?'

'Absolutely. They believe they too are the scrappy underdog, even if they've come from a home where silver spoons were inserted into their mouths when born.'

Marlowe paused halfway up the auditorium on the right-hand side. There was an empty row here, and he didn't feel like moving closer.

'Not going to the front row?' Steele asked with a smile. 'Best view in the house.'

Marlowe shook his head.

'I think I'm fine here,' he replied. 'I'll catch you later, yes?'

'Absolutely,' Steele nodded, shaking Marlowe's hand and walking off to the front of the ballroom.

Marlowe watched the man walk away, an intrigued expression on his face. He had expected to be classed as a persona non grata, but Steele welcoming him actively gave him the impression that either something else was at play, or Steele was actually being genuine.

Marlowe noted there were a few other members of the funeral contingent who were spending more time glancing at him out of the corner of their eyes, or trying to make out they weren't looking at him while doing so, than they were looking at the stage. He hadn't meant to disrupt anything—

Was that true?

Marlowe considered this. There was a thought, an option to do this, to follow Emilia Wintergreen's orders and destroy Orchid, even though he no longer worked for her, but currently Marlowe still didn't know what was going on – and because of this, he didn't feel comfortable being the usual agent of chaos that he was.

He checked his watch. It was almost noon and, as the dial of his watch clicked to the hour, the lights changed, and a man walked onto the stage.

Marlowe recognised him. It was Ichabod, dressed in a full black suit, white shirt, and black tie, looking like a slightly tall, gangly undertaker as he stepped up to the lectern at the front, as, behind him, a giant image of Taylor Coleman filled the wall.

Marlowe had to take a moment to compose himself. He hadn't expected to feel anything, but this was such a visceral moment, he felt like he'd been punched in the gut.

Was this because he had lost his father? And was he still calling Taylor Coleman 'father' after his death?

Ichabod stared around and nodded.

'Good morning,' he said. 'Or afternoon now, I should say. As many of you know, my name is Byron Coleman, and I am the son of Taylor Coleman.'

He looked around the auditorium.

'Many of you here have come to pay your respects to my father, who was taken tragically from us with lung cancer. Some worked with him through his global corporation, *Arachis*, and others through his various philanthropic endeavours. And I thank you all for attending.'

Various philanthropic endeavours. Marlowe almost chuck-led, as this explained how people like Pearson could turn up without a domino mask on. If asked, she could simply say *"oh no, I'm not part of any secret organisation, or worked with an arms dealer, I worked with Coleman to help repopulate red pandas"* or some other suitably noble reason.

Marlowe wasn't certain, but he was absolutely convinced that, as he said this, Ichabod had glared up at Marlowe.

'As many of you know,' Ichabod continued, looking back out at the auditorium, 'My father had many business interests. Some of them were less ethical than others.'

Marlowe sat forward at this; he had a feeling he knew where this was going, but he wanted to make sure he was hearing correctly.

'One of my father's last wishes was to ...' Ichabod paused, smiling.

'I tell you what,' he continued, his voice softening as he looked back at the giant image of Taylor Coleman behind him. 'Let's hear it from him.'

At this, Ichabod stepped back from the lectern, and the image on the screen of Taylor Coleman burst into life – and Marlowe realised it had been a frozen frame of a video message.

'Good evening,' Taylor Coleman said out of the speakers, while his face on the screen matched the words. 'Or morning, or lunchtime, or whenever it is that you're watching this. If you are watching this, then it's pretty bloody clear I've passed on, died, kicked the bucket, you name it, I've done it. It's not really a surprise – I've been told I've only got months to live, but it's still weird to talk about it like this.'

Marlowe examined the image on the screen. This wasn't the Taylor Coleman he saw in Versailles, the one with the oxygen bottle in the wheelchair. This was more the Taylor Coleman he'd met in New York before the cancer had gathered too much of a hold on him, which meant this had to have been recorded several months ago. Marlowe wondered if Taylor had even considered what was going to happen with his estranged son at this point.

Had this video been made before he sent a hitman out to gain Marlowe's attention, or shortly after?

On the screen, Taylor Coleman, unaware of Marlowe's internal monologue, had carried on speaking.

'I've been very lucky over the years,' he said. 'Although the cancer inside me says that perhaps I haven't been so lucky with the items and machinery I've worked with.'

Marlowe winced at this. *Machinery.* That was a polite way of explaining the high-ordinance illegal arms he'd been playing with, many of which had radioactive sources that had caused his cancer.

'But I'd always said,' Taylor continued on the screen, 'that when I was gone, there were too many legacies I was leaving, too many black marks against me, and something needed to be done about this. I'm known for my philanthropy. I'm known for my work with military ordinance and machinery. I'm known for the advice and consultancies I've given countries over the years and far more. But, I've made my money from war, and I'm not ashamed of it. If it wasn't me, someone else would have made just as much.'

He shifted in his seat, and Marlowe could see that even the action of talking was physically hurting him here.

'But what I *am* ashamed of is that I didn't do more with the money I made. I didn't try to better the world I lived in more than I had. And that is why my son, who I'm hoping is standing somewhere near this video, has been made executor of all aspects of my life. He will dismantle my companies, selling them off, moving the funds into more philanthropic areas. If ever there was a black cloud over me and my name, my son will remove it.'

There was a muttering and a murmuring of discontent from the auditorium, and Marlowe knew this was most likely members of Orchid, realising that one of their principal assets was about to be removed. After all, Taylor Coleman mentioned consulting to countries and military arms, but he also supplied terrorists and secret organisations with the same equipment and ordnance. Was this why Orchid needed a few dozen million here and there from people like Gabriel Rizzo?

On the screen, Taylor continued.

'Obviously, I don't know what the response to that is,' he said. 'But, knowing many of the people who are likely to be sitting in the audience wherever this is being shown, you're probably pissed off about it. And I get that. But I'm dead. So I don't care. My last will and testament has already been dealt with by now, and if everything has gone to plan, we are having this in a swanky ballroom in a brand-new Las Vegas casino, created by my friend and business partner, Gabriel Rizzo.'

There was a small and reluctant round of applause at this, and Marlowe could see Gabriel smiling to the side, trying his best to build a sense of humility to his expression, while happy that he was being singled out.

'Gabriel Rizzo is a scumbag peacock who thinks he's bigger than he is,' Taylor said, to an intake of breath from the audience. 'Sorry, Gabriel, I'm sure you're here, but you know I'm telling the truth your father never could.'

There was nervous laughter, and Marlowe could see that Gabriel Rizzo was furious.

'But, in all ways, if you're a scumbag peacock, or a scumbag warlord, or a scumbag whatever, it's amazing how making money changes your reputation,' Taylor continued. 'Your casino will make a lot of money for many people, and once it *makes* that money, your reputation will magically change. I wish you all the best, my friend. But I'd be lying if I didn't expect you to end in failure.'

On the screen, Taylor Coleman chuckled, a laugh which morphed into a coughing fit.

'Because let's face it, you're going to make a lot of money from this casino, and then spend it on something absolutely stupid, and I wouldn't have you any other way,' Taylor eventually finished.

Gabriel couldn't tell if he was being complimented or insulted, and Marlowe had to hide a smile of his own, as Gabriel Rizzo gave a little bow to a video message on a screen in front of him.

But the show hadn't finished yet.

'While here, I want you all to respect Gabriel's casino as neutral ground,' Taylor continued. 'No grudges, no blood spilled, unless by mutual agreement. Understand?'

There was a murmuring of dissent after this, and Marlowe couldn't hide his smile.

People didn't like the dead telling them what to do, it seemed.

'I want the Coleman name to be known throughout the world as a philanthropy source where people can feel safe,' Taylor's video message explained. 'I know this sounds contradictory to what I've done over many years, but I truly feel we can get this done. My son and my family will provide the answers to this, and I look forward to seeing what they come up with.'

At this, there was a louder round of applause, even from the people unhappy with the situation. After all, you didn't want to be seen as the person who didn't applaud charity work.

'There is one more thing I'd like to talk about,' Taylor said. 'I have the greatest children, but I've not been the best of fathers. And I have one estranged son whom I recently spoke to in New York.'

He leant forward on the screen, and Marlowe felt a chill down his neck. *This was after he sent the hitman, after all.*

'Thomas, if you're there, I'd like to speak to you now,' his dead father said.

11

FATHER / SON

MARLOWE FROZE AS THE GHOST OF HIS FATHER SPOKE TO HIM through the means of technology.

'Thomas, I was a dreadful dad to you, and I don't know if I'm going to see you again before I die,' he said. 'Probably not, after how our last chat went, but if, somehow, you're here, know that when I die, you'll be given a gift that many people here will wish to have had. A position of authority in an organisation you probably won't like. Now, I told you in New York it was a gift you wouldn't want, and I'm telling you the truth. I'd be honest if I wasn't considering giving you this hereditary position, because it means that your half-brothers and sister won't have to deal with the issues that you would deal with – but the truth of the matter is, I know that of all of my family, you, Thomas, are the only person who could deal with what you're given.'

Marlowe stared in horror at the screen.

'You are your mother's son more than mine, and that has made you strong, stubborn, bloody-minded. And those character aspects are what will get you through this. I hope, in the same way that my son will be taking my company and making the best of it and turning it into something light rather than dark, you can take what I give you and do the same.'

Taylor started coughing at this point, grabbing a glass of water from someone to the side, taking a sip, clearing his throat, and then looking back at the screen.

'I'm bored with this,' he said. 'I'm never going to see it, and I don't really care who's watching it right now. The fact of the matter is this: all of you who made money from me, it's not happening anymore. *Arachis* is closed for business. If I owe you money, you'll be paid. If you owe me money, you'll be paying. If you have any problems in relation to this, I suggest you speak to my sons, both legitimate and bastard. Thank you for coming to my wake. I hope you're not celebrating too hard that I'm dead.'

And with this, the video stopped.

There was a smattering of reluctant and confused applause, as the people sitting in the auditorium weren't too sure if they were supposed to celebrate this or still be sympathetic. Marlowe didn't clap his hands; he was staring at the screen.

Had Taylor Coleman just told him to turn Orchid from the organisation it was into something positive? It certainly felt that way.

Ichabod returned to the lectern.

'My father has set up several things for the next two days as part of his funeral and wake, ending with the launch party of our partner's casino.' he said. 'This is in conjunction with Gabriel Rizzo, who I believe is a fine, upstanding member of our community, regardless of what my father, in his medicine-induced state, might have said.'

Marlowe noted Rizzo straightened at the utterance of his name, and that Ichabod had still named him as "our" partner, rather than naming as the partner of his late father. Which gave the impression that Ichabod and Gabriel were still working together.

Marlowe was wondering more and more whether Ichabod was truly happy to be free of Orchid's High Council.

However, Ichabod was still talking.

'You will be invited to share your memories, help us work out the future of *Arachis*, and have your own networking sessions, which I'm sure many of you will want.'

Marlowe wasn't really paying attention. He was now staring at the image on the screen of Taylor Coleman, still trying to work out what had been said.

'... Thomas Marlowe.'

There was a small round of applause, and Marlowe looked up, realising that Ichabod had just called him to the stage.

Not really wanting to do this, but with everyone now staring at him, Marlowe rose awkwardly, making his way down the stairs and up onto the stage from the side entrance. Facing the audience, Ichabod held his hand out for Marlowe to shake. Marlowe knew this was nothing more than theatre, but he took the hand and shook it, anyway.

'We only found out about our half-brother recently,' Ichabod explained to the people watching. 'And as such, we find it strange to have such a relationship, but I would not refuse my half-brother his moment to speak about our father.'

Marlowe froze as the audience applauded. He hadn't expected to make a speech; he had hoped to be standing at the back, avoided and ignored, but now he knew he had to say something, if only to tell people to go away.

'My name is Thomas Marlowe,' he said into the microphone. 'And, as you all now know, Taylor Coleman was my father. Many of you have spoken to him over the years, and some of you have been close friends and family to him, but for me, I only met him three or four times in my life. The last real time I met him was when I was eighteen years old, and he came to celebrate my birthday in an unorthodox way. The next time I saw him was over fifteen years later, when he tried to have me murdered, just to gain my attention.'

He had expected some kind of intake of breath, but instead he got laughter.

Of course he would. People knew Taylor Coleman; they knew what he was like. Having someone state he was being targeted for death purely to gain his attention was probably something that many of them had already experienced in their past.

Marlowe straightened.

'I spoke more with my father the last two times I met him, than I probably did in my entire life,' he continued. 'And I'll admit right here and now that I don't actually know who my father was. The man I met on my eighteenth was not the same man who left me and my mother when I was a child, and he certainly wasn't the same man who faced me in a Paris garden when I asked for his help.'

He watched the crowd as he spoke and saw several faces nod or express interest at the last line.

Orchid's here in force, he thought to himself.

'My father did give me a gift,' he said, realising that actually, he'd already decided on this. 'A mighty, terrible, earth-changing gift ... and it's a gift that I intend to use.'

He leant closer to the microphone, lowering his voice, but allowing it to carry through the speakers.

'And, if you have a problem with that, then just like my father, you can try to gain my attention by doing something big, because otherwise, I'm just going to ignore you all. I'll be around. Let's have a chat.'

Marlowe turned and nodded at Ichabod, noting his stony expression, and walked offstage. He decided not to stay in the auditorium, and walked up the steps, exiting out of the middle door, noting as he did so that both Pearson and Steele were smiling widely as he passed.

Obviously, both of them were now trying to work out how to use him in their own agendas.

Pulling out his phone and checking for any messages he'd missed while in the auditorium, he had made it five steps away from the door when a woman walked over. She wasn't wearing black, but was in business attire, and Marlowe noticed she hadn't approached from the auditorium, which meant that she hadn't been part of the funeral, or welcome at the funeral.

She watched Marlowe for a long moment, as if deciding whether he was the person she needed to speak to, and then walked over to him.

'Mister Marlowe?' she asked, as if confident she was speaking to the right person, but aware there could be a problem here.

'I am,' Marlowe frowned, observing her. 'Have we met?'

'No,' she replied, reaching into her pocket and pulling out a leather wallet. 'But I think we're going to become firm friends very soon.'

She opened up the wallet and revealed the badge and ID of an Interpol officer.

Marlowe felt a sudden surge of curiosity. *Was this the officer that Clarissa had mentioned?*

'Are you here because of my father, or because of ...'

'Oh, I'm here because of you, Mister Marlowe,' the woman said. 'My name is Sandra Reilly, I'm a level three special agent in Interpol, and I'd like to talk to you about a few things that we're investigating.'

'Really,' Marlowe tried to keep his voice light and amused by this, as he closed his phone and placed it into his outer jacket breast pocket. Her accent had a slight Dublin twang, but there was an element of Parisian twang to it. Possibly Irish born, but she'd been based in Europe for a while. 'And what sort of things would they be?'

'We have a few incidents that we're looking into,' Reilly said.

'Explain "incidents" to me,' Marlowe smiled. 'As I think you'll find that some of these are covered by the Official Secrets Act. I was—'

'You *were* under the auspices of Her Majesty's Government, now *His* Majesty's Government,' Reilly replied. 'But you are no longer under those auspices, and as such, all MI5 related shenanigans you may have been playing with are now open to scrutiny. Which means, Mister Marlowe, we're going to be having a little chat about some unsolved murders on British soil, in particular in a service station off the M4, and a separate murder outside a roadside diner near Cambridge.'

Reilly gave another smile.

'So,' she said, 'how would you like to start?'

12

PAST CRIMES

MARLOWE WATCHED REILLY CAREFULLY. SHE HAD AN ANGLE here, and he hadn't quite worked out what it was, because there was no way an Interpol officer would be trying to take him down for things he'd done in protection of the realm.

As she'd spoken, they'd walked over to a coffee stand at the side of the casino area. A queue was waiting for their coffees to be made, but there were a few seats and chairs that could be sat at. Marlowe waved for Reilly to sit down.

'Please,' he said, 'explain to me what this is.'

'I've been following you for a while, Mister Marlowe,' Reilly replied, settling down and placing her hands on the table, folding them on top of each other. 'I was involved in a Taskforce looking at a dead Eastern European by the name of Stefan Chechik. He was found in his car on a country road north of Duxworth, near the A505. You might remember him.'

'Don't recognise the name,' Marlowe forced a smile. He remembered him very well. Chechik had been an assassin hired in relation to the Rubicon list. Marlowe had fought

Chechik in Cambridge, and had then followed him out of it. Eventually, he'd allowed Chechik to "see" he was being followed while heading south on the M11, and after Chechik had moved onto the A505, he'd then faced him in a service station. They'd spoken, and Chechik had left with him, thinking he had Marlowe secured, but Marlowe had prepared the SUV they were heading to in advance, convincing Chechik he'd been given a nerve agent.

He convinced Stefan Chechik a little too well, however, and the assassin had bit down on a cyanide capsule, inconveniently dying, and after wiping any footage of the meeting, Marlowe had eventually driven out to a country lane, miles from anywhere, leaving Chechik's body in the car, before wiping the scene clean.

More importantly, Marlowe knew that Reilly *also* knew everything he'd just considered.

'The problem is, Mister Marlowe,' Reilly continued, 'I know that isn't the truth. I know you were in a roadside restaurant with Stefan Chechik shortly before he was found dead, and that you left together. I know this because you returned to this location shortly afterwards, waving a Special Branch ID badge and demanding to see their security cameras, claiming you'd lost a valuable phone with critical ID on it, and then watching footage that, I will point out, would have proven the meeting, and leaving shortly before a newly placed malware virus destroyed the last twenty-four hours' worth of it.'

'But, if there is no footage,' Marlowe replied, 'there is no proof of a meeting.'

Reilly smiled.

'No, you're correct,' she said. 'However, the manager you spoke to recognised you when I showed a photo, and I know damn well it was you. Shortly after that, an organisation that had been involved with Chechik tried to kill multiple dignitaries in Westminster. You were there "saving the world," according to my Government sources.'

'Sounds like whoever killed this person helped save lives,' Marlowe started, but Reilly held a hand up to stop him.

'Whether or not you save the world, Mister Marlowe,' she said, 'that's not my decision. I'm investigating a murder. You could have said it was self-defence, but to do so, you would have had to have raised it with the police. You didn't. You hid the body, you tried to hide your tracks, removing security footage – and for me, that sounds like murder.'

'Or they, hypothetically bit down on a suicide pill, killing themselves.'

'Hypothetically?'

'Hypothetically.'

'Hypothetically or not, suicide pills are from the realm of spy books and movies, Mister Marlowe,' Reilly replied icily. 'And as such, do not exist in this investigation. One thing we did find was your rather visible Jaguar seen on ANPR cameras on the A505, shortly before the incident. The same Jaguar, I hasten to add, that was seen in the Heston services off the M4 motorway a few weeks later, when Grayson Long was murdered in an explosion.'

Marlowe kept his expression blank, but secretly he was groaning. Grayson Long had been a hitman sent after Marlowe by his father, who had tried to kill him in the Heston services. Marlowe, realising he was being followed, had set up a trap and, after killing Long, he had used a car bomb that *someone else* had tried to murder him with to detonate in the vehicle, hoping to make sure any evidence aimed at him would be gone.

However, at the time, even though it was late at night, or rather early in the morning when this happened, and the people witnessing the event were small in number and likely filled with a lot of people being tired or worse for wear, Marlowe was aware the death of Grayson Long was going to land on him. Even more so later on when he met with Taylor Coleman in the Tick Tock Diner in New York, learning Long had been sent to him deliberately to fail, purely so Marlowe could find a clue that led him to the diner and his father.

Luckily for Marlowe, that part of the story, a photo with an address and time on the back had been taken from the scene.

'Interesting thing about Grayson Long,' Reilly continued. 'Even though your London police believed he'd been killed as some kind of West London gangland war, we know he received a cash payment from an unnamed source, which, when Interpol looked into it, we learned came from a subsidiary of a company owned by your father, Taylor Coleman.'

'Still never heard of him,' Marlowe lied.

'Well, let me tell you about him. He was part of a two-man group with Vanessa Cale, his fiancée. You may have heard of her.'

'Name doesn't come to mind,' Marlowe shrugged.

'Really?' Reilly pulled out her phone now and opened up an app on it. On it was a photo of the Tick Tock diner in New York. Marlowe recognised it. It was his meeting with Taylor Coleman. There, to the side, and not part of the conversation, was Vanessa. Marlowe knew she was there because he'd told her about it. She'd decided to kill him because she'd been informed he was the man who killed her husband. Marlowe had explained that Taylor had done this, and she'd changed her mind.

'Maybe you should speak to her about what happened,' Marlowe suggested.

'Interesting fact about Vanessa Cale,' Reilly said. 'She died in New York, days after her partner was killed. Her body was found, shot dead, during an event at the Lotte New York Palace Hotel. The same event, by the way, where Nathan Donziger was arrested and where you were seen to be.'

Marlowe shrugged once more.

'What happened in New York was part of a joint MI5 and CIA—'

He stopped again as Reilly raised a hand.

'MI5,' she said. 'That's right, you're an MI5 agent. Tell me again the remit of MI5.'

Marlowe sighed. He knew where this was going.

'MI5's remit is directed to protect British parliamentary democracy and economic interests, as well as stopping counter terrorism and espionage within the United Kingdom.'

'Within the United Kingdom,' Reilly continued. 'That means things happening on UK soil, doesn't it?'

'Yes,' Marlowe continued.

'In fact, if it was an international event, MI6, your sister organisation, would have been involved instead, is that correct?'

Marlowe nodded.

'So, why is an MI5 agent dealing with something in New York?' Reilly smiled. 'Why aren't you passing it to a relevant department?'

'I was asked for personally,' Marlowe replied. 'It was following the events at Westminster.'

'I see, I see,' Reilly started flicking through her phone still. 'And you had no knowledge of Vanessa Cale.'

Marlowe suspected he was being led down a road and so shrugged.

'There were many people involved in the scene,' he said. 'There's a chance I could have met her. I recognised her when you showed the photo.'

'Ah, that would explain this then,' Reilly said. She opened up another photo, this one from the security camera of the lobby of the Lotte New York Palace Hotel, which showed Marlowe and Vanessa walking together.

'Oh yes,' Marlowe nodded. 'I remember her now. I wondered where she'd gone. She never told me her name, or that she was involved with any hitmen, like ... what was his name again?'

Reilly chuckled, placing her phone down.

'I have your face linked to a gun battle in Clontarf in Ireland, and of course, we've all seen the footage of you stabbing a fellow agent on the A40 after a road chase that caused countless accidents and millions in damage.'

Marlowe narrowed his eyes at this.

'I was on—'

'I know, I know,' Reilly replied. 'You working on super top-secret spy stuff, on behalf of your government, and he was a traitor, or a terrorist, or some other utterly shite "get out of jail free" type of bad guy.'

She leaned closer.

'I don't care about what your government did with you,' she said. 'I know you killed Stefan Chechik and Grayson Long. And if you didn't kill Vanessa Cale, you were definitely involved in her death. So how about we talk a bit more about this—'

'How about you cut the crap,' Marlowe said now, his voice tightening. 'And tell me what this is really about. You've had me sitting here for at least five minutes. Interpol doesn't have the reach for some of the stuff you're throwing here; this is CIA level bullshit. And not once have you tried to arrest me. If you had me for these offences, you would have taken me out before I even got to Las Vegas. And if you had seen the file on Chechik, you'd see the cause of death was "death by cyanide."'

'You know that how?'

'He was a person of interest in a case,' Marlowe replied. It wasn't a lie; he just wasn't pointing out he'd been there when it happened. 'and I read the report. One that you would have known if you read the MI5 one, rather than a CIA one based on guesswork and stolen intel.'

Reilly placed her hands on the table.

'Cut to the chase,' she mused, nodding. 'I like that. I know that if I went for you, arrested you for these crimes, it'd get lost in the courts. Your government would throw up blocks. You might have been working on your own at this point, Mister Marlowe, but I know that it would have raised a few ghosts in the process. What I really prefer is getting my hands on Gabriel Rizzo.'

So this was the Interpol agent hunting Rizzo.

'Many people do,' Marlowe leant back at this. 'Why do you think I can help you here?'

'Because I have you by the short and curlies,' Reilly replied. 'You're going to help me take Gabriel Rizzo down by the end of this week. I want him in my custody.'

'That could be hard,' Marlowe said. 'There's a lot of people gunning for him right now.'

'Oh, I'm sure there are,' Reilly said. 'I know you were seen facing off with him. Rumours bounce around. I also know you're with Roxanne Vasquez, a lawyer who was also seen to be arguing with him and, by the way, was also seen to be at the Lotte New York Palace Hotel, so could even be arrested as an accomplice, maybe have her life dismantled easier than yours can be—'

'You leave her out of this,' Marlowe hissed.

'I'm sure you already have a plan to take him down in your own way,' Reilly ignored the threat, a small smile playing at her lips.

'And what would my own way be?' Marlowe asked.

At this, Reilly simply watched him, miming a gun with her finger, pointing it at Marlowe.

'Stefan Chechik. Grayson Long. Vanessa Cale,' she said, miming gunshots. 'Need I say more?'

'So you're saying if Gabriel Rizzo ends the week in your custody, this gets forgotten?'

'Well, I'll need a little more,' Reilly smiled.

'Like what?'

Reilly leant closer, and even though she whispered the words, they came out clear and echoing.

'So, let me explain to you what I need. You want to hurt Rizzo? I see that. If it was me, I'd be taking what he loves, his money.'

'Sounds like a plan.'

'It sounds like a plan you've probably already considered,' Reilly replied simply. 'Mister Marlowe, from reading your file, I believe you intend to hurt Mister Rizzo, in the process robbing the Gold Strike Casino of several million dollars' worth of profit, thus stopping Mister Rizzo from paying a lot of debts to some very important people, including his own family.'

Marlowe said nothing, staring at her.

'I would like you to provide me with that money,' she finished.

'I'm sorry?' Marlowe did a double take.

'I don't think I said anything out of the ordinary there, Mister Marlowe,' Reilly straightened back up, now comfortable in the fact that no one was overhearing her. 'It's very simple. I want Gabriel Rizzo, as well as the money that you make from any heist you pull. Call it a finder's fee if it helps you sleep at night.'

'There's no money to be made from the heist, if it was even going to happen,' Marlowe said. 'It'd be a revenge job.'

'Then you won't mind passing it on then, will you?' Reilly smiled.

Marlowe sat back on the seat, glaring at the woman in front of him.

'What if we don't get the money out?' he asked. 'What if we don't succeed?'

'Then you'll probably be dead and the mission will be off the books, so no one will know we had spoken.'

'What if we don't manage to get the money but succeed? Maybe the hotel burns down or something else happens?'

'The deal is the same. I want the money.'

Marlowe shook his head in disbelief at the situation.

'The plan I was thinking of was just attacking the vault,' he said. 'Causing disruption.'

'Whatever's in the vault would be nice to have.'

Marlowe sighed.

'I don't really have a choice here, do I?' he asked.

'Not really,' Reilly shrugged, almost apologetically as, reaching into her inside jacket pocket, she pulled out a recording device.

'Here we go,' she said. 'Let's make a little contract, shall we? You just speak into this device and confirm that you'll be providing me with the money.'

Marlowe took the device, glaring at Sandra Reilly.

'Fine,' he said, turning it on. 'I, Thomas Marlowe, hereby state that any money we gain from the vault of the Gold Strike Casino will be passed to Interpol agent Sandra Reilly.'

Reilly nodded.

'I think we need a little more,' she said. 'I'd like you to add that it's not just money. You could, after all, be finding a way to get around paying, if there are stocks, bonds, or jewellery, even.'

Marlowe choked back a laugh.

'You're kidding me,' he said.

Reilly just stared at him.

'Fine,' Marlowe replied, returning to the recorder. 'I promise to give all the money, stocks, jewellery, gold, and any other items of definite worth that we personally remove from the Gold Strike vault,' he said. 'How's that sound?'

'That works for me,' Reilly nodded. 'Keep an eye on your phone, Mister Marlowe. I'll contact you shortly.'

Marlowe forced a smile.

'I think we can do that,' he said.

'Good,' Reilly rose, throwing down a business card with her number on it. 'Because I'd hate to start destroying the lives of the people around you.'

Marlowe watched her walk off and forced the bile and anger back down. Chechik, Long, Cale, they'd all been parts of his past he hoped were long gone.

Parts that MI5 and Emilia Wintergreen had promised would be scrubbed.

Rising, he took a deep breath to calm himself.

Looked like those days were gone now he was out of the boys' club, he thought to himself. *Best play nice, and watch your back.*

Feeling more centred, he turned and walked back to the ballroom.

After all, he had a wake to get back to.

13

CLOSE QUARTERS

As expected, the auditorium was now empty, and Marlowe had seen several groups wandering off, conspiratorially talking to each other.

Deciding to catch up with Trix and see if she'd heard anything, he pulled out his phone, but stopped as he noticed Gabriel Rizzo, a goon on either side, walking towards him.

Gabriel had obviously seen him and had waved his goons back as he approached.

'Mister Marlowe,' he said. 'My condolences on the loss of your father.'

Marlowe nodded.

'Thank you,' he replied. 'Congratulations on your hotel.'

'So, do we pretend that last night didn't happen?' Gabriel smiled. 'Do we do business or do we decide to keep away from each other in peace?'

'I'm not your enemy,' Marlowe said, straightening slightly. 'I came to you yesterday because my friend was being hassled by you. And if she's left alone, we have no problems.'

Gabriel nodded.

'At some point in the next day or so, before this all ends,' he said, waving around the casino; Marlowe assumed he meant the wake rather than the casino itself ending. 'I'd like to talk to you about your plans for Orchid.'

Without waiting for Marlowe to respond, Gabriel continued.

'You heard your father's video message. He's allowing you to shape Orchid into a weapon of your own desire. My question is, what kind of weapon would it be?'

'I think you're taking more from that message than there was,' Marlowe forced a smile. 'I'm not Orchid. There are a lot of people who have their own opinions on what needs to be done; I'm just one of them. A seat at the High Council doesn't necessarily mean control of the High Council.'

'True,' Gabriel nodded. 'But let's call a spade a spade here. We've already seen if someone goes against you on the High Council, they get taken down.'

Marlowe knew Gabriel was commenting on what had happened to Lucien Delacroix. In response, he gave a little bow.

'Delacroix was a rabid dog, a billionaire who thought he should be in control of the world,' he said. 'He was actually proof that no one person should be in control of anything. If Orchid wants to change with the times, I'll listen. But if they decide to go the other way ...'

He leant closer.

'Then I'll burn them down.'

Gabriel took an involuntary step back and then composed himself. The smile returned to his face.

'I look forward to seeing that happen,' he replied. 'Orchid has been kind to me. I'd hate to see them falter if the wrong types get into power.'

'Yes, they've funded quite a lot of this, haven't they?' Marlowe looked around. 'I hope you can afford to pay them back.'

At this, a conversation now on more comfortable ground, Gabriel's face broke into a beaming smile.

'Mister Marlowe,' he asked, almost mockingly. 'Concerned for my casino? Don't you worry at all. With the launch we have in two days, the gambling that's been happening this week, Taylor Coleman's wake attended by countless billionaires, all with large pockets for gambling ... I think I can safely say any debt that we owe will be sorted.'

'Good to hear, but one question I will ask – just curious – what happens if you *can't* pay Orchid back?' Marlowe's voice was colder, more blunt now. 'Your casino was created before I joined the High Council, and if I'm going to be changing the way Orchid works, I want to make sure the money's there to do so.'

He glanced around, checking to see if the goons had come close or not, and was grateful to see that they were still vaguely there in the background, keeping their distance.

'You'd better make sure the money's there,' he said. 'Orchid might be unhappy. There are other Rizzos they can work with, after all ...'

Gabriel Rizzo chuckled.

'Don't worry, Mister Marlowe,' he replied casually. 'My sister won't be gaining my empire just yet. I'm sure you already know the problems I have with my family. A man like you is always well informed. You leave your business to yourself ... and leave my business to me.'

At this, Marlowe gave a mocking bow.

'Enjoy the rest of your stay, Mister Marlowe,' Gabriel replied. 'Don't forget, you do have a room here if you so need to rest. I know that bereavement is so *taxing*. And you never know what's coming at you from around the next corner.'

'A threat?'

'A warning,' Gabriel replied. 'I had a visitor today. You have people looking to remove you.'

'So I've heard,' Marlowe narrowed his eyes. 'Are you part of that list?'

'Not yet.'

With this stated, Gabriel Rizzo walked off, and Marlowe stared after him.

He had forgotten he had a room here.

At the moment, nothing seemed to be happening in the main casino, and gambling was irrelevant to his interests. Had the other members of Orchid returned to their own rooms? Or was there a small queue outside of his forgotten room, waiting for him to turn up?

Walking over to reception, Marlowe grabbed himself his room's plastic RFID card, gaining his room number in the process. It was on a high floor; he had expected nothing less, as he started towards the casino's elevators.

If anything, he could grab himself a glass of water from the minibar, knowing it at least hadn't been tampered with.

As he approached the elevators, however, he realised that somebody was walking along beside him. No, not beside him, more to the left and a few steps behind, making it look as if he was there on his own cognisance, but matching Marlowe almost step for step.

Marlowe didn't want to turn and look. At the moment, there was every opportunity this could be a potential ally, waiting for a secluded moment to speak.

Or an assassin, ignoring Taylor Coleman's wishes.

As they passed one of the machines, Marlowe grabbed a

small glance in the chrome on the side of it, recognising the figure following him. A small shiver went down his spine, adrenaline hitting his system as he now recognised an assassin known as *Quaid*, who primarily worked in Brazil.

He stopped, turned, and looked at him.

'Quaid,' he said, the utterance of the name enough for an introduction. Quaid was tall, slim and blond, in his early forties and tanned from sunny Brazilian days. He looked like an athlete, maybe a baseball player, in a black suit and t-shirt, and in a way Marlowe realised he technically was an athlete – it was just that his sport of choice was *death*.

'Marlowe.'

'Following me or just happening to go the same direction?'

'I'm heading to the elevators,' Quaid said. 'I couldn't give a damn where you're going.'

Marlowe nodded. He knew that was utter bollocks, but didn't want to call the assassin on it just yet.

'Here for the wake?'

'Taylor Coleman's family looked after me many times over the years,' Quaid replied as they started walking together now, towards the elevators again. 'It was only fair that I came to pay my respects.'

He ignored Marlowe's expression, looking away, unconcerned with the man beside him.

'I liked your speech.'

'I wasn't expecting to give one,' Marlowe replied.

'Oh, you could tell,' Quaid mocked. 'You've polarised Orchid quite nicely, though. Half of them are convinced you're the new messiah, the other half want you gasping for breath like a fish on a river bank, as the last breath leaves its body.'

'That's scarily specific,' Marlowe said as he pressed the button, waiting for the elevator to arrive. 'Has anybody spoken to you about that?'

'Yes,' Quaid replied. 'Three. I won't give you the names, but there's a hit out on you already. You won't find it on any dark net forum, though. It's more of a gentleman's agreement kind of hit.'

'Did you accept it?'

'If I did, would you care?' he asked. 'Besides, I hear the Gravedigger's in town. I'd be more worried about that if I were you.'

Marlowe chuckled.

'I have no fear of bogeymen, and I heard there were to be no murders during the wake,' he said. 'My father demanded that nobody fulfilled grudges in his video eulogy.'

'This isn't a grudge,' Quaid said as the doors opened and three elderly Americans here for the gambling walked out past them. 'I think you could class this as ... well, more that this is more of a threat to their very existence.'

'You take this elevator then,' Marlowe smiled. 'I'll wait for the next one.'

'Scared of me?' Quaid grinned, touched. 'Don't worry. Unlike you, I don't have one of those fancy coins that allows me to bring guns into this place.'

Marlowe gave a small nod.

'They are convenient,' he said, refusing to confirm whether he had or didn't have a weapon on him.

Knowing what the meaning was, Quaid chuckled, as the two of them entered the elevator.

'You're wrong about the deaths,' he said. 'People have been dying since we've arrived.'

'Oh yes?' Marlowe asked.

'There's an arena downstairs. It's being used for the fight tomorrow night. Orchid members have been bringing their own bodyguards in, having them fight like gladiators, betting on the outcome,' Quaid explained, and Marlowe could tell from his tone that he wasn't a fan.

'To the death?'

'Not by design,' Quaid replied. 'They've spent money on their bodyguards. The last thing they want to do is kill them off. It's more like it used to be back in the day of ratters.'

'Ratters?'

'You know, in your native London, where people would have rats in pits and set dogs on them. If the dog got injured, they'd be taken home and looked after. But they still gave sport.'

He looked as if he wanted to spit to the side at this, a distaste in his mouth.

'But a couple bled out before they could be treated,' he continued. 'Don't worry yourself, this was all planned by your father. If you recall, he said, "no blood spilled, unless by mutual agreement," and these fights are definitely by mutual agreement.'

Marlowe pressed the button for his floor, glancing back at Quaid.

'Fourteen,' Quaid nodded at the button. As he pressed it, Marlowe noticed it was two floors above him. It meant that Marlowe would leave first.

'Well, it's good to see you, Quaid,' he said.

'I wish I could say the same about you,' Quaid replied.

The elevator doors shut with a definitive click, sealing Quaid and Marlowe in a steel box ascending slowly. Quaid, his eyes cold, drew a SOG Pentagon FX fixed blade knife from a forearm sheath, its dual edges razor sharp.

'I thought you couldn't bring weapons in?' Marlowe asked, almost sighing with dismay that he was going to have to fight in here.

'I can't,' Quaid shrugged. 'I was given this, asked to finish the job with it.'

'And I can't change your mind about this?'

Marlowe considered drawing his CZ and ending this quickly, but knew the gunshot would draw unwanted attention.

Quaid shook his head.

'You're MI5, or at least ex-MI5,' he replied. 'You know how this works. You go down, or I do.'

'You sure you want to do this here?' Marlowe asked, nodding at the elevator car's camera in the corner.

'Nobody's watching,' Quaid replied with a smile. 'I was told the elevator specifically was a perfect kill zone.'

'And who told you that?'

'The people who want you dead.'

'And they are?'

Quaid shook his head.

'Beyond your pay grade,' he said, flipping the SOG into a reverse hammer grip. Marlowe knew he was about to strike, so uncoiled his steel bracelet defence chain, a metre of deadly, flexible metal.

Quaid attacked first, his blade slicing through the air in a vicious arc.

Marlowe dodged, the chain in his hand whipping out, clashing against the knife. They moved quickly, their actions efficient and deadly, both trained by organisations that prided themselves on their skillset in combat. The sound of metal on metal rang out, and Marlowe's chain proved effective, not just blocking but also striking, leaving shallow welts on Quaid's arms.

The assassin pressed the attack, slashing quick backhand knife and elbow strikes. Marlowe kept pace, his movements fast and precise, using the chain to create a barrier of spinning and constantly moving steel. In a split-second decision, he lashed out; the chain wrapping around Quaid's wrist, pulling the knife-hand wide. Marlowe then struck, his fist connecting with Quaid's jaw.

Staggered, Quaid regained his balance, his glare intensifying.

'You little prick,' he hissed, landing an elbow strike that slammed Marlowe into the elevator wall. The confined space was becoming a definite challenge, limiting Marlowe's ability to use the chain. Quaid pressed on, his SOG blade a blur of steel, and nicking Marlowe's forearm.

But Marlowe adapted, using the walls for leverage, his counterattacks swift and chaotic as he swung the chain, whistling through the air as it wrapped around Quaid's ankle, unbalancing him.

Marlowe capitalised on this, delivering a sharp blow to Quaid's knee. Quaid faltered but recovered, kicking off the chain and lunging blade forward, forcing Marlowe to deflect and counter.

The two were locked in a deadly ballet, each move critical, each second vital. In a final, calculated move, Marlowe feigned a wrong step. Quaid, sensing an opening, lunged with full force – but Marlowe was ready. He sidestepped, using Quaid's momentum against him. With a swift, precise motion, he whipped out the chain, striking Quaid in the throat.

The assassin gasped, his blade clattering to the floor as he stumbled back. Seizing the moment, Marlowe closed in, using the chain to ensnare Quaid's weapon arm, pulling it back and exposing his torso. In a fluid motion, Marlowe delivered a powerful punch to Quaid's solar plexus, knocking the wind out of him. As Quaid doubled over, gasping for breath, Marlowe struck again, a targeted blow to the side of the head with the chain, now wrapped around his fingers like a knuckleduster.

Quaid staggered, disoriented and weakened, and Marlowe didn't hesitate. Moving behind, he wrapped the chain around Quaid's neck, pulling it taut. The assassin struggled, clawing at the steel, biting into his flesh, but Marlowe's grip was unyielding. With a final exertion of strength, Marlowe tightened the chain further, cutting off Quaid's air supply.

Seconds later, Quaid's body went limp, his struggle ceasing. After a few seconds more, Marlowe released the chain, letting the assassin's body slump in the corner as he rose, staring up at the camera.

'You happy now?' he hissed, but turned, expecting another attack as the elevator reached its destination, and the doors slid open, revealing the grim scene.

St John Steele stared in horror at Marlowe, standing over Quaid's prone form.

'You killed him?'

'No, he's sleeping,' Marlowe left the elevator, watching Steele carefully. 'And no blood spilled. Well, maybe a little. What are you doing here?'

'I came to your room, looking for you,' Steele replied as the elevator doors closed, continuing up to the next floor. 'But now it seems I need to stop some kind of mutiny. Do you know who sent him?'

'Apparently it's above my pay grade,' Marlowe said as Steele pressed a button, and entered a different elevator.

'I'll fix this,' he said. 'After all, until they hire a new one, I'm still technically the Arbitrator.'

As the doors shut, Marlowe stared at the doors, working through the events of the last few minutes. He'd assumed Quaid had taken the elevator as a convenient location to kill him, but that had been removed with one line.

'Nobody's watching. I was told the elevator specifically was a perfect kill zone.'

They knew Marlowe would be in the elevator. They made sure the cameras were off.

'Don't forget, you do have a room here if you so need to rest. I know that bereavement is so taxing.'

Could this have been set up by Gabriel Rizzo? Seen publicly to be allied with Marlowe, or at least civil, while sending someone after him?

No. Quaid had mentioned pay grades, and there was no way Rizzo was high enough to demand that kind of loyalty.

So who was?

With that question, Marlowe went to his room before anyone else appeared. Also, his arm was still bleeding, and he needed to treat the wound.

Heh. Maybe blood had been spilled after all.

14

ALLIANCES

'MASON QUAID,' TRIX SAID, LOOKING OFF-CAMERA AS SHE typed on the keyboard off screen. 'Jesus, Marlowe, you really do pick them, don't you?'

Marlowe smiled, sitting back on the sofa, his phone up in front of him as he took the video call with Trix.

'I didn't choose this,' he said. 'Quaid decided. He was paid to kill me.'

'Do you know who sent him?'

'It's kind of what I was hoping you could tell me,' Marlowe replied.

Trix carried on typing.

'Born in America. Spent most of the last ten years in Brazil. Special forces. Worked with Rattlestone ...'

She looked back up.

'You don't think this is Trisha Hawkins?'

'I don't think so,' Marlowe shook his head. 'This is something more relevant to Orchid. He said to me it was above my pay grade, which means as far as I'm concerned, he thinks it's somebody above me. And, as I'm High Council ...'

'Yeah. But he might mean pay grade as in seniority,' Trix replied. 'You *are* the new boy on the block, after all.'

She stopped.

'That's interesting.'

'What?'

'He's worked as a bodyguard for the Colemans. Not just an assassin.'

'Okay, so he has a connection to Taylor. I knew that already—'

'Not Taylor,' Trix looked back up at her camera, and by default at Marlowe. 'Byron Coleman, his son. The one you call Ichabod.'

She scrolled on her screen.

'Says here that he was brought on close protection for Byron Coleman during an arms exchange. Daddy was obviously working on something, and wanted to make sure his son couldn't be used as collateral. They were in Brazil and he brought in Quaid. It looks to me like Quaid and Byron sparked quite a good relationship.'

Marlowe cursed softly as a phrase Quaid spoke returned to his thoughts.

'Taylor Coleman's family looked after me many times over the years.'

The family. Not Coleman himself.

'Did they keep the professional side going as well?' he asked, irritated he hadn't seen this.

'There're several jobs marked down here that Quaid took and completed ...' Trix paused, looking up. 'Jesus Christ, Marlowe. I think your half-brother's been using him as a hitman.'

Marlowe leant back on the sofa at this. Ichabod had struck him as somebody who wanted out of the family business, but at the same time, he knew *everything* about the family business. There was every opportunity for him to get involved in whatever his father was doing.

'Are you sure your half-brother didn't want this High Council seat?'

Marlowe shrugged.

'Maybe Taylor didn't discuss it with him. Might have thought he was doing Ichabod a favour, throwing me under the bus. Either way, I think it's a conversation we need to have,' he said. 'Do you know where he is right now?'

'He's in your hotel playing poker,' Trix replied. 'I've got him on the cameras.'

'You've hacked into the cameras?'

'It's not that difficult, Marlowe,' Trix smiled.

'Either that or Gabriel Rizzo wants you to believe so.'

'Well, if he does, he's an idiot,' Trix leant back on the chair, turning her attention away from the screen and back onto the camera. 'Listen, I've been thinking. This whole thing with Roxanne is distracting you.'

Marlowe shook his head.

'If anything, the deal with Roxanne is actually focusing me,' he said. 'It's everything else that's distracting me. Hitmen being sent by members of Orchid, a rogue Interpol agent who wants me to steal millions of dollars for her—'

'I thought she wanted Gabriel Rizzo?'

'With the aforementioned millions of dollars from him, sure,' Marlowe chuckled. 'Let's not class this as anything it isn't. Reilly wants money. And if I don't sort it, then bad things are going to happen. And somehow she's got intel on me that only the CIA, or MI5 would have, so she's being helped somewhere.'

'Vic Saeed?'

'I think he's on the side of the angels for the moment, but it won't hurt to check him out.'

'Maybe we could hire Quaid to take her out once he wakes up,' Trix suggested. Marlowe wasn't sure if she was serious or not.

'Let's keep that in our pocket, shall we?' he replied.

Trix shrugged.

'St John Steele?'

'Was on my floor, but claimed he was waiting to speak to me. Would have been handy, though, if I was dead,' Marlowe mused. 'He could have quickly pulled my body out, dumped it in my room. I think I need to keep an eye on him.'

'No offence, Marlowe, but I think you need to keep an eye on pretty much everybody you've dealt with,' Trix laughed. 'I'll see what I can find at this end. Oh, one more thing.'

'Yes?'

Trix looked uncomfortable, and Marlowe knew this was probably something she didn't want to talk about.

'You're going to need help with your plan.'

Marlowe winced. He'd been expecting this conversation. He was hoping he wouldn't have to have had it this early on.

'I'm aware,' he said. 'I'm guessing you have thoughts?'

'You're hamstrung,' Trix explained. 'Hamstrung by locations and people.'

'How do you mean?'

'There aren't many assets of yours in Vegas right now,' Trix was typing again. 'And I can't see Orchid helping you take down the guy who's supposed to be giving them money.'

'I'm not sure,' Marlowe replied. 'He's pissed a lot of people off, and I think ...'

He paused.

'You've already worked out who I need, haven't you?'

'Someone who already watches Orchid,' Trix replied. 'I reckon if you call her—'

'Don't say the name," Marlowe held up a hand, grimacing. 'If you say the name, she turns up just like the devil.'

Trix started chuckling.

'Sasha Bordeaux is probably there already,' she said. 'She's going to have seen that you've arrived. She knows it's Taylor's funeral and she's going to be watching to see who turns up from Orchid. Plus, if she's around, Brad might be there, too. And I think of all the people you know, Sasha Bordeaux is one of the few who will actually help you take down Orchid rather than try to arrest them.'

Marlowe grimaced again, aware that Trix was watching him through the phone's camera.

'She annoys me,' he said. 'She irritates the hell out of me.'

'That's because you can't read her,' Trix replied with a smile. 'How many times have you met now? Two? Three? Five? And you still don't know her name?'

'I know her first name,' Marlowe said. 'It's actually Sasha.'

'Only because she told you,' Trix laughed. 'Face it, Marlowe, she's a better spy than you are, and that pisses you off.'

'She's got more money at her disposal,' Marlowe snapped. 'I've never been given a private jet to fly around in.'

'I don't think you've ever had an opportunity to ask for one,' Trix replied. 'Maybe you should ask Wintergreen next time you speak to her.'

'I somehow don't think that's happening for a while,' Marlowe said, sighing. 'Okay, I'll tell you what. Make some enquiries. See if you can find her if she's in the area. If she is, arrange a meeting.'

'Done already,' Trix said, and although there was a little

bit of smug triumph in her tone, Marlowe could sense some embarrassment.

Probably because she went behind your back, knowing you'd complain about it for ages, he thought to himself. *Clever girl.*

'Send me the where and when,' he sighed. 'And then get back to the shopping list I arranged.'

'Already on it,' Trix brightened. 'Although I still don't understand why we need to fix up a wheelchair ...?'

MARLOWE DECIDED HE DIDN'T LIKE REYNARD MASSEY FROM the moment he met him.

It didn't help that although Sasha Bordeaux had passed Trix an address and time for the meeting, she hadn't bothered turning up herself, leaving Reynard as her surrogate. One that looked more irritated to be there than Marlowe was when he eventually arrived.

The diner was cheap and cheerful, everything you'd expect from an establishment providing such a service. Marlowe had entered, having taken off his black suit and replaced it with a pair of jeans and his leather jacket. He still wore the black shirt, the cuts to his sleeves hidden, but if you saw him, you wouldn't have thought he'd been at any kind of funeral memorial service that day. He was simply a man looking for the "special of the day and a cup of joe", as they said in the movies.

Reynard Massey, however, had the look of a bookish librarian. He wore a charcoal-grey suit made from what looked to be some kind of wool blend, definitely not the kind of thing to wear in the Las Vegas heat unless you could guarantee super-cool air conditioning; a thick white shirt and a dark-blue striped tie, which looked very much as if it was some kind of group or university colours. They were blue and silver and for a second Marlowe wondered if he was from one of those fictional houses in one of those fantasy boarding school books. Although if he was CIA, he was likely to be more the gothy dark house than flouncy, optimistic hero house.

He was stocky, but not fat, his head square with short hair at the sides and a tuft of brown or dirty ginger, slightly curly hair on top. He looked to be in his forties, wore rimless glasses, and was pale-skinned, the tan of a man who wasn't allowed to see daylight. In fact, he looked like a rather bookish vampire, if all was said and done.

Marlowe approached slowly, looking around to see if Massey was on his own, or if he'd brought anybody with him. The last time he'd met Sasha Bordeaux in a bar, the moment she'd left, half the bar went with her. Massey had obviously been informed of Marlowe's arrival, or at least had been told to look for the confused-looking bearded man who was hunting for a woman rather than a bespectacled man.

He waved a hand.

'Marlowe,' he said, and Marlowe was surprised to hear that his accent was East Coast, more Massachusetts than New York. Marlowe walked over, glanced around, and then sat facing Massey.

'I've got to say, Sasha, your makeup department's gone out of the way this time.'

'You're funny,' Massey replied, his face completely dead-pan. 'I read you were funny in your file. I'm glad to see it's true.'

'You're the second person who's read my file in as many hours,' Marlowe forced a smile. 'I'd like to read it someday.'

'Sorry, CIA paperwork is highly classified.'

'Too classified for Interpol?'

Ignoring the veiled accusation, Massey leant back in the booth, waving over for the server.

'Want anything?'

'I'm not here for lunch,' Marlowe replied.

'Good, because lunch was ages ago. I meant, did you want a coffee?'

Marlowe nodded, and as the server walked over, Massey asked for two coffees to be brought over.

Settling down, he looked back at Marlowe.

'I'm Massey. Reynard Massey. You know why I'm here?'

'Because Sasha didn't want to be.'

'The woman you know as Sasha Bordeaux is unfortunately indisposed until later this evening,' Massey replied. 'I know you're shocked to hear this, but apparently you're not her only pet project.'

Marlowe nodded at this.

'I kind of guessed,' he replied. 'And I'm also guessing that Reynard Massey isn't your name, either. Do you have the same fixation as she has on comic characters, or is this something different?'

'Reynard is a fox, named after the one I had as a child and based on the Twelfth Century trickster fox of legend,' Massey replied. 'And Massey means "gift of God" and was my mother's name.'

'Wait,' Marlowe paused. 'Reynard is a fox you had as a child?'

'Yes,' Massey replied, frowning. 'Do you not have foxes in England?'

'Yes, but we don't really keep them as pets.'

Massey shrugged.

'It was less of a pet and more of a visiting friend,' he said. 'But Reynard is the name of the mythical trickster fox, and so we named him that, and later on I decided to use it as my own name. It adds an air of mystery.'

'And Massey is your mother's maiden name?' Marlowe started chuckling. 'Your first pet and your mother's maiden name. That's your porn star name, not your super spy name.'

Reynard Massey glared at Marlowe.

'As I said,' he replied, 'I love your sense of humour.'

Marlowe got the distinct impression that Massey was not liking anything about Marlowe, which was fine because Marlowe was starting to feel there was something off about the man in front of him – although it could have just been the fact he'd hoped to see Sasha, and was stuck with Massey instead.

Massey smiled at the server as she returned with two mugs of coffee, placing them down and, taking some sweet-eners from his pocket, he quietly clicked three into the coffee before stirring. Marlowe noted he didn't take any cream or milk to place into the coffee, which meant he either took his coffee black or was lactose intolerant.

'Your friend, Trixibelle Preston,' Massey continued, taking a sip, deciding it was a little too hot for the moment. 'She says you need help.'

'Not so much help, more friendly assistance,' Marlowe replied. 'In the past, Sasha has given help where she can, and usually whenever our targets have been aligned.'

'Though, you've screwed her over in the past as well,' Massey said. 'I've read your jacket. I've seen what's happened when you've previously crossed swords with the CIA and Miss Bordeaux.'

'Good,' Marlowe replied. 'Did you also see that she set me up on a plane once? And she also ...'

'We don't need to go through the history lesson,' Massey said. 'Suffice to say, Miss Bordeaux has said I should give you whatever you require.'

He leant forward, elbows on the table.

'What is it you require, Mister Marlowe?'

'I was hoping to know where Brad Haynes was,' Marlowe replied. 'I could really do with his help right now.'

'Perfect. Mister Haynes is in Vegas,' Massey said. 'Well, he will be in an hour. He was in Los Angeles and he's been tasked to whatever you require. I also understand you were looking for some muscle for some kind of caper.'

'Not so much a caper,' Marlowe replied. 'I'm getting revenge on someone, and—'

'I know,' Massey interrupted again. 'Your friend Roxanne Vasquez ... Miss Bordeaux mentioned her as well. She's having problems with Gabriel Rizzo.'

'Yes,' Marlowe replied.

'We'd like to have a chat with Gabriel Rizzo,' Massey said, straightening up now, trying his coffee again, and finding that it was no longer burning his tongue, taking a bigger sip. 'We have some requests.'

'I'm sure you do,' Marlowe replied, his tone icy.

'We understand you're looking to run some kind of heist operation on Gabriel Rizzo to stop him from gaining money to pass on to his paymasters.'

'Not quite the same, but I can go with that,' Marlowe said, wondering just exactly how much Trix had said, and how much had been expertly guessed by Bordeaux.

Or was Massey working with Reilly?

'We'll provide you with help to do what you need to do,

but there are two requirements. The first is that we gain Gabriel Rizzo at the end.'

'I can't give you that,' Marlowe said.

'And why would that be?'

'Sandra Reilly of Interpol,' Marlowe replied. 'She's already asked for dibs on Gabriel Rizzo once this all ends. I'm guessing she's going to be pulling him out before Orchid fillet him and leave him out in the sun.'

Massey scratched at his chin with an annoyed expression on his face.

'The higher ups won't like this,' he said.

'I don't care what she likes,' Marlowe replied, noting that Massey hadn't named Sasha there. 'I'm telling you the truth. I have a choice of either pissing off you or pissing off Interpol. I'm kind of caught between a rock and a hard place here.'

'You need to decide what's worse, the rock or the hard place,' Massey said. 'Because we *do* want Gabriel Rizzo at the end.'

'Okay, I'll see what I can do,' Marlowe nodded. 'What's the second thing?'

Massey smiled, leaning a little closer to Marlowe, but it felt odd, as if he was trying to lower his voice and get a message across with nobody else in the diner realising what he was doing.

'We want Orchid,' he said. 'Not destroyed. It's too valuable for that. But we want it working for us.'

'You're kidding me!' Marlowe shook his head. 'There's no way I'll manage that.'

'Then we want your brother,' Massey said quickly, and Marlowe had the distinct impression the first request was made so unworkable that anything alternative sounded better. 'You give us Byron and Gabriel together ...'

Marlowe slumped back in the chair. He needed the help to break Gabriel's security, but at the same time ...

'Fine, I'll do my best.'

'And we want your intelligence officer.'

Marlowe rose at this, angry.

'There's no way Trix—'

'Not the Brit,' Massey shook his head. 'The real one. Clarissa, or whatever she's calling herself these days. Sasha wants her too.'

'Off the table,' Marlowe replied coldly. 'You want her, you go get her yourself. Or are you too scared to?'

Reynard Massey finished his coffee, grimaced slightly at the taste.

'Oh, you should know,' he said. 'The Gravedigger's in town. I hear he's looking for you.'

'Not the first time I've heard that today,' Marlowe shrugged. 'I'm not that worried.'

'You should be,' Massey finished before he rose from the table. 'Especially as he's one of many targeting you.'

Marlowe was amused to see at least three other men rise up at the same time Massey did, as Massey nodded a farewell to Marlowe, turned, and walked out of the diner.

Marlowe sat back in the booth seat. He had expected to get shafted, but Massey's shafting was made with a smile on his face – and, considering Marlowe might have been against the guy from the start for personal and selfish reasons, it wasn't unexpected. Reilly had been unexpected, but at the same time Marlowe couldn't help wonder if the two were connected somehow. The only way Marlowe could win in this situation was to *not* win. Anything that was gained from the vault would immediately go to Reilly's bank account rather than Interpol or the CIA. This was fixable, and Marlowe had a plan for that.

The problem Marlowe had, however, was the other request. The CIA wanted Gabriel Rizzo, but so did Interpol, if Reilly was to be believed. If Marlowe was to keep Rizzo from Interpol, then he and many of his friends would be targeted. If, however, he kept it from the CIA, then it looked very much like worse things would happen.

Marlowe sniffed, took a deep breath, and rose from the chair. He'd almost made it to the door when the server stormed over to him, waving a piece of paper.

'Oh no, Sonny,' she said. 'You ain't leaving till you've paid your bill.'

'My bill?' Marlowe asked.

'The coffees you and your friend had, and the three specials his bodyguards ate,' she said. 'He told me you were paying.'

Marlowe, furious now, checked the amount and passed over a wad of ten-dollar bills.

'Keep the change,' he said.

'There's barely enough here for a tip,' the server snapped.

Marlowe smiled.

'You want a tip?' he asked. 'Never trust the CIA.'

15

TEXAS HOLD'EM

Returning to his suite at the Horseshoe Casino, Marlowe took some time to explain to Trix what had happened. Trix was as angry as he was, but frowned as she watched him dress for the wake once more.

'You don't seem as angry as I am about this,' she said. 'What do you know I don't?'

Marlowe shrugged.

'I don't know what you mean,' he replied.

'Yeah, you do,' Trix said. 'You're playing something. You're looking at angles, or finding a way to screw over everybody.'

'Let's just wait until Brad arrives,' Marlowe shook his head. 'We'll work out what to do after that. To be honest, I'd rather do this without MI5 or CIA involvement, but we're short on funds and friends right now. And, as I'd said to our new friend at Interpol, if we clean the vault, she gets it all.'

'But if we don't get anything out of the vault, then she doesn't get anything,' Trix countered. 'And if we don't do the heist, we don't—'

'No,' Marlowe sighed as he interrupted. 'There's a lot of

players now wanting to be involved in this, and between the CIA and Interpol, I'm just hoping I can work out how to surf the wave long enough to get this sorted. If Brad calls by, let me know.'

———

MARLOWE RETURNED VIA A CAB TO THE GOLD STRIKE CASINO, once more passing through security, and once more keeping his weapons with him. However, when he arrived this time, the people in funeral attire seemed a little more wary of him. He wondered if the information had got out about the attack by Quaid, and whether people now would think twice before going against Taylor Coleman's wishes.

Ichabod was still at the poker table when Marlowe arrived, even though it was a good couple of hours since Trix had given his location. Marlowe made a point of sitting down at the table and looking around. He wasn't surprised to see that everybody else on the table was Orchid, several of whom were High Council. It seemed that Byron Coleman, Ichabod to his friends – well, at least to Marlowe – was hanging around with a very exclusive level of clientele.

Ichabod glanced up, saw Marlowe and his expression tightened, almost with dismay.

'Didn't think I'd make it?' Marlowe asked. 'Neither did I. It's been a busy day.'

'I'd heard you had a run-in with a bodyguard.'

'No,' Marlowe said, passing out a pile of bills, easily five grand worth, to the dealer, and waving for some chips. 'I wasn't attacked by a bodyguard, *brother*. I was attacked by a hitman, one that you apparently have an excellent relation- ship with.'

Ichabod said nothing, but Marlowe noticed a slight twitch of the eye at the word "brother."

'Quaid has worked for my family for many years,' he replied. 'But he's a contractor. He freelances for many people, in the same way that you do.'

'So, you're saying that you had no knowledge of his attack?'

'No, I didn't know about it,' Ichabod continued, looking up at Marlowe. 'Also, we have informed him that his presence at this event is no longer required. He went against my father's rules.'

Marlowe took his cards and checked them. They were low, not really worth playing, so he placed them down and folded immediately.

'It seems people don't want me in Orchid,' he said. 'I feel like I shouldn't be here.'

'If you have the coin, you have the right to be on the High Council,' Ichabod replied. 'You hold that coin up anywhere, and Orchid will have to back down. My father's DNA links you. Did you ever read *The Three Musketeers?*'

Marlowe frowned at this; he hadn't expected a literary conversation.

'When I was younger,' he replied. 'Although I prefer the films. I quite liked the Disney one with Kiefer Sutherland.'

'In the books, the Milady De Winter is given a letter,' Ichabod continued. 'A pardon from Cardinal Richelieu. He needs her to do a job, so she's given a pardon that says "C'est par mon ordre et pour le bien de l'Etat que le porteur du present a fait ce qu'il a fait," or in English—'

"'It is by my order and for the good of the state that the bearer of this has done what he has done,'" Marlowe replied.

If Ichabod was annoyed at being interrupted, he hid it well.

'Yes. The pardon was signed Cardinal Richelieu. It's a get-out-of-jail card that d'Artagnan gains later in the book. Then at the end, when he's about to be sentenced to something terrible by Richelieu, he pulls it out and points out that whatever d'Artagnan does is on Richelieu's command, so technically Richelieu himself is as complicit as d'Artagnan was.'

'I remember the scene,' Marlowe said. 'The movies rarely use it, though. Mainly as it means d'Artagnan ends up working for Richelieu at the end.'

'The coin is similar,' Ichabod said, ignoring the critique. 'To have the coin in your hand means you are High Council, and if you are High Council, you are working for the betterment of Orchid.'

Marlowe nodded.

'So, hypothetically ...' he paused, as the hand ended and a new pair of cards was dealt to him, this time a King and an Ace. 'If I was to say, hypothetically, I did something terrible, and I went against Orchid, the fact I have the coin in my hand stops me being ... What? Punished for it?'

'To an extent, yes,' a woman to the side of Marlowe said. Looking across, Marlowe didn't recognise her, but she seemed familiar. She was young compared to the others in the room, probably mid to late forties and Asian, maybe Japanese in looks, with a short black bob.

'I don't think we've met,' he said.

'We have,' she replied. 'In the *Crime City* server meeting room, where you proved to us that a *mutual acquaintance* had gone off on a mad scheme.'

Marlowe smiled. The comment, made as a throwaway line meant the woman had been one of the High Council members who had "virtually" seen the faked-up meeting room that Marlowe had made for them.

She must have, therefore, been one member who sided with him.

'Were you on my side or not?' he asked.

'You're still alive. And so am I.'

'Only just, in my case,' Marlowe shrugged.

The dealer was going around the table now, and Marlowe threw a couple of chips in, matching the bet that Ichabod had started.

'Your father wanted you out of the business,' he said, looking back at Ichabod.

'My father didn't ask me what I wanted,' Ichabod replied. 'And if he had asked, I would have told him I was a far better prodigy than he ever expected you to be. I see your bet and I raise five hundred.'

He placed another chip on the table. Marlowe watched Ichabod carefully.

'Yeah,' he replied. 'You wanted *this*, didn't you?'

As he spoke, he pulled the Orchid coin out of his pocket, holding it in his hand, turning it in the light. He saw two of the other people on the table flinch at the revelation of the coin, but of the ten people sitting around it, the other six seemed unfazed by its appearance. Marlowe wondered how many High Council members were actually sitting at the table.

'If you want this coin, you can have it right now,' he said. 'When you gave it to me at the fountain, you knew then I didn't want it. You could have hidden it, kept it, and I'd have never known.'

'Orchid would have known, and my father gave it to you,'

Ichabod replied. 'Your DNA gives you the right. You're on the Council.'

Marlowe leant back onto his chair, observing the man facing him.

'You want this so badly,' he replied. 'And I have never wanted it at all. Why do you think your father – *our* father, I suppose, gave it to me?'

'Because he didn't want me involved in this. It's as simple as that, so don't go thinking you meant more here,' Ichabod replied with a hint of arrogance in his tone now. 'My father loved *me*. You were an accident after a one-night stand. He knew that by giving you this responsibility, this coin, the people who hated him – the people who had an agenda against me and my future endeavours – would have to aim at you instead.'

Marlowe threw a five-hundred dollar chip onto the table.

'Therefore, in that case, I match your bet,' he said.

By now, two of the others had folded, placing their cards aside, so only four people remained in the hand. Ichabod waited for the next card to be placed down, and seeing it was another king, placed two more chips onto the table.

'I raise a thousand,' he said. 'Let's see where your money is, *brother*.'

He looked around the table, and then returned his gaze to Marlowe with a smile.

'You're on the High Council, my father's old seat, *your* father's old seat, but you're not part of Orchid,' he said. 'I've known these people and lived in this world for most of my life. And because of this, I know I don't need a coin or a fancy title to exist in this scenario.'

'Are you sure?' Marlowe said.

'I am.'

'Good,' Marlowe looked at the cards. 'It's my bet, I believe.'

Ichabod nodded, and Marlowe took the Orchid High Council coin and, making sure everyone saw, he placed it onto the baize.

'I see your thousand and raise you whatever you think this is worth.'

There was a moment of stunned silence at the table. The remaining two players outside Marlowe and Ichabod immediately folded, knowing there was something going on here they wanted no part of.

Marlowe placed his cards down, folded his arms, and stared with a smile at his half-brother.

'If you claim not to want this,' he said, 'place your hand down, fold it and lose. If you want the coin, you know what you need to do.'

There was a long, awkward pause. Eventually, Ichabod, licking his lips, staring down at the coin, nodded, grabbing his chips and pushed them into the middle of the table.

'All in,' he said. 'Show me your cards.'

'Show me yours first,' Marlowe said as he looked at the cards on the table. Two aces, a king, an eight, and a nine. The suits were all over the place. There was no way a flush could be made. But Marlowe knew that his king and his ace meant he had a full house of three aces over two kings.

Ichabod turned his cards over.

An ace and an eight.

'Aces and eights,' he said, pointing at the three aces and the two eights in his hand. 'Known as the "dead man's hand," after Wild Bill Hickok.'

Marlowe turned his own cards over.

An ace …

And a *four*.

'You win, brother,' he said, standing up. 'Congratulations.'

As he moved away from the table, he noted that although every other table there was loud and filled with excitement, the table of High Council Orchid members was silent.

As Byron "Ichabod" Taylor took his place on the Council High Council, he picked up his father's coin, held it up to the light, and then placed it into his own pocket. This done, he looked across at Marlowe, who stared back at him.

'I don't know what you're playing at,' he said, 'but you've just given away a major part of your game.'

'I play many games,' Marlowe said, waving around. 'It's a casino, after all.'

As he turned and continued away from the poker table, Marlowe saw, to the side, St John Steele staring at him.

'You've signed your death warrant, boy,' Steele said softly as Marlowe walked past. 'He can have you killed now.'

'And how will he do that?' Marlowe asked.

'You've just made him High Council, in the same way that his father made you High Council,' Steele was angry, strangely more angry than Marlowe had expected him to be. 'He can command anybody to do things now. You've given him exactly what he wanted, and with Gabriel Rizzo on his side, he can carry on what his father wanted him to move away from.'

'That's his choice,' Marlowe said. 'Quick question, though. These coins, what's so important about them? Are they all the same? Can you forge one?'

Steele laughed.

'You want to forge a High Council coin now?'

'No, I'm just curious whether they can be,' Marlowe asked.

Steele shook his head.

'Each one is unique,' he said. 'Linked to a member of the High Council's own genetic code – if you twist it a particular way, it opens a slot, and you place your blood, your DNA into it. You don't need to, obviously, if you're a direct DNA descendant. Some of Orchid haven't done this since the coins were first minted, being passed down parent to child.'

He looked back at the poker table.

'If you hold it, you are in power. If you lose it, or if someone takes it from you, and manages to not only open it but alter the DNA inside, then you aren't anymore.'

He waved at the table.

'You were in power, Marlowe, and now you are not,' he sighed. 'And I thought you were going to be a fun distraction for a while.'

'Don't count me out yet,' Marlowe smiled. 'The House might think it always wins, but I feel lucky today. What happens if someone takes the coin but doesn't change the genetic coding?'

'Chaos, Mister Marlowe,' St John Steele stared over at Ichabod now, with the expression of a man wondering what he was missing. 'Nothing but chaos.'

16

OLD ENEMIES

THE REST OF THE DAY PASSED UNEVENTFULLY, POSSIBLY BECAUSE Marlowe had given away his only bargaining chip and was no longer a member of the High Council as far as Orchid was concerned.

Returning to the Horseshoe Casino, he found Roxanne and Trix waiting for him.

'How was your day, darling?' Roxanne grinned, sitting on the sofa. 'Tough day at work?'

'I lost everything in a poker game, a man tried to kill me in an elevator, I was screwed over by both Interpol and the CIA, and I spoke to the entirety of Orchid's High Council, telling them they were on my watch,' Marlowe said. 'So, pretty average, really. How about you?'

Roxanne shifted in her chair.

'There was this really creepy guy who was eyeing me up all day,' she said. 'Works for one of the Chicago law firms that's turned up. Thought he'd have a chance at seducing me, poor bastard.'

'Why poor bastard?' Marlowe asked, raising an eyebrow.

'Because I arrived around that point,' a fresh voice spoke, and Brad Haynes walked into the room.

Marlowe grinned as Haynes, already comfortable in the suite, walked over to the bar, pulled out a bottle of beer, and passed it across.

He was in a New York Yankees top over jeans and combat boots, as muscled and stocky as ever, and old enough to be Marlowe's dad, with salt and peppered thick hair in a short cut, and a strong jawline. Marlowe had once described him as "Captain America after working as a rock band's roadie for a decade", and the description still fit, even though he was back with the CIA.

Still, as an ex-Navy SEAL, you probably couldn't drum that out of him.

'I understand you can't do without me,' he said with a grin as he walked over to the sofa and settled down beside Roxanne.

'I heard you were having a nightmare in Los Angeles and needed a way out,' Marlowe replied.

'Well, anything that gets me in the field is good,' Brad shrugged.

'I've got one question, though,' Marlowe said, walking over to a chair and sitting down on it. 'Reynard Massey.'

'Oh God, that guy is such a tool,' Brad snapped. 'Honest to God, bangers to biscuits, that guy is the greatest waste of space the CIA has.'

'How is he Sasha's number two?'

'Is that what he told you? He's only her second in command when he does the jobs that she doesn't want,' Brad smiled wider as he said this. 'So, if you've met him, that means she doesn't want to know you, man. Take the loss and move on.'

Marlowe was surprised, but he felt a brief pang of disappointment. If Sasha Bordeaux didn't want to see him, that meant his influence on her was minimal.

Watching his face, Brad couldn't stop laughing.

'Oh man, look at you, like a puppy dog who's lost his favourite ball or has a cone on his head, which means he can't lick his nuts anymore,' he chuckled evilly. 'Reynard Massey isn't anything to do with Sasha. The problem is that Sasha's deep on a mission at the moment, and wasn't going to be here until later today. So, they sent him in her place. He's nothing but a glorified step monkey.'

'Well, he's a step monkey that's making his own plans, and has access to my file.'

Brad shook his head.

'If he reckons he's seen it, he's either lying, or he stole it,' he said, looking a little awkward. 'I looked for it before leaving. It's missing.'

'Missing lost, or missing stolen?'

Brad shrugged.

'Maybe Interpol stole it,' Trix suggested. 'They seem to know everything.'

'Possibly,' Marlowe said, turning back to Brad. 'Did you hear about his deal?'

'Yeah, he wants Gabriel Rizzo with a sack on his head, dumped in a black site. Just like Interpol.'

'No, *she* wants all the money we take.'

'You're kidding,' Brad sat up at this point. 'You can't do that. That's my retirement fund.'

'Are you spending money we don't have already?' Marlowe raised an eyebrow.

'Damn right I'm spending money we don't have. It's the only way to spend money,' Brad said. 'Let's be honest, from what I've heard from Trix, this ain't going to be happening. We're going to get shot, taken out, murdered, blown up, you name it. This is Orchid's money you're about to steal.'

'No, it's Gabriel Rizzo's money,' Marlowe replied. 'That Orchid lent it to him is not my problem. Talking of which ...'

He looked back at Trix.

'Any news on the others?'

'We have a couple of options,' Trix said. 'It'd be better if I knew what your plan was.'

'Still gestating,' Marlowe said.

'Is it going to gestate even more now you've given away your chip?'

'Casino cameras,' Marlowe grimaced.

'Damn right, casino cameras,' Trix half rose. 'You gave your Orchid High Council chip to your brother. And I know you had a winning hand. Where did the king go, Marlowe? The king that you had with the ace. The king that would have given you a full hand, aces and kings, to defeat his aces and eights?'

'Let's just say I have a plan,' Marlowe replied.

Trix stared at him, her brain working through the issue ... and then she smiled.

'Oh, you bastard,' she said. 'Yeah, that's the sort of thing you'd do. I hope he chokes on his good fortune.'

'Hang on, so can someone explain to me what these coins are?' Brad frowned.

'They're kind of get-out-of-jail-free cards,' Marlowe said. 'If you're standing around Orchid members and you have one of these coins, it means you're a member of the High Council. Big thing, important. From what I can work out, the coins are each linked to the person who holds it, biometrically. My father—'

He winced.

'Still feels weird calling Taylor my father, but biologically, my father held the coin and passed it to me. The coin is linked to my DNA. Therefore, the coin would have been linked to Byron's DNA.'

'Who the hell is Byron?'

'Oh, I called him Ichabod last time you were around.'

'Ah, the gangly guy, your half-brother. Is he as ineffective as he was last time?'

'Actually, Ichabod's proving to be a different person to the man I thought he was.'

'Is he looking to be his father's son, by chance?' Trix said. 'Because let's face it, Marlowe, we've all been waiting for that.'

She pulled up something on the second screen beside her laptop, nodded to Marlowe to look at the TV on the wall, and mirrored her screen onto the TV.

It was an image of Ichabod, or rather Byron Arthur Coleman, as the name next to the face suggested.

'This is an Orchid report on him, one of the encrypted files I picked up from the game server before I flew out, and only just opened,' she said. 'As you can see, he's not squeaky clean. He's been doing a lot of things for his father in the time his father's been ill, and with what we're seeing here, I think we can all agree he's been getting used to it. He's enjoying what he's doing.'

'Did Taylor know Orchid had this file on his son?'

'No idea. Maybe he did, and that's why he wanted him as far away from the cabal as possible,' Trix replied. 'Oh, wait. I have something else for you as well.'

Trix brought up another image. It looked to be some kind

of bank statement, but Marlowe wasn't sure. There was no name on it, and the data was scrubbed.

'What am I looking at?' he said.

'This is the only financial record I can find of Gabriel Rizzo's deal with Orchid to build the Gold Strike Hotel and Casino,' Trix said. 'Interestingly, going into it, the deal was arranged by Taylor Coleman and Gabriel Rizzo.'

'That makes sense,' Marlowe replied. 'They worked together, and they were friends.'

'Yes, but it was never finalised by Taylor, and after digging, I also found this.'

A new image appeared on the screen now. It was a telegram, and on it was a message from Taylor Coleman to Byron Coleman:

```
Do not agree with the casino idea, whatever
        he suggests. Walk away.
```

'So, Taylor Coleman didn't broker the deal,' Marlowe replied. 'It was Ichabod.'

'Yes. And here's another thing,' Trix said, tapping on the screen, the TV now showing even more images and documents. 'Over the last five years, Taylor Coleman had slowly restricted his arms business. He'd been closing up shop effectively, making sure that anything that could land on him was gone. What he hadn't realised is, as he'd been doing this, his son's been building it back up secretly to the side. Everything Taylor believes he sold on paper was actively moved into Ichabod – I mean Byron's – account. Also, I thought you'd want to see this.'

Another document came up.

'What is this?'

'This is the company that Byron Arthur Coleman created to hold everything,' Trix replied. 'It's called *Prodigy*, and it's a partnership with Byron – or Ichabod – and Cody Donziger.'

'Jesus,' Marlowe replied. 'Bloody Donzigers again. Where is he now?'

'Back in Manhattan, after his plea deal took out pretty much everyone,' Roxanne said. 'I know that for a fact because I recently found out more about the trial that's coming up. Everything's been landed on Nathan's lap. Apart from some "Me Too" level cancelling from his drug orgies with minors, all of which was paid off, Cody's probably going to get away with a lot of stuff, do some rehabilitation, community service. His old company's in ruins. He has nothing left from the Donziger name. So it makes sense that he's found a way to claim new money.'

'The first-born sons naming themselves "Prodigy" is a bit on the nose,' Brad muttered. 'Better they name it "Nepo" or something similar.'

'This company employs goons off the books,' Trix said. 'Goons including this guy, Walton Diggs.'

'Why are we looking at him?' Marlowe asked.

'Oh, that's simple,' Trix smiled. 'He's the guy who set fire to Lexi Warner's house.'

'You're sure?' Marlowe sat up.

'Bangers to biscuits, Marlowe,' Trix said, winking at Brad as she said the line he'd uttered earlier.

They were interrupted as Roxanne's phone rang. Glancing curiously at it, she picked it up.

'I don't recognise the number,' she said, as she swiped across and started the call. 'Hello?'

She paused.

'Yes, this is ...'

She stopped, her face paling.

'Thanks,' she said. 'As their legal representative, I'm asking you to hold them as long as you can. I'll be there immediately.'

She disconnected the call, looking up at Marlowe.

'Lexi Warner's awake,' she said. 'But they're taking her to another hospital.'

'Who are?' Marlowe asked.

'That's the problem,' Roxanne replied. 'I don't know. And the woman who called, she's the nurse on call, and she doesn't understand why she's being moved either. She's still in a weakened state.'

'Rizzo,' Trix said. 'It's got to be.'

'Which hospital?' Marlowe was already moving.

'It's the Sunrise Hospital and Medical Centre,' Roxanne replied. 'It's ten minutes by car.'

Marlowe glanced at Brad. 'Did you ...?'

'Rental's in the car park,' Brad nodded.

'Let's go, then.' Marlowe grabbed his CZ, clipping the holster to his belt.

'You expecting trouble?' Roxanne asked.

'People we have no idea of are trying to kidnap one of the key witnesses against Gabriel Rizzo,' Marlowe said. 'Yeah, I'm expecting trouble.'

'Marlowe, there's more,' Trix said, looking from the computer screen. 'The Gravedigger. I think I have an image. He was in the casino—'

'One issue at a time, Trix,' Marlowe was running for the suite's door now. 'One issue at a time.'

THE SUNRISE HOSPITAL WAS BUILT TO THE NORTHEAST OF THE Las Vegas Strip and, in the early evening, the traffic had made it harder for Marlowe, Brad, and Roxanne to get through. However, Brad had shown that this wasn't his first time in Vegas, and using the back streets and alleyways, they had got through in under ten minutes.

There were ambulances out front as they arrived. Marlowe still didn't understand how ambulances worked in America. In the UK, you had the National Health Service, so if an ambulance arrived, you knew it would take you to the hospital. But in America, ambulance firms competed against each other for jobs.

Each ambulance he could see out the front looked different, with different markings and logos.

There was no way to decide which one could be the ambulance that Roxanne's contact had informed her about.

Roxanne was already running into the main ER, looking around frantically.

'Lexi Warner,' she shouted out. 'Does anybody know where Lexi Warner is?'

Nobody really paid her attention, so Marlowe upped it, holding up his Marshal's badge.

'US Marshals,' he shouted. 'Where's Lexi Warner?'

At this, there was more interest. And one of the scrub nurses, running across to them, pointed down a side corridor.

'Two paramedics just took her that way,' she said. 'They were supposed to be coming out the front, but one nurse on duty had stopped them, said they needed to wait a moment. There was a bit of a tussle, and—'

'They're going for the back entrance,' Brad interrupted. 'They know we're after them.'

'Thank you,' Marlowe replied to the scrub nurse. 'If you see them coming back this way, pull the fire alarm.'

'I can't—'

Marlowe leant close.

'*Pull the fire alarm.*'

'I'll do it,' Roxanne took the car keys from Brad. 'Get Lexi. I'll meet you back at the hotel.'

Marlowe nodded and, as Roxanne continued speaking to the nurses, he started running down the corridor with Brad, scanning the rooms as they passed. There was every possibility that the two men who were with Lexi Warner, the so-called paramedics, had realised they were rumbled and were looking for a place to lie low. This could turn into a hostage negotiation situation.

Marlowe was hoping it wouldn't. It would be a lot quicker, and a lot easier if they just found and stopped them.

'No bodies,' he shouted to Brad. 'Unless we have to.'

'You always kill my fun,' Brad muttered. Marlowe wasn't sure if he was joking or not.

'We're in a hospital,' Marlowe replied. 'We don't want this public. Remember, we're trying to take Gabriel and Orchid down quietly, not in the news.'

'Marlowe, everything you *do* ends up in the news,' Brad smiled. 'It's one of the reasons I tolerate you.'

'Tolerate? That's high praise,' Marlowe chuckled as they turned, running further into the bowels of the hospital. There was a clatter ahead of them, around the corner to the right. The sound as if, for example, a gurney had been run into a wall.

Marlowe raised his gun, turned the corner, and then ducked back as rounds *spanged* around him.

Brad looked at him, his own back to the plaster.

'This whole no-killing rule,' he said. 'Do *they* know about this rule?'

'Doesn't look like it,' Marlowe replied, as he turned and fired back.

17

EMERGENCY ROOM

MARLOWE AND BRAD, PISTOLS IN HAND, NOW SPRINTED through the sterile, echoing corridors of the Sunrise Hospital, their steps echoing in the otherwise quiet night, the sound ricocheting off the walls. Ahead, two men dressed as EMTs, one short and stocky, the other stick-thin and balding, manoeuvred a gurney at a breakneck pace, currently with an almost conscious Lexi Warner on it oblivious to the chaos.

'Always a hospital, or somewhere with long bloody corridors,' grumbled Brad, checking his pistol. 'Why can't these things ever happen in a donut shop?'

Marlowe smirked, backing against a wall as more rounds echoed around the corridor.

'You just want an excuse for a snack,' he said. 'Plan?'

'Flank and spank,' Brad suggested, but he couldn't elaborate on this as, without breaking stride, Stick-Thin fired over his shoulder, the round whizzing past Marlowe, embedding into the wall.

'Take cover!' Marlowe yelled, veering into a nearby room.

Brad followed, more rounds pinging off the door frame as they disappeared from sight.

Inside the room, they quickly assessed their options.

'We can't let them get to the exit,' Marlowe said, peeking through the door's window.

Brad nodded, his jaw set.

'I'll flank them through the adjacent corridor. You just sort out the skinny bitch.'

Exiting out of a back door, Brad headed down a side corridor to circle around. This done, Marlowe waited for the sound of Brad's departing footsteps to fade before he stepped back into the corridor, moving with a predator's grace. It didn't last long, however, as Stick-Thin had expected something, firing in Marlowe's direction, with Stocky continuing on with the gurney. He didn't get further, either, as Brad, emerging from a side entrance slammed into him at speed, Stocky's own weapon going flying and the gurney, with Lexi still on it, careened into a wall, coming to a jarring halt.

It was a split second's distraction, but it was enough for Marlowe, as he sprang from his cover, firing. Stick-Thin staggered back, hit, but he wasn't down. He returned fire, a round grazing Marlowe's arm, causing him to drop the CZ. Gritting his teeth against the pain, Marlowe closed the distance, and landed a solid punch, sending Stick-Thin reeling.

'That's for making me run,' he panted, a follow-up kick sending Stick-Thin crashing to the floor, motionless.

Meanwhile, Brad had Stocky pinned down. In a desperate attempt, the shorter man reached for his dropped gun, but Brad was quicker. He slammed his fist into Stocky's face, knocking him out cold.

Marlowe, nursing his bleeding arm, joined Brad.

'I hope Lexi here appreciates the workout she's given us,' the older man said. 'Next time, I pick the venue.'

'Agreed. But first, let's get out of here,' Marlowe replied, as the sound of approaching sirens could be heard in the background. 'After I get an answer.'

Marlowe knelt down, his knee resting on the torso of the shorter and stockier impostor EMT.

'You're in a hospital,' he said. 'The best place you could be with a gunshot wound. You're going to answer some questions first, though, as I'm not going to get a chance to talk to you again.'

He leant closer.

'Who sent you?'

'Get off,' Stocky groaned, struggling. 'I didn't do anything.'

'You shot at us and tried to steal a woman who, until recently, was in a coma,' Marlowe pressed a little harder now, resting his weight more on his knee. 'Who sent you?'

Stocky groaned again.

'I can't say. She'll kill us.'

'She?' Marlowe leant closer. 'Why did you need her? Was it to tie up loose ends? If you wanted to silence her, you could have smothered her in her bed. No one would have seen. Why try to take her somewhere?'

'She wanted ... leverage ...'

The man glared at Marlowe, before his eyes rolled into his head, and he passed out.

Brad tugged at Marlowe's arm as Marlowe checked the man's pockets.

'Come on, the sirens are going,' he said. 'We need to get out of here. I know a place.'

'What kind of place?' Marlowe rose, pulling out a wallet. Opening it, he frowned.

It was cheap, and it looked fake – but it was an Interpol ID.

Was Sandra Reilly the "she" the man had just spoken about?

'CIA safe house, ten miles out of town. It's got a clean room we can use as a makeshift ward,' Brad replied.

Marlowe, grabbing his dropped CZ, looked over to Brad, now pushing the gurney out of the back entrance. There was an ambulance waiting, probably connected to the other two EMTs.

Marlowe walked to the driver's side, where a woman driver sat, a short, blonde bob swept out over her eyes, looking confused at him. He understood why – the army tattoo on her wrist meant she was more likely a mercenary than a driver. And Marlowe didn't look like either Stick-Thin or Stocky.

'I'm busy,' she said.

'I know,' Marlowe raised his CZ, pointing it at her. 'Your friends aren't coming. I suggest you get out and make your own way back to Rizzo.'

At the mention of the name, the woman frowned, swallowed, nodded, and after opening the driver's door and exiting the vehicle, left as quickly as she could. Marlowe frowned – she hadn't reacted how he'd expected when hearing Rizzo's name, but that was a question for later. With the driver now removed from the equation, he helped Brad get the now-waking Lexi Warner into the back of the ambulance as he pulled out his phone.

'Who are you?' Lexi asked warily, watching them.

'It's okay,' Marlowe smiled, texting Roxanne, telling her Lexi was rescued, and she should head back. 'We're friends of

Roxanne Vasquez. We're getting you out. Gabriel Rizzo won't be harming you anymore.'

Lexi nodded.

'Great,' she said, the drugs still in her system, already slowly passing back out. 'One question, though ... who the hell is Roxanne Vasquez?'

———————

IT WAS LATE IN THE EVENING BY THE TIME MARLOWE RETURNED to the suite, Brad beside him. Lexi Warner was now secured with a reluctant CIA operative, and Marlowe had his own questions he wanted to ask.

As he entered, Roxanne rose.

'I can explain,' she said, already looking to head him off at the pass.

Marlowe smiled; it was a dark, bitter, distrusting one.

'You're getting ahead of the game, are you?' he said. 'You know Lexi's already spoken to us, don't you?'

Trix, who hadn't been paying attention up to this point, looked up from her laptop.

'What's going on?'

'Roxanne didn't know Lexi,' Marlowe explained. 'Or rather, Lexi didn't know Roxanne. It's why she offered to stay back and bring the car to the hotel, rather than face her. There was no "visiting a friend", there was no "getting revenge". Roxanne used me again for her own means.'

Roxanne shook her head.

'I never said I was friends with her,' she replied. 'I said she was someone I knew of, and she was someone in the industry. I only really looked into the arson attack.'

'You didn't mention that you *weren't* friends with her,'

Marlowe walked across to the bar and grabbed himself a beer. 'I've gone out of my way for you, and you've been lying to us again. It feels a little like it was when you had your personal crusade against Nathan Donziger. So, how about you start again and really tell us what the hell's going on?'

Roxanne reluctantly sighed.

'Clarissa aimed me at her,' she said. 'It wasn't the random encounter I claimed it was. Clarissa wasn't a name given to me by Lexi, as Clarissa worked with my dad back in the day when he was working with the CIA.'

Marlowe glanced at Brad.

'I don't know who he worked with,' he replied. 'This could be true.'

'It could also be completely made up,' Marlowe snapped. 'You need to tell me more.'

'Clarissa worked in the information gathering side of the Agency. She was older than my father, but they worked together frequently. About two months ago, Clarissa contacted me and said she had something I might be interested in. Sent me details of Gabriel Rizzo, and how he was cosying up to Cody Donziger while building a new casino. She had somebody inside who was giving her information.'

'Lexi Warner.'

Roxanne nodded.

'I had a convention in Vegas that I'd been invited to, and I accepted the invite knowing it would get me here, give me a chance to see what Clarissa was up to.'

'And what was Clarissa up to?'

'Gabriel Rizzo was working with the authorities,' Roxanne started. 'He'd been pulled up on some gaming charges or something, and the casino looked like it wasn't going to happen. So, he threw a few people under the bus to make sure that the wheels were greased.'

'What sort of people?'

'Orchid.'

Marlowe chuckled.

'So your whole "what the hell is Orchid" was a lie as well?'

'No,' Roxanne admitted. 'I only knew it as a name. It could have been a corporation, maybe a men's club. I didn't know. Clarissa honestly thought she said, "War Kids." All I know is that Gabriel Rizzo had given information on several of the investors. It'd spooked Orchid, and they were looking for a culprit, but he'd gained himself time to carry on building the casino. But then something happened a few weeks back. Something big that changed the situation.'

'Taylor Coleman died,' Trix said.

Roxanne nodded.

'Coleman's son, Byron, who you call Ichabod, looked to inherit everything as the eldest legitimate son. I started looking into it.'

'And that's when you found out about me,' Marlowe shook his head with amusement. 'That must have been quite a shock.'

'I realised that if Coleman's wake was happening at the same time as Rizzo's launch event, there was every chance you'd be here. I knew if I was going to do anything, I had to do it now.'

'So the whole "looking for a private investigator at the airport" story was a lie?'

Roxanne's face reddened as she nodded.

'I'd made a calculated guess as to when you'd arrive, and watched all flights from London for the last day or two,' she admitted. 'I saw you arrive, and followed you.'

'You could have just asked me.'

'I didn't know whose side you were on!' Roxanne exclaimed. 'I was hearing rumours you'd joined with your father! I didn't know if you'd help me, or turn me in!'

'Hence why you ran, when you saw me with two of Rizzo's men,' Marlowe nodded. 'You should have trusted me. So what happened between you finding out I was involved, and me finding you in a boutique?'

'I went to see Lexi, but they'd burned the house down.'

Marlowe leant closer.

'Was it arson? And before you answer this, remember, I've already spoken to Lexi Warner.'

Roxanne shook her head.

'They were looking for something,' she said. 'Walton Diggs had been told that there was a disc Gabriel needed destroyed. Gabriel was paranoid his family would try to take his business, so he monitored his office: cameras, microphones, saving everything, in case he could use it. However, even the most paranoid can forget for a moment, and apparently he took a call in the office and during it gave away the fact he was talking to the feds.'

'Ouch,' Brad chuckled. 'Whoopsies.'

'He managed to remove everything once he realised, but between the action and the realisation, it'd been a couple of days, and in that time somebody had gained a copy of it.'

'That somebody being Lexi?'

Roxanne nodded again.

'She'd seen the footage purely by chance. She was trying to work out the timings of a meeting and used the footage from his office to get a time and date. When she heard the phone conversation, she realised it was gold, and burned it onto a CD.'

'Why not a USB drive?'

Roxanne shrugged.

'They check for stuff like that, but people still have music CDs in their cars if they're old. She probably thought she could get it out easier if it looked like a CD mix-tape. Either way, she then took that CD with her, hiding it in her house.'

'Why didn't she pass it to the feds?' Trix asked.

'Because she realised how much that CD was worth,' Roxanne replied. 'She went to Clarissa and asked her to broker a deal with Byron Coleman, as he'd been mentioned on the recording. Said she had something on his partner he would want to hear. The price was half a million.'

'Yeah, he was never going to pay that,' Marlowe shook his head. 'Clarissa should have known that.'

'I don't think she knew him that well, but she knew Gabriel had investors placing millions in, so assumed this was a drop in the ocean. Anyway, Byron went straight to Rizzo. He wasn't playing games and didn't care about secrets. Rizzo realised he was being screwed over by Lexi and sent his man in to find it. While he was hunting through her house, Lexi arrived home. Diggs knocked her unconscious, leaving her for dead. Then he burned the house down, trying to make it look like a gas explosion. But Lexi managed to escape, collapsed, and that's when the police and the fire engines arrived.'

She trailed off.

'And then she was in a coma from then on. The CD was in the house when it burned down. The proof's gone.'

'Is it still on the casino server?' Trix was already typing.

Roxanne nodded.

'They keep all security in their main office,' she said. 'She'd saved it in a file she'd marked, hidden in her expenses subdirectory. No one's realised yet as far as I know, and as far as Clarissa believes, it hasn't been found.'

'This is why you were pushing for me to help you. You knew Trix would be beside me. That's what Clarissa wanted Trix's help for half an hour for, right?'

'I knew she could hack into the server, find the data,' Roxanne nodded. 'Proving Gabriel Rizzo was working for the feds would cause a massive problem with his family.'

'Why do you care so much about the family?'

'Because he's working with Byron Taylor, and Byron Taylor's working with the Donzigers,' Roxanne snapped. 'Just because Nathan's having everything thrown on him doesn't mean the story is over. You might have walked away, Marlowe, but I still have to deal with that every single day. And while the Donzigers can still exert any kind of power, I've got to stop them. They killed my father. I'm not letting that go down.'

Marlowe went to snap back, but paused and nodded.

He could understand that level of need for revenge.

'All of this is because Cody Donziger is in bed with my half-brother,' Marlowe chuckled.

'So, what now?' Trix asked.

'What now?' Roxanne rose from her sofa, pacing as she snapped angrily back. 'We do nothing. You had a coin. You were on the High Council. I could have used you to force your way in. And what did you do? You gave it away in a stupid bet. Now we have to find a way to get into the system, and there's no way you can do that without doing a full-scale attack, so maybe we do have to do your heist after all.'

Marlowe watched Roxanne, waiting for her to finish. Once she had, sitting back down, her face glowering at him, he nodded.

'The original plan was to remove Gabriel's money,' he said. 'Interpol wanted the money. The second plan was to have him taken by Interpol for questioning, but now we also have the CIA wanting him, and they don't share their toys, and we don't trust Interpol after their boss seems to have my CIA-stolen file for bedtime reading. Now, the third plan is to find proof that he worked with the feds, therefore causing problems with all of his relationships.'

He looked across at Trix.

'Hasn't really affected the game plan, has it?'

'You tell me,' Trix replied. 'You're the one with the damn fool idea.'

Marlowe laughed.

'Trix is hacking into the system anyway,' he said. 'If Clarissa knows where it is, then we'll be fine.'

'And how do we get this Clarissa to tell us this?' Trix asked.

'That's easy,' Marlowe said. 'She gave me information in return for half an hour with you. Let's see how well your social engineering skills are.'

'My what?'

Marlowe spoke to the room now as he replied to Trix.

'I mean play nice, Trix. We need to turn Clarissa into one of our assets before she does the same to us.'

18

DIRT POOR

IT WAS GETTING ON IN THE EVENING NOW AND ALTHOUGH Marlowe's arm, freshly bandaged and sewn back up rather expertly by Brad, wasn't hurting as much as it had earlier, Marlowe would have preferred nothing more than to lie down and get some sleep.

However, there was still one more event to get involved with, according to the wake "schedule" Marlowe had seen when he'd arrived earlier that day. So, with a heavy heart and a reluctant stride, Marlowe returned to his black funeral suit to return to the Gold Strike Casino.

He didn't wear his black shirt this time, not because it was soiled or dirty, but more because it had been torn open during a gunfight in a hospital and the sleeve had been slashed in a knife fight in an elevator, and he didn't really want to explain this to anybody. He picked a dark-blue shirt; it was as reverent as he could find for the moment and, after removing a couple of other items from his person, he made his way back to the casino.

The doorman at the entrance looked sheepish as he

waved Marlowe over to the queue through the security cordons.

'I'm sorry, sir,' he said, 'but I've been told we have to put you through the metal detectors this time.'

'That's fine,' Marlowe smiled, holding his hands up. 'I didn't bring it with me. I knew that giving up my coin meant that I'm back with the masses, and there's no place I'd rather be.'

He had expected this the moment he'd given away the coin, and his CZ in its holster was back at the Horseshoe Casino. He still had his security chain around his wrist, and he waved it at a guard who, confused as to what it exactly was, reluctantly let Marlowe through when he explained it was actually his prayer beads, and he was part of a *deeply religious British sect of Catholics that could only use iron because of the nails in the cross.*

It was all nonsense, but the guard, knowing Marlowe had been one of the "special people" for most of the day, just assumed that it was fine, and what British people did. Marlowe was happy about this; the last thing he wanted to do was go back into the casino unprotected. He didn't know what was going to happen; Quaid had attacked him and tried to kill him, most likely on the orders of Marlowe's half-brother Byron, or, as he was now *deliberately* going to call him, Ichabod. But Ichabod probably had his own plans in play right now, especially now he owned a High Council seat.

Marlowe didn't begrudge him that. If he had spent his entire life under Taylor Coleman's fist, being brought up in the world that Taylor Coleman had lived in, Marlowe probably would have done the same. After all, he grew up in a world of his mother's, where spies and soldiers saved the world, and now he was doing it even though he was likely no longer eligible for MI5 level security clearance.

The evening was supposed to involve some entertainment. There had been rumours that one of the resident singers would perform, or maybe a magician, but Marlowe didn't care. He just wanted to make sure that his face was seen and, if possible, to get a brief trip backstage, maybe even to where the vault was.

St John Steele was talking to a woman beside a bar as Marlowe walked towards them. She was the same woman who'd been at the poker table earlier. Seeing Marlowe, Steele smiled.

'Marlowe,' he remarked. 'I didn't think we'd see you again.'

'Really? How come?' Marlowe queried. 'Or was it because I gave away my coin?'

'More that two hitmen had the crap kicked out of them in the backlot of a hospital,' Steele replied. 'Know anything about it?'

Marlowe shrugged, shaking his head.

'Not that I can think of.'

'So, if I squeeze your arm, you're not going to wince?'

Dammit. He knew about the gunshot. Who else knew?

'If you squeeze my arm, Steele,' Marlowe smiled, 'I'll assume you're trying to ask me for a date, and you might not be sure what you'll be getting.'

Steele chuckled. He knew as well as Marlowe did that Marlowe was the person who had saved Lexi Warner's life. Marlowe didn't yet know if Steele had an interest in the game he was playing, but the impression he'd had so far was that St John Steele wasn't the biggest fan of Gabriel Rizzo, and Marlowe was hoping he'd get the benefit of the doubt.

The woman, meanwhile, simply smiled at him. Marlowe knew she was High Council; she remembered him from the virtual world, but as of yet, he didn't know who she was.

'Tom Marlowe,' Steele said, pointing at the lady. 'Have you met Sonia Shida?'

'I think I would remember,' Marlowe smiled, taking a bow and kissing Shida's hand. 'It's a pleasure to meet you, Shida-San. In this world, at least.'

'It *was* a pleasure to meet you,' Shida replied. 'Until you gave away your only bargaining chip.'

'As I said to Mister Steele,' Marlowe smiled. 'This is Vegas, and there are more chips out there to be used.'

'I look forward to seeing what chips you find next,' Shida smiled. 'Will you be joining us this evening for the entertainment?'

'No one's explained to me where or what it is yet,' Marlowe shrugged. 'I wasn't sure if I'd even get in having, you know, given up my coin.'

'Oh, I assumed you'd been told,' Steele said, genuinely surprised. 'You don't have to have a coin to go to the entertainment. As long as you're one of the combatants, you can enter.'

'Combatants?'

'Yes,' Steele shrugged. 'The entertainment is a gladiatorial arena held under the stage, but they also gamble on other fights. Your brief battle with Quaid lost a lot of people money.'

Marlowe didn't quite know how to respond to this and Steele, seeing this, continued to chuckle.

'Mister Rizzo has been setting contests up throughout the day,' he explained. 'Members of the Orchid High Council and other dignitaries have been able to bet on a whole variety of things. Whether someone's going to win or lose, or if someone is going to start a fight on the casino floor, and if a fight happens, who's likely to win. They had you down twice today. The first time was with Quaid, the second when you faced your brother.'

Marlowe nodded, grasping the scheme of things. He'd also heard about the underground fights earlier that day, and knew there had been a couple of deaths, too.

'The contest tonight is about fighters brought in to thrash each other senseless,' Steele continued, his voice dripping with contempt. 'Mostly UFC rejects, mere cannon fodder. You'll understand once you're there.'

'Are you planning to attend?'

Steele glanced at Shida, who gave an affirming nod.

'The alternative is to stay up here with the ordinary folks,' she commented, hesitating slightly before the word "ordinary", giving Marlowe a clear sign she preferred being where the air was more exclusive.

Marlowe nodded in agreement and gestured forward.

'Lead the way,' he invited.

The route involved navigating through the casino's back rooms, passing through the high-stakes poker areas, where whales congregated to play games with stakes soaring into the hundreds of thousands. Marlowe steered clear of these rooms; he had already spent much of his budget on an earlier poker game that day. But he always believed in the adage "you have to spend money to make money", in this case, the "money" being professional credit and making a statement.

Two guards initially moved to stop them but, upon recognising their faces, they simply waved them through. Marlowe surmised that his passage was either because of the presence of two high-ranking members of Orchid, or perhaps they recognised him.

Maybe they had even placed a bet on him during the day.

They descended some stairs and entered a small arena with seats on all sides. It resembled a black walled basketball gymnasium, with UV lights and LEDs giving it the look of an old *Laser Tag* venue he used to play in when he was a kid. Marlowe had seen similar venues, often converted into wrestling rings for pro wrestling events. Tonight, the arena's centre was occupied by a ring resembling the octagon style of UFC, encircled by chain-link fences, designed to prevent anyone inside from escaping the imminent brutal confrontation.

Marlowe, having previously experienced such rings undercover, knew firsthand the pain of being thrust against those fences.

A fight was underway; a tall, muscular albino man, towering at over six and a half feet and almost as broad, struggled against a more agile, gymnastic fighter, a white luchador mask on his head. This opponent was faster, employing a technique known as a "Superman punch", leaping up and using the chain-link fence to rise him higher than usual, and then momentum and gravity to propel his attack. The punch landed squarely on the albino man's chin, and despite Marlowe's initial assessment of the albino's resilience, he fell to one knee as his adversary swiftly capitalised on the moment, locking him in a submission hold.

The albino man tried to rise, using his significant size to dislodge his opponent, but overbalanced, and with his legs locked into the hold, he was eventually forced to tap out, signalling the end of the fight.

Marlowe was impressed, even more so when, after the

fighter pulled the luchador mask off, he realised the victor was none other than Gabriel Rizzo.

Gabriel, basking in the applause, grabbed a microphone.

'Thank you,' he said. 'It's always a pleasure to showcase my jiu-jitsu skills. Let's give it up for Parker here, a commendable adversary. And of course, all bets are finished, and winners receive their profits from the pool, as per usual.'

Marlowe wondered how much Gabriel had bet on himself here, and as the crowd applauded, Marlowe felt as if he was being watched. Glancing back at Gabriel Rizzo, he noticed him listening intently to something through an almost hidden earpiece.

The cheeky bastard. He's got an earpiece feeding him information. He didn't win that fight on his own; they told him his opponent's weaknesses.

'I see we have a special guest,' Gabriel finally announced, his gaze fixed on Marlowe in the third row. 'A man who today gambled away his entire future on a single card turn.'

A spotlight swung across the auditorium, illuminating Marlowe's face. He winced, shielding his eyes with a hand.

Gabriel smiled.

'Mister Marlowe also cost quite a lot of us some money today,' he announced. 'His elevator altercation with Mister Quaid ended in a no contest.'

'No contest?' Marlowe retorted, surprised by this claim.

'Yes, regrettably, the footage in the elevator carriage cut out before we could discern the victor of your skirmish,' Gabriel elaborated with a smile. 'We classified it as a draw.'

Marlowe, fully aware that Gabriel knew the truth about what transpired with Quaid, and had probably bet considerably against him while also being at stake for any winnings against him, shook his head.

'Inform those who lost their bets that it wasn't a draw at all,' he countered. 'Considering I left Quaid unconscious on the elevator floor, I'd claim it as a convincing win.'

'If only you had a witness,' Gabriel remarked with mock sadness.

'I saw it,' Steele interjected. 'Mister Rizzo, I was on the twelfth floor waiting for the elevator when it opened. I saw Mister Marlowe exit, and your comrade, Quaid, was lying there, sound asleep.'

'Mister Steele,' Rizzo smiled. 'If only you were still the Arbitrator, your words might have some bearing on what actually transpired there.'

'I don't require any authority,' Steele replied. 'I'm just merely stating what I witnessed.'

Marlowe was impressed; Steele hadn't needed to defend him, and his willingness to do so showed there was more at play than mere camaraderie. Marlowe had suspected Steele wasn't a fan, but this gesture suggested a deeper agenda.

Gabriel Rizzo, however, wasn't finished and raised a hand.

'Mister Marlowe, it seems you might, hypothetically, have emerged victorious in your encounter, much like I did in mine, but we'll never know for sure. Would you be interested in a few rounds with me right now? I'm still in prime condition.'

Marlowe shook his head.

'I'm fine, thank you,' he replied, declining the offer.

'Afraid I'll best you?' Gabriel taunted. 'Or perhaps you're worn out from *extracurricular* activities?'

Marlowe knew Gabriel was provoking him, he also most likely knew about the injured arm, but tonight was not the time for confrontation.

'I concede this match to you, Mister Rizzo,' he said. 'I

don't want to cost the house any more winnings when I defeat you. Perhaps another time.'

'Perhaps,' Rizzo said, turning back to the crowd. 'It appears MI5's finest is too timid to face me. Who will challenge me next?'

'If my brother's too frightened, I will do it,' Marlowe was surprised to see Ichabod emerge from one of the front row seats, shedding his shirt to reveal a surprisingly muscular torso for his gangly frame. Marlowe had initially pegged him as a scholarly assistant, but now he realised Ichabod was far from it.

The crowd cheered and applauded as Ichabod clambered into the ring.

'Betting begins from now until the first punch,' Gabriel smiled. 'And remember, the house always wins, so spend your money wisely.'

Marlowe stood up.

'Not interested in watching the bout?' Shida asked, half amused.

'Not in the mood,' Marlowe replied. 'But thanks for the invitation. I hope we can reconnect later. For now, I'm quite weary and will call it a night.'

His intention wasn't actually to end the day; it was merely an excuse to leave the fight arena. Once outside, he wandered the back corridors, hoping to uncover secrets before being found and escorted back to the main casino floor by the guards. Disappointingly, Marlowe found little of interest; Rizzo had evidently ensured everything was securely compartmentalised.

However, after ten minutes of uninterrupted wandering, and just as he was about to return to the casino, a guard he'd encountered earlier in the day on the security line appeared, surprised to see him.

'Mister Marlowe, you shouldn't be here,' the guard stated.

'I know,' Marlowe replied with a smile. 'But I couldn't resist exploring. I've got a million dollars in diamonds somewhere down here. I don't know where they've stashed it.'

'Something like that would be in the vault, sir,' the guard responded, pointing down to the right. 'Two levels down.'

'Any chance of seeing it?'

The guard almost laughed.

'Sir, it's not just a case of it being more than my job's worth; it's a matter of life and death.'

Marlowe nodded in understanding.

'It was worth asking.'

He made his way back to the casino, guided by the guard. Back on the floor at the rear of the casino itself, he paused as Gabriel Rizzo, now donned in a boxer's robe and surrounded by men, approached him.

'Marlowe,' he said, his face glistening with sweat, 'you should have stayed. Your brother was quick to lose, but keen to learn. Unfortunately, nobody bet on him, so I made little from it.'

'Well, I'm sure you'll be an excellent mentor to him in future fights,' Marlowe replied.

'I was merely a conduit. I'm assuming you were in an investigative mood?' Gabriel inquired, looking down the corridor, the security door still open.

'Not at all,' Marlowe responded. 'Although I will admit I'm curious about how you've managed all this, why you did it, and what your plan is when it all crumbles around you.'

'You think this will collapse around me?' Gabriel surveyed his surroundings. 'Why would you think that?'

Marlowe shrugged, gauging how far he could push the conversation without endangering himself.

'Maybe because there's evidence out there showing you're betraying your associates to the authorities?' he suggested.

Gabriel Rizzo's expression flickered.

'Lexi Warner is a deceitful woman,' he retorted. 'Yes, I'm aware you're keeping her safe. Do whatever you wish with her. She's a liar. And when my lawyers are through with her, she'll have nothing left.'

'She's already lost everything, even half her face,' Marlowe pointed out.

'So what?' Gabriel scoffed. 'Why should I care about her accusations?'

'Because she wasn't confiding in the authorities,' Marlowe revealed. 'She was speaking to your family.'

That revelation visibly unsettled Gabriel.

'She spoke to my sister?'

Marlowe wasn't certain if she had, but it was a calculated guess. If she'd started with Byron, it was only logical she also moved on to other people with an axe to grind. Angelina Rizzo was the most likely option.

'I wouldn't know,' Marlowe feigned ignorance. 'I've been preoccupied with my father's wake.'

Gabriel chuckled.

'Tomorrow is the last day of the wake, and in the evening the official launch of the casino,' he said. 'Everything will be resolved then.'

'I agree,' Marlowe replied. 'From what I can see, everything will be.'

Gabriel appeared as though he might speak further, but then paused as he saw a man was walking towards them; he wore a charcoal suit, white shirt and shaded glasses. Gabriel seemed surprised to see him there, however.

'This isn't a good time for your charter,' he said.

The man nodded, looked at Marlowe for a long moment and then smiled, walking off.

'Friend of yours?' Marlowe asked.

'More a fan of yours,' Gabriel smiled. 'Calls himself the Gravedigger. Maybe you've heard of him?'

Marlowe looked back after the man.

'I have. I thought he'd be taller. And younger.'

Gabriel laughed at this, but then stared at Marlowe for a moment before shaking his head sadly.

'It's such a shame, Mister Marlowe, that you won't be joining us for the festivities,' he said.

'And what's that supposed to mean?' Marlowe asked, frowning.

'You were brought here for two reasons,' Gabriel explained. 'The first was that it was your father's wake, and we had been requested the honour of your visit. The second, more simply, was that you were a High Council member of Orchid and had the right to attend.'

Marlowe said nothing, but had noted the use of "we" in the statement. And did Gabriel mean "brought here" as in allowed entrance into the casino, or was he involved in the fake invite in the first place?

Continuing, Gabriel gave a shrugging motion, which looked vaguely ridiculous in the boxing robe he was wearing.

'Unfortunately, Mister Marlowe, you are now neither invited, nor expected,' he explained. 'Your family, as much as it is, no longer requires you to be here. And your coin has been passed on to its rightful owner.'

Marlowe felt a sliver of ice slide down his spine at this.

Looking around, he realised that the gunmen surrounding Gabriel were now watching him.

'Ah, I see,' he smiled, realisation now on his face. 'You never wanted me here anyway, I get that. But now I've done my job, haven't I? I've given Byron his coin and now I can just piss off into the sunset. Is that right?'

'Bravo, Mister Marlowe,' Gabriel slowly clapped his hands together. 'You'd make a fine detective.'

'So, what happens now?' Marlowe asked.

'Now?' Gabriel shrugged, once more looking ridiculous in his attire.

'Yeah. Now.'

'Now you're no longer of any use to us,' Gabriel explained, as he pulled out a phone. 'You've got no friends, no allies. And unless you had the coin, we have no interest in you being here. You are just a burnt spy, Mister Marlowe, looking for relevance in the Twenty-First century.'

'And what about you?' Marlowe retorted.

'Me?' Gabriel started to laugh. 'Mister Marlowe, I don't know if you've noticed, but I own one of the newest and most exciting casinos in Las Vegas. At our official launch, I will make tens, if not hundreds, of millions of dollars. My debt to Orchid will be paid. And my partner and I—'

'You mean Byron Coleman.'

'Yes, Byron and I, we'll sit back and count our percentage. We do have one more use for you, though.'

Marlowe went to speak, but Gabriel held a hand up.

'Before I do what I'm about to do,' he said, 'please be aware, I know that you're trying to take me down. I'm aware you think you can stop me when you don't even know who I am.'

'I know who you are,' Marlowe started, but Gabriel held his hand up again, pausing him.

'All you have is the opinion of a woman,' he said almost dismissively. 'A woman who's gone to war with me purely because of people I do business with.'

'That's how most wars start,' Marlowe replied. 'You should read a history book one day.'

'Oh, I have,' Gabriel smiled. 'I've read them all, front to back, left to right. I know.'

'She might have more than just words,' Marlowe didn't mean to say it, but Gabriel Rizzo had irritated him. At this, however, Gabriel just laughed.

'You mean the super-secret recording she burnt to disc?' he asked. 'It's gone, turned into slag. Destroyed in an absolutely preventable fire.'

He leant closer.

'Or do you mean the original file, hidden by Lexi Warner on my own server, and deleted two days ago? Whoops. That's an issue.'

Marlowe felt his world's axis shift.

Gabriel knew.

In return, Gabriel smiled, opening an app on his phone. Marlowe didn't know what the app was, but he quickly realised its function, as when Gabriel Rizzo spoke into his phone, his voice echoed through the casino's Tannoy.

'This is management,' he said. 'We have a new game for those in the know. Fox Hunt, Thomas Marlowe, game ends at midnight, a hundred thousand dollars to the person who ends the fox. Betting begins now until the moment he's ended – or midnight, whichever comes first.'

Marlowe said nothing as Gabriel Rizzo went to put the phone away in his robe's pocket.

'You're no longer welcome here, Mister Marlowe,' he said. 'I expect you gone from Vegas, either feet first, or by your own accord, by first thing tomorrow. Until then, have fun, little fox.'

Before he could say anything else, though, Marlowe lunged forward, grabbing the phone before it was placed away, pressing the same button.

'New betting option,' he shouted into the phone as he backed away from the guards. 'Gabriel Rizzo will lose tens of millions of dollars tomorrow from his own vault when Thomas Marlowe steals everything he has from him. Betting starts now.'

He tossed the phone back to Gabriel with a smile.

'You once said you thought I'd be more exciting,' he said. 'How's that for exciting?'

Before Gabriel could reply, staring in stunned silence at Marlowe, the doors to the casino opened and Marlowe backed through them, watching them close, barring him from Gabriel and his men.

Looking around, Marlowe could already see the eyes on the casino floor turning to him. People who knew what was going on were obviously Orchid; regardless of what Marlowe just did, what Gabriel Rizzo had done was place a hundred grand hit on Marlowe's head.

A fox hunt was just that: he was the fox, and he was being hunted.

And worse than that, "ending" the fox meant killing Marlowe.

19

FOX HUNT

MARLOWE LOOKED AT HIS WATCH; IT WAS JUST BEFORE NINE IN the evening. He had three hours to stay alive.

The only thing in his favour was most of the people who'd come at him wouldn't have weapons, as only Orchid members of the High Council with their fancy coins and special privileges had weapons, and they were more likely to bet on the outcome rather than affect it.

The problem was, right now, apart from a small metal bracelet around his wrist, Marlowe didn't have a weapon either.

So, now the hunt would begin.

Marlowe decided to take the hunt into the streets, rather than remain in the casino. Although people in the streets might have weapons, there would be more tourists, more civilians, and more opportunities for him to blend into the crowds than in the casino. Here, he stood out conspicuously, and he knew that, with Gabriel Rizzo's top-notch security system, hiding anywhere in the casino, even his room – which he believed would now be checked out and barred to him – would be futile. If he found a place to take cover, he was convinced that someone on a Tannoy would announce his location.

Having seen enough of what he needed, Marlowe knew what his next move would be. All he had to do was survive until the following day, until the launch of the casino itself.

Of course, this meant getting out, and the closest casino exit was still across the casino floor.

A couple started towards him; the first was a man, unloosening his tie and pulling it off, coiling it around his hands like a garrotte. Marlowe knew that they intended to take him down. He let his security bracelet uncoil and held it like a whip, facing them.

'Mine will hurt more than yours,' he said.

The man smiled, pulling a roll of quarters from his pocket, now changing tactics, knotting it to the end of the tie and swinging it like a ball and chain. Marlowe realised that there was a strong chance now that his chain wouldn't hurt as much as *that* would.

'Look,' Marlowe said, 'I'm not gonna fight with makeshift weapons. Gabriel Rizzo isn't the man you think he is.'

He stopped as the woman now pulled out a wicked-looking hunting knife, licking her lips with anticipation.

Marlowe reassessed the situation quickly. *There was no way she would've got that through security unless she was a member of the High Council.*

'I see,' Marlowe smiled. 'You're one of the ones that sided with Delacroix, I suppose?'

The woman simply smiled.

'You were always a mistake,' she said. 'Ever since you were born. Taylor said that many times, you know.'

'Ah, so you're an old friend of the family.'

Marlowe was shifting to the side now, trying to find a better location to attack from. Somewhere he could block her thrust, but behind him, he could already see figures moving in.

Other Orchid members looking for their prize.

He had to get out of the casino, and fast.

To the side, he could see St John Steele watching him. He couldn't work out whether Steele was happy or sad at the situation. He'd hoped it was sad, but Steele didn't look like he was about to come and assist Marlowe at any moment soon, so Marlowe prepared to attack.

The noise of a slot machine pumping out its winnings, a siren spinning above the top of it, and the cheers of the gamblers around it couldn't have come at a better time. It was completely random, and Marlowe used the moment of distraction to turn and sprint towards the side entrance.

His hunters, who for a moment had been distracted by what was happening beside them, swore under their breath as they chased Marlowe through the casino.

Security wasn't following. They didn't need to. As far as Gabriel Rizzo was concerned, he'd turned the other members of Taylor's wake, mainly low-level Orchid members, into his own security force to take out his problem.

Marlowe shook his head at this; Gabriel Rizzo was relying on Orchid to keep this quiet from the "normal" people there, right before his launch – there was a risk he could lose business if things went wrong here.

He'd underestimated Marlowe. He thought this would end quickly.

Well, he'd learn he'd made a terrible mistake.

Marlowe's breath was ragged, his senses heightened as he navigated through the chaotic Las Vegas casino floor. The cacophony of slot machines and roulette tables created a dissonant backdrop to his desperate escape. Clutching the steel security chain, his only defence, Marlowe's eyes darted for his next move.

His pursuers were relentless. Devoid of firearms, they were now armed with makeshift weapons, turning the casino's amenities against him.

He took cover behind a blackjack table as one of his hunters, a middle-aged, slightly overweight man, swung a jagged broken wine bottle at him. Marlowe retaliated with a fierce lunge, the chain lashing out with precision, striking the hunter's wrist.

The bottle shattered against the gaudy carpet, and Marlowe seized this moment, trying to kick the table forward. It was secured to the floor, but the scattering chips and cards momentarily confused another attacker, giving Marlowe a window to strike an elbow to the throat, sending the new target to the ground, grabbing at his neck as he gasped for breath.

Near the craps tables, Marlowe found himself once more surrounded. He rolled a portable dice table towards one assailant, creating a temporary barrier. The hunter stumbled over the table, finding herself off-balance. Marlowe swung his chain, wrapping it around the woman's neck and pulling her down with a thud.

The impact of her nose crunching against the edge of the table with a gush of blood echoed through the casino, and Marlowe winced as it happened.

As he pushed through the crowd Marlowe's eyes locked onto the bar area. It was risky, but offered new opportunities. He dashed towards it, weaving through the panicked crowd.

A hunter armed with a pool cue emerged, swinging it like

a spear. Marlowe ducked under the swing, feeling the air shift above him. He countered with a quick jab to the hunter's abdomen, followed by a brutal sweep of the chain, knocking the cue stick away.

Another Orchid member, wielding a pair of silver tongs likely snatched from a nearby buffet, lunged at him. Marlowe parried with the chain, its clinking sound mingling with the chime of the surrounding slot machines. He swept the member's feet with a low kick, causing him to crash onto a poker table. Cards and chips flew into the air like a startled flock of birds.

Marlowe went to move on – but the fight wasn't over yet. The member, undeterred, rose swiftly, swinging the tongs with renewed ferocity.

Marlowe ducked and weaved as he grabbed the broken pool cue, thrusting it like a spear. Spotting an opening, he lunged forward, ensnaring the member's wrist with the chain and yanking it with all his might. The tongs clattered to the floor, as, with a swift flick with the blunt end of the cue, Marlowe sent the man sprawling over the poker table, unconscious.

The woman who'd pulled the hunting knife, now returning into the fray after checking on her husband, moved in to attack now. Having reached the bar, however, Marlowe grabbed a bottle of whisky, hurling it at her. The bottle clipped the blade and smashed as she ducked behind a slot machine, showering her with shards and liquid.

She moved to attack, but Marlowe grabbed a Zippo lighter from the bar, flicking it on and tossing it at her. Screaming, she ran from this, unaware that, unlike in the movies, it was the vapour that burned, not the liquid itself.

This was why, in a flaming alcoholic drink, the flame floated above the liquid. Thank God she didn't know that.

Marlowe didn't stop to watch the effect, or wait to see when she'd realise she'd been conned; he vaulted over the bar, using it as cover. Behind him, glasses and bottles became weapons in the hands of his pursuers.

A new hunter, a mountain of a man, bald and in his sixties, wearing a black suit and tie, emerged at the end, brandishing a heavy brass lamp from the back of the bar like a club. He swung wildly, the still-connected lamp casting erratic shadows on the walls.

Marlowe, running on instinct, flicked out and caught the lamp with his chain, twisting it to wrench the lamp from the mountain's grip. The lamp flew sideways, shattering against a drink's pump. The hunter, now unarmed, charged with a roar.

Marlowe countered with rapid, precise strikes of the chain, each link biting into the man's flesh. Even though he was way larger, the hunter recoiled and, as Marlowe passed him into the VIP area, he seized a nearby velvet rope used for crowd control and whipped it around the man's legs, bringing him down with a thud.

A quick "knuckleduster" chain strike to the temple ensured the mountain of a man stayed down, and Marlowe needed more than anything to pause, take stock, and regain his breath.

No time.

Emerging from the other side of the VIP entrance, Marlowe faced two more hunters, another husband and wife team from the looks of things. He feigned a desperate lunge, misleading them, and then spun around with his chain extended. It wrapped around the husband's leg, yanking him off his feet. The wife charged, but Marlowe was quicker, delivering a swift knee to the gut, followed by a chain strike to the back, leaving them both on the carpet, groaning and regretting their life choices.

The exit was in sight, the neon lights of the Vegas strip calling out to him. Marlowe sprinted, his energy depleting but adrenaline spurring him on. A final hunter, wielding a bar stool, attempted to block his path; Marlowe sidestepped, redirecting the hunter's momentum into a slot machine, which erupted in a frenzy of lights and sounds as his face went through the glass front.

With a final push, Marlowe burst through the side door. The cool night air hit him like a wave. He was out, but his safety was far from guaranteed. The pursuit was far from over and, as he looked back at the entrance, he could already see hunters approaching.

There was the sound of a horn and Marlowe glanced back onto the road outside. A convertible Mustang was parked, the windows tinted, the roof up, the driver unseen.

Until the driver's window came down, and Sasha Bordeaux stared at him.

'Are you getting in or what?' she asked with a smile.

Relieved, Marlowe ran to the car, climbing into the passenger seat and closing the door as the Mustang revved into life, speeding off down the Vegas street.

'You're a sight for sore eyes,' he said, pulling out his phone.

'I always am,' Sasha replied simply as Marlowe sent a single text.

> We're blown. Get out now. Go to backup location.

A moment later, a text appeared from Trix.

What backup location?

Find one.

Marlowe sat back on the seat, working out his options.

Weirdly, he was exactly where he expected to be right now. Tomorrow was going to be an interesting day indeed.

If he survived until then, of course. Glancing back, he saw two sets of lights weaving through the traffic, following them.

'You're popular tonight,' Sasha grumbled as she turned onto the strip, accelerating from the pursuers.

'Hundred grand hit,' Marlowe explained, as if it was the most obvious answer.

'Really?' Sasha smiled, her eyes locked on the road. 'For that, I might take you in myself.'

The roar of the engine echoed through the night as Sasha floored the Mustang, its tyres screeching against the asphalt. The neon lights of the Las Vegas Strip blurred past, creating a kaleidoscope of colours. Even though his seatbelt was on, Marlowe couldn't help himself and gripped the dashboard, his eyes scanning the rearview mirror.

The hunters were relentless, their vehicles a menacing presence in the night.

Sasha swerved onto the Strip, weaving through the late-night traffic. The iconic Bellagio fountains erupted in a choreographed dance to the right, a stark contrast to the chaos unfolding on the road. An SUV, one of the hunter's vehicles, closed in, its headlights bearing down on them like a predator.

'Watch out!' Marlowe shouted as a black sedan, the other

hunter's car, attempted to box them in. Sasha's instincts were razor sharp, however, and she took a sudden hard left, turning onto a side street. The sedan overshot the turn, crashing into a row of parked scooters with a cacophony of crunching metal and alarms.

They sped past the Fremont Street Experience, the LED canopy above casting an array of dynamic lights over them as they tried to escape. The hunters were persistent, two more vehicles joining the fray, their engines growling in the night.

'I suppose having a hit put on you during an Orchid convention really isn't the best thing to happen,' Sasha said, almost conversationally, cutting the wheel sharply. The Mustang slid around a corner, narrowly missing a late-night hot dog stand, sending condiments and napkins flying.

'I've had better days,' Marlowe winced as they screeched around a woman in the street, screaming after them as they continued on. They now raced past the Mirage, its volcano erupting in a fiery spectacle. Sasha dodged in and out of lanes, her face a mask of concentration. The hunters were losing ground now, their cars mere shadows in the Mustang's tail lights. As they approached the Luxor, Sasha made a split-second decision. She veered off the Strip, taking them down a less-travelled road.

The hunters hesitated, losing precious seconds, and Sasha pushed the Mustang to its limits, the engine screaming in protest.

The road led them to the outskirts of the city, where the bright lights of Vegas gave way to the dark, quiet desert. The hunters were mere specks in the distance.

Sasha kept the pedal to the metal until the pursuers were no longer visible.

Finally, she eased off the accelerator, the Mustang's engine settling into a low purr.

'If you wanted me to take you somewhere secluded, all you had to do was ask,' she said, her voice a purr as well.

Marlowe smiled. Filled with adrenaline, there was a cockiness to Sasha Bordeaux.

He liked it.

———

'So, what now?' she asked after a few minutes of driving, pulling up beside a motel, turning the lights off and watching up the road.

'We need to keep out of sight until midnight,' Marlowe replied. 'Rejoin the others tomorrow morning and start the last part of the plan.'

'Just under two hours to kill,' Sasha said playfully, looking at the motel sign beside them. 'What shall we do?'

Marlowe had an immediate reply, but bit it off before he spoke. Sasha was in her mid-to-late thirties, red hair in an overgrown bob style, with minimal makeup and currently a Harvard sweater over jeans. She was incredibly attractive and knew it, and Marlowe had a feeling she felt the same about him – but she was a CIA operative so secret that she used DC characters' names as IDs, and not even Washington seemed to know her true identity.

Almost as if she could sense what he was thinking, Sasha smiled.

'You know what?' she said simply, unclipping the seatbelt. 'You need to stop planning. Think less. Live in the moment.'

With this said, she leant over, kissing him. It was a full-on kiss; no simple peck, a real toe-curler of a smacker, leaving Marlowe breathless as he sat back.

'Want to get a room?' she asked.

Marlowe simply nodded dumbly.

'Good, because I've been up for almost forty hours and I'm shattered,' Sasha smiled, breaking the spell and climbing out of the car. 'You can pay for it. After all, I saved your ass.'

Marlowe took a moment to compose himself and then chuckled.

'Bloody CIA,' he muttered.

20

CLEAR OUT

From the moment she read the text, Trix knew it was time to go.

She'd already worked out something had happened, as she'd lost the live feed of the casino half an hour before this, and had been trying to reconnect as the message came through.

Within seconds of her telling the others, she'd already folded up her computer system, her laptop, her screens, and her spare keyboard and mouse, which went into her bag, while Brad went over to the fold-out bed in the main room and grabbed Marlowe's bags, already packed. Trix had laughed when she first saw that; she didn't understand how you could go to a hotel and not unpack your bags, but Marlowe would take out what he needed, pack everything back up, and come back the following day when he needed more.

It was only now that Trix realised why he did such a thing.

When he needed to run.

Within five minutes of the message arriving, Trix, Brad, and Roxanne were all in the elevator, heading down to the main reception of the Horseshoe Casino. Brad had a car; he'd used it earlier on, but already they were worried it had been picked up and tracked by now. If so, there was a problem with moving it.

Because of this, Trix had already made sure there was another booking in a fake name that she could use to gain a car if required, but as it was she decided instead to go for the closest option, moving them to a hotel only a matter of steps away.

The one good thing about the Las Vegas Strip was that you didn't need a car if you stayed in the centre, and staying in the centre was currently what she wanted to do.

Within an hour of the text, she'd gained a remodelled Classic King Suite at Paris Vegas, comprising one king-size bed, and two separate rooms with queen-size beds in, placing it on another of Marlowe's fake identities, and using one of his fake credit cards. She didn't feel bad about this; she wasn't going to be taking money off Marlowe soon, as the character who owned the credit card didn't technically exist. She also didn't feel too bad about ripping off the hotel because they were making a fortune, regardless.

Ten minutes after they'd arrived at the new suite at the Paris Vegas hotel, Trix had already reset up her command centre, Brad had already requisitioned one bed, and Marlowe had been informed of the location via a message board for a UK sci fi show that they often used for dead drop codes. Worryingly, nothing came back for at least half an hour, and then a single message:

Speak tomorrow. M.

Marlowe had obviously gone to ground, and Trix was concerned about Marlowe's status, until Brad started laughing, checking his own texts.

'You don't need to worry about pretty boy,' he said, nodding at the room next door where Marlowe's duffel and cabin bag had been left. 'He's shacking up with Sasha Bordeaux!'

Trix raised an eyebrow.

'She's just sent me a message,' Brad turned the text to show Trix.

> Saved the Brit's life. Now forced to listen to him snore tonight. Reconvene tomorrow.

'I don't think that's the night-time connection he thought he was going to get,' Trix grinned. 'But at least he's alive. Do we know what happened?'

Brad shook his head.

'Sasha doesn't leave messages with information on it,' he said. 'She hasn't even mentioned where they're staying. The only reason I know she's talking about Marlowe is that she's said "the Brit" in the message.'

Roxanne now walked into the main room. Trix wasn't sure, but she thought she could see an element of jealousy in Roxanne's face.

'Don't worry,' she said. 'I don't see any passionate nights of romance for Marlowe or Sasha Bordeaux tonight.'

'I don't care either way,' Roxanne straightened, her voice almost accusatory as she looked around the room. 'No, really, couldn't care. He can do what he wants. He's a grown man. He's got a beard. Grown men have beards.'

Realising she was rambling, Roxanne sheepishly walked back into her room.

Trix looked back at the computer. Something had gone horribly wrong. She didn't know what it was yet, but she hoped that by the time they reconvened at eight the following morning, she would know exactly what it was that had caused Marlowe to move hotels.

With a yelp of triumph, she reconnected to the Gold Strike servers; they weren't live, still, but she could at least go back into the saved feed, and check what had …

She paused as she watched the carnage on the casino floor.

Trix didn't know what had happened, as she didn't have sound, but she could see Marlowe running for the door, hunted by several already identified Orchid agents. The fights were brutal, short, and close range.

'Oh shit,' she muttered as she watched. Brad and Roxanne both walked over, staring at the screens.

'He's been outed,' Brad said, simply. 'He's burnt. If he got out, he can't go back.'

'Look at Rizzo,' Roxanne growled, pointing at one screen. 'He's loving it.'

'Why's he cosplaying as Rocky Balboa?' Trix looked up. 'Dammit, I'd rather we knew the full story than watch half of it.'

There was a beep, and a message appeared on Trix's burner phone.

'It's Ryan Gates,' she said, reading it. 'The guy who sorted Marlowe's gun out.'

> Gold Strike Casino having fox hunt until midnight – Marlowe the fox. 100k hit on him from what I hear.

Brad read the message, his face furrowing as he realised

the meaning.

'Sasha has him, so all they have to do is stay out of sight until the "game" is over,' he said. 'Although it's really annoying she didn't say where they were.'

'Why?' Roxanne asked, confused.

'Because I could really do with a hundred grand right now,' Brad winked.

IT WAS LATE IN THE EVENING, OR EVEN EARLY IN THE MORNING, when Gabriel Rizzo finally went to bed.

His bed, right now, was in the palatial Penthouse Suite of the Gold Strike hotel, and it was a literal fortress. You couldn't get into the location without a key card, and only his men had those.

This was why he was actually both surprised and impressed when he found the Gravedigger sitting in one of his suite's armchairs, waiting for him.

'You might not realise it from my jovial expression and pleasant demeanour, Mister Rizzo, but I am incredibly unhappy with you,' he said.

Gabriel looked around the room. He'd told his guards to take the night off, relying on his own security systems in case someone broke in. To find himself now unarmed in his own suite, with a man known for killing people for the simplest of grudges, was not an ideal situation.

'The fox hunt,' he said simply.

The Gravedigger nodded.

'The fox hunt,' he replied, shifting in his chair. 'I came to you professionally and with the greatest of respect, Mister Rizzo. I didn't have to. I could have taken out my charter without your knowledge, without your permission, but I came to you and asked for your help, your advice.'

He rose, facing Gabriel now.

'What I didn't expect was for you to take my target and turn him into some casino game of yours. Christ knows what your investors must think, knowing the regular people in your casino were almost fodder in some high-stakes murder brawl.'

Gabriel Rizzo raised a hand to pause the Gravedigger.

'I get what you're saying, but we made sure everyone there gained recompense for the "improvised street theatre" we mistakenly provided,' he replied. 'And what can I say? I was caught up in the heat of the moment, and it seemed like a good idea at the time.'

'The road to hell is paved with "it seemed like a good idea at the time", Mister Rizzo,' the Gravedigger responded.

'But,' Gabriel said, raising his eyebrows, trying to defuse the situation with a mocking smile. 'He didn't die, did he? It's gone midnight, the game is over and somewhere out there, Tom Marlowe is running around being alive, so you can just take your charter and kill him at your own leisure.'

'But I can't now, can I?' the Gravedigger countered. 'Because you made him run. I've checked his hotel suite, there's nobody there. There's no luggage, no tech; it's empty. The only thing he didn't do was check out. He's in the wind, Mister Rizzo. He's running. Maybe he's stopped now, but that just means he's somewhere out there that I don't know.'

Gabriel nodded, realising the gravity of the situation.

'I get that,' he said. 'I see that can be a problem, and I apologise. I hadn't considered he would listen to my words and actually run for his life.'

'You *told* him to run?'

'I might have suggested that he leave Vegas and never come back again. It looks like he's listened to my words.'

'You told my charter, knowing I had a job here, to leave?' the Gravedigger's voice was softer and for the first time, softer didn't mean better. 'Mister Rizzo, you have cost me a lot of money.'

'Well, maybe you should have gone for the fox hunt,' Gabriel shrugged. 'You could have gained your charter and made a hundred grand in the process—'

He flinched as the Gravedigger slammed his fist onto the side table.

'I kill when I decide,' the Gravedigger retorted. 'Not when you decide. You've cost me a lot of money, affected my reputation and made my work harder, purely because you wanted to have a joke at Tom Marlowe's expense. You need to make this right.'

'And how do I make this right, Mister Gravedigger?' Rizzo asked. 'Do I call you Mister Gravedigger? Is it just Gravedigger? Is it Digger?'

He stopped. He realised he was probably annoying the man.

'You've told Tom Marlowe to leave. You've said he's banned from the events. He no longer has an Orchid coin, and now you're playing your own games.'

The Gravedigger rose from the chair and now moved towards the door, and Gabriel had a sigh of relief as he realised the Gravedigger wasn't targeting him today.

'Invite him back tomorrow, or later today, I should say,' the Gravedigger explained. 'Make him think he's welcome. He doesn't have to be. He doesn't have to stay long. But if you get him back here tomorrow, day or night, I will end Tom Marlowe for you, at no extra charge.'

'He made a bet,' Gabriel protested. 'He said he'd be back tomorrow night and steal my money from the vault. If I bring him back in, he could do that.'

'Well, you'd better hope I kill him first then, eh? This wasn't a request. Do it, or I offer your family my own "no extra charge" job. And you won't like it.'

This stated, the Gravedigger nodded, walked out of the door and shut it behind him, leaving Gabriel Rizzo alone.

It was at this point that Gabriel Rizzo realised he'd been holding his breath.

Stumbling over to the phone, he dialled reception.

'Find me my men,' he said. 'Any of them. I think I might need security after all.'

MARLOWE HAD TRIED TO SLEEP, BUT THE NIGHT HAD BEEN warm, and he'd been sleeping on a rather uncomfortable and ratty chair, while Sasha slept in the bed – the second time in a row he'd performed such a chivalrous action.

If he was being honest, he didn't think she got the better deal though, as the bed itself was lumpy, with a mattress that he thought was older than he was. Still, the motel did what it needed to do, providing them cover for the night. By six in the morning, he'd given up on sleep and was up, working out what to do next. Marlowe had slept little during the night, and because of this, he'd spent the hours of darkness planning, working out what he needed; later that day was the opening of the Gold Strike Casino. This was what Gabriel Rizzo had been planning, and Marlowe needed to know exactly how to stop him.

Sasha woke, stretched, and stared at him.

'You look like shit,' she said.

'You talk in your sleep,' he retorted. She didn't, but the flicker of concern on her face was worth the lie.

'Bullshit,' she eventually decided. 'One of my many lovers would have told me.'

'Your many lovers might have been spying, using your snores and mumbles—' Marlowe started, but stopped, laughing as a well-aimed pillow slammed into his head.

'You're planning,' Sasha rose, looking at the scattered notes. 'What's the plan?'

'Revenge,' Marlowe smiled as Sasha picked up a sheet of paper, reading it.

'You're stealing the money?' She shook her head. 'I thought better of you. That's just playing into Reilly's hands.'

'You know Reilly?' Marlowe was surprised.

'She came to us a few days back, offered her services. Seems she has a real crush on you,' Sasha replied. 'I didn't speak to her, it was Massey who brokered the arrangements. In the end, though, I told him to step back from it. You might be a cold-blooded rogue, but you're *my* cold-blooded rogue.'

Marlowe gave a weak smile, but one thing now made sense.

Massey had been dealing with Reilly.

Massey had to have given her the file that gave the information she needed. But why?

'I said I was taking it from him, not stealing it,' Marlowe shrugged. 'Currently I have a plan that does this nicely.'

He sighed, sitting back on the sofa.

'The problem is, I've seen the security,' he said. 'If I'm getting into the back rooms, I need biometric approval. And that's going to be difficult after yesterday, and my idiot bravado.'

'The bet you made?'

'The bet I made. And the vault is likely to open about an inch for viewing inside, no more without Gabriel himself there.'

'So, you need a new plan?'

'The plan I have works,' Marlowe grinned. 'I just need to get it working. Also, I need to make sure when everything's done and dusted, Gabriel Rizzo actively begs you to take him out of Vegas before anyone manages to kill him.'

'And Reilly?'

Marlowe looked back at the paperwork.

'I'm still working on that,' he said. 'It involved killing two birds with one stone, but I'm not sure who the other bird is, yet – but I think it could be Massey.'

Sasha stretched, walking over to the bathroom. She looked into it, grimaced, and then walked back.

'I think I'll be showering in my own hotel,' she said. 'You?'

'Trix will have sorted me a suite,' Marlowe replied, rising to meet her. 'I'll shower there.'

'Shame,' Sasha purred, but Marlowe ignored it, walking over to the desk and gathering his items.

'I don't play around with people who don't give me their real names,' he said, looking back at her. 'So, the next time you want to play "show me yours", you'd better come ready for show and tell.'

'Killjoy,' Sasha replied as she grabbed her own things. 'I suppose you want a lift back to Vegas?'

'It'd be nice,' Marlowe smiled sweetly.

21

AIR SUPPLY

MARLOWE HAD ARRIVED AT THE PARIS VEGAS HOTEL SUITE around nine that morning. The original plan had been to bring Sasha with him, but while driving to the Strip, they'd discussed the events of the previous day, and with Marlowe's comment about Massey taking point with Reilly while she wasn't there weighing on her mind, she'd decided she needed to check a couple of things – primarily, how *Gabriel* had known what Marlowe's plans were. Marlowe thought he knew this, and was concerned about Reynard Massey acting independently – he'd even voiced this concern to Sasha on the drive back. She'd at first disbelieved him, saying he was overreacting, but after a couple of calls had looked back to him, concerned.

'Someone's making a move on me,' she said, and the indignance in her voice was palpable. 'Reynard's the likely subject, but I can't work out—'

'That's the second bird,' Marlowe sighed, leaning his head against the headrest of the seat. 'I think you'll find he's cosying up to Interpol, using me as a way to lose you points with Langley. I get taken off the board, it hurts you, strengthens him. Or, at worst, distracts you.'

Sasha said nothing to this, not even a joke to say he'd overestimated his value, and Marlowe knew it was because she was thinking the same thing. Thus Marlowe had been dropped off outside the fake Eiffel Tower that led to the Paris Vegas hotel.

He hadn't entered, however.

Instead, he walked back across the strip, over to the Bellagio fountains, staring up at them. They weren't performing one of their timed, multicoloured music shows this early in the day, but the fountains were still impressive when they were off.

Marlowe needed some time alone; it was the following day now, so as Sasha had said, the damn fool "fox hunt" would be over now and he could stand in public without being taken out. At least, he could stand there and not be taken out by someone who wasn't there deliberately to take him out.

He took a deep breath and considered his options.

Had he kept his cards too close to his chest this time?

He was keeping secrets within secrets, and his concern was that he was keeping people who could help him at arm's length.

Why?

Marlowe considered this.

Because it was *personal*.

When Marlowe had first joined Section D, the "Botany Bay" of the Security Service, he'd done it voluntarily, to the amazement and some disbelief of his peers. Usually the screw-ups, the people who were too good to be fired went there, and for years the rumours had been that instead of being named "D" because it was the fourth unit to be created, Section D instead meant Section *Disavowed*.

It wasn't true, though. Marlowe had joined it because his mother had been part of it. And, when Emilia Wintergreen had pulled him over from the Royal Marines, she explained that by leaning into this myth she gained more leeway in operational status, as her team was believed to be mavericks. When they went off books, she could raise her hands and shrug, the narrative already created.

Because of this, over the years, he'd taken on mission after mission, dangerous op after even more dangerous op for Emilia ... before multiple injuries pushed him out of the field. Though, even then, he continued off the books. In the last couple of years he'd saved all of Westminster, stopped a Russian sleeper ring, removed the Donziger Corporation from the map, and used the same mission to remove Trisha Hawkins, defeated *Fractal Destiny* – okay, in his defence, he might have started that as well – and stopped Lucien Delacroix from removing the President of the United States.

All of these had been business as usual, and Marlowe knew that if he'd failed, he'd get nothing more than a small plaque, likely behind the charity box, in an unknown MI5 Church in London, the equivalent of the anonymous "star on the wall" in Langley.

But, for the first time, he was actively going against *family*.

Regardless of their lack of contact over the years, Byron Taylor – Marlowe still couldn't help calling him "Ichabod" – was still Marlowe's blood. Orchid had been Marlowe's right, also by blood. And Gabriel Rizzo ...

What was the problem with Rizzo?

This had been bothering him for a while now. On one side, Rizzo had made his bed the moment he sent Quaid to kill Marlowe, followed by the "fox hunt" he'd begun, a game created after he'd "outed" Marlowe's plans.

'I know that you're trying to take me down. I'm aware you think that you can stop me when you don't even know who I am.'

He'd gone against Marlowe, not because of a loyalty to Ichabod, but because Marlowe had got involved in Roxanne Vasquez's problems. And after a night of planning, the solution to these problems seemed to involve not only removing money from Gabriel Rizzo, which Marlowe wasn't worried about, but also by outing the fact that he was a federal informant, and was actively working against Orchid.

But if he was an informant against them, didn't that make him an ally to Marlowe?

Marlowe didn't like that thought, but it was valid. If Marlowe was still trying to bring down Orchid, as per the remit given to him by Emilia Wintergreen, then surely Gabriel Rizzo was an asset, something to be used.

Unless Gabriel Rizzo's plan for outing Orchid was for the wrong reasons.

This was more likely. Gabriel Rizzo and Byron Taylor were working together, with Cody Donziger along for the ride. Like Delacroix before them, they had the arrogance of wealth and influence, all from families with a "don't screw with us" reputation. If they were shaping Orchid into their image with *Prodigy*, that was an image Marlowe didn't want to see.

So, what was the plan? If he let Rizzo continue, then Orchid wouldn't be the organisation it was now. He'd win, but it'd be fractured, hobbled even. That was a win for Marlowe. But if he stopped Rizzo, then Orchid would stay as it was, but the more extreme end of it might be removed.

'I hope, in the same way that my son will be taking my

company and making the best of it and turning it into something light rather than dark, you can take what I give you and do the same.'

The words spoken by the recording of Taylor Coleman returned, as Marlowe watched the tourists around the fountain. He still couldn't be sure if this was a tacit suggestion to make Orchid better, or whether Taylor was playing a part.

But what if he did make Orchid better? What if he could remove the rotten apples from the cart and keep Orchid aimed more as a peacekeeper of some kind? What were the options if he attempted this? And, if he found such a backer, what could someone like Tom Marlowe, with Trix Preston beside him, do with an *unlimited Orchid budget?*

Marlowe shook his head. This was how nightmares started; the "what if" thought that began everything that would lead to disaster.

Taking a deep breath and letting it out, Marlowe knew what he had to do. That night was the launch of the Gold Strike casino. It needed to do well, and was the whole reason the highest echelon of Orchid were there, planned in advance by Ichabod and Gabriel; all to gain them more money.

Marlowe had to find a way to stop this.

First, the obvious option, and the one he'd already considered at length, was to remove the money. If Rizzo couldn't pay, then he was screwed. And if he couldn't pay, then either Cody or Ichabod would have to cover the debt, and that would severely hurt them. If they couldn't cover it, then they were all screwed. And Marlowe would bring popcorn for that.

Then there was the fact Interpol wanted the money.

Fine, they could have it. Marlowe didn't care if Reilly

gained the cash, but he was annoyed at being strong-armed by a corrupt agent. If possible, he wanted her removed from her role, preferably after the dust had settled. Maybe even with Reynard Massey if he was playing both sides.

But Marlowe had a plan for that.

Reilly talked about wanting Rizzo in her custody, but Massey had also wanted this, and from the sounds of things, was using this possibility, and Reilly herself, knowingly or unknowingly, as a way to remove Sasha from his career ladder. Marlowe liked Sasha, regardless of the games she played, and he wanted to help her, but there was no way on earth he actually *trusted* her.

But then he trusted Massey less.

Still, again ... he had a plan for that.

He needed to do this fast and surgically. It had to be a stealth strike in all but name, using the pieces he'd already placed into action—

He stopped as a man walked towards him from the side of the Bellagio fountain.

He was in his late fifties, stocky and tanned. His short black hair was cut in a side parting, and he wore a charcoal-grey pinstripe suit, comfortable-looking black brogues, a crisp white Oxford shirt, and a tie, with photochromic lenses over his eyes.

Marlowe had seen him in the Gold Strike, talking to Rizzo. And he knew exactly who he was.

'Marlowe,' the Gravedigger said with a smile. 'We meet at last.'

He turned and looked out over the Bellagio fountain's man-made lake.

'The sun is red over Moscow, and my lighter has run out of fuel.'

'I think you're enjoying this a little too much, Gates,' Marlowe said as he looked across the lake with the new arrival.

'Hey, you give an actor a role, he'll take it as far as he can,' Ryan Gates smiled. 'One question, though. Should I be worried if the real Gravedigger appears? I'm guessing he's real because everyone who meets me shits their pants.'

'The Gravedigger is real, and if he turns up, leave him to me,' Marlowe smiled. 'What do you have?'

Gates looked around to check they weren't being monitored.

'He's allowing you back into the hotel,' he said. 'He realises his impetuous idea cost me – well, the Gravedigger – a charter, so he's making it up to me.'

'And your friend?'

'Atkins? He's already speaking with the sister, Angelina. The family pretty much want Gabriel gone; he's an embarrassment to them. Only the fact he has Orchid's ear is keeping Gabriel alive. If he loses that, and "circumstances" mean he goes, then Angelina arrives the following day and life goes on. Atkins wants his life to go on, too, and is happy to work for any of the family, so he's happy to help where he can.'

He passed Marlowe a scrap of paper.

'This is where you'll find Walton Diggs,' he said. 'If anything was found before the fire, he'll have it. Also, he was – is – a loyal soldier for Gabriel Rizzo, hence why he was used to look for the disc. He's trusted. Close to the source. Which means—'

'Which means I can use him to get through the biometrics, into the rooms we can't get into,' Marlowe nodded. One issue he'd had was working out how to get past the various biometric doors and locks. Sure, Atkins would help, probably for a payout, but Marlowe didn't want to cause him any issues when Angelina arrived. After all, Marlowe was still intending to screw over the hotel she would be inheriting.

It looked like Walton Diggs would be getting a visit later that day.

'Oh, and you'll need this,' Gates added, passing a key over. 'It's the key to the upper levels. The suite, the office, Atkins gave me his, and I used it last night, so make sure if you get caught with it you throw someone else under the bus.'

'Thanks,' Marlowe said, taking the key. 'That actually helps with something tonight.'

Ryan Gates shifted, and Marlowe could see he looked uncomfortable.

'Look,' he eventually said, looking at Marlowe. 'I get what you're trying to do, but they won't let you in, armed, without one of those fancy coins. And you can't say anything to Orchid High Council, or any of the big hitters in the room without one. Because you gave your brother the one your dad gave you—'

'You mean a coin like this?' Marlowe interjected, pulling a blackened Orchid High Council coin out with a slight smile on his lips. 'Yeah, I thought about that. I think this'll do me just fine.'

As Ryan Gates stared at him, open-mouthed, Marlowe placed the coin away with a grin.

'Don't worry,' he said. 'I have a plan for that.'

WHEN MARLOWE FINALLY MADE HIS WAY TO THE KING SUITE IN the Paris Vegas Hotel, he found Trix was there at her desk, Clarissa sitting beside her, in her wheelchair.

'Taking my side of the bargain,' Clarissa smiled as Marlowe looked at her. 'You said I got half an hour.'

'Take as long as you want,' Marlowe smiled. 'If you're able to find what we're looking for, you're saving us a lot of hassle.'

Clarissa nodded and carried on looking into the system, with Trix tapping on the keyboard, jabbing at the screen here and there, saying, 'That one, click there,' and such like to the younger woman.

As they returned to their task, the suite and the people in it fading from their attention, Brad walked out of the bathroom, drying his hands on a cloth.

'Still alive, then?' he asked with a smile.

'For the moment,' Marlowe replied.

'So, tell me, Brit, do you feel stupid for going off half-cocked last night?'

Marlowe nodded.

'It wasn't one of my best moments, I'll agree,' he said. 'But it did what I needed to have done.'

'And what would that be?'

'I got a chance to look around the back of the area, and I have an asset that I know I can use.'

'And who would the asset be?'

Marlowe smiled.

'Oh, I think you could probably work that out yourself if you had a really good look.'

Brad considered it.

'Someone in Orchid who's friendly to you,' he said. 'Maybe Pearson, possibly that Steele guy?'

'Could be,' Marlowe said. 'Either way, we'll know tonight.'

'Why tonight?' Brad walked over to the bar's fridge, this time in a sideboard, and pulled out a can of sparkling water, tossing another to Marlowe.

'Because tonight, I intend to piss Gabriel off in the biggest possible way,' Marlowe grinned. 'Tonight, I'll be taking his money from him on his launch night extravaganza.'

He walked over to his bag, opening it up, pulling out a couple of items.

'Now, if you don't mind, I need to have a shower,' he said.

'Oh aye?' Brad grinned. 'Did you get all sweaty last night?'

Marlowe smiled in response.

'More covered in bed bugs,' he said. 'Or God knows what. We ended up staying in one of those motels where the last thing you want to do is wave a blacklight around. I kind of feel grimy.'

'You didn't want to use the shower there?'

'There wasn't a door,' Marlowe laughed. 'And the last thing I wanted to do was reveal everything to Sasha Bordeaux. Who, by the way, needs to speak to you at some point.'

'Good or bad?'

Marlowe paused, considering this.

'Depends how you feel about Reynard Massey taking over everything.'

Brad was already moving, grabbing his jacket.

'The hell with that,' he said, pulling it on as he walked to the door. 'Will you try not to die before I come back?'

'Can't promise, but I'll do my best,' Marlowe nodded.

As Brad left, Marlowe looked back at Trix as she swore loudly.

'Rizzo told me he'd deleted the file,' he said. 'I'm guessing he was correct?'

Trix focused an angry gaze on him.

'Looks like it,' she said, grumbling as Clarissa sat back in her chair.

'He's outplaying us and I don't like it,' she said. 'We need to find the original disc.'

'I thought it was burnt up in the fire?' Roxanne walked in from one of the side bedrooms. She was in nothing more than a wrapped towel, and Marlowe had to look away quickly before she accused him of staring at her.

And he *really* wanted to stare at her.

'Walton Diggs is apparently brokering something big on the dark web,' Clarissa rubbed at her chin. 'Off the books, real quiet. Talk of the family being interested. Which means we might need to have a word with him, perhaps?'

'Already on it,' Marlowe replied. 'Right after I shower and change, I'm paying him a visit. And, if you're interested in putting on the old espionage hat again, I might have a little job for you later.'

Clarissa smiled.

'I can do that,' she said. 'What about tonight's launch?'

'I have a plan about that,' Marlowe said, walking past Roxanne as quickly as he could, and heading for the shower.

The sooner he was out in the field again, the better.

22

NOISE ABATEMENT

Unsurprisingly, Walton Diggs lived in yet another less-than-savoury area of the Las Vegas suburbs. Marlowe wasn't even too sure whether he should call it the suburbs because the term conjured images of gardens and families living together, waving across the roads as they picked up their freshly delivered newspapers from the pavement. This, however, was a downtown complex; dirty, broken, and unappealing. The sun had faded the walls of the building, and the once vibrant colours were almost white and bleached.

Marlowe had used a car that Trix had picked up under one of his fake names, driving up and parking the rented Mustang half a block away from the address. He was amused that he too now had a Mustang, following the previous night, but it wasn't as swanky and filled with extras as Sasha's had been. Marlowe had even wondered whether she had a flicked-out secret glove box which had switches for things like ejector seats and smoke grenades like a James Bond Aston Martin.

It wouldn't have surprised him if she did.

The house was small, with a dirty, unkempt garden leading up the path. There was a shutter blind over the main entrance, the windows were possibly covered by a newspaper on either side, and if it wasn't for the rusted and battered car parked down the side, Marlowe would have believed that nobody had been there for years. It looked abandoned.

Climbing out of the Mustang, Marlowe closed the door and walked over to the house. He didn't knock. First off, he walked around the side to see if there was anybody around the back. He could hear music playing inside, but that wasn't necessarily proof that somebody was in the house.

After checking around, looking for any exits and possible chase locations, and using a shovel for a use it wasn't created for, Marlowe walked back to the front and banged on the door.

After a minute with no answer, Marlowe banged again.

'Walton!' he shouted. 'Turn your goddamn music down! I've told you a dozen times!'

The phrase had the desired effect, and Walton Diggs, believing this to be one of his neighbours complaining about his music, pulled the door open, ready to have a confrontation – and then paused as he stared at the bearded man, smiling at him, pointing his CZ pistol directly at his face.

'There you are,' Marlowe said. 'In you go. Back, back, nice and slow. Hands in the air where I can see them.'

Walton stepped back as Marlowe followed him into the dilapidated house.

'Anybody else here?' Marlowe asked as he closed the door behind him, looking around quickly.

'Look,' Walton began, licking his lips and shaking his head. 'I promised Big John I'd pay him. I'm a man of my word. Trust me.'

'You think I'm here over a gambling debt?' Marlowe couldn't help but smile at this.

'Well, what else would it be?' Walton frowned.

Marlowe paused, mouth shrugged in a De Niro manner, and then looked closer.

'So, no one's actually here?' he said. 'Shame if someone set fire to the place.'

'Ah, shit!' Walton exclaimed, finally realising what this was about. He looked over at Marlowe again, his hands still at his side. 'Dude, that wasn't my fault. I had nothing to do with it. I was just following orders.'

Marlowe nodded.

'I also get that you weren't supposed to be disturbed, were you?'

'Who are you?' Walton asked, nervous but calming a little, now he realised it wasn't some debt collector ... even though the gun was still in his face.

Marlowe took a moment to look around the house. He noticed at the side was a small laptop. Next to it, plugged into the USB drive, was a portable CD player. It was one of those CD-DVD-ROM burners that used to be on the sides of laptops, but were no longer built into the laptops themselves. That Walton had it plugged into his laptop meant that recently he'd been examining, or at least playing, a CD or DVD.

'I ain't done anything,' Walton continued, still trying to work out what was happening here. 'You can go back and tell Rizzo.'

'You think I work for Rizzo?' Marlowe asked. He knew Walton had kept the CD. It was a calculated guess from seeing the external CD drive. 'Let me tell you what I think happened. You went to Lexi Warner's house to find a certain disc. While you were searching, possibly even after you found it, Lexi Warner turned up unannounced. You panicked, struck her with something, maybe an item from her house. Maybe the butt of your gun? I don't know, but you knocked her unconscious. Then, realising that she'd seen your face, you set fire to the house.'

Marlowe shrugged at this point.

'Maybe you were supposed to set fire to it, anyway. Either way, the house burned down, Lexi would die in the fire, and nobody could be a hundred percent sure the CD-ROM hadn't been destroyed with her. So, now you go back to Gabriel Rizzo and tell him, "Sorry, boss, the disc got destroyed." Rizzo, he's happy with that. It means that whatever he had hanging over his head no longer worries him. But you know differently.'

He pointed at the drive.

'You come home, you check the disc, you see it's got a file on it – a video file of Gabriel Rizzo sitting in his office, talking to the FBI.'

At this, Walton's eyes narrowed.

'Who the goddamn hell are you?' he hissed. 'Nobody knows about this.'

Marlowe played a card. It was another guess, but he knew Walton wouldn't be going to the feds with this information. He'd be trying to sell it to the highest bidder, and at the moment, based on the comment by Clarissa earlier, there was one family in particular that would pay over the odds for anything that would remove Gabriel.

His own.

'Angelina Rizzo knows about him,' Marlowe smiled. 'You told her when you started mouthing off about how much it was worth.'

Watching Walton's face as he spoke the name, Marlowe knew he'd struck gold.

'I told her I'd contact her,' Walton eventually said. 'She didn't say she'd send any muscle around.'

'She doesn't trust you,' Marlowe replied, shrugging again, relaxing his gun, making Walton think he was now talking to someone on his side. 'Do you blame her? You work for Gabriel.'

'I don't work for Gabriel no more,' Walton said. 'He tried to throw me to the dogs after this happened when that bitch stayed alive. He told me I had to go and kill her.'

'Let me guess, you sent the two guys and the girl, the fake EMTs?'

Walton shook his head.

'I outsourced it,' he said. 'The hospital's small, no one really gives a shit about it. I thought they could go in, grab her, wheel her out.'

'And then what?' Marlowe asked, remembering the shovel outside by the door. 'Gonna go out to the desert, dig a hole, dump a body in it?'

'If that's what it took, yeah, sure,' Walton nodded. 'But they screwed up. There were these guys there, an East Coast bouncer and ...'

He slowly trailed off as he took in Marlowe, standing in front of him.

'... and a bearded guy.'

Marlowe knew without a doubt that his ruse was now over. In fact, Walton didn't give him a chance to even consider this. The moment he realised that the man standing in front of him was the same man who had stopped the hitmen from taking and killing Lexi Warner, he leapt into action, diving out of the room before Marlowe could bring his gun back up.

'Shit,' Marlowe muttered to himself. He didn't want a runner, but also, he knew Walton had two choices: get out of the house as quickly as possible, or find a weapon and use it in return.

Marlowe ran towards the kitchen door. This was the exit he'd found earlier, and the one that he'd sorted out before entering through the front door. Walton had obviously realised that the door was unable to be opened, blocked by something outside. He didn't realise it was a large shovel placed through the bars, blocking the door from being pulled in.

Aware now he had nowhere left to run, Walton looked around the kitchen urgently, and Marlowe knew he was hunting for a weapon.

'This doesn't have to end like this,' he said, placing his CZ down on the counter. He didn't want to fire the weapon; the last thing he wanted was to draw more attention, but he also wasn't going to let Walton Diggs find something to kill him with.

As it was, Walton grabbed what looked to be a lump of sharp metal with two handles on either end. It was curved and reminded Marlowe of the weapon that the Klingons in *Star Trek* would use, with a vicious-looking double-handed blade.

It was only once Walton Diggs held it up that Marlowe realised it was actually an extra-large pizza cutter.

Of course it is, he thought to himself. *Why would anybody have some kind of space-age weapon when a chunk of metal to cut a pizza into pieces is just as good?*

The problem was, Walton Diggs now had eighteen inches' worth of solid, sharp, heavy metal in his hand and was swinging it around frantically, using the wooden end like the handle of a sabre.

Marlowe wasn't a novice when it came to close combat melee fighting with blades, but at the same time, it had been a long week and a sleepless night, and he didn't want to keep this going any longer than necessary. The blade's manic swinging had meant Marlowe had ducked to the side, now out of reach of the CZ on the counter. Walton, realising this kept Marlowe at bay, the blade accidentally clipping the gun and sending it clattering across the floor, stopping either man from using it, and realising he had no other option, Marlowe went to unclip his chain – and then realised it was no longer on his wrist.

Somehow, in the chase to the kitchen, the clasp must have undone, and the chain had fallen to the floor.

He didn't have a moment to go hunting for it, or the gun, as Walton was already swinging again. Instead, Marlowe grabbed the first thing he could pick up, which turned out to be a wooden rolling pin. The pizza cutter slammed down on the counter, leaving a wicked-looking gash in the top. Marlowe realised this was a lot heavier than he had realised; it was coming down with the force of a meat cleaver, about three times the length, and with an anger and force given by the man behind it, that was fatal if touched.

Marlowe took the opportunity to swing back with the rolling pin, catching Walton on the side of the head. This staggered the man back, but after a second, he shook his head and charged back at Marlowe.

'I just want the disc,' Marlowe managed to get out before the blade slashed past him.

He almost ran for his CZ on the kitchen floor as it was now getting to the point where just shooting this bloody man would be easier, but instead, he took the rolling pin in both hands, blocking a downward swing, the double-handed pizza cutter slicing into the wood, and then twisted with his hands, pulling the blade out of Walton Diggs's grip for a moment.

However, he too was overextended as he did so, and stumbled slightly backward, banging his hip against the counter beside him – meaning Walton could once more grab the weapon, swinging it again. But he missed, then grabbing Marlowe's hand, pulling it forward and bringing down the blade with immense force, looking to cut Marlowe's hand off at the wrist.

Marlowe, however, yanked back, and the blade, instead of hitting Marlowe, went deep into Walton Diggs's own wrist.

As the fresh blood started spurting upwards, and Walton started screaming, Marlowe pulled away, Walton's grip no longer holding his own wrist. This was because the pizza cutter was deeply embedded into the wooden surface, and Marlowe couldn't help but notice that part of Walton's own forearm and hand were on the other side, with Walton now stumbling back, gripping the stump of his arm, staring in horror at the blood spurting out at the end for at least three seconds before he screamed, a mixture of shock and intense pain.

Marlowe had seen this on the battlefield, when soldiers losing a limb would have a moment of complete shock, not feeling the pain of the injury. Sometimes, it was only once they saw the wound that the full impact of what had happened hit them.

Marlowe held up the rolling pin in a surrendering motion.

'We need to get that cauterised,' he said. 'You need to stop the bleeding. We can get you to a hospital.'

But Walton Diggs wasn't listening. Screaming, he pulled a dishcloth around his stump. He staggered back from Marlowe, whimpering, his eyes wide, his face now covered in blood. Marlowe hadn't realised, but he was covered in blood as well, the spurting arm having drenched the front of his shirt.

'I'm not ... I can't ...' Walton started, but his words were broken and nonsensical.

Marlowe held up a hand.

'Diggs, it doesn't have to be like this,' he repeated. 'We can get you to ...'

Walton Diggs, in his mind, had decided to escape rather than attack, and had grabbed the door behind him, opening it and turning to run. However, Marlowe assumed that during the fight he'd got himself turned around, and instead of running out into the house again, he'd instead stepped onto the steps that led to the basement – his foot finding no purchase as it hovered over the space between the top step and the next one, overbalancing him.

This, added to the shock of his hand being cut off, meant Walton Diggs tumbled backwards, once more yelling out in horror as Marlowe saw him fall out of sight, followed by the sound of him tumbling down the stone steps into the basement.

Quickly, Marlowe followed, looking down into the basement. It was pitch black, but the switch at the side gave him a light that he could turn on. Once he did so, he could see at the base of the stairs the prone and obviously dead body of Walton Diggs.

He'd landed badly on his neck, his arm still spluttering blood, his eyes glassy, staring at a strange angle, his head almost eighty degrees off-kilter.

Marlowe stepped back.

It would look like an accident if he hadn't accidentally cut his own hand off but, looking back into the kitchen, Marlowe realised there was no way he could make this look like anything other than what it was. At least he hadn't fired a round. Either way, the kitchen was beyond repair. Marlowe's prints and Walton Diggs's blood were all over. Luckily for Marlowe, he hadn't been cut, and his blood hadn't merged with Walton's, but his fingerprints would be everywhere.

Quickly, Marlowe grabbed a cloth, wiping down what he could, and picked up his CZ from the floor. He was about to leave, grabbing the rolling pin as well, but then paused, staring at the severed hand.

Well, he'd wanted something to get past the biometric details in the casino.

Walking back, he opened the drawers looking for some kind of freezer bag, finding a Ziploc of the right size. He gingerly placed the severed hand into the bag, sealing it up. Finding a paper grocery bag, he placed it inside, adding the rolling pin into it as well.

Marlowe walked over to the laptop. He pressed a button at the side of the USB drive and, as it opened, he saw a flash of silver within. Closing the USB drive back up, he unplugged it from the laptop, placing it in another pocket. He was about to move on when he saw an envelope on the chair under the desk. Pulling the chair back, he opened it, and saw a wad of dollar bills.

Probably the advance payment for the fire at Lexi's house.

Flipping through it, he reckoned there was probably twenty grand's worth there, and slipped it into his pocket.

At this point, Marlowe decided that subtlety was over-rated here so he walked to the stove and yanked the gas pipe out of the back of it; the hiss was audible, the smell unmistak-able. This done, he rooted about in the drawers until he found a matchbook, then walked into the hallway and, placing the book on the base of the staircase balustrade, he lit one match, allowing it to burn down. Knowing once it hit the others it'd be a big enough flame to ignite the now rapidly building gas, and Marlowe quickly turned and left, closing the front door behind him. He hoped this was a neighbour-hood where people didn't peer out their windows, but just in case, he kept his head down. Climbing back into the rented car, adjusting his jacket so it covered the bulk of visible blood, Marlowe returned to the Vegas Strip.

Walton Diggs' dilapidated house exploded into flames before he turned out of the street.

But as everyone ran out to stare at it, nobody watched the mustang leaving.

And that was just how Marlowe wanted it.

23

MISSION POSSIBLE

Trix Preston stared down at the severed hand in the Ziploc bag for a good minute, silent and speechless, before looking back at Marlowe.

'And what exactly am I supposed to do with this?' she asked.

Marlowe, now changed out of his blood-covered shirt and into something new, walked out of his room.

'You had a collection of eyes,' he said, referencing Trix's hobby of scanning retinas and turning them into acrylic fake eyeballs, using the data in the eyes to break through security settings. 'I assumed you could do the same with hands.'

'You assumed? Does this *look* like an eyeball?' Trix retorted, pointing at the bloodied item. 'Honestly, does this look like *anything* I can make an acrylic version of?'

Marlowe shrugged. 'I just—'

'You just ...' Trix held a hand up to stop him. 'This is the problem with soldiers. You don't think.'

She stared back at the hand.

'I suppose I could make a silicone mould,' she said, now

thinking about it. 'You could place it over your wrist. It would cover the palm, the fingerprints. It depends if the lock is more complicated, though, on how it works. If it relies on skin temperature, silicone wouldn't cover that. I'd have to find a different way of doing this.'

She looked up at Marlowe.

'This isn't *Mission Impossible,*' she said. 'You keep forgetting this.'

Marlowe nodded apologetically.

'Can you do something here?' he asked.

'Give me ten minutes. Let me look at what I've got in stock,' Trix rose, walking out of the suite's main living area.

Clarissa smiled, watching her go.

'She's clever,' she said. 'Dangerous, too. Wouldn't want to be on the side she takes a disliking to.'

She looked over at the hand.

'Did you ...?'

'He amputated himself,' Marlowe replied. 'Swear to God. I didn't do it.'

'Doesn't matter either way,' Clarissa muttered. 'Lexi will be happy to hear what happened to him.'

'On that note, has anyone heard from her?' Roxanne asked, looking back from the window, where she seemed to stare out across the Strip like some kind of avenging guardian.

Marlowe shook his head.

'She's being looked after by the CIA, but let's just say I'm not holding that much faith in them at the moment,' he replied.

A moment later, Trix walked back into the room with a frown on her face. Marlowe could see she wasn't happy.

'You know, they always said that whatever you want in

Vegas, you can get,' she said. 'But if you want some kind of silicone printer, it seems you can't get one without some kind of twenty-four-hour turnaround.'

'It was a long shot,' Marlowe said, almost appealingly.

Trix glared at him.

'If this had been Soho, we could have had this done in half an hour.'

'If this had been Soho, we wouldn't have needed to,' Marlowe replied, shrugging.

Trix walked back to the Ziploc bag and looked at it, clicking her tongue against the roof of her mouth.

'You can still use it,' she said. 'It's just you're gonna have to take it with you.'

'Take the severed hand with me?'

'Yeah. I can plastic-coat the end so it doesn't drip, but it'll smell by tonight.'

Marlowe shook his head.

'I don't think so.'

'What's the plan then?'

Marlowe went to ignore the question, but then sighed to himself for a second.

'I'll be going through the front door of the casino,' he said. 'As well as you, and you if you're up for it.'

The last part was said to Clarissa.

'The hand?'

'That? It'll be carried by Brad.'

'I'm sure he'll be overjoyed.'

'Text him now, and see how fast he takes to find the printer you need from the CIA,' Marlowe suggested with a smile.

'Actually, that could work,' Trix rubbed at her chin as she considered this.

'I noticed you didn't mention me in this,' Roxanne spoke now, turning from the window, folding her arms as she stared at Marlowe. 'Don't for one second think you're leaving me here.'

'I have plans for you. Don't worry,' Marlowe shook his head. 'I have plans for everybody.'

'And when are you going to tell us what they are?' Roxanne snapped.

Marlowe went to reply, but paused as his phone rang. Frowning, he pulled it out and checked the number.

It wasn't one he recognised.

Answering it, he didn't speak, allowing the person calling to make the first move.

'Mister Marlowe,' the voice of Interpol agent Reilly spoke. 'I didn't think you'd answer.'

'And why would that be, Agent Reilly?' Marlowe said, so that the others in the room knew who he was talking to.

'We thought you might be out in the suburbs,' Reilly replied. 'I understand there's been an explosion. A terrible house fire.'

'Really,' Marlowe tried to sound disinterested, but didn't really care if he came off one way or the other.

'It seems Walton Diggs blew up in his house,' Reilly replied. 'It's quite a mess. He seems to have lost quite a few body parts in the process. They're scattered over a hundred-yard area.'

'That sounds terrible,' Marlowe replied, stifling a yawn on the phone. 'Who's Walton Diggs, exactly?'

'Come on, Mister Marlowe. You know exactly who he is. And how it's a fitting end for him to be caught in a fire in his house.'

'I wouldn't know,' Marlowe glanced around the room. 'I don't know anything about fires in houses.'

'I'm becoming quite an expert,' Reilly replied. 'I've been spending time in a CIA safe house, talking to a woman who was in one. She's not really answering, she's been put back in a medical coma, but we're having quite a nice one-sided chat. I hear you stopped her from being kidnapped last night.'

Marlowe looked at Trix. She couldn't quite hear the conversation, but she could see that there was a problem.

'You're working with the CIA now?' he asked into the phone.

'Yes. An agent Reynard Massey contacted me, suggested we should work together,' Reilly said back. 'I think you've met him.'

'We've had the pleasure,' Marlowe said, trying to slow the conversation so he could work through it, work out all the angles. 'He's the one who gave you my file, isn't he?'

'I read so many, I forget.'

'Of course you do. You ought to be careful of him, Reilly. He wants the same thing as you do.'

'I know,' Reilly replied, and there was a hint of smugness in her tone. 'Well, not everything I want. After all, his requests aren't so financial. He's just looking at his own promotion prospects. But he seems to believe he's gaining Gabriel Rizzo at the end of this. Where I seem to recall, you were promising him to me.'

'For questioning?'

'For silencing.'

'You'll get what you deserve,' Marlowe said with a smile, wondering what she meant by her comment. *Why would Reilly want Gabriel Rizzo dead?*

'Now, Mister Marlowe, that doesn't sound friendly,' Reilly

snapped. 'That sounds a bit more like a threat than anything else.'

'It's only seen as a threat if you think you should be threatened,' Marlowe replied. 'By tonight, everything will be sorted out.'

Reilly laughed down the phone.

'So good doing business with you, Mister Marlowe. I'll tell Lexi you said hello. Don't worry about speaking to her before tonight. I know you're very busy.'

'If anything happens to her ...'

'What do you think I am?' Reilly replied, shocked at what he was stating, her tone showing she was majorly insulted. 'I'm no EMT driver being told to leave at gunpoint. I'm an agent of Interpol. I'm whiter than white, and if you say anything else that differs from that, I'll have you extradited back to the UK and arrested for half a dozen crimes. You'll never see the light of day again.'

Before Marlowe could reply, however, Reilly continued.

'Oh, one more thing. Rizzo. He keeps bearer bonds in his office. Worth a few million, I heard. I'd like those added to the pot. Tick-tock.'

The phone went dead.

Marlowe wanted to scream.

'It seems we have two enemies now,' he said. 'And they're working together to take down the third.'

'Enemy of my enemy is still my enemy?' Trix suggested.

'Seems like it,' Marlowe grumbled, but then paused.

How had Reilly known about the EMT driver being told to leave at gunpoint; unless she was there?

'Trix, what happened to the fake EMTs?' he asked.

'Nothing,' Trix shook her heard. 'Apparently, you kicked one out of the van, and by the time the police arrived, the other two were gone. Likely to an off-the-books doctor if you shot one.'

'And nobody gave a statement?'

'Why?' Trix folded her arms, watching Marlowe. 'What did the bitch say?'

'She knew I forced the EMT driver out at gunpoint,' Marlowe mused. 'But if they were gone, nobody would have told the authorities. Or her. She could have been told by Lexi, but she was half out of it on pain meds, and is unconscious again.'

'So, you're thinking the only way she'd know was if she spoke to the EMTs?'

Marlowe nodded.

'Which would mean she would be involved in trying to silence Lexi. Diggs told me he outsourced the hit.'

Marlowe considered this, shaking his head, looking to move on for the moment.

'Right then. I think it's time to tell you my plan. Trix, do you, by chance, have a blueprint of the casino?'

'I thought you'd never ask,' Trix grinned, pulling up a rolled, poster-sized sheet of paper, which she unrolled onto the dining table, using ornaments to hold the corners. 'What else do we need?'

Marlowe considered this. A moment from Epping came back into his mind, when he'd used C4 to blow up Razor's cars. It hadn't been the destruction of the vehicles that had finished that confrontation; the explosives in the doorway did nothing more than scare the wannabe gangster, but the smoke and flames, the explosion and the power, the *threat* that it was somewhat worse than people believed? That was everything. That was something that could be used here to the same effect.

Thank you, Monty. Helping you has actually helped me, he thought to himself.

He looked back, realising Trix was still waiting.

'Sorry, just thinking back to Monty, and how I can use something from Essex here,' he replied sheepishly.

'Okay, so what does Monty think we need?' Trix raised an eyebrow.

'A silicon mould from the CIA, some explosive wire, and a necklace that looks like diamonds, but is actually earbuds and detonation caps,' Marlowe smiled. 'In around eight hours.'

'That's a tall order,' Trix raised her eyebrows, glancing at Clarissa.

'It's doable,' the older woman said with a smile. 'Anything else?'

'I need some of your uranium glass, too,' Marlowe smiled. 'Pretty much all of it, actually. I'll pay its value. Oh, and also some tuxedos and cocktail party dresses. We need to look good tonight.'

'You want me to find a suit to make you look good?' Trix laughed. 'That might take a little longer than eight hours.'

BRAD HAD ARRIVED AT THE SAFE HOUSE SHORTLY AFTER SASHA had, although he didn't know her by the name Marlowe did. That said, "Sasha" was correct.

And currently, Sasha was standing outside the house, hands on hips, and a mask of fury on her face.

'You okay?' he asked. 'You don't look okay, if you don't mind me saying.'

Sasha turned her furious gaze onto Brad now, and he almost stepped back.

'They've taken Lexi Warner,' she said. 'The whole place has been cleaned out.'

'That can't be true,' Brad exclaimed, almost walking past her and entering the safe house to confirm this. 'We were here yesterday. The place was working fine. There were agents in there, we left her in their care.'

'Oh, there were agents here,' Sasha nodded. 'But this morning Reynard Massey gave them the order to move out. They've gone to one of a dozen other safe houses, taking her with them.'

'Surely if the CIA wanted her moved, he would have ...'

Brad trailed off as he realised what had happened.

'He's gone off the books.'

Her mouth set, her lips tight, the woman known as Sasha Bordeaux nodded.

'Massey's making a play for my job,' she explained. 'Which usually I'd be fine with. Ambition isn't a bad thing, and all that. But he's made an alliance with that rogue bitch from Interpol. He's gone into business for himself. And he's about to cause some major problems.'

Brad nodded.

'If he's working with Agent Reilly, then things could go south very quickly,' he mused. 'You know she's only about the money, right?'

'Aren't we all?' Sasha gave Brad a smile, looking at her watch.

'It's just gone noon,' she said. 'The party tonight starts in seven hours. We have slightly less to find our rogue agent and work out what the bloody hell is going on.'

She looked up at the sky; the sun shining down through a cloudless canopy.

'If Massey realises he'll make more money by giving Lexi Warner in, this whole thing could go south real quickly,' she muttered, before turning and walking back to the car. 'I thought today would be simple. A nice little heist, the destruction of a global network, an asset placed in my lap. I didn't expect a bloody CIA mutiny.'

She glowered as she returned her attention to Brad.

'What?' she snapped.

Brad was smiling.

'I was wondering if you knew where I could get a silicone printer at short notice?' he asked. 'It's part of a plan to screw over Reilly, so it'll help ruin Massey's day, too.'

'Why in God's name would you want one of those?'

'Apparently, Marlowe needs to print a dead man's hand.'

'Of course he does,' Sasha sighed. 'Of course he does.'

IN VEGAS, CLANDESTINE MEETINGS WEREN'T EXACTLY COMMON. Marlowe was also aware that there was pretty much nowhere in Las Vegas where one could *have* a clandestine meeting without somebody somewhere realising what was going on. The simple fact that you were looking for somewhere quiet in one of the busiest and most bustling places in America stood you out more than meeting somebody in the middle of a busy thoroughfare.

This was what Marlowe hoped, anyway, as he walked down the main street towards the Cosmopolitan Hotel and his meeting, arranged for four-thirty in the afternoon, in

Ghost Donkey, a Mezcal and Tequila bar on the second floor of the food court.

He'd put the message out, but didn't know if his contact would be there. Things were about to draw to a close, and now was the time when alliances could be broken or even reformed. And he was mildly surprised and a little happy to see St John Steele sitting at a booth in Ghost Donkey as he entered. Steele was wearing a zip cardigan hoodie over jeans and a baseball cap on his head. It was obviously some kind of attempt at disguising himself, but Marlowe almost wanted to laugh out loud. Even wearing casual clothing in a Mexican-themed Tequila bar speakeasy, Steele looked as if he was attending a business meeting.

You can take the man out of Orchid, but you can't take Orchid out of the man.

Next to Steele were two women. To his left was US Senator Alison Pearson. To his right sat Sonia Shida. Neither of them had gone with the fake disguise, both wearing casual yet effective business attire. It almost looked, with Steele between them, as if some bored rich billionaire had gone out for a day with his lawyers.

Maybe that's what he's going for, Marlowe thought to himself as he walked over, nodded, and sat down. He had seen no agents or guards around and wondered whether the bodyguards of these three very high-ranking members of Orchid even knew they had escaped to meet with the fallen son of Orchid.

'Thank you for meeting me,' he said.

'The fox hunt is over and we're bored,' Shida looked up with the slightest of smiles on her face. 'We were hoping you would be interesting. The location for the meeting is a good start.'

'I hope I'm of interest, too,' Marlowe grinned.

A server walked over and took some drink orders, walking away. Marlowe noted that every single person at the table had ordered a non-alcoholic drink.

'I understand you had a plan to take down Gabriel Rizzo,' Shida said. 'Are you going to tell us what it is?'

She looked at her watch.

'After all, we're talking less than four hours now.'

'No,' Marlowe replied, holding his hand up to stop them from asking any follow-up questions. 'Not because I don't trust you or anything, but simply because I need you to have plausible deniability when this all goes down. If things go wrong and I fail, I don't want you guys standing next to me in the firing squad line-up.'

'And that's appreciated,' Steele put in. 'So, what exactly are you looking to do and how can we help?'

'You're aware that Gabriel Rizzo owes money to Orchid?'

'Yes, but that should be paid by the end of today,' Steele waved around the now filling-up bar. 'Vegas is busy as it's a fight night this weekend at one of the other casinos. And the Orchid high rollers alone would bankroll what he needs at the Gold Strike.'

'*They* need,' Marlowe corrected. 'He's in league with Cody Donziger and Byron Taylor. They've created some kind of consortium called Prodigal, and with Byron now with an Orchid coin, they intend to take Orchid in a new direction.'

Pearson nodded.

'We'd heard similar,' she said. 'But we've spent decades in the shadows, and the amount of billionaires who thought they could do something like this—'

'The problem is,' Marlowe added quickly, 'he's also

playing another angle. Gabriel Rizzo has been talking about Orchid to the FBI.'

At this, Shida almost stood up angrily.

'He *what?*' she asked.

Marlowe nodded.

'I thought that would get your attention,' he said. 'It seems he's been working with the FBI, keeping them on his side, while at the same time giving out details of prominent Orchid members. I think one reason he's having his party is to take out some of you. Anyone who's against his plan, probably.'

He gave a pointed look around the bar's table. Each of the people facing him knew they were in Gabriel's crosshairs.

'Have you got proof of this?'

'A disc,' Marlowe nodded.

'The one he tried to kill the lawyer for,' Pearson stated as fact rather than as a question, and Marlowe wasn't surprised that they knew about this. He turned to Pearson, nodding.

'I see you're already well informed,' he said.

'I was told it was burned in a fire.'

'The man who started the fire took the disc before he left.'

'And you know this because ...'

'Because I took it from him before I left him to burn in another house fire.'

There was a moment of silence as the other three people around the table took this in, and then St John Steele chuckled.

'What do you need from us?' he asked. 'You do seem to find yourself in a bit of a situation, after all.'

'And what kind of situation would that be?' Marlowe asked.

'You gave away your coin,' Steele replied, as if it was the simplest thing in the world.

'This one?' Marlowe looked innocently around the table as he placed a blackened Orchid coin onto the surface. 'I think you'll find I never gave anything away.'

The three members of Orchid stared down at the coin as if it would bite them.

Eventually, Steele picked it up, examining it.

'It's an excellent copy,' he said. 'I can't tell if it's original or not.'

'It's original.'

Marlowe forced himself not to laugh as all three members suddenly tapped at pockets, checking that he hadn't stolen their coin.

'So, someone's missing their coin,' Steele nodded to himself. 'What's your plan?'

'I want to know the rulings of the High Council,' Marlowe replied. 'When my father gave me the coin, there was no rule-book, no explanation of what you needed to do in certain situations. But I'm guessing that over the years, the decades, the whatever, when an Orchid High Council member goes off the rails, there must be a way that you can remove them. There must be a rulebook.'

'There are accords and codes,' Pearson nodded. 'Not many, but they exist. It all depends on what you intend to do with it.'

Marlowe placed his elbows on the table as he leant closer to the three people watching him.

'How about I tell you exactly what I intend to do,' he said. 'And you explain to me the rules and accords I'll need to do it?'

The server walked back over with their non-alcoholic

drinks, and Steele took his, sipping it, smiling, and then raising it to Marlowe in a toast.

'Here's to a very interesting evening,' he said.

Marlowe's phone buzzed, and he held up an apologetic hand as he saw the name calling.

'Sorry, a moment,' he said, moving away from the group as he took the call.

'Sorry to interrupt your team bonding session, but I have something,' Trix said down the line. 'I've opened the CD, and listened to the recording of Gabriel and his handler.'

'The FBI?' Marlowe asked.

'No,' Trix replied. 'It's not the FBI. There's more to it, but listen to this.'

There was a click, and then the audio of the recording fed through the phone. It was Gabriel Rizzo's voice, caught on the camera's audio.

'Wait, you promised me Interpol would take care of me if I did what you said. I'm not giving up any of my leverage ...'

There was a pause.

'Screw you, Reilly,' he said suddenly, anger in his voice. *'You're just lining your pocket. I want you to get me out of this, make sure I walk clean, or I tell everyone what you've been up to, and how your little "retirement fund" is growing.'*

Marlowe didn't need to hear anything else.

Gabriel Rizzo wasn't informing to the FBI. He was informing to Interpol – in particular, Special Agent Sandra Reilly.

Lexi Warner had a recording with Reilly on it.

Reilly knew the fake EMTs had tried to take Lexi.

Finally, it was all making sense.

Disconnecting the call, he looked back at the others. Reilly wanted money, but she also knew Rizzo was a loose thread. He needed to go. That's why she wanted him. And Lexi Warner, the only other person alive who knew this, was another that needed to disappear.

Marlowe dialled a number quickly.

'It's me,' he said. 'I need your help. How do you feel about going to work?'

———————

24

OPENING NIGHT

Even though it was away from the main Strip, tonight the Gold Strike Casino gleamed like a jewel in the heart of Las Vegas, its neon lights casting a vibrant glow against the dark desert sky. The grand opening was a magnet for the city's glitterati, drawing in high rollers, celebrities, and media from all corners, not to mention the Orchid members and friends of Taylor Coleman, who'd stayed a day or two more, just to attend.

Flashing cameras and the buzz of excited chatter filled the air as limousines lined up, depositing guests onto the hastily positioned red carpet that led to the casino's lavish entrance. The façade, worked on overnight and now an intricate blend of modern and classic design, shimmered with golden accents that promised a night of unparalleled luxury and thrill to the attending guests and dignitaries.

Inside, the casino floor was already alive with the clink of glasses and the distinct chime of slot machines, while freshly cleaned chandeliers hung from the ceiling, casting a warm, golden light over the bustling crowd. Roulette tables, blackjack, and high-stakes poker games were in full swing, each table surrounded by eager spectators and serious players alike. For a change, and unlike the previous few days of "bedding in", this evening cocktail servers in elegant uniforms weaved through the crowd, offering champagne and exotic drinks, while a soft melody played by a string quartet filled the background, adding a touch of sophistication to the lively atmosphere.

In Marlowe's eyes, however, it was as fake and gaudy as one of Gabriel Rizzo's loud suits.

Vegas would have had its fair share of launch parties and openings over the years, but nothing as expansive and exciting in recent years would have been as close as the launch of the Gold Strike Casino, apart from maybe the Sphere, but that was more concert venue than casino. It felt strange, considering the fact that the casino had been open for a few weeks already, but tonight, Gabriel Rizzo was obviously going for some kind of award, as even approaching from a distance, Marlowe could see the lights shining into the sky. The electric bill for this day alone was likely to be more than the last month combined.

He wasn't surprised to see that Gabriel had also beefed up the security. He'd expected this; not only was this the biggest day of his year, and not only had Marlowe effectively told Gabriel he was about to rob him, but there was a chance that many of the Orchid high rollers who had come in for Taylor Coleman's funeral wake and stayed were also there today to spend serious money. Around fifty million was owed to Orchid alone, so Marlowe knew the estimated profit for the day, added to the soft launch, was likely to push towards nine figures.

Walking up the red carpet to the door, however, he found

himself mixed in with a variety of impatiently waiting guests. There were cameramen and paparazzi photographers, hangers-on and crowds looking to see who was arriving. The chances were that Gabriel Rizzo would have also pulled in an extensive amount of celebrities and named guests to arrive, to add a piece of Hollywood flair. But the security, having spent several days checking guests for guns while allowing high-ranking Orchid members in with their blackened coins, had now been ramped up. If someone was going to rob the casino, it would be tonight, the biggest night of its year, and Marlowe knew very well that he might not be the *only* person trying to do this today.

He also knew the chances were they were all for *him*.

Ryan Gates, in his guise as the Gravedigger, had been told that Marlowe was no longer a person of interest for Gabriel Rizzo. But Gabriel had only done this because he believed the Gravedigger was going to kill Marlowe. Which for Gabriel meant a win-win situation, and the guards would watch anxiously for Marlowe's return.

Either way, they'd get that in a matter of moments, because the plan was simple. Marlowe, for all intents and purposes, was the diversion for the event.

Looking to the side, he smiled as his date for the evening arrived. Roxanne Vasquez looked breathtaking in her cocktail dress; Marlowe wore his tuxedo well, but Roxanne transcended in her clothing. She walked up, gave Marlowe a peck on the cheek, and looked around.

'I see you've gone full James Bond,' she said, nodding at the tuxedo. 'Shame about the beard.'

'I'm not losing the beard for anything,' Marlowe replied. 'I quite like the beard.'

'I'm sure you do, because someone has to,' Roxanne

smiled at a cameraman who was taking photos of the guests walking down the red carpet, waving at the prettier ladies to show a leg or smile for the camera. The chances were these would appear on some stock image website, but Marlowe didn't care. After all, if anybody saw one of these, and asked why Thomas Marlowe was attending the opening of a casino, he could point out the fact that his family had technically been investors.

Which sounded weird for a council house kid from West London.

'Will we get in?' she asked.

'I don't see a problem,' Marlowe said, as they started towards the door. There was likely a strict guest list tonight, but anyone trying to score a ticket hadn't got a Trix Preston and her hacking abilities in their corner. Marlowe noticed a couple of the guards, the ones that had already spoken to him as he'd entered the casino on the previous days, frowning as they saw Marlowe and Roxanne arrive. They knew who Roxanne was as well, and they knew that her arrival would probably mean nothing more than complications.

Marlowe walked up to the side of the lines, where one guard shook his head.

'Mister Marlowe,' he said, 'I'm afraid without a coin you have to ...'

He paused as Marlowe pulled a blackened Orchid coin out of his pocket, holding it up.

'I know,' he said with a flashing smile. 'Which is why I brought my own.'

'I'm sorry,' the guard frowned. 'I was told ...'

'Whatever you were told was incorrect,' Marlowe stated. 'Now let me and my date for the evening go through. You don't need to check us, but if you want to, I'm more than happy to be frisked. I haven't brought a gun. I don't need one today. I'm with friends.'

It was a lie, he had the CZ in its concealed holster, but Marlowe knew the coin meant he didn't have to "show and tell" here. In fact, the line would go to the control room, and Gabriel Rizzo would be informed.

The guard was about to reply, and Marlowe could see several others moving closer, possibly getting ready to argue as well. But stage two was about to begin, because outside, moving towards the main entrance, was his own distraction.

Outside, walking down the red carpet, was Trix Preston. She wasn't wearing a dress, instead a tailored black tuxedo over a black bra, a beautiful silver and diamond necklace around her throat. She called out as she walked, making sure people moved out of the way of the wheelchair she was pushing, in which a smiling Clarissa waved to the cameras, in an ankle-length black and gold dress of her own.

The wheelchair was as basic as you could get, but still the guards stood in front of it as they reached the entrance.

'Name?'

'Trixabelle Preston, and Clarissa—'

'Just Clarissa,' the named woman interjected. 'You don't need anything else. We're on the list.'

The guard nodded, and looked back at his superior, who picked up a handheld metal detector.

'If you move to the side, we're gonna have to check you—' he started, but Trix, expecting this, and still in front of the press, raised her voice.

'Oh! Victimise the physically disabled person? What a shock!' she exclaimed, looking around. 'A woman too? I see the men all walk in fine!'

'Your friend can't walk—'

'Are you saying my friend here, a war veteran who lost her leg in the line of duty, can't walk?' Trix pantomimed for the crowd. 'You haven't even looked!'

At this, Clarissa raised her skirt to her knees, showing her prosthetic leg.

'I can walk perfectly fine,' she said. 'But it hurts, and I'm old.'

'Not too old to be treated as a terrorist, though!' Trix said as the guard, realising a scene was about to kick off, started to quickly scan the wheelchair, more as a courtesy than anything else.

Inside, watching, Marlowe pointed at the scene outside.

'You're giving Rizzo some bad press there,' he said. 'That woman is known to us, a US veteran, and lost her leg in an IED explosion. I see CNN are taking an interest—'

He stopped as, walking up behind Trix, was Senator Pearson.

'Leave this poor woman alone!' she exclaimed, looking to the press, now focusing on her. 'We should be honouring our veterans, not accusing them!'

She looked back to the guard as the ones Marlowe had been speaking to, already realising she was a Senator and a wielder of one of the magic coins, left Marlowe and Roxanne alone, both running to bring the news story into the casino before it became the front page.

This done, Marlowe and Roxanne simply slipped back into the crowd, heading into the casino, walking over to the cashier's station, where Marlowe placed the twenty grand in bills he'd gained earlier that day across.

'How would you like it?' the cashier asked, already counting the notes.

'Large denominations,' Marlowe smiled. 'And keep a hundred for yourself.'

As the cashier started placing chips onto the counter, Marlowe motioned for Roxanne to take them as he walked away, looking up at one of the ceiling cameras.

And smiled.

IN THE SECURITY ROOM, GABRIEL RIZZO STARED DOWN AT THE image of Marlowe, gritting his teeth as he did so.

'Tell the Gravedigger his bloody charter is here,' he hissed. 'And that I want this done quick and quietly.'

IN A VAN ACROSS FROM THE ENTRANCE, INTERPOL SPECIAL agent Sandra Reilly stared at the doorway, her fingers tapping on the dashboard in a mixture of irritation and annoyance.

Reynard Massey, sitting beside her, frowned as he looked across at her.

'What?' he muttered.

'Why should something be wrong?' Reilly stopped tapping as she looked at him.

'You've been staring so hard at that crowd, I'm expecting laser beams to shine out of your eyes,' Massey replied. 'You need to settle in as this could take a while.'

Reilly sighed, looking back into the van, at the eight suited and armed Interpol agents in full combat gear, helmets already on and ready to go.

'It'll be soon,' she said. 'Marlowe and his woman are already in, and their tech girl's taking granny for a night out.'

She looked back at Massey.

'I don't see Haynes or your boss, whatever her name is,' she replied.

'She's on her way to Langley to stop my coup for her job, and Haynes is probably knee deep in bourbon now, aware his golden goose has flown,' Massey was staring back at the crowd now, the very thing he'd admonished Reilly for. 'Neither of them are threats, although I'm starting to regret working with you.'

'That makes two of us,' Reilly nodded, looking back at her team.

'Where did these guys come from anyway?' Massey frowned, following her gaze. 'I was under the assumption Interpol wasn't armed in the US, and don't have assault teams.'

'You're an expert now, are you?' Reilly was amused by the comment. Massey straightened, his hands on the wheel.

'I was always taught Interpol was purely an information gathering, investigative body.'

'Well when you actually *join* Interpol, you can tell me if I'm wrong here,' Reilly said, pulling out a Glock 17. 'Because I'm armed, my men here are armed, and I don't see you complaining, as these "armed men" will help you get what you want.'

She looked back at the assault team.

'Trix Preston, Roxanne Vasquez and Tom Marlowe are terrorists, armed and dangerous,' she said. 'They are to be terminated with extreme prejudice on my command. You understand?'

'You want them killed?' One man at the back of the bus spoke. 'I thought you said to keep them alive?'

'I changed my mind. Is that a problem?'

'No, ma'am,' the Interpol agent said, settling back. 'On your command, we execute the threat.'

Reilly nodded, sitting back in the seat. Her command would be the moment Thomas Marlowe gave her the money and bearer bonds he'd stolen.

It was true; the agent had been correct – she'd told Marlowe she would keep his friends and family safe if he followed her commands. But she wasn't an idiot. He was MI5, and so were a lot of his contacts. The Preston woman was a grade-A hacker, too. Last thing she wanted was either of them on her back.

No, the wise thing was once Tom Marlowe gave her what she wanted, she'd make damn sure there were no loose threads before she started her new life as a multi-millionaire. And having someone else do it meant she never had to find out if Tom Marlowe was better than her, face to face, with his life on the line.

Massey observed her.

'Changing the rulebook?' he asked.

'What do you care?' Reilly snapped back. 'You want your promotion? I'm giving it to you.'

She smiled, leaning closer.

'I worry about Miss Warner, though,' she said. 'I know you moved her somewhere safe, but if your boss is compromised in any way, she might know the places you moved the asset to.'

'Your suggestion?'

'I have an Interpol safe house,' Reilly suggested, almost as an afterthought. 'Nobody in the CIA knows it. Take her there, and I'll send Interpol in to watch her.'

'Interpol doesn't have safe houses on US soil—'

'There you are, telling me my job again,' Reilly mock

sighed. 'Okay, I have *personally*, on Interpol's behalf, arranged a safe house that is uncorrupted by your CIA moles. Better?'

Reynard Massey considered this, and then nodded. It was a wise move, but more useful to him, as if anything happened to Warner in an Interpol safe house, the CIA were shielded.

He would be shielded.

'Give me the address,' he said. 'I'll make it happen.'

Reilly read out the address of a warehouse in the suburbs, and then sat back, watching the front of the casino once more as she pulled out her phone, secretly texting.

> You failed before, you get a second chance.
> They're on their way. Don't screw it up.

This sent, she glanced around the van, watching the agents for a moment, before sighing, cricking her neck to release tension.

Tonight was going to be a long, but profitable night.

25

CHIP DOCTORING

ONCE SENATOR PEARSON HAD HELPED ESCORT TRIX AND Clarissa through security, they spent no time in moving to the next stage as the Senator left them alone.

Walking through the casino, Clarissa in front of her, Trix made a beeline for the toilets at the back of the casino, beside the elevators.

However, a suited guard, watching them approach, held a hand up.

'Sorry ladies,' he said. 'The party's that way.'

'Yes, but the toilets are behind you,' Trix replied, pointing at the entrances to the side.

'There are other toilets—' the guard didn't get any further as Trix now squared up to him, hands on her hips.

'Are you telling me you're refusing a disabled war veteran a chance to go to the toilet in one of the few wheelchair accessible cubicles in the entire goddamn building?'

The guard wanted to argue a reply to this, but instead sighed, stepping to the side, and letting them through.

With a smile, Trix wheeled Clarissa through the bathroom doors, closing them behind her as she walked Clarissa up to the end cubicle.

It wasn't the accessible one; that had been a ruse, and with the door to the cubicle now open, Trix placed the toilet seat down, turning back to Clarissa, who'd wheeled the chair to face her.

'Sorry,' she said as she knelt in front of Clarissa, unlatching her prosthetic leg.

'My idea, so I can't complain, really,' Clarissa smiled as Trix took the leg away, pulling out rolled fabric cloths from the hollow interior. As she did this, Clarissa leant forward, pulling a flat box from between her and the cushion. It was the size of a laptop, and as she passed it to Trix, it was opened to reveal a monitor screen with Velcro backing.

Backing which connected to the industrial strength Velcro, Trix was now sticking to the wall of the cubicle.

'Will it hold?'

'Only has to last an hour,' Trix shrugged, opening a second wrapped roll as Clarissa pulled off both armrests of her wheelchair, the first revealing a small oscillating saw, the other a drill with an extremely small titanium drill bit, only a couple of millimetres in diameter.

Trix took the saw and, with four quick cuts, took out a piece of the plasterboard at the back of the cubicle, exposing a junction point of wires. Exposing two of them, she clipped two bulldog clips to them, connecting these to the monitor, now precariously Velcro-ed to the wall. From her own pocket she connected her phone to this, and the monitor burst into life, showing six small security camera footage images.

'We're in,' she smiled as she passed the saw back to Clarissa, but paused as the door to the bathroom opened, and the guard stood there, stunned.

'What the hell are you doing?' he asked, reaching for his radio, but jerked back as a taser jammed into his spine, his eyes rolling back as he fell unconscious to the floor.

Behind him, turning the taser off, Roxanne entered with a smile.

'Walking in on a girls' bathroom? Creeper,' she said, pushing him in and closing the door behind her.

Clarissa pulled out some zip ties from a hollow tube in her chair, and Roxanne swapped them for a handful of casino chips.

'How many do you need?' she asked, already tying the unconscious guard up.

'We have twenty detonators,' Clarissa replied, but then shook her head. 'I mean nineteen, as the Brit has one. These should do fine.'

Taking a strip of duct tape from Trix and covering the guard's mouth, Roxanne now manhandled the body into the last of the cubicles, securing him to the toilet pipes.

'Now what?' she asked, turning to Clarissa, who was using the small drill to pierce the edge of the chips, drilling inch-deep holes, before taking inch-long pieces of wire and sliding them in. 'Will those hurt people?'

She pulled off her necklace and passed it over.

'No,' Trix was now opening up a folding Bluetooth keyboard. 'Some flames, lots of smoke and noise. We want to scare people, not kill them.'

Clarissa passed the chips to Roxanne, who, taking small caps from the necklace, was placing them on the ends of the wires, sealing the chips back up. Once all nineteen were done, she looked back at Trix, who was working on the keyboard, using the box that had held the monitor inside as a tray table, as she sat on the toilet seat.

'Comms,' she said, and Roxanne removed three of the "diamonds" in the necklace, passing them across.

'Check check,' Trix said, placing one into her ear.

'Comms one active,' Roxanne replied, inserting her own.

'Comms two active,' Clarissa replied.

'Comms three active,' a new voice spoke. 'You done the chips?'

'Of course we have,' Roxanne snapped irritably. 'You don't get to have all the fun.'

'Good,' Marlowe replied down the line. 'Now, go spend them badly and lose all over the place. Moving on to part two.'

Roxanne smiled at Clarissa, who had her leg reattached and her wheelchair back to looking like one.

'Shall we?' she asked with a wave of the hand.

'Don't mind if we do,' Clarissa replied, as she allowed Roxanne to wheel her out of the door.

MARLOWE HAD PLACED THE EARBUD IN THE MOMENT ROXANNE had left him, after an embrace that allowed him to take one from her hastily put-together necklace. He was glad it didn't need to look exact – Roxanne would be under less scrutiny than he would be, which was good, as she had a taser and he had nothing, not even his security bracelet, which he now believed was still in a Las Vegas motel room.

As he walked across the casino, however, he saw St John Steele and Sonia Shida walking towards him.

'Best not to be seen with me,' he suggested cautiously as they fell into step.

'If Gabriel doesn't realise we're on your side by now, he's

an idiot,' Steele replied with a sniff. 'Besides, I have my own ways to screw up his cameras.'

'You set things up?' Marlowe asked.

'Doctored the special champagne the moment they opened it,' Shida replied. 'You sure it's harmless?'

'Pretty sure,' Marlowe shrugged. 'It's more for effect than anything else. You have the devices?'

'Of course,' Steele shook his head. 'You forget who has the experience here. Your attempt at a beard doesn't make you the grown up in the room.'

By now they'd walked up to the back doors, the ones that led to the rooms for the high rollers, the Venice Ballroom and the games area.

The guard was packing – Marlowe could see that immediately. And, probably more vital for the moment, he was glaring at Marlowe with recognition.

'Coin holders and guest list only,' he said, checking the small tablet he had in his hand, before looking back at Marlowe. 'And you ain't on the list.'

Steele and Shida showed their coins, and the guard stepped to the side.

'I'm a combatant,' Marlowe offered, but the guard moved into his way.

'Not important this time,' the guard sneered. 'You might be allowed back into the casino, but if you're not on the list and you don't have one of those fancy coins, you can—'

He stopped, however, as Marlowe held up a coin.

'There,' he said, a dark smile crossing his face. 'Now get the hell out of my way.'

The guard faltered for a moment, frowned, and then stepped back.

'More than my pay grade, anyway,' he muttered.

With a nod, Marlowe walked past, joining the other two as they walked into the back areas of the casino.

They said nothing, focused on their own thoughts as they entered the upper entrance of the arena. It was the same as before, with tiered seating leading down to a cage fighting arena, two UFC fighters already fighting within it.

A suited woman, smiling and with a tray of crystal champagne glasses on her tray stepped forwards.

'Good evening,' she said. 'Please, enjoy a glass of Moët & Chandon Imperial Vintage, 1946 collection.'

Marlowe, Steele and Shida took a glass of the incredibly expensive champagne each. Marlowe smiled when he saw that neither of them drank from their glasses, though.

'Have fun,' Steele said to him, raising his glass. Marlowe bowed his head slightly before turning to the steps, down to the arena.

Showtime.

As Marlowe went to pass, however, Steele grabbed him by the arm.

'You know if you do this, things won't be the same again,' he stated, glancing around the small arena. 'If it works, half of Orchid will be on your side, but if it fails ...'

Marlowe nodded.

'I know,' he said. 'And I'm aware what you're putting up with.'

There was a sudden cheer as one fighter in the arena threw the other one against the chain fence, flipping him over with a solid jiu-jitsu throw, and the people in the seats jumped up, knocking Marlowe to the side, pushing him into Steele, spilling some of the incredibly expensive champagne onto Steele's jacket.

Steele laughed, pushing him back.

'If I'd have known you wanted to give me a hug, Mister Marlowe, I'd have worn a better jacket,' he said, adjusting himself and wiping his lapel. 'We talked about dating yesterday, so don't tease me again.'

Marlowe smiled.

'See you on the other side,' he said, turning and making his way down to the middle of the arena.

He carried on walking, several champagne-drinking members of Orchid watching him with both confusion and curiosity as Marlowe climbed over the railings, walked up to the arena, and opened the door to the cage.

'Leave,' he said, his tone commanding.

The two UFC fighters, still not finished but also not paid for anything else, shrugged and walked out of the cage to a cacophony of boos and hisses from the surrounding people. The fight hadn't finished. Marlowe had cost a lot of people money.

Marlowe turned to address the crowd.

'You all know who I am,' he said loudly, allowing his voice to echo around the room. 'And a lot of you probably know why I'm here. I hope you've all made your bets because it still stands. Gabriel Rizzo will lose tens of millions of dollars tonight from his own vault. Will I do it? If I do, he'll still have to pay out, as the house doesn't always—'

There was a commotion to the side, and Marlowe saw Gabriel Rizzo running down the steps.

'Get him out of here! I want him removed!' he shouted.

Two guards emerged out of nowhere beside the cage and walked towards the door, but Marlowe held a hand up.

'I am here by the right of birth and blood,' he stated loudly. 'You cannot stop me from speaking, for you are not

Orchid High Council, and this hotel is owned by us until you pay your debt.'

Gabriel paused at this. Marlowe's attitude and words, especially the use of the word "us" gave a confidence he hadn't been expecting. The guards also had stopped by the door, turning to their boss, waiting to see what his suggestion was. Gabriel waved them down and continued over the barrier, walking up the steps and into the cage, facing Marlowe.

'Big words,' he said. 'And I'm impressed that you're happy to say them in front of so many distinguished guests, but we all know that you gave away your heritage yesterday when you lost your coin in a poker game with your brother.'

There was a rumbling around the audience, mumbles and mutterings of Orchid members as Marlowe took this in, nodding, before reaching into his pocket.

'Do you mean *this* coin?' he asked, removing it and holding it up for all to see.

At this, the room electrified as the crowd, realising something was going on, leant closer, their voices rising, and Orchid High Council members straining to see if the coin was real or not.

Gabriel went to take the coin, but Marlowe snatched it back.

'As I said,' he snarled, 'you are not Orchid High Council—'

'I am,' another voice shouted, and Marlowe saw Ichabod walking down the steps, two goons with him. By now, the barrier had been moved, and he walked straight through, climbing up the steps, pulling out his own coin.

'I am the hereditary High Council member of the Coleman clan,' he said. 'Through this coin, given to me by you when you lost at poker yesterday. Whatever you have is a forgery, and as such is punishable by expulsion and even death, as per the accords.'

'I am glad you mentioned the accords,' Marlowe smiled, still holding his coin up to show the audience. 'You say I lost? I didn't lose. I threw the game, so you'd have *that* coin. This is the real Coleman clan coin, which means, *brother*, that you are a pretender to the High Council, holding a coin that isn't yours and isn't connected to you in any way.'

The crowd shouted at this, demanding some kind of resolution.

'I claim by right of the accords, under subsection five, paragraph two, that this man, Byron Coleman, has willingly and knowingly lied to you about his position in the Orchid Organisation,' Marlowe shouted now, addressing the crowd. 'I'm happy to have my coin examined.'

He turned his attention to Ichabod.

'Are you?'

'Of course I am,' Ichabod replied, but now his voice was more cautious, distrusting. He'd worked out something was going on; he hadn't quite understood the rules, and now he realised he'd walked into an arena with a man who had more parts moving right now than he thought.

'I can confirm it,' the voice of St John Steele echoed around the arena as both Steele and Shida walked through the open barriers. 'I was the Arbitrator, and until a replacement is made, I am *still* the Arbitrator.'

He looked across, waving for a suited man to come running over, a box in his hand.

'Bring me your coins,' he commanded.

Marlowe and Ichabod both passed their coins over, Marlowe passing his to Steele and Ichabod doing the same to

Shida, who held hers up so that no one could accuse her of tampering. Marlowe then walked to the side of the cage, placing his champagne flute down as Steele turned to face the watching audience, making sure that the camera that usually showed the fight on the screen above had focused on his own hand, as he took a device from the suited man next to him.

'The coins carry the DNA of High Council families,' he informed the audience, in case people weren't aware. 'Many coins have DNA that lasts generations. Taylor Coleman's DNA was the first of his clan in this coin. If this is truly the Coleman coin, the DNA will match Thomas Marlowe or Byron Coleman, as they are his sons, and will carry the same DNA markers.'

Marlowe waited as the man who had run over to Steele now walked over to him with a needle. He held out his finger and allowed a prick of blood to be removed. This was swabbed onto the end of a Q-Tip, and wiped onto the left-hand side of some kind of device, no larger than a cigar cutter. Steele, meanwhile, had taken a small thin key and placed it against the edge of the coin. Marlowe couldn't see how it worked and hadn't seen any holes in the coin, but guessed it must have been something to do with magnets, because once this was done, he could twist the top of the coin anti-clockwise; a quarter turn, before a small tray slid out of the edge of the coin, in the same way that a SIM card holder would pop out on a phone.

Steele took a second swab from his assistant, slightly damp from some liquid placed on it, and quickly wiped on the blackened coin's tray before returning the tray back into the coin, locking it once more. He then took the swab, and wiped the other half of the device, now with two samples: Marlowe's on the left, and the coin's on the right.

He pressed a button; the audience waited.

There was a beep and a green light.

'This is the coin of Taylor Coleman,' Steele announced, looking around. 'The DNA samples match.'

'There's no way ...' Ichabod muttered, turning now and looking at Gabriel for support. 'I couldn't—'

'Is Robert Chester Crown the Third in the audience?' Marlowe shouted.

There was a slight commotion, and a hand raised.

'I'm Robert Chester Crown the Third,' a small, rotund man in his forties replied nervously.

'You lost your coin, didn't you? Several days ago, when you first arrived at the casino?'

At this, and now knowing his secret was out, Robert Chester Crown the Third stood, nodding.

'I did,' he replied. 'I didn't tell the High Council, I hoped to get it back. I thought I'd been pickpocketed, assumed I'd be extorted for its return. I've been hiding in my room all week, only got in here because I came in with some others.'

Marlowe pointed at the coin.

'There's no point testing Byron Coleman for that coin,' he said. 'I'd check Robert Chester Crown the Third, instead, as it's his coin.'

The crowd made a noise. Ichabod held his hand up.

'You knew!' he shouted angrily. 'You knew this wasn't my father's coin, and you gave it to me anyway, made me think I'd beaten you!'

'I never told you it was your father's coin,' Marlowe replied. 'I just held the coin up and said I'd play for it. I'd found it on the floor when I first arrived. I was going to give it back to its rightful owner, but as you can see, there's a lot of rigmarole in finding that out.'

He turned back to Robert Chester Crown the Third.

'Come and pick up your property once you're confirmed as the owner, and keep it somewhere less likely to fall out in the future,' he said before glancing back at Ichabod.

'You tried to destroy my life,' he said. 'You thought you were playing a great game when your father went. You believed that Taylor Coleman and everything he did was lesser than what you could do in his place. You used me, you used everybody here.'

'I did no such thing!' Ichabod cried out.

Marlowe gave it a long moment, watching the crowd before looking back at Ichabod.

Now.

'You teamed with people to try to kill me, and hated me for something I never wanted,' he said, loud enough for all to hear. 'And now, brother, as the true Orchid High Council member, and going on your recent comment of your crime being punishable by expulsion and even death, as per the accords, I challenge you to *single combat.*'

26

SEWER RATS

When Marlowe had spoken about a party at a swanky Vegas launch event, Brad Haynes had assumed he would attend as a guest. However, now clad in his maintenance overalls and trudging through the sewers under Las Vegas, he found himself muttering curses under his breath, determined to seek revenge on the man who had relegated him to wading through filth to save the world.

This wasn't the worst job Brad had undertaken, but it certainly wasn't high on his list of preferred summer holiday activities.

With another grumble, he followed the GPS device in his hand until he located a set of stairs welded to the wall.

At last. Hallelujah.

Ascending the stairs, he halted at a door. It was a maintenance entrance, but one he could easily access with a couple of specific lock picks and a security dampener. Within seconds, and hoping Trix Preston had turned any external alarms off, he had it open, slipping from the foul-smelling sewer into the lower basement of the Gold Strike Hotel.

Once inside the building's bowels, he quickly shed his overalls to reveal a black suit underneath. It wasn't a tuxedo like Marlowe's; it was more akin to a utilitarian security guard outfit, complete with a white shirt and black tie. Thus prepared, and with his bulky holdall now back over his shoulder, he made for the furthest door. He hoped the area would be deserted, and with the party in full swing above, it seemed his wish was granted.

Tapping his ear, he performed a comms check.

'Online.'

'You're right on time,' Trix's slightly echoey voice responded.

'Where are you?' he inquired.

'In a toilet cubicle,' she replied, 'helping provide that wonderful aroma you've been enduring for the past half-hour.'

Brad chuckled.

'Can you see me?' he asked, looking up at one of the cameras along the route.

'I can, and I've looped the feed so no one else will,' Trix answered. 'You've got about three minutes to reach the back door.'

Nodding, Brad quickened his pace towards a lone metal door at the end of the corridor, beside which was a biometric scanner.

'Do I need a passcode?' he queried.

'Possibly. I saw a guard approaching one of the entrances from the casino, so zoomed in as he placed his hand against the scanner and then keyed in four digits. 2-3-7-8.'

Brad approached the security console, delving into his bag and extracting a silicone hand mould, courtesy of a pissed-off CIA asset technician earlier that afternoon.

Fitting it snugly, he shook it around so it didn't feel too tight.

At least he didn't have to bring the dead man's hand, he thought to himself as he placed his now covered palm on the scanner. A yellow line moved down it before turning green, and the keypad flashed blue. He entered the number Trix had provided, and the door clicked open.

'Looks like your taxidermy skills worked,' he said. 'How many more doors like this?'

'Unsure,' Trix replied. 'Keep the glove on, just in case.'

'Any other allies nearby?'

Trix chuckled down the line.

'Afraid not. We're rather short on friends here,' she said. 'Good luck.'

With the holdall firmly on his back, feeling the weight of the equipment inside, Brad stepped through the door, and into the more secure back rooms of the Gold Strike basement.

———

Ichabod glanced around the arena, and Marlowe could see he was trying to work out how much shit he was in right now. Marlowe didn't really care if a fight actually happened; he just wanted all eyes on him, distracting everyone from everything else that was happening outside the small arena's doors.

'This is stupid,' he muttered. 'We're all businessmen—'

'The accords were called,' Steele shouted out.

'Blood demands blood,' Pearson echoed from the other side.

Sighing, Ichabod went to take off his jacket—

Only to find Marlowe moving in already, kicking hard between his legs.

As he went down to his knees, clutching at his balls, Marlowe swung down, connecting hard on Ichabod's jaw, sending him to the floor, almost knocked out.

Pushing him onto his back, Marlowe placed a knee on his throat, and leant down, whispering, so nobody could hear him.

'You were never going to beat me,' he whispered. 'I threw the hand, so you'd walk right into this. You think you were born for this? I was trained for it. Over years. By the best in the world. You're over, Byron. Tonight, Gabriel will be over. And next week? I'll be coming for Cody Donziger. So, if I was you, I'd start running, because if I see you again, brother or not, I'll kill you.'

This said, he now rose, facing Gabriel.

'I know all about you, too,' he said. 'Your friendship with Interpol agent Sandra Reilly, for example.'

There was a muttering in the audience, and Gabriel's eyes narrowed.

'That's a lie, and if you had any proof—'

He stopped dead as Marlowe pulled a CD case out of his jacket's inside pocket, the material specially widened for the purpose.

'Like this?' he asked with a smile. 'Walton Diggs kept it. He was looking to sell it to your sister. I'm sure the Orchid High Council would like to listen to it – if you weren't trying to kill them first.'

At this, the audience stopped muttering; you could now hear a pin drop in the small arena.

'Did you enjoy your champagne?' Marlowe shouted now, walking back to the edge of the fighting area, picking up his glass and holding it up. 'The Russians are known for poisoning their traitors and people who speak out against them. A favourite being polonium-210, a poisonous radioactive isotope.'

He allowed the background noise, the muttering and the shouting to build.

'Taylor Coleman was an arms dealer, and he knew how to find polonium-210,' he continued. 'And Byron, his son, worked with his business partners to poison you all with small doses of it.'

He looked back at Gabriel, now frowning at him, trying to work out Marlowe's game plan here. But Gabriel didn't have to wait long, as Marlowe looked over at Steele.

'Do you have it?' he asked.

Steele nodded and waved for his minion to return. This time the minion had a new device in his hand; it was portable, and featured a distinctive flat, circular probe, resembling a pancake in shape. It was connected to a compact body, housing electronics and a digital display screen on the facing side.

'This is a Geiger counter,' Marlowe explained. 'Known as a "pancake" one because of the design. It's specifically designed to detect alpha and beta particles, as well as low-energy gamma rays.'

He held his champagne glass up.

'You were probably given this when you came in, told it was a super expensive champagne,' he continued. 'Made you want to really try it.'

Shida took the Geiger counter, turning it on. The familiar Geiger "clicks" heard in film and TV started, as the device took in the surrounding base line radiation. However, as she took it closer to the glass, it became louder, the clicks coming through faster.

Marlowe could see people with glasses staring in horror at them.

'Now you might think this was just aimed at me,' he said, nodding at Steele, who now placed his own glass against the device, the machine once more going crazy.

At this point, more people were looking uneasy in the audience as Marlowe looked up at the camera filming him.

'Whoever's in the booth,' he started, waving his hand around. 'I know you have UV lights here. Turn them on.'

The lights dimmed, and the UV lights lit everyone up as they flashed on. The whites of shirts and overly whitened teeth glinted in the purple half-light—

And several of the champagne glasses in the hands of Orchid members glowed a muted green, as did several lips on faces.

The lights turned back on as the Orchid members shouted excitedly and urgently, having seen this on each other's faces.

'Don't worry, you've not taken enough of a dose yet,' Marlowe replied. 'But I'd stop drinking the champagne.'

'I don't know what you've done,' Gabriel hissed, pulling a Glock 17 out of his jacket pocket and aiming it at Marlowe, then glancing around the small arena, watching several of his guards pulling out guns, aiming them at the suited guests. 'But I'll see you swing for this.'

He turned to the audience.

'He's playing with you,' he said. 'He's lying through his teeth.'

'He's not Orchid, no matter what coin he holds,' Ichabod,

climbing to his feet and rubbing at his jaw growled, pulling out his own gun. 'And now he's going to die.'

'Yeah, about that,' Marlowe smiled. 'I don't think that's going to happen right now.'

———

ROXANNE AND CLARISSA HAD PALMED OUT ALL NINETEEN OF the chips, making sure almost every single one of them was in the hands of a dealer thanks to terribly planned bets, ones which left them broke, before meeting back at the bar.

'We're done,' Roxanne said into her earpiece. 'What now?'

'Now you need to get Lexi Warner to safety,' Trix said through the earbud. 'I've got intel saying Reilly's given the CIA a new safe house address to take her to, and you can guarantee she's sending someone to end her.'

'Send me the details,' Roxanne was already wheeling Clarissa towards the main entrance. 'Will you be okay alone?'

'Just save her,' Trix replied. 'And don't worry about the address, Marlowe provided you with some help.'

Roxanne stared at the main entrance, and the stocky man walking towards them.

The *Gravedigger*. She'd seen him on the CCTV, but in person he was even more imposing.

'Okay, now I'm really impressed with your planning skills, Marlowe,' she whispered.

'Ladies,' he said with a bow. 'Your carriage awaits.'

There was a buzz, and Clarissa looked at her phone.

'You guys go,' she said. 'I'd just keep you back.'

She indicated the wheelchair.

'You okay on your own?' Roxanne looked around the casino.

'Girl, I've been okay for decades,' Clarissa laughed. 'Get out of here.'

Roxanne nodded and then ran off with Gates, while Clarissa started wheeling the other direction. The text was something she'd been waiting for, permission of sorts to go for broke.

Reaching the door to the back rooms, no longer guarded, she rummaged under her seat, pulling out the remnants of a silicon hand – this had been the first attempt at Walton Diggs' prints, but hadn't worked on Brad's larger hand.

It worked on Clarissa's though, as she placed it on, slamming it against the sensor and typing in the four-digit code.

The door clicked open, and with a smile, Clarissa entered the back rooms, closing the door behind her.

Marlowe was causing chaos outside, and also in the basement.

Her target was elsewhere.

BRAD HAD MADE HIS WAY THROUGH TWO LEVELS NOW, EACH time using the code and the fake hand to gain entrance, but he knew his luck would run out soon. Therefore, it was with a sense of relief he found himself outside the casino vault.

Closing the door behind him, he walked over to the keypad.

'I could melt this,' he suggested.

'Not an option,' Trix replied in his earbud. 'Do me a favour, attach the small square device you have in your bag.'

Muttering, Brad placed the holdall on the floor and

unzipped it, opening it up and pulling out a five litre plastic bottle, attached to a feed sprayer. It was the kind of sprayer you'd use on a garden, de-weeding – you'd pump the pressure up, and then pull the trigger, releasing the weed killer.

But that wasn't what he was looking for. Deeper, under some ammunition, was a small black square, the size of a wireless charger. Magnetic, it snapped onto the side of the pad, and Brad stepped back as it lit up, numbers scrolling across the screen.

'How long will it take?' he asked, watching the door in case any new arrivals appeared.

'A minute, ten minutes, who knows,' Trix replied, and Brad got the distinct impression she was enjoying herself. 'It's a Babbage series forty. You miss a step, a glass screen drops and the air is removed from the vault.'

'So don't miss a step,' he started, but stopped as the security pad beeped, and the door started opening.

An *inch.*

As the door stopped, Brad ran for it, pulling at the metal door, but it was stopped tight. Looking through the inch gap, he almost wanted to cry, as he could see through the slit into the lit vault, where in the middle were pallets of dollar bills, millions of dollars' worth, topped off with high denomination bearer bonds on a shelf to the side.

'What the hell?' he muttered.

'Fail safe,' Trix replied. 'Only Gabriel can get any further.'

'And you knew this?' Brad shook his head in frustration. 'You expected this?'

'Of course I expected it,' Trix replied haughtily in his ear. 'So grab the weedkiller and get to work. An inch is all we need.'

Reluctantly, knowing what was now about to happen,

Brad sighed and started pumping the bottle, building the pressure.

'You're a goddamned killjoy,' he muttered as he did so. 'You know this, right?'

MARLOWE HELD THE CD UP AS HE FACED GABRIEL.

'You want this?' he asked. 'You have to work for it. You kill me? A heart rate sensor sets off a pre-set email, and everyone gets a copy of the audio. This CD moves over twenty feet away from me? Same sensor inside it detonates the case, and in the process sets the email off.'

Gabriel looked unsure, as if he didn't believe this, so Marlowe shrugged, pulling out a phone.

'You need proof,' he said. 'I get that. The explosion would be small, but violent. Let me show you. Three, two, one ... now.'

Before Gabriel could say anything, Marlowe clicked the button on the side of the phone – and faintly, in the distance, a series of explosions could be heard.

'What the hell?' Gabriel spun to see the audience now running for the doors. Being poisoned was one thing, being blown up was another.

'I've just destroyed your casino,' Marlowe smiled. 'And any digital money you own has now been frozen by the CIA and the FBI. Not Interpol, as we know how much she loves your money.'

Gabriel bit his lip in anger as he raised his gun, but stopped as his phone went. He answered, listening to the frantic sounds coming through it. Marlowe knew without a doubt this was one of his men, telling him the casino was now filled with smoke and fire, as nineteen separate explosions had all gone off at once.

They'd been set off by Trix, not by his phone, but the theatre was everything.

'What do you want?' he asked reluctantly.

'I want you to step down and allow your family to replace you,' Marlowe said, holding up the disc as Ichabod went to fire his gun. 'Nah-uh. You kill me, you screw over your friend there, and your entire business deal dies.'

'Sounds like it dies anyway,' Ichabod growled.

'Not at all,' Marlowe shook his head. 'The vault's still got money in. Or maybe it doesn't, I've stolen your cash from it, and now you also owe everyone who bet on me. And the house always covers its bets, isn't that the saying?'

'I need to get to the vault.' Gabriel turned to leave, but Marlowe shook his hand, waving the case.

'I'll be going with you,' he replied.

Gabriel went to argue, but then stopped as his phone buzzed. He read the message and then smiled.

'Fine by me,' he said. 'Let's see if you or I pay out tonight, Mister Marlowe.'

Marlowe wondered what had just happened, but Trix, in his ear, gave him the answer.

'Interpol agents just breached the casino,' she said. 'Reilly and Massey are leading them. You need to—'

The voice stopped, and Marlowe paused, tapping his ear.

'You there?' he whispered.

Nothing.

At his voice, Gabriel looked back, a dark smile on his face.

'Sounds like someone just lost their eyes and ears,' he said. 'I do hope she wiped her ass before we shot her in the head.'

TRIX STARED UP AT THE ARMED GUARD, GUN AIMED DIRECTLY AT her face.

'Do you mind?' she asked with mock indignance. 'This is the ladies' room!'

The guard took a moment to lean in, staring around the cubicle, seeing the tech on display. He then leant back out, peering into the third cubicle, seeing the secured and unconscious guard there.

'Oh, you're so dead,' he snarled as he turned to face Trix, raising the gun up again, his finger tightening on the trigger as he waited for the command to fire.

27

CAVALRY

Trix swallowed, closing her eyes.

So this is how it ends.

However, there was a pause as the door to the bathroom opened, the gun rising slightly as the armed guard looked back at it.

'Change of plans,' a new, suited guard leant into the bathroom, nodding his head out into the casino. 'It's chaos out here and Interpol are in. Leave her.'

'I was told to get rid of her, and I don't know you,' the guard snapped, glaring back at the newcomer.

'Oh, yeah, sorry. My bad. I should have introduced myself. I'm Brad. I'm the distraction.'

'The what—'

The guard didn't get to say anything else, as Trix took the opportunity to wedge her taser between his shoulder and neck and turn it on, the shock jerking him back, his hand dropping the gun and his eyes rolling back into his head as he collapsed, twitching to the floor.

'We're blown,' Brad said. 'The chips have detonated, the

smoke's been added to by Interpol grenades. We need to use this to escape.'

'Clarissa?'

'Nowhere to be seen. I thought she was with you?'

Trix shook her head.

'I hope she knows what she's doing,' she replied, checking the feeds – as expected, they'd all gone dead now, but she'd planned for this. Hopefully, they were still uploading to a cloud server she'd set up. 'Marlowe?'

Brad paused, pushing his lips.

'He's on his own,' he muttered. 'Just as he asked.'

ONE THING YOU COULD SAY ABOUT THE CIA WAS THEY WERE efficient and fast, as the RAM van pulled up outside a warehouse just outside of Las Vegas. The term "safe house" didn't always mean a house, more a safe location, and because of this, they weren't that concerned at the surroundings Interpol had given as the two CIA agents climbed out of the front, walking around and unlocking the back doors.

Inside the van was a fully tricked-out ambulance. From the outside, you wouldn't have guessed what was going on; it resembled those stealth "van life" vehicles that digital nomads, usually making YouTube videos, drove around the world in. Inside, there was a gurney that clicked into a bed, with Lexi Warner on top and secured, unconscious again with a selection of cabinets and boxes to one side, and seats for a doctor and an EMT. The CIA agent and his colleague had been in the driver's cabin, separated by only a small window into the van.

Now, looking up as he opened the back doors, the driver

saw the door to the warehouse open, revealing three strangers. The first was a woman, slim with a short blonde bob, followed by two men. One was stick-thin and balding, and looked like he'd been in a fight, while the other, shorter and stockier, was favouring his side, as if he'd been punched in the side, or shoulder. The woman, obviously in charge, held up what looked to be an Interpol ID, but from the distance, the agent couldn't see it properly.

'Are you the ones Reilly sent to us?' she asked.

The agent nodded.

'I'm Special Agent Carson,' he replied. 'I was told to bring Miss Warner here, so you ...'

'Yeah, we've got it,' the woman interrupted, not giving her name or rank. 'You can just leave her there.'

'I'm sorry, ma'am, but we can't just "leave her" anywhere,' Carson said, glancing back at the doctor who was now climbing out of the van, helping the EMT beside him pull the gurney out, the legs locking open as it hit the car park asphalt.

'You don't need to see anything,' the Interpol lady retorted. 'I know what Reilly ordered. Your safe house was compromised; this one isn't. I'm not having any of you in here; I don't trust any of you. Give us the woman, turn around, and go home.'

'Our doctor ...' Carson began, but was cut off again, this time by the taller of the agents.

'We have our own doctors,' he said, a hint of amusement in his voice. 'Trust me, we all have EMT training.'

This seemed to be a private joke among the three Interpol agents, as they laughed.

Carson was starting to feel uncomfortable.

'I'd feel better if ...'

'I don't give a damn what you feel,' the woman snapped. 'You were given an order; if you don't like it, contact Massey and tell him you want to complain. I'm sure he'll deal with it after he sends you to Denver or wherever CIA agents go when they piss off their superiors.'

Carson clenched his jaw to avoid replying. He looked to the other CIA agent, but saw no agreement with the Interpol agent's words, and the doctor, deciding enough was enough, was already wheeling the gurney over to the Interpol agents. Carson was about to protest when another car, a Mustang, entered the car park, flashing its lights and beeping its horn.

It screeched to a stop, and Roxanne Vasquez jumped out of the passenger seat. Carson recognised her from the case files he'd been dealing with earlier that week.

'Don't give them Lexi,' she yelled. 'They're not real!'

'They're not *what?*' he asked, turning back to the woman, who, realising the ruse was over, had drawn her gun.

'She said we're not real,' she announced, firing the gun. 'Well, this is awkward.'

Roxanne and Ryan had driven like demons to get to the safe house after Trix had sent the address to Ryan Gates. They arrived just in time, too, it seemed – just as the confrontation was beginning.

The CIA agent, standing beside the gurney, was speaking, but the woman, likely the female EMT Marlowe had encountered the previous night, drew her weapon.

Roxanne couldn't identify it, assuming it was either a Glock or a Sig Sauer, the types Marlowe often used, and had shouted that she "wasn't real" – which was probably not the brightest idea at the time. As the woman fired, everyone dived for cover, and Ryan Gates drew his own gun, providing covering fire for the confused CIA agents, who backed out of the line of fire, using the back door of the van as their cover. As this happened, the shorter of the two imposters grabbed at the gurney, trying to pull it back into the warehouse. Roxanne, unarmed but determined, sprinted towards the gurney, yanking it out of his reach. Surprised, he attempted to pull back, forgetting he had a weapon for a moment. After a few tugs, he remembered, raising his gun.

Roxanne acted on instinct, a palm strike to the side of the man's chest – she'd remembered Marlowe and Brad saying one man had been shot, and if the woman was the same one from the previous night, the odds were this was the same man they shot, which meant even with a vest on, he'd be tender there.

He was more than tender, and he screamed in pain and anger as Roxanne went to strike again – but, before he could act, a round struck him between his eyes, and he collapsed, glassy eyes and dead.

Roxanne noticed one of the two CIA agents had fired and was now re-engaging in the fight. However, the fall of their colleague seemed to demoralise the other two fake Interpol agents, who raised their hands in surrender.

'This isn't worth the money,' the woman declared. 'I didn't sign on to die. I'm not some fanatic.'

'Then you can tell us what's going on,' Gates demanded, walking over and snatching the gun from her hand.

The woman laughed bitterly.

'More than my pay grade,' she said. 'But I do know whatever's happening, it's going on right now, and at the Gold Strike.'

Roxanne looked back at Gates – he didn't need to look back as he threw over the keys to Roxanne.

'Finish the story,' he said as she ran for the car, and the casino.

MARLOWE WAS PUSHED INTO THE VAULT ROOM FIRST, HIS HANDS in the air, as Gabriel Rizzo walked in behind him, gun aimed directly at the square of his back.

The vault room was surprisingly empty, with nothing more than a small canister in a corner which was hidden, almost out of the way. The vault door itself, however, was a different story. The foot-deep steel of the door had been cracked, and even on entering through the door and staring across the room, Gabriel could see that the lock had been tampered with.

'No, no, no,' he said as he ran across, noticing that the door was only open with an inch gap. At this, his worries and concerns turned into laughter as he looked back at Marlowe with a smile.

'You failed,' he said, holding his hands out, the gun no longer aimed at Marlowe. 'You failed. No payout for the idiots who believed you, who bet on you. All this time you thought you had everything planned, and all you managed was an inch.'

'All you need sometimes is an inch,' Marlowe said, shrugging.

Gabriel had expected Marlowe to be a little more contrite at this devastating loss, and frowned, looking back at the door.

'No,' he said, 'there's no way you got anything out of there.'

'Maybe, maybe not. You won't know until you have a look.'

Nodding, acknowledging the comment, Gabriel turned to the door, still watching Marlowe out of the corner of his eye as he did so, and slid his hand into the gap where the second ID scanner was hidden. His hand scan done, he then tapped in the code, a different one to the one that Marlowe had seen before from the other guards on the keypad.

Slowly, the vault door opened.

As Marlowe stood there at the entrance, he saw the contents of the casino's vault.

Pallets of dollar bills, high denomination, stacked into wads, and placed in columns, a good four feet in height and width, faced him. To the side, on a metal shelf, were sheets of bearer bonds, likely fifty or a hundred grand's worth per sheet. He could see gold bars at the back and maybe some jewellery, but not that much. The focus in the vault was on cash, which was logical, because the cash had been coming in constantly throughout the entire day.

At this, Gabriel Rizzo started to chuckle.

'There's close to a hundred million dollars there,' he said, 'and that's just this week's takings. Easily enough to pay my debt to Orchid.'

Marlowe shrugged.

'Currently,' he replied as Gabriel turned the gun back onto Marlowe now.

'I believe you have something of mine in your pocket,' he said.

Marlowe sighed, pulling out the CD case. Gabriel looked at Marlowe, looked into the vault, and then grinned.

'I'd tell you to throw it in,' he said, 'but you've already told me there's a distance limit on it.'

At this, Marlowe chuckled, shaking his head.

'You actually believed that I could put some kind of distance detonation device inside a CD?' he asked in disbelief. 'It was only to get you to bring me here.'

Gabriel Rizzo frowned as Marlowe, before he could say anything, tossed the CD case onto the top of the pallet of money.

Gabriel flinched – nothing happened.

'See? No explosion,' Marlowe smiled.

Gabriel watched Marlowe now, and Marlowe knew he was trying to work out what Marlowe's game plan was. Marlowe was too calm for someone who'd been caught out. Upstairs, chaos was happening, and Gabriel knew he had to sort something out fast, while his casino haemorrhaged money. Marlowe could see the cogs in his head turning as he looked from vault to Marlowe.

'What have you done?' he said.

Marlowe sniffed the air.

'Can you smell petrol?' he asked as he pointed at the canister half hidden in the room's corner. 'It's faint. No, wait. It's more like some kind of accelerant.'

Gabriel was still slow to what was going on and looked down at the canister in mounting horror, as Marlowe grinned a dark, vicious-looking smile.

'I told you that if that CD case went over twenty feet away from me, it would blow up,' he said. 'Which currently isn't happening, as I'm about what, fifteen, sixteen feet from it.'

'No.'

'Yes,' Marlowe nodded, almost sadly, taking two large steps away from the door – and as Gabriel Rizzo went to stop him, the twenty feet limit was reached, and there was an explosion inside the vault, where the device inside the CD had detonated in a tiny amount of flame and smoke.

'If you remember, the bet I made was that you would lose tens of millions of dollars tonight from your own vault,' he said, a hint of sadness in his voice. 'Looks like the house lost.'

Gabriel looked back at the vault as the dollar bills, soaked in accelerant provided by a weed sprayer, burst into flames from the small ignition, the flames licking at the ceiling and catching the bearer bonds on the sides; the fire spreading around the vault, the accelerant having been sprayed liberally and to the very end of the canister.

'No!' Gabriel screamed, but he had taken his eye off the ball, or, rather, the pissed-off spy standing directly in front of him. With a scream of anger and rage, Marlowe charged at Gabriel, moving in close before the man could raise his gun back up.

The two of them scuffled to the floor in a tumble of arms and legs; Gabriel's gun skidded across the ground, slamming against the corner. Marlowe didn't need to grab the gun; he had his own. However, as he reached for his CZ in his side holster, he realised it was missing.

It could have come out of his holster at any point over the last half an hour, especially when he was in the arena – more likely, it had fallen out a second earlier as he charged Gabriel but, quickly glancing around the room, Marlowe couldn't see it. Nevertheless, he needed to work out what to do now without his weapon, instead deciding to go for hand-to-hand combat, slamming down with his fist, punching hard into Gabriel's jaw.

Marlowe didn't know Gabriel's fighting style, but he had watched him in the arena the previous night and knew that

Gabriel had MMA history, or at least training. This meant that if they stayed close and grappled, there was every chance that Gabriel could find some way of grabbing a sleeper hold on Marlowe. So instead, he moved fast. Another punch to the face, a knee to the groin, pulling Gabriel up and slamming him face-first into the wall.

'You sent people after me,' he growled as the smoke filled the room. 'You played a fox game with me as the target.'

Slam.

Gabriel's face was thrown into the other wall.

'You thought you were powerful enough to destroy people's lives on a whim.'

Whuff.

A punch to the solar plexus sent Gabriel doubling over, the air punched out of his body.

Marlowe pulled him up, staring at him.

'You allied with the wrong people, Gabriel,' he said. 'You tried to *kill* the wrong people.'

At this, Gabriel Rizzo started chuckling through blood-stained teeth.

'You think *I* was the one who wanted you dead? You meant nothing to me, Marlowe. Your brother wanted you dead. Cody Donziger wanted you dead.'

'And yet still I stand.'

Marlowe went to continue, but Gabriel had gathered a bit of energy, and as Marlowe went to push him against the wall he spun, kicking out, taking Marlowe's knee.

Marlowe fell to one knee as Gabriel threw down what was the same move he'd used in the ring, a Superman punch given from a height.

The force of the blow rocked Marlowe. He hadn't expected such a solid punch. It made him stagger across the vault room. As he stumbled against the wall, Gabriel had every opportunity to work on this to gain an advantage, but he was already running to the vault door, staring at the flames, conflicted, trying to work out what could be saved.

'It was a mixture a friend of mine created,' Marlowe said, chuckling, wiping his face, clearing the blood from his mouth. 'Creates an exothermic reaction when mixed with oxygen, and can reach temperatures of up to three thousand degrees Fahrenheit, almost as hot as thermite. Another friend of mine coated the dollars in it for a good fifteen minutes before we came in.'

He clambered to his feet now.

'You're not getting any of that back,' he continued. 'If you're lucky, the jewels and the gold will be melted but intact, but by then I think you'll find the police, the FBI, maybe even Interpol will be involved.'

Gabriel turned and glared at Marlowe.

'You're working with her,' Marlowe said, rubbing at his jaw. 'I know. I heard the tape. She wanted the money, but it looks like she didn't get it either.'

Gabriel glanced back at the money burning away in front of his eyes.

'You only have one choice now,' Marlowe continued. 'You have to give up. There's nothing there for you. No insurance will cover this money, or cover your bet losses. Orchid won't believe that it's gone because there won't be anything left by the time the money burns – nothing left but ash. They'll believe you've taken the money, tried to run with it.'

He waved around the room.

'Your only chance now is to start anew. Your men are already waiting for your sister to take over. Orchid won't work with you anymore. Cody Donziger and Byron Coleman are once more nobodies,' he said. 'You've lost. Your only game plan now is to claim immunity with the authorities. And if you come with me now, I'll make sure that happens.'

Gabriel wanted to scream and shout at Marlowe, and Marlowe could see this clearly on his face. But he knew also that Marlowe was telling the truth; there was no other opportunity here for him.

Sighing, he turned back to Marlowe—

There was an explosion from the vault, the flames engulfing him as he did so.

Marlowe quickly realised there must have been something liquid and flammable in the vault he hadn't figured on – no, that wasn't completely true; he'd guessed there could be items like expensive perfumes or spirits in there, flammable liquids, explosive at the temperature, he just didn't figure anyone would stand directly in front of the vault as the items exploded.

The scream Gabriel made as the liquid fire licked at him was louder and more shrill than Marlowe had ever heard from anyone as, engulfed in flames, Gabriel staggered back.

Marlowe, however, had already pulled off his jacket and was jumping onto Gabriel, smothering the flames, patting them out as the burning man passed out from the pain. The clothing that Gabriel wore was burned, and he had bad-looking burns appearing on his face, but compared to Lexi Warner, he'd got off lightly.

Marlowe picked the unconscious Gabriel Rizzo up, with a last look at the burning millions, and a quick scan for his missing gun, he grabbed Gabriel's discarded Glock 17 and left the vault room to its demise.

28

BURN IT DOWN

ON THE CASINO FLOOR, IT WAS CHAOS. THE SMOKE FROM THE grenades, mixed with smoke thrown by Interpol agents as they moved through the main area, caused an almost blindness for the agents as they made their way past screaming and terrified gamblers, watching for their targets.

Seeing this, Brad and Trix kept to the back wall, staying low to avoid inhaling the smoke.

'You know the plan,' Brad said.

'I wrote the plan,' Trix nodded.

They were about to discuss further when an armoured Interpol officer appeared in the smoke, his helmet and mask keeping the smoke out of his eyes and mouth, facing them, gun in hand.

Brad straightened up.

'Then fulfil it,' he said. 'I'll speak to you later.'

Before Trix could reply, Brad had already decided his next plan of action, and started moving towards the armed officer, the smoke engulfing them both. Trix, hoping Brad had played his cards right and made the correct decision, turned and continued along the wall, pausing a minute later as she heard gunshots behind her.

Brad was a big boy and knew what he was doing, but the uncertainty of the outcome lingered in her mind.

There was a chance this entire plot could go terribly wrong.

However, as she neared the door, she drew to a stop, because a gun rested against the back of her head.

'Miss Preston,' Interpol Agent Sandra Reilly said, her voice muffled by the gas mask she wore over her mouth and nose. 'How good of you to finally turn up.'

Trix slumped against the wall.

For now, her job was over.

Roxanne had returned to the Gold Strike Hotel in the Mustang, leaving Ryan Gates with the CIA agents, helping secure the fake Interpol agents. She knew he'd be okay, as he'd saved the agents lives so he obviously had to be on their side, and a call to Sasha would sort things, but she also wondered whether what she now did was more of a mistake, as she kept her foot down on the accelerator through the Las Vegas strip, horn blaring, tourists diving out of her way as she turned off, heading eastwards.

Screeching up to the front of the Gold Strike, she disregarded the need for valets or parking permission; the crowds of terrified patrons streaming out of the hotel and casino showed the futility of seeking assistance.

Upon entering the casino, Roxanne pushed through the escaping gamblers and guests into a world of smoke and noise. She'd grabbed a CIA coat from the hire car, likely Brad's, as the Las Vegas evening was too cool for nothing more than a strapless cocktail frock. With it on, passing through the now discarded metal detectors, she realised, unsurprisingly, they didn't go off, as she entered the main casino area once more.

The fruit machines were oblivious to the chaos, the sounds of gunshots echoing in the open and fogged area, still playing their music, and casting a blue, red, and yellow glow in the smoke.

It was strangely reassuring, but she paid them no mind as she focused on her task.

There was the sound of talking to the right of her, and she turned, making her way over. After a minute of blindly groping through the smoke, Roxanne eventually faced Trix Preston, standing still against a wall.

'Are you okay—' she started, but the words trailed away. The smoke was clearing and, next to Trix, Roxanne could see a woman with a gas mask and a windbreaker jacket similar to Roxanne's own, but with hers bearing the Interpol logo.

This must be the infamous Sandra Reilly, she thought to herself.

'We're not the enemy here,' Roxanne said as Reilly turned her gun towards her.

'I'm the one to decide who's the enemy or not,' Reilly replied with a smile, motioning with her pistol for Roxanne to join Trix. 'And currently, you're high on my shit list.'

'There's two of us and one of you,' Roxanne said. 'You can't kill us both.'

'Roxanne, please,' Trix said, a pained expression on her face. 'Don't give her ideas.'

'It's okay, Preston, she's just giving us some bad maths,' Reilly smiled. 'She's assuming I only have one gun.'

As she spoke, two Interpol agents, helmeted and

armoured, appeared through the remaining smoke, rifles ready.

Roxanne looked at them, placing her hands on her hips.

'Are these Las Vegas SWAT?' she asked. 'Because I seem to recall my law school training states you can only use assets from a local agency.'

'You as well?' Reilly shook her head in disbelief. 'Christ, you Yanks are anal about shit like that. All you need to know is these armed men are loyal to me.'

Roxanne wasn't listening, looking back at the two figures.

'So, are all Interpol agents as corrupt as this woman?' she asked. 'Is that why you're here, breaking the law? Are you even Interpol? Did she pick you off the street?'

Neither agent replied. The taller of the two glanced at Reilly.

'Is the order given, ma'am?' he asked, his voice European.

'Marlowe isn't here yet,' Reilly shook her head. 'As I said in the van, he's the one I'm waiting for.'

Roxanne laughed.

'Do you seriously think he's bringing you the money? The entire plan was to destroy it.'

'You'd better hope he didn't,' Reilly replied. 'Because if he *has* burned my money, then you'll die.'

Roxanne mouth-shrugged as she leant against the wall.

'Lexi Warner says hi,' she said. 'Your fake agents failed. In the end decided the hassle of being tied to you was more than their pay grade.'

She looked at the two armed agents.

'You should consider joining them—'

She flinched as Reilly whipped her pistol against her cheek, sending her staggering back.

'Next time I pull the trigger,' she hissed. 'Shut up, stand there and wait.'

Roxanne rubbed at her cheek, seeing it'd been split open at the lip.

'You'll pay for that, you bitch,' she muttered.

'The only person paying here is your boyfriend,' Reilly sighed, looking back into the fog. 'Just as soon as he brings me my bloody money.'

THE JOURNEY UP FROM THE LOWER LEVELS TOOK LONGER THAN Marlowe expected. He hadn't factored in that he'd be dragging the burned and unconscious Gabriel Rizzo with him. But as he entered the corridor that eventually led into the casino, he paused.

Byron Coleman, still Ichabod in Marlowe's mind, stood watching him, a gun in his hand.

'You've destroyed everything,' he said. 'You've taken everything I planned and thrown it away.'

'No,' Marlowe replied, sighing. 'I'll guarantee you still have the money you made from your father. You'll have the profits from his death and the sale of *Arachis* assets. What I've taken from you is your access to an organisation you had no right to. What I've taken from you is a company you created with enemies.'

He placed the unconscious Gabriel Rizzo down for a moment.

'Your choice now is whether you want to risk everything on revenge against me, or escape out the side door and start afresh. We can always have this fight some other time.'

'If I don't kill you now, the Gravedigger will kill you,'

Ichabod smiled. 'He was so pissed at Gabriel starting the game on you last night.'

'He's also not the Gravedigger,' Marlowe shook his head. '*He's* in Ukraine at the moment.'

Ichabod pursed his lips, trying to hold his anger at bay.

'That's how you knew what was going on,' he said. 'You had a mole.'

'I had more than one mole,' Marlowe replied. 'I had half of Orchid on my side.'

'That leaves the other half against you. This isn't over yet,' Ichabod glanced down at the burned body. 'Let me take him. He's my friend. You've got your revenge.'

'Be aware that there are Interpol and CIA agents outside waiting for him,' Marlowe motioned for Ichabod to take the body. 'If you take him, you'll be taken by them.'

Ichabod looked down at Gabriel, then back at Marlowe, and smiled.

'Then you take him,' he said. 'I can always make more friends. Until next time, *brother*.'

And with that, he turned and left into the smoke-filled corridor, pulling a key from his pocket as he did so. Marlowe recognised the key; it was the same style as the one used by a guard the first time they took Marlowe to Gabriel's office; the one that controlled the elevator.

Ichabod was going for the briefcase of bearer bonds.

'Good luck, brother,' Marlowe muttered, half under his breath.

There was a groan, and Marlowe looked down. Gabriel had awoken and had probably been feigning unconsciousness, hearing every word of the previous conversation.

'Looks like your friends aren't who you thought they were,' Marlowe said as he hefted him up. 'Pretty much a good time to start a new life, maybe make some new friends. And I know just the person who can help you with that.'

Marlowe gently carried the still groaning Gabriel Rizzo through the casino. The smoke was thinning, but it was still thick enough to limit visibility to fifty or sixty feet before fading into whiteness, the sounds of shouting and crashing in the background creating a strange white noise effect as they walked through the discarded poker area. Thus, Marlowe was unprepared for the sudden appearance of a crowd of people by the wall. In particular, two armed Interpol agents in full tactical gear, one aiming their weapon at him, the other covering Roxanne and Trix ...

And Agent Reilly standing in the middle, hands on hips.

'You've brought me Gabriel Rizzo,' she said. 'But you don't seem to have brought me the money.'

'The money was several pallets in size,' Marlowe replied. 'There was no way I was bringing you that.'

'And the bearer bonds?'

Marlowe looked at Gabriel Rizzo.

'This man has serious burn injuries,' he said. 'He needs to be seen by a doctor.'

'And he will be,' Reilly replied. 'After you explain to me where my money is.'

Marlowe sighed, gently placing Gabriel down.

'Your money's gone,' he replied. 'Burned up. You can go check downstairs if you want, but all you'll find is a smoking pile of ashes. Maybe some jewels, a couple of gold bars. Not enough for the life you expected, and certainly not enough to live it out in an extradition-free country.'

Reilly narrowed her eyes.

'You promised me,' she said.

'I promised you whatever I took from the vault would

be yours,' Marlowe said. He pointed at Gabriel Rizzo. '*That* is what I took from the vault. I kept my word. It's not my fault you didn't phrase it right. Feel free to check your recording.'

Reilly didn't need to. She knew she'd been played. She started to laugh.

'You know what this means, don't you?'

Slowly, Marlowe nodded.

'I do,' he replied. 'But I'd rather go out this way than have you believe that you'd won.'

He looked around the now empty casino.

'Massey?'

'No idea,' Reilly shrugged. 'I aimed him at the arena. You know, to keep him out of the way. Between us, I think he was regretting the arrangement we had. I know I was.'

'Clever,' Marlowe nodded. 'It's what I would have done. Did he give you the file on me?'

Reilly nodded.

'I'd never even heard of you,' she said. 'I'd heard about Westminster, and of course seen the A40 footage, but I didn't put it together until Massey explained.'

'When did you meet?'

'A couple of weeks back,' Reilly shrugged, more relaxed. Marlowe assumed it was because she held all the cards right now. 'He had a roadblock in the way of his promotion, and I'd been working Rizzo.'

'Why didn't he go to the FBI?'

'Moles,' Reilly laughed. 'Claimed he had three on his books already. Interpol though? We were incorruptible.'

'How little people know,' Roxanne muttered.

'I realised very early on though that what he had was crap,' Reilly replied. 'He was talking about secret cabals and shit, and I reckoned he was one of the tinfoil hat brigade. Decided to get what I could from him.'

'You extorted him.'

'I like to call it incentivised,' Reilly shrugged. 'But then he shit the bed, recorded us, said my name. I needed to clean up his mess, and here was a CIA agent who had the answer. He needed his boss embarrassed, and her favourite pet was turning up to a wake.'

Marlowe bristled at the "pet" line, but kept quiet.

'So, you read the file, saw my worth and decided to use me against Rizzo.'

'I outsourced it to you, true,' Reilly shook her head. 'But I now realise you should never let a man do a woman's job.'

She glanced at the two Interpol officers beside her.

'Is the order given?' the first said. He'd been asking this question since the van, and now finally, he got it.

'The order was never mine to give,' she said with a smile. 'It's yours to decide.'

With this stated, the two Interpol agents looked at each other, decided this was a "yes", and then opened fire on Marlowe, Trix, and Roxanne.

However, the moment it happened, it suddenly looked as if Reilly hadn't wanted to do it.

As the bodies now lay on the casino carpet, the smoke still half-obscuring them, she gave out a yell of anger and frustration as she turned to the two armed Interpol agents.

'What did you do?' she asked, frowning. 'I gave no order!'

'But you said—'

'I know what I said,' Reilly replied. 'I gave you the option to make your own decision. One that ended in murder. How will that look on both of your reports?'

She leant in.

'You're *mine* now. Heart and soul,' she replied, nodding at Gabriel. 'Take the asset out and find someone who can patch him up.'

As the two agents gathered up the barely conscious, moaning Gabriel, Reilly took a deep breath, letting it out.

Of *course* she wanted them dead – they were loose ends. With Marlowe, his tech bitch, and the mouthy lawyer gone, the disc burnt to ash and Gabriel Rizzo now under her control, there was nobody who could tie her to any of this, apart from Lexi Warner, and she could easily close that down. Even the agents who'd performed her bidding could be used there, if needed. But she needed to have plausible deniability in case the shit hit the fan.

And the shit *always* hit the fan.

Reynard Massey would soon realise he'd made a terrible mistake, but by then everything would be over. She'd lost the money, sure, but Rizzo wasn't stupid. He would have squirrelled away something somewhere – she could still come out of this a millionaire once he gave it all up for his life.

Plus, with the witnesses gone, she could even keep her professional life for a while longer.

Hell, she might even get a *promotion* out of this, after all – before she retired for the life of luxury.

29

OUT OF THE FIRE

BY THE TIME THE NOW RATHER CALM AGENT REILLY EXITED THE casino, the crowds had eased down, but the Las Vegas police had now arrived, and both FBI and local officers were milling around, trying to sort things out. Reynard Massey, along with a couple of CIA agents next to him, were doing their best to control the situation, but she knew he was out of his depth. She'd realised that the moment she'd seen him for the first time.

Massey had effectively given her full control, and allowed her to fill the van with her own people. He was with some freshly arrived CIA agents now, sure, but it was too late. He'd expected to gain Rizzo as a prize, prove he was better than his bitch of a boss, but all he was walking away with now was a casino in flames.

Sucks to be you, Reynard. So much for being a cunning fox.

An FBI officer, seeing Agent Reilly, stormed over to her.

'What the hell do you think—' he started, but stopped as Reilly held up a hand.

'Interpol doesn't need to tell you what we're doing,' she

explained. 'We were part of a joint campaign with the NSA and CIA. It was national security, above your pay grade. All you need to know is we've taken down a terrorist organisation, and we'll be arranging to have the terrorists moved for questioning.'

She turned, shouting at some EMTs beside an ambulance.

'I need to take your vehicle,' she shouted. 'We have a downed asset.'

As she did this, the two uniformed Interpol agents wheeled a gurney, with the unconscious and badly burned Gabriel Rizzo on it out of the doorway towards the ambulance. At that moment, Reynard Massey, realising Reilly was in his vicinity, also started marching over to her.

'This was your plan?' he inquired. 'Utter chaos?'

'I didn't think it would go so far,' Reilly replied honestly. 'And I didn't hear you complaining when you thought you were going to get promoted.'

Massey glared around the forecourt, taking in the full scale of what had happened.

'Marlowe?'

'Dead,' Reilly replied. 'I don't know how. I think it was during the chaos within, possibly by Gabriel Rizzo himself.'

One of the EMTs was running over to the ambulance, helping Gabriel into the van. Reilly turned to two Las Vegas police officers walking out of the casino, ignoring Massey for the moment.

'Everything okay?' she asked.

'All clear,' the closest officer said. 'Everyone's out, bar some old woman, and we're helping her now.'

'And the dead?'

The police officers looked at each other, confused.

'There's no dead in there,' the closest one replied. 'The smoke's clearing. We would have seen them.'

Glancing back at Massey for a moment, shaking her head, Reilly turned her ire back to the officers.

'There are three bodies by the side wall in the casino,' she said. 'One of them is a New York lawyer. The other two are British nationals, both of whom work for His Majesty's Secret Service. You might want to ...'

'They told you, they've already looked,' the FBI officer she'd first argued with interrupted. 'And I don't know what you're playing at, but I don't appreciate your games.'

Reilly frowned.

'What the hell do you mean by that?'

'The casino is clear.'

The police officer nodded, stepping forward.

'Ma'am, we know what we're doing, unlike your guys ...'

'Unlike my guys?'

'Half a dozen of your Interpol guys, out like babies, piled in a corner,' the other police officer laughed, punching his partner's arm. 'One was draped over some guy in his under-wear, snoring away!'

Reilly turned and faced Massey.

'What did you do?' she demanded.

'Me?' Massey shook his head. 'I did nothing. You told me you had this sorted. You promised me promotions. But all I'm seeing here is ...'

He trailed off as he looked back at the ambulance.

'I'll be with you in a minute,' he said, leaving Reilly alone as he marched off again. Reilly sighed, holding back her fury. She'd guessed Marlowe would try to screw her over, but this was even more annoying.

He was dead. She saw him die. It was why she'd relaxed,

walked outside—

It was why she relaxed. Why she took her eye off the ball.

'Oh, you bastard,' she muttered to herself, looking around, but then stopped as she spied the entrance to the casino again. There was an old lady being wheeled out by the FBI in a wheelchair; a woman that Reilly recognised.

'You,' she called out, walking over. 'You came in with Trix. Where have you been? Why did it take you so long to get out?'

Clarissa glared at Reilly and then pointed at the wheelchair.

'None of your bastard friends in their oh, so scary tactical gear and guns helped me,' she retorted. 'I had to hide behind a slot machine until you stopped shooting.'

She started to move away, but Reilly grabbed at her.

'My men ...' she began, but Clarissa yanked away with a pull on the wheel, turning round and smiling darkly at Reilly.

'Your men?' she questioned. 'Do you mean your Interpol agents who were with you in the van? You had eight, didn't you? Doesn't look like you have eight anymore.'

Reilly looked from Clarissa to the two police officers, now taking statements from witnesses. In the chaos, she'd assumed her agents were still inside, or somewhere else. The police had claimed they were disabled, and dumped in a back room – but by who? Certainly not some ancient bitch with no leg.

There were only two Interpol agents now, and they were still dealing with the ambulance, helping Gabriel onto the bed as a doctor climbed in behind him.

Raymond Massey stood beside the ambulance, looking as if he was going to be sick.

'Hold on a moment,' she shouted, running over to it. 'That's my collar. He's my asset to be interviewed.'

The Interpol agent standing closest turned, blocking her way. He was the one who'd asked about the order back in the van, who'd shot Marlowe in the casino.

'I think not, ma'am,' he said, and for the first time, Reilly realised his accent, European at first, was now decidedly more British than before.

'Give me your name and rank before I end your bloody career right here, right now,' she snapped angrily.

The Interpol agent nodded, pulling off his helmet and mask. Behind it was the face of a man in his late sixties, maybe seventy – although he looked good for it, with close-cropped grey hair, and a nose that had seen many fights and breaks over the years. He rubbed his hands through his hair and looked around.

'My name? It's Marshall Kirk,' he said. 'I don't really have a rank, as I'm kind of retired at the moment, but I'm sure you know who I am.'

He smiled.

'After all, you seem to know so much about Thomas Marlowe from the file Mister Massey here shared with you.'

Byron Coleman had always ensured he had a back exit available. He knew from the start that there might be people with a grudge against his father who could take it out on him. It was one reason he was glad Marlowe had appeared in the first place; it was always sensible to provide two potential targets for someone aiming at the heir to the Taylor-Coleman fortune.

He needed to thank whoever faked the invite – once he found them. And then? He'd kill them.

As it was, he could hear the chaos above him as he hurried down the back corridors of the Gold Strike casino, clutching a thin, metal briefcase. It contained over two million dollars' worth of bearer bonds, and there was no way he was letting it go anytime soon. He'd retrieved it from Gabriel Rizzo's office the moment he'd left Marlowe, right after all hell broke loose, knowing things were going south. Now he was quickly making his escape. He'd lost money on this, but at least with the briefcase, he'd have some funds to plan his next move.

He halted as a figure emerged in front of him.

St John Steele, a gun in his leather-gloved hand, confronted him.

'Mister Coleman,' he said. 'I'm sorry to be the bearer of bad news, but your journey ends here.'

Byron laughed.

'You're not the Arbitrator anymore, St John,' he retorted, hugging the briefcase now. 'And more importantly, as you've all made such a point of stating, I'm not a member of Orchid. I'll do whatever I damn well please, and you're not getting this.'

Steele advanced, gun still raised.

'You don't understand,' he replied. 'I'm not after the bearer bonds in that briefcase. I'm here to say your race is over. Your journey has ended, and it's time for you to join your father.'

Byron laughed, then stopped, realising Steele's seriousness.

'What the hell is this?' he demanded. 'My father and you were allies.'

'Your father and I worked together, nothing more,' Steele countered. 'And now that's over. Your arrogance, your belief that you were above everyone in Orchid. It all led to this. I saw your ambitions during Lucian Delacroix's takeover. You thought you could join him, or if he failed, were destined to surpass him.'

He shook his head.

'You were correct on one of those points, though. Now you'll join him.'

St John Steele punctuated this by firing three quick shots from his gun into Byron's chest, directly above the briefcase.

Byron, in shock, stared at his bleeding shirt, then collapsed, gasping, as the briefcase fell to the ground beside him. Steele placed the gun – a Czech CZ 75BD pistol – next to Byron's body. It wasn't a weapon he typically used, having only picked it up once, and his prints wouldn't be found on it, having wiped it down when he gained it from Marlowe in the arena, before pulling his gloves on.

Granted, this also meant Marlowe's fingerprints would be hard to find, but Steele wasn't looking to have Marlowe arrested by the authorities; he had a bigger game to play here, one which started with Marlowe being blamed for his brother's murder.

Byron had been right, the poor, blind fool. St John Steele wasn't the Orchid Arbitrator anymore.

Now, he was planning on becoming something *bigger*.

There was a noise further down the corridor, and Steele stopped, wondering if he was about to be found. However, it seemed to be nothing more than background noise from the chaos upstairs. Deciding he was finally safe, he picked up the blood-spattered metal briefcase and opened it.

Bloody fool hadn't even locked it.

After a moment of examination, however, he tossed the briefcase away, allowing it to clatter against the corridor wall, the sheaf of blank A4 printer paper within it fluttering across the floor as he did so, angrily rising to his feet.

The bearer bonds he knew should have been inside had been taken.

Looking back at Byron Coleman's body, he wondered if the idiot son had even bothered to check the case before taking it. Probably not.

He sighed, looking up at the ceiling before laughing.

Marlowe. It had to be.

Marlowe was the only other person who could have done it. But when? There was no way; Marlowe hadn't even been in the office that evening, he didn't have a key to the office elevator, and the authorities would have stopped anyone leaving with bearer bonds – even if he survived against a pissed-off Gabriel Rizzo without his precious CZ pistol.

He could hear sirens in the distance. This was a conversation for another time.

Steele looked down at the gun.

Thomas Marlowe and St John Steele would have that conversation very soon.

AGENT SANDRA REILLY STARED IN HORROR AT MARSHALL.

'But there were two of you,' she said.

'There were,' Marshall waved for the other agent who'd exited with him to walk back. The agent was already pulling off his helmet and mask, and Reilly saw the familiar face of CIA agent Brad Haynes grinning at her.

'I found this on an unconscious officer,' he said, pointing

at his uniform. 'It's amazing how many unconscious Interpol people there are in a back room in that casino right now.'

Marshall shrugged as Reilly stared back at him, finally realising what the police officers had been talking about.

'I got a bit carried away with a taser and a shit ton of smoke,' Marshall admitted. 'They'll be okay in the morning, though.'

Reilly reached for her gun, but Marshall held a hand up, waggling a finger in a "nuh-uh" gesture.

'I wouldn't,' he warned. 'You're surrounded by FBI, police, and *actual* CIA. Proper authorities, not rip-off artists who want to steal and get away with it. And, the moment you start anything, we'll have to tell them *everything*.'

'You have nothing on me,' Reilly snapped, glancing around for any potential allies. Doing this, she saw Reynard Massey looking like he had been kicked in the bollocks, walking towards her, waving for the two Las Vegas police officers to come over to him.

'Arrest this woman,' he said. His voice had lost all the commanding lustre it had earlier. It was almost as if he was commanding the men to do something that he'd been ordered to do. As Reilly looked back at the ambulance, she saw a woman climbing into the back, closing the doors.

She knew the woman. It was Reynard Massey's boss. *The woman who changed her name depending on the day and the weather.*

Reynard Massey watched Reilly carefully.

'I unfortunately won't be able to see what happens to you,' he said, 'as I've been recently transferred.'

Marshall made a mock-horrified look.

'Oh no,' he said. 'Surely being found to have sided with a corrupt Interpol agent, giving sensitive CIA files to her, and having lost an informant in the process didn't cause you any trouble?'

Brad patted Massey on the shoulder.

'Couldn't happen to a nicer man,' he said. 'Send me a postcard when you get to wherever it is in the Arctic Circle they're sending you.'

Reilly had moved backwards, realising that she was trapped no matter what, but in doing so, she walked back into the FBI agent, now standing behind her.

'We'd like to have a word with you about a video message we've just received,' he said. 'You are Sandra Reilly of Interpol?'

'Yes,' Sandra's muscles slackened and her shoulders slumped as she realised she wasn't getting out of this. 'I was set up.'

'I'm sure you were,' the FBI agent replied. 'But until we know for sure, I'm afraid you're coming with us, ma'am. You see, we have you conspiring with hitmen to not only abduct and kill a witness *twice* but also extort money from an agent of a foreign country.'

'An agent of a foreign ...' Reilly trailed off.

Bloody Tom Marlowe.

'I haven't done anything like that,' she said. 'This is all ...'

She paused as Brad Haynes pulled his phone out, clicking play.

'There's no money to be made from the heist, if it was even going to happen,' Marlowe's voice said. *'It'd be a revenge job.'*

'Then you won't mind passing it on then, will you?' Reilly spoke. As the conversation continued, Brad looked sadly at Reilly.

'Did you honestly think that while you were recording him, he wasn't recording you?' he asked.

Reilly thought back to the moment they met; Marlowe had been on his phone, placing it into his outside breast pocket as she started speaking – she was so confident she'd caught him unawares, she hadn't even considered he'd instantly started recording as he placed it away.

'Shh,' Marshall pulled at his arm. 'I like this part.'

'Whatever's in the vault would be nice to have.'

'I don't really have a choice here, do I?'

'Not really. Here we go, let's make a little contract, shall we? You just speak into this device and confirm that you'll be providing me with the money.'

'Fine, I, Thomas Marlowe, hereby state that any money we gain from the vault of the Gold Strike Casino will be passed to Interpol agent Sandra Reilly.'

Brad turned it off.

'There's more, but we both know how it goes. And it can be listened next to the other recording, the one just sent to the FBI, where you tell ... Now, what was it ...'

Marshall pulled his phone out now, showing a paused video image of Gabriel Rizzo in his office.

'Let me help you there, partner,' he said as he pressed play.

'Screw you, Reilly, you're just lining your pocket. I want you to get me out of this, make sure I walk clean, or I tell everyone what you've been up to, and how your little "retirement fund" is growing.'

'Ooh, that doesn't sound good,' he paused it again, shaking his head as the FBI agent grabbed Reilly's hands, cuffing them behind her back.

Reilly shook her head.

'I don't get it,' she said. 'You shot him, you made me think he was dead.'

'Of course we did,' Marshall replied. 'If you thought there was still any chance of not getting away with everything you did, you wouldn't have walked out so cleanly. You'd have left through the side, or found a way to cover your back. This was the only way to have you trussed and tied like a turkey.'

Marshall Kirk smiled at Reynard Massey, who still looked like he was about to throw up. He'd watched Massey storm over to them, confused when he'd seen Sasha Bordeaux appear to the side. He'd then seen the message on her phone, that from the President himself, Anton McKay, explaining that whatever she did was on his behalf – as she told Massey he was now demoted, and could step down after he'd performed one last task for her.

Like many people in Vegas, Reynard Massey had banked everything on the roll of a dice. But unfortunately for him, they had come up snake eyes.

'So, where's your man?' Massey sighed, looking back into the casino.

Marshall Kirk shrugged. 'You know Marlowe,' he said. 'He's probably not even in the state anymore. His job's done.'

GABRIEL RIZZO WAS HALF UNCONSCIOUS AS THE AMBULANCE started towards the hospital, sirens blaring, and Sasha Bordeaux leant close to his ear.

'Hello, Gabriel,' she smiled. 'We're about to become close friends. My name's René Montoya, and we're going to have a lovely talk about family ...'

30

DEBRIEFINGS

As it was, Marshall Kirk hadn't been correct; Marlowe was still in the state, and by the time Brad and Marshall had given their debriefs, removed their fake uniforms and escaped before anyone could ask the questions they should already have asked, Brad returning to wherever Sasha was, and Marshall returning to the King suite of the Paris Vegas Hotel, Marlowe was already there and waiting.

The story had been very simple. Sasha Bordeaux had explained to Washington that she had found out about a rogue Interpol agent turning an unsuspecting and naïve CIA agent named Massey, and had set up her own team to sting them out. This way, Marlowe and his friends weren't officially involved in any paperwork, more so than just attending a funeral – or a conference in Roxanne's case, and more importantly, couldn't be targeted for anything illegal.

It also gave her full credit, but Marlowe didn't care about that. He was happier to keep his name out of the spotlight.

It was another hour before Marlowe learnt of the death of his half-brother.

It had been Clarissa who found out about this and, as she arrived in her wheelchair, she gave Marlowe the news. Byron had been found shot in a backroom corridor of the hotel, an empty briefcase beside him.

Marlowe had punched the wall in anger; he'd been surprised by how much the news had affected him if he was being honest. Ichabod hadn't really been the closest of family. For a start, family rarely tried to have you killed.

He must have gone for the bearer bonds, Marlowe considered. He'd seen the key in Ichabod's hand and had assumed that was his plan, anyway. Ichabod was looking for something to get out of the whole mess, perhaps thought it was his property, but then someone found him in the corridor, shot him and took them – or at least whatever was in the briefcase – before running off.

Roxanne, sitting at the table, looked up at Marlowe.

'You don't seem surprised.'

'That he went for the briefcase, or that there was nothing in it?'

Marlowe replied with a raised eyebrow.

'A bit of both.'

Marlowe shrugged.

'I'd made arrangements,' he replied casually.

'There's one other thing,' Clarissa said. 'Your gun you've been using for the last few days, it's not a normal one, is it?'

'It's not a Sig or a Glock if that's what you mean. It's a Czech gun. A CZ 75BD. Problem?'

Clarissa nodded.

'They found it next to the body. It's the gun that killed him.'

Marlowe felt a sliver of ice go down his spine. He'd lost

his gun earlier that night. To have it kill his brother and be left beside the body was definitely a message.

'Do they—'

'I'm not sure about anything,' Clarissa interrupted. 'All I know from my sources is they have the gun, but they can't find fingerprints. Whoever used it wiped it down, probably to take their own off.'

She narrowed her eyes.

'Unless you were down in the back corridors at some point?'

'Only with Gabriel. And trust me, we didn't find Ichabod – Byron – when we were down there,' Marlowe shook his head. 'But there ... there was a moment when I entered the back rooms with Steele and Shida. When I was walking down to the arena, there was a commotion, someone knocked me and I bumped into Steele.'

He trailed off, thinking back to the moment.

'If I'd have known you wanted to give me a hug, Mister Marlowe, I'd have worn a better jacket.'

St John Steele had not only stolen his gun, but had possibly even killed Ichabod for the money, blaming Marlowe in the process.

'The gun can't be linked to you, right?'

'No.'

'Can it be linked to the Gravedigger, or whatever his real name is?'

'Ryan Gates,' Marlowe replied. 'And no, I asked him when I picked it up, and he said whoever it'd be linked back to is buried in an Arizona desert, so I think we're safe there.'

He stopped, thinking through the situation.

'The police won't be able to pin anything on me,' he said. 'But Orchid will take this as some kind of message, either for good or for bad. If it was him, then St John Steele is doing his best to cause some kind of unrest, a conflict in the group. I'm not exactly sure how we should play this.'

Trix watched Marlowe as she spoke.

'Must have been a shock to find that the briefcase was empty,' she said. 'Do you think Ichabod knew?'

'He wouldn't be carrying it down corridors if he knew, I would have thought,' Marlowe replied. 'I'm sorry to hear he's dead, but he wasn't exactly proving himself to be a fine member of my family.'

'So, what do you think happened to the bearer bonds?' Trix looked at Clarissa now. 'Would you know, by chance?'

Clarissa chuckled as she leant forward.

'Do me a favour,' she said. 'Pull out my back seat.'

Trix did so and found a cardboard folder wedged between the back of the wheelchair and the cushion itself. It was slightly larger than A4 and fitted the space perfectly.

'Tell me that's not what I think it is,' Trix whispered.

Clarissa passed the folder over to Marlowe, who opened it up, revealing a wad of bearer bonds, each one worth fifty thousand dollars.

'Is this a job interview, Mister Marlowe? Because I'm impressed. I'll hire you. What are your rates? I have a briefcase of bearer bonds just waiting to be spent. Tax free and everything. Name your price. It'll be double, triple the pittance MI5 give.'

'I saw the case when I was up there with Roxanne the first night,' he said. 'Rizzo offered me some of them to work for him, and when Reilly asked for it as an additional incentive to her blackmail, I guessed it was something more than I'd considered. Maybe even millions more than thousands. While you were sorting out the casino, I had Clarissa go up to his office and, well, let's just say acquire it for me.'

'How?' Marshall asked. 'You said there was a key needed?'

'Ryan's mate Atkins gave him his key so Ryan could go to Gabriel's bedroom and scare the piss out of him,' Marlowe explained. 'He gave it to me to pass back. I just did it in a roundabout way, via Clarissa.'

'Jesus,' Trix was flicking through the bonds. 'There's almost four million here.'

'Three million actually,' Marlowe said, looking back at Clarissa. 'A million was payment for the task and for the help she's given us.'

Clarissa smiled, nodding at Marlowe as he counted out a thick wad of sheets of bearer bonds and passed them to her.

'This'll keep my network going very well,' she held them up, actually examining the bonds she'd stolen, as if expecting them to be forgeries. 'You ever need anything, Marlowe? You call. I kind of owe you now.'

'Yes, you do,' Marlowe smiled as the door to the suite opened, and Brad Haynes walked in.

'Christ,' he said, staring at the wad of bearer bonds. 'I thought we didn't steal anything?'

'We stole nothing from the vault,' Marshall laughed from the sofa as Brad stared hungrily at the papers.

'What do you ... I mean we ... do with them?' Brad asked, looking around nervously. 'If the CIA finds out I actually stole ...'

'Don't worry, we'll keep you out of the spotlight,' Marlowe replied. 'We cash our ones in once we're back in the UK.'

'*Our* ones?'

Marlowe nodded as he passed one of the bearer bonds to Roxanne.

'I know you did this for vengeance, but do what you want

with this. Use it to help cover costs for Cody's financial destruction, even.'

He then passed another small pile of bearer bonds over to her.

'These are for Lexi Warner's medical bills. Half a million won't cover all of it, but I'm getting the feeling she'll probably have Angelina Rizzo offer to help – for any extra info Lexi might have on her brother.'

He then turned to Brad.

'Here's fifty grand for you,' he said. 'I know you did it on behalf of loyalty to America and the CIA, but what Sasha doesn't know won't hurt her.'

'Only fifty?' Brad grinned, taking the bearer bond.

'You were the one who wanted to keep out of the spotlight,' Marlowe shrugged. 'Another fifty goes to Marshall here, for his exemplary service, and the last one goes to Ryan Gates for helping. It's the least I can do for losing his gun.'

'So that's seven hundred grand gone, which leaves you, after expenses and Clarissa here, just over two million,' Roxanne looked up from the bond. 'What are you going to do with it?'

'Trix and I split it down the middle,' Marlowe replied. 'We'll end up with about a million each.'

'I'm liking the sound of this,' Trix grinned.

'You're not going to like the next part,' Marlowe shook his head, as if about to give some terrible news. 'We each get to keep one bond, like the others, but the rest go into an operations fund.'

'Operations fund?'

'Yes,' Marlowe looked around the room. 'Orchid is still out there, and Orchid is now angry. It looks like St John Steele tried to set me up for murder – not with the police, but with *them*. There's a civil war coming, and it's bigger and more dangerous than we thought it would be.'

He pointed at the bearer bonds.

'This is the start of a war chest. To take them down, we're going to need an army. And armies take time to train and cash to keep.'

'So we start the army with a small team,' Marshall said. 'You know I'm up for it. Tessa too, if you want her.'

At Tessa's name, Marlowe saw Roxanne twitch a little.

'Must feel weird, hearing the name of the other girl-friend,' Trix spoke in a mock stage whisper. 'Well, the *other* other girlfriend, anyway.'

Roxanne gave her the finger.

'I can't be in your war,' she said, looking back at Marlowe. 'I need to take down Cody Donziger.'

'Who's part of this, which makes *you* a part of this, whether or not you like it,' Marlowe shrugged. 'This war isn't happening tomorrow, I might not call on you for months, years even. Just know this bearer bond is an advance for your time down the line.'

'There are easier ways to get a date, Marlowe,' Marshall Kirk laughed. 'Hell, for this bearer bond, I'd date you myself!'

There was a lightening of the tension in the room, and Marlowe relaxed a little – but a moment later there was a beep from Trix's laptop, as she typed on the keyboard.

'Here,' she said, turning it to face everyone. 'Footage from the back corridors from earlier. I kept everything recording to a cloud as we made our way out, and it's just returned. Look.'

On the screen was Ichabod, facing another tuxedo-wearing figure, briefcase to his chest. The other figure fired three times, and Ichabod went down.

Marlowe leant closer; it wasn't the scene that interested

him; it was the killer. His face was pixelated in real time, just like the intruder in his apartment, days earlier.

'Recognise the tech?' Trix asked him. 'And the gloves?'

Marlowe looked closer at the buckle on the gloves; the same one his own CCTV had picked up.

'It's Steele. I'm sure of it, but we still need more proof,' he said, nodding. 'We thought the tech was from the Coleman family, but this is him, it means either Steele worked with them ...'

A thought came to mind. A line spoken by Steele earlier that evening.

'Besides, I have my own ways to screw up his cameras.'

'Or he's somehow stolen the tech,' Trix continued before Marlowe could comment on this. 'And, if he is the pixelated man, it means he's the one who sent you the fake invite in the first place. What do you want to do?'

Marlowe leant back against the suite's bar.

'I need a drink,' he said. 'I think we deserve it.'

He stopped as a new thought came to light.

'Did the footage work, by the way?'

Trix smiled and cast her laptop to the screen. On it, terrified gamblers and patrons ran out of the door, taken from a CCTV camera.

'The Gold Strike had full spectrum cameras,' she said, typing code into a box. 'Which means, with a few keystrokes, we can move into the ultra-violet spectrum ...'

The screen turned black and white, almost as if the camera was now a night vision camera, but instead of a green tinge, it was purple.

'Watch,' Trix said as, on the screen, she rewound the footage to the start, where the first gamblers came running out.

However, this time, several of them had glowing lips.

'The uranium glass did its job,' she smiled. 'I don't think Steele and his friends even knew what you were planning with it.'

'He thought I was using it as a distraction,' Marlowe said, looking over at Marshall. 'But while they played with the dust, adding it to a couple of bottles, you did a stellar job with the glasses.'

Marshall grinned and held up his own glass, as Marlowe looked back to the screen. The plan he'd told everyone had been to make the high-ranking members of Orchid – effectively anyone who'd been invited into that back arena – think Gabriel was trying to kill them. That would create chaos, and Marlowe knew that was what sold Steele and the others on it.

What they didn't know, however, was before they placed dust on a couple of glasses, or poured small amounts into full champagne bottles to complete the ruse, Marshall Kirk had already entered the kitchens and used a gel-like compound, mixed with the dust to coat almost every glass to be used that evening. It had been a time-sucking job, and he'd only just made it into his Interpol uniform after finishing, but now every single person who'd even sipped at the champagne, people who, by having champagne in the first place belayed their status in Orchid, were running out of the casino, easily identifiable under the UV light.

'Make a list, check it twice,' Marlowe said, straightening. 'I want to know who each of these bastards are.'

'To take them down?' Brad asked.

'Hell no, to see if they're a potential ally,' Marlowe smiled darkly, holding up the blackened coin of the Orchid High Council, flipping it in his fingers. 'If St John Steele wants to cause chaos and dissent in Orchid, I want to be right there, watching.'

'You know this won't be all of Orchid?' Trix asked, concerned. 'Some people would have stayed away.'

'Yeah, but we'll be able to cross reference. Work out who's connected to who, who else is in that group we may have missed, and eventually we'll have them all.'

This now stated, Marlowe tapped the screen.

'Go back to that footage,' he said. 'Ichabod's death.'

Trix tapped on the keyboard, and the scene reappeared of Ichabod, the case to his chest, facing the pixilated, gloved man.

'Now use full spectrum.'

Trix pressed a button, the screen turned purple.

And, on it, the pixelated man's tuxedo lapel started to glow.

'I spilled champagne on his lapel when I was bumped, and he took my gun,' Marlowe growled. 'That's definitely Steele.'

He sighed, straightening.

'It's late, it's the city that never sleeps and I need a drink,' he said. 'Who's up for a stroll around town?'

31

EPILOGUE

As it was, only Brad and Roxanne agreed to accompany Marlowe; Marshall had claimed jet lag was finally kicking his arse, Clarissa had disappeared to speak to some contacts about the best way to invest a sudden windfall, and Trix was simply unwilling to leave the safety of the suite, utterly convinced Marlowe would find some way to get himself into trouble the moment he stepped out onto the Strip.

Marlowe hadn't been worried about reprisals; the chances were anyone of note had made a point of leaving Vegas the moment the shit hit the fan, and Steele wouldn't want Marlowe dead before whatever plan he had came to fruition, but he still kept the Glock 17 he'd taken from Gabriel. It was a little weird, but even though he preferred the Sig Sauer, and the Glock was a suitable alternative, he missed the CZ 75. Either way, if anything did happen, he was sure that between him and Brad, who was no doubt packing half a dozen different weapons, they'd be able to sort anything else.

The drink had actually been quite sombre for a victory

lap; Roxanne was distracted by the fate of Gabriel, concerned he'd be unpunished for his actions, while Brad was constantly checking his phone.

'What is it?' Marlowe eventually erupted after the fifteenth or sixteenth check. 'You've either booked a hitman or an Uber. Which is it?'

'An Uber,' Brad smiled, showing the screen. 'Feeling a little "third wheel" here, so thought I'd go check out the safe house we have Gabriel at.'

'Can we come?' Roxanne looked interested at this, but Brad shook his head, laughing.

'Some things are only for the CIA,' he replied almost apologetically. 'But don't worry, if he doesn't have electrodes attached to his toasted balls by the time I arrive, I'll make sure it's sorted pretty damn quick.'

He rose, looking down at Marlowe.

'Long way down the road since we met outside the *Jolly Sailor*,' he said. 'At least this time I'm not on the run. Although *you* might be.'

Marlowe raised his glass of bourbon in a toast.

'We'll see,' he replied. 'Thanks for the help. Pass on my thanks to your boss, too. Although from what I hear, she should be thanking me for saving her job and getting her further up the CIA chain of command.'

'Higher ranking means bigger favours,' Brad winked. 'If you have any other get-rich-quick schemes, let me know.'

Then, with a nod to Roxanne, Brad Haynes left the bar – and the post-mission drink.

Marlowe leant back in his chair, stretching.

'And then there were two,' he said. 'Up for another?'

Roxanne shook her head.

'Early start in the morning back to New York,' she said,

nodding to the bag beside the chair. 'Got my things, got a room near the airport, and I'll be off at some ungodly time tomorrow morning.'

'You sure that's safe?' Marlowe frowned. 'I mean—'

'Gabriel's in custody, his sister will probably arrive first thing tomorrow, and I want to be as far away from here as I can be by then,' Roxanne laughed. 'Anyway, I should leave, allow you your booty call with the CIA fox.'

Marlowe chuckled.

'I make it a rule never to sleep with people I don't know the full name of,' he said piously. 'I don't think I'll be making any such calls tonight.'

Roxanne bit her lip, considering her next words carefully.

'Then come back to my hotel,' she said matter-of-factly. 'At the worst, you can make sure I don't die one more night.'

'Is there a sofa?'

'I don't rent suites,' Roxanne laughed, rising. 'It's a simple room. You can sit in an uncomfortable desk chair ... or you can share my bed.'

Marlowe rose to meet her.

'Close contact security?' he considered the option. 'It might be very *hands on.*'

'Oh, for God's sake, Marlowe,' Roxanne leant across, kissing him hard on the lips before pulling back. 'Just come back with me and shut up, okay?'

Marlowe laughed.

'Shutting up, ma'am,' he said, as the two of them left the bar, hunting a taxi to the airport.

Montgomery "Monty" Barnes wasn't used to being woken up in the middle of the night, but the banging on his door was urgent, so grabbing a weapon, he slowly and creakily made his way down the apartment corridor to the thick, wooden door that protected him from the outside world.

He almost reached it when it exploded in on the corridor, an enormous explosion of fire and noise, sending Monty backwards, tumbling across the floor, his shotgun falling from his flailing grasp, as he was left just in his underwear and a tatty string vest, looking up in anger at the man who walked in through the smoke-filled gaping hole in his doorway.

'What the hell do you think you're doing?' he shouted. 'Is this how you were taught to treat your elders?'

'Jesus, you're like a hundred,' the man said in surprise, stepping into the hallway's half-light. 'But age aside, I've been told you're the man who can get me what I want.'

'And what the bloody hell is that, then?' Monty snapped back, the bluster and anger a mask for the absolute terror he now felt as the man leant over, picking up the fallen shotgun.

He was slim, wearing a sweater under a pea coat, jeans over Timberland boots. He had a baker's boy cap on, blue tweed, that obscured most of his brown and silver peppered short hair. His face was pockmarked and scarred down the left-hand side as, weapon in hand, he crouched beside Monty Barnes, aiming the weapon directly at his face.

'I'll make this quick,' he said. 'The police will get calls about your door right now. You should do something about it.'

'Yeah, I'll get right on it,' Monty muttered, wincing as his side ached, the knife wound from a few days ago having reopened under the bandage. 'Who the hell are you?'

'I won't give you my name, Mister Barnes, but I will give you the name I'm known by,' the man smiled. 'I'm called, in your profession, the Gravedigger, and I've just arrived from a very uncomfortable trip from the Ukraine.'

'Oh, shit,' Monty recoiled in terror as the Gravedigger leant closer now, barrels still aimed at Monty's face.

'Oh shit indeed,' the Gravedigger said, his voice calm and unemotional. 'And respecting my elders or not, I've been talking to a contact of yours, a Raymond Gibson.'

'Razor? He's no bloody contact of mine—'

'Either way, he was very helpful in passing me your details,' the Gravedigger continued. 'Through him, I hear you can tell me where I can find Thomas Marlowe, for I very much desire to speak with him.'

Tom Marlowe will return in his next thriller

BROAD SWORD

Order Now at Amazon:

Mybook.to/broadsword

Released 27th May 2024

Gain up-to-the-moment information on the release by signing up to the Jack Gatland VIP Reader's Club!

Join at http://bit.ly/jackgatlandVIP

ACKNOWLEDGEMENTS

When you write a series of books, you find that there are a ton of people out there who help you, sometimes without even realising, and so I wanted to say thanks.

There are people I need to thank, and they know who they are, including my brother Chris Lee, Jacqueline Beard MBE, who has copyedited all my books since the very beginning, editor Sian Phillips and weapon specialist Eben Atwater, all of whom have made my books way better than they have every right to be.

Also, I couldn't have done this without my growing army of ARC and beta readers, who not only show me where I falter, but also raise awareness of me in the social media world, ensuring that other people learn of my books.

But mainly, I tip my hat and thank you. *The reader.* Who once took a chance on an unknown author in a pile of Kindle books, and thought you'd give them a go, and who has carried on this far with them, as well as the spin off books I now release.

I write these books for you. And with luck, Tom Marlowe will be around for a very long time.

Jack Gatland / Tony Lee,
London, January, 2024

ABOUT THE AUTHOR

Jack Gatland is the pen name of *#1 New York Times Bestselling Author* Tony Lee, who has been writing in all media for thirty-five years, including comics, graphic novels, middle grade books, audio drama, TV and film for *DC Comics, Marvel, BBC, ITV, Random House, Penguin USA, Hachette* and a ton of other publishers and broadcasters.

These have included licenses such as *Doctor Who, Spider Man, X-Men, Star Trek, Battlestar Galactica, MacGyver,* BBC's *Doctors, Wallace and Gromit* and *Shrek*, as well as work created with musicians such as *Iron Maiden, Bruce Dickinson, Ozzy Osbourne, Joe Satriani* and *Megadeth.*

As Tony, he's toured the world talking to reluctant readers with his 'Change The Channel' school tours, and lectures on screenwriting and comic scripting for *Raindance* in London.

As Jack, he's written several book series now - a police procedural featuring *DI Declan Walsh and the officers of the Temple Inn Crime Unit*, a spinoff featuring "cop for criminals" *Ellie Reckless and her team,* a third espionage spinoff series featuring burnt MI5 agent *Tom Marlowe*, an action adventure series featuring conman-turned-treasure hunter *Damian Lucas*, and a standalone novel set in a New York boardroom.

An introvert West Londoner by heart, he lives with his wife Tracy and dog Fosco, just outside London.

———————

Feel free to follow Jack on all his social media by clicking on the links below. Over time these can be places where we can engage, discuss Declan, Ellie, Tom and others, and put the world to rights.

www.jackgatland.com
www.hoodemanmedia.com

Visit Jack's Reader's Group Page
(Mainly for fans to discuss his books):
https://www.facebook.com/groups/jackgatland

Subscribe to Jack's Readers List:
https://bit.ly/jackgatlandVIP

www.facebook.com/jackgatlandbooks
www.twitter.com/jackgatlandbook
ww.instagram.com/jackgatland

Want more books by Jack Gatland? Turn the page...

LETTER FROM THE DEAD

"BY THE TIME YOU READ THIS, I WILL BE DEAD..."

A TWENTY YEAR OLD MURDER...
A PRIME MINISTER LEADERSHIP BATTLE...
A PARANOID, HOMELESS EX-MINISTER...
AN EVANGELICAL PREACHER WITH A SECRET...

DI DECLAN WALSH HAS HAD BETTER FIRST DAYS...

AVAILABLE ON AMAZON / KINDLEUNLIMITED

THE THEFT OF A **PRICELESS** PAINTING...
A GANGSTER WITH A **CRIPPLING DEBT**...
A **BODY COUNT** RISING BY THE HOUR...

AND ELLIE RECKLESS IS CAUGHT IN THE MIDDLE.

JACK GATLAND

PAINT
— THE —
DEAD

A 'COP FOR CRIMINALS' ELLIE RECKLESS NOVEL

A NEW PROCEDURAL CRIME SERIES WITH
A TWIST - FROM THE CREATOR OF THE
BESTSELLING 'DI DECLAN WALSH' SERIES

AVAILABLE ON AMAZON / KINDLE UNLIMITED

JACK GATLAND

THE LIONHEART CURSE

HUNT THE GREATEST TREASURES
PAY THE GREATEST PRICE

BOOK 1 IN A NEW SERIES OF ADVENTURES
IN THE STYLE OF 'THE DA VINCI CODE'
FROM THE CREATOR OF DECLAN WALSH

AVAILABLE ON AMAZON / KINDLEUNLIMITED

EIGHT PEOPLE. EIGHT SECRETS.
ONE SNIPER.

THE
B⊕ARD
ROOM

HOW FAR WOULD <u>YOU</u> GO TO GAIN JUSTICE?

NEW YORK TIMES #1 BESTSELLER TONY LEE WRITING AS

JACK GATLAND

A NEW STANDALONE THRILLER WITH
A TWIST - FROM THE CREATOR OF THE
BESTSELLING 'DI DECLAN WALSH' SERIES

AVAILABLE ON AMAZON / KINDLE UNLIMITED

Printed in Great Britain
by Amazon